The PLEASURE LIST

THE PLEASURE LIST
Copyright © 2020 by Emma Mallory
All rights reserved.

The Pleasure List is a work of fiction. Names, characters, business, places, events, and incidents are the products of the author's imagination. Any resemblance to actual persons, living or dead, or actual events is purely coincidental.

The author acknowledges that product and company names are trademarks™ or registered® trademarks of their respective holders. Use of them does not imply any affiliation with or endorsement by them.

ISBN 9789083228105 (Paperback)
ISBN 9789083228112 (eBook)

First paperback edition February 2022

www.emmamallory.com

To my late mother who always encouraged me to chase my dreams.
Ik hou van je tot de maan en terug, mama.

PLEASURE
/ˈpleʒ.ər/ *noun.*

A feeling of happy
satisfaction and enjoyment.

CHAPTER 1
Jordan

All my life, I had struggled. I had struggled to pay tuition and to go to college, struggled with loss and grief, struggled with relationships. And right this moment, I was struggling my way through this job interview.

"So, last question," the woman on the other side of the desk said as I shifted slightly in my seat, happy that this interview was finally coming to an end. I almost let out a breath of relief, but I managed to keep it in. It was probably not a good idea to show her how ready I was to go home.

I had a hard time concentrating on the words the brunette in front of me was saying anyway, constantly catching myself staring at the weird proportions of her face throughout our conversation. The Botox hid her age well, but it was overly done, so she looked...*different*.

"Ms. Sawyer?"

I blinked a few times, breaking out of my trance and focusing on her dark eyes. "My apologies, could you repeat the question, please?"

She nodded, though her face didn't give me any hint of what she was thinking. "What's the color of money?"

The color of money?

It was a weird question, but I'd heard many people say companies use these questions to test their applicants, and we'd rehearsed them in college too. You'd think I would be confident to in answering them.

The obvious answer would be green if you lived in the US, but it really depended on the country. Euro bills could be all the colors of the rainbow, just as many others around the globe. Or was she looking for a different answer?

This was taking me too long, so I just decided to follow my instincts.

"That would depend on the country," I said confidently. Mrs. Martin nodded, writing something on the notepad in front of her. I couldn't see what it was, but her face looked somewhat satisfied with my answer, so I smiled in relief.

I jumped when the room was suddenly filled with the excruciating sound of my ringtone.

Shit.

My cheeks burned up and Mrs. Martin raised a brow—*kinda*—placing the pen next to the notepad before folding her hands together on the table.

"I am *so* sorry." I reached for the pesky device in my purse, my face probably resembling a tomato at that point. Reading my best friend's name, Ashley, on the screen, I shut it off, not risking it ringing again, even though the interview was practically over.

"Well, Ms. Sawyer," Mrs. Martin continued and I nodded, straightening up in my seat. "Before we end the interview, I was wondering if you have any questions for me."

Oh, shit. I should ask something really smart. Of course, I drew a blank instead.

"What are the work hours?" I blurted out, and Mrs. Martin raised her brows, *again.*

"As I mentioned before, work hours are from eight to five," she answered, somewhat annoyed.

God, she must think that I'm really dumb.

"Ah, yes. That was all." I smiled, relieved when the corners of her mouth curled up too—*or as much as they could.* The nerves in my stomach fluttered but in a good way.

"Well, then." Mrs. Martin stood up from her seat and I did the same, trying not to trip in the four-inch heels I had decided to wear. I had borrowed them from Ashley, who assured me they were the comfiest pair she owned. "Thank you for coming. We'll get back to you by the start of next week."

"Thank you so much for this opportunity." I shook her hand and followed her to the exit.

"You're welcome. Have a good day," she replied, practically shoving me out of her office and shutting the door behind me.

I took one look at the closed door before I walked down the hallway towards the elevators.

Surely, I finally had a shot. The job wasn't much and the pay wouldn't be great, but *God*, I really needed all the money I could get. Hopefully, starting at the front desk, I would be able to work my way up and have a job that matched my degree for once. I had been searching for something for months now. The part-time job behind the bar wasn't doing much for me anymore, but finding something else proved to be harder than I thought.

As I took one of the elevators down, surrounded by people in sharp suits and pencil skirts, I turned on my phone and waited for the messages to come in. *Three missed calls from Ashley.*

I pressed call and brought the device to my ear, rolling my eyes at her persistence. I loved her, but sometimes she could be a little much.

The phone barely rang once before she picked up.

"Finally," she huffed and I scoffed.

"Hey, Ash. What's up?" I chirped, my voice dripping with sarcasm, earning a few looks from the up-tight businessmen and women standing next to me.

"Well, how did it go?" she asked and I smiled, leaving the elevator faster than seemed natural when the doors slid open to the ground floor. I rushed out of the big office building and took a deep breath before answering her question.

"Honestly, pretty good." I beamed, "but didn't I tell you it was going to be *at least* an hour?"

I heard a shriek on the other side of the line and pulled the phone from my ear, not wanting to go deaf.

"I'm so happy for you! But you know that my offer still stands?" she asked, ignoring half of my words and making me sigh as I made my way down the street. Ashley was the one who came from a rich family, and from an outsider's perspective, it must've looked very weird that we were best friends.

"Yes. And you know I appreciate it, but I'm still not going to accept."

"Ugh, *fine*," she droned. "You're so stubborn. Maybe we can celebrate tomorrow?"

I groaned, knowing that fighting her was pointless since I was going to agree to go in a few seconds anyway. Ashley had a way with words, and even though I definitely still had my spine, she was able to talk me into practically anything.

So, I said, "sure."

I walked towards the parking lot next to the building, feeling actually really professional in my improvised pencil skirt, holding my phone to my ear. Almost as if I belonged here, having an important conversation instead of talking to my best friend about drinks. *Well, that was important too.*

"We can go to that new place...what's it called?" she continued.

"What, The Red Martini? I can't afford that." I groaned. I could literally *feel* my last dollars fly out of my wallet.

"You know I'm like, rich, right?" *Here we go.*

"Ash, I appreciate it, but I'm not a charity case."

"Yes, you remind me of that at least once a week. But it's my treat, really, I have something to tell you anyway," she chirped and I raised my brows. What was so important that she wanted to tell me in person?

I walked to my car, putting the key in the door and unlocking it. I had this red Mini for as long as I could remember and I still loved it. To be honest, I couldn't afford a new car, so I didn't really have a choice.

"Ok, fine. Meet you at nine?" I asked, struggling to get the door of my car open. It took special care to get it open—this car was all kinds of shabby.

"Yes, I'll ring Bailey as well."

"Oh, Ash?" I shifted my weight from one foot to the other, desperate to get them out of these heels. "I'll bring your shoes around soon. Thanks for lending me them."

"Of course," Ashley exclaimed. I remember when we picked out the outfit I was wearing. I had finally given her the chance to dress me and of course, she had taken this opportunity with open arms. "Any time."

"Ok. See you tomorrow," I said before hanging up the phone, finally able to concentrate on that stupid door.

I drove to my tiny apartment on the dodgy side of town, singing along with the music obnoxiously loud and almost running a few people over. It sounded worse than it was, but driving just wasn't my strong suit.

Once I made it home, I parked my car in the same spot as always, close to the front door and in view of the only camera in the street. I killed the engine, made sure the emergency brake was on, and stepped out, locking my car twice.

It wasn't like it was actually worth anything anymore, but I definitely didn't have the money to buy a new one. *That, and it was my baby.*

Finally in the foyer of my building, I closed the front door—*which needed an extra pull*—and made my way up the stairs.

"Hi, Mrs. Hellen," I greeted to the older lady who was always watering the millions of plants in the hall.

"Hello, Jordan. How did your job interview go?" she asked and I paused on the stairs. I studied the checkered blouse she was wearing, another statement piece she undoubtedly got at the old thrift shop down the street.

"It went well!" I replied, shifting my gaze back up to her eyes.

"Good. What was the name of the company again?" she went on, not a care in the world that the pot of the philodendron she was watering was overflowing.

My face fell ever so slightly, but I quickly regained composure when I remembered the name.

Yes, I just came from there and I had sent the company numerous emails, but it wasn't an easy name. *Sue me.*

"Cendose Incorporated. Something with finances."

She chuckled. I turned around and continued up the stairs, smiling when I heard her mutter under her breath, "something with finances."

―

That evening, I stood in front of my closet, looking at the few items of clothing I had to choose from for tonight. I had taken a quick shower after dinner and put on a matching lingerie set. *I mean, you never know.*

I grabbed the few dresses I had and laid them on my bed.

Why was choosing an outfit so hard?

Bailey, the third member of our little best friend club, had set me up with a rich guy for a date in a fancy restaurant, even though I thought I had made it clear that I wasn't looking for a boyfriend. Honestly, I only agreed because I was in desperate need of a good fuck.

I looked at my options, trying to figure out which one was

most likely to get me laid but decent enough to wear to a fancy restaurant. Most of the time I looked like I came out of the gutter, but I wasn't looking to embarrass myself tonight. Especially since I knew the other ladies at the restaurant would be dressed to perfection.

I nodded to myself and picked up the red body con dress that I had bought a million years ago on a whim, holding it in front of my chest and looking in the mirror.

Yes, this is going to work.

I stepped into the dress, pulled it up, and arranged the thin straps on my shoulders. I didn't have the biggest boobs, but my *just-shy-of-a-b-cup*-breasts filled the fabric decently. My ass, however, stretched the dress a little bit, so it was rising a bit further up than it was meant to, but I didn't mind. As long as I didn't walk around with my ass on full display, it was fine.

Walking into my tiny en suite bathroom, I stood in front of the mirror debating what to do about the dark mess on my head. I dried my black waves and let them flow down my back, covering my tattoos. For make-up, I just put on some eyeliner and nude lipstick, and I was done. I never really was the make-up kind of girl, but putting on some lipstick on a night out, I enjoyed.

I closed the bathroom door behind me and grabbed my phone, looking at the time. With just a few minutes left before my cab was here, I quickly grabbed all the items of clothing that were scattered around my room and stuffed them into my closet. Folding clothing was exhausting and if I was being honest, I was lazy.

Then, I put on a pair of black, strappy heels that were hanging by a thread and I was surely going to regret wearing, and left my bedroom, ready for the night of my life.

CHAPTER 2
Jordan

After paying the driver, I stepped out of the cab and walked up to the restaurant, finding the red ropes and big modern sign in front slightly intimidating. I took a last breath of the fresh air, the light breeze clearing my mind before I stepped into the warm, busy restaurant.

My heels clicked against the dark, mosaic ceramic flooring as I walked up to the hostess, nervously pulling the hem of my skirt down as far as possible.

"Welcome to *Latmeyer*. Do you have a reservation?" the blonde asked with a big smile on her face, years of training clearly paying off. *I could never.*

"Yes, hi. I think the name was Polley?" I said, scanning the restaurant for my date even though I had no idea what he looked like.

Almost immediately, my eyes were drawn to a *gorgeous* man leaning against the bar with a drink in his hand. He was wearing dark grey slacks and a white button-up, the sleeves neatly rolled to his elbows.

Was my mouth watering?

I watched the muscles in his arm tense as he brought his drink to his lips, his eyes flickering to mine. A smirk appeared on his face, as well as small dimples that enhanced his chiseled jawline even more. His dark blond hair was carefully pulled back, the sides shaved into a fade, and a light stubble covered his jaw.

He was fucking perfect.

And that shirt...it would look beautiful on my bedroom floor.

"Jordan?" Another man who was looking me up and down at my side rudely interrupted my staring.

He was a little less handsome compared to the god I was making eyes at a few seconds ago—but definitely not hideous to look at—and I realized he was the one I was supposed to be meeting. To say I was disappointed was an understatement, but I sucked in a breath and quickly painted a smile on my face.

"Yes, hi," I replied, my cheeks heating up because I was fantasizing about the other man's face between my legs.

"I'm Chris," the guy in front of me said and I nodded. At this point I had completely forgotten that I was actually having a conversation with the hostess before I got distracted.

"I'll show you to your table," she said, still with the same smile on her face.

Chris smiled at me before we followed the hostess to our table, of course in the middle of the fucking restaurant. I didn't have a phobia for large open spaces, but something a little more secluded would be better.

"Please take a seat. Your assigned waiter will provide you with your menus shortly, as well as taking your drink order," she said as I sat down, Chris doing the same on the opposite end of the table. The white cloth felt like silk against my bare legs, and the lavish tableware made me feel like we were dining with the queen herself.

"Thank you," we said in unison before the hostess walked back to her station.

"So, Jordan," Chris started. I looked up, making the mistake of letting my gaze travel to the bar for a second. Pretty Boy was watching us with a mischievous grin, and I rolled my eyes, my previous infatuation rapidly turning to annoyance.

"Something wrong?" my *actual date* asked and I quickly averted my eyes.

"No, sorry. What were you saying?" I smiled, taking this opportunity to take him in. His dark eyes gave him an innocent and kind look, but my gut was telling me he was quite the opposite. And the way his brown hair was slicked back with way too much gel didn't sit right with me either. Then again, you shouldn't judge a book by its cover.

"What do you do?"

I raised my brows. I didn't want to let him know that he startled me with the question, but I couldn't help that I was.

What was I even going to say? *'Well currently unemployed but hopefully in two weeks sitting behind the front desk of the company you can probably buy.'* I think not.

Before I could answer, one of the waiters appeared next to our table, sporting the same perfect smile as his coworker.

"Welcome to *Latmeyer*. My name is Danny. I will be your waiter for the evening. I have your menus," he said as he opened one of the leather-bound menus before handing it to me. He did the same for Chris and placed a wine list on the table. "Can I get you an aperitif?"

God, yes, alcohol. I had a weird feeling that I was going to need it.

"I would like a martini, drop the lemon in and no olives, please," I said and Danny nodded, directing his gaze to my table partner.

"And for you, sir?"

"A whiskey on the rocks," Chris ordered, not giving our waiter a single look as he spoke. *Yikes.* Instead, he kept his eyes on me. Maybe this was his way of flirting or something? If it was, it wasn't working.

"Perfect, I'll be back shortly with your drinks," Danny said and he walked towards the bar, a place I was still very much avoiding with my eyes.

"So what do you do?" Chris continued, unfortunately not dropping the question. He was as determined to know as I was to change the subject.

Right.

"I'm transitioning. What do you do?" I answered quickly, hoping he would leave it.

"Well, I'm a lawyer at *Fero & Polley*, my father's law firm," he said with a smug grin, sitting back in his chair as Danny returned with our drinks.

"Thank you," I smiled up to him and I grabbed my glass before it could touch the table, taking a big gulp.

The alcohol burned down my throat, and I regretted my pace when I tasted the drink, the martini actually being the best one I ever tasted in my life. Maybe I could get one or two more out of Chris tonight.

"I'll come back in a minute to take your dinner orders if that's ok with you," Danny said and I nodded. I had a lot of respect for him. He remained friendly, even though my dinner date had no intentions of showing Danny any of the aforementioned respect.

"Yeah, yeah, thanks," Chris mumbled as he waved Danny away. "I'm actually in the race to become senior partner." I narrowed my eyes for a second, before realizing he had picked up where we had left off with our conversation. He really *did* like talking about himself.

"Oh, that's—"

"Yeah, the position comes with a massive raise, too," he interrupted me.

I rested my chin on my palm, not caring that my elbow was on the table. *Just give it a chance, Jordan. He's just proud of his achievement. I guess.*

"I'll be working longer hours, of course. But it'll all be worth it when I get my salary increase." He smirked before taking a sip of his drink.

"Eh, yeah," I mumbled, my face lightning up when I spotted Danny coming our way once more.

"Did you make your decision?" he asked, folding his hands in front of his chest.

"Yes, I would like—"

"I'll have the filet mignon with asparagus, and she'll have the Caesar salad," Chris said and he closed his menu, daring to smile at me as he did.

Excuse me?

"I will not have the Caesar salad," I retorted. "I would like the fillet steak with brussels sprouts and some extra garlic bread on the side, please." I closed my menu in the same fashion as Chris had done, smiling at him.

"Excellent choice," Danny said, taking our menus and nodding one more time before walking away.

"I thought you'd like the Caesar salad," Chris stated, pouting like a child as I resisted the urge to roll my eyes, again. *We met like half an hour ago, how could he possibly know what I like?*

"Well anyway..." Chris continued talking about himself, but I had zoned out, my gaze unintentionally going back to Pretty Boy at the bar. He was still leaning against it, but he wasn't alone anymore. To his left there was a beautiful woman with straight, dark hair and a perfect face, sitting on one of the stools, sipping her cosmopolitan and occasionally touching him on the arm.

How did she get so lucky while I got stuck with this asshole?

My lips parted when Pretty Boy looked over, his brows raising and a playful twinkle shining in his eyes.

I quickly redirected my gaze to Chris, who was still talking about himself and hadn't even noticed that I wasn't really paying attention.

And why was Pretty Boy looking at me when he had this perfect girl at his side? With her perfect nails, perfect, full lips, and perfect tits.

Meanwhile, I'm here with my chipped nails and small boobs.

The entire restaurant was able to tell that he was *very* out of my league, but I had to admit I felt some sort of satisfaction about the fact that he kept looking over.

I was grateful when Danny returned with our meal, finally giving me something to focus on that was actually interesting.

"Thank you," I said, the sweet and smoky smell of my dinner filling my nostrils. *Fuck, I think I just had a mini orgasm.*

I drowned out Chris' babbling while I ate my meal, the salty and juicy flavors doing everything for my mood. So far, I was going to smack Bailey for setting me up on this horrible date. I was interested to see where she dragged this dickhead from.

I tried to eat my steak as slow as I could, as Chris had barely touched his food, but it was so fucking good.

"But then he said that Angela was better fit for the job," Chris continued and he chuckled humourlessly. "As if—"

He coughed when I raised my brows, waiting to see if the following words out of his mouth were going to be the last straw. With all the red flags that had gone up since our date started, I expected the worst.

"As if she's better than me," he corrected, even though it was clear that he meant something else.

If it weren't for the fact that I really needed him to pay—and that I didn't have the balls to storm out—I would've left already. So I smiled painfully.

I managed to make it through dessert without crushing my teeth or ripping my hair out, but aside from the fact that Chris' favorite topic was himself, he was also incredibly boring. I almost cheered when he raised his hand, signaling to Danny that we wanted the check.

"I had a lovely dinner, Jordan," he said as he took out his card, and I almost spit out the sip of my third martini that I was drinking, coughing and trying not to choke. *Lovely din—*

"Right," I rasped, before downing my glass. Danny walked over, taking Chris' card and settling the bill, giving me a pitiful smile when he walked away without a tip.

"We could set up a second date if you'd like," Chris said, looking at me with hooded eyes, and I tensed up when I felt his foot go up my leg.

I really wanted to have sex, but definitely not with him.

My chair scraped across the floor when I pushed it back and stood up, flipping my hair over my shoulder.

"That would be a no," I replied, my eyes quickly shifting to the bar, not seeing Pretty Boy anymore. *Eye candy gone too. Probably having sex with miss perfect right now. Lucky girl.*

Chris stood up as well, guiding me to the exit with his hand on my back, just above my ass. I hadn't given him any sign that he was allowed to do that, so I quickly shoved his hand away. He was terrible at reading people, *that's for sure*.

"Well, I could at least take you home," he tried and I sighed.

"Chris, someday you're going to make some poor girl very happy, but it's not me," I stated before I moved my mouth closer to his ear. "And we aren't going to fuck either."

I clearly hit a nerve, because he took a step back, looking down at me with a scowl. His confident and flirty demeanor vanished, and I took a step back.

"I wouldn't fuck you in a million years," he sneered before he stormed out of the restaurant. *What a dick.*

Never in my life have I been on such a horrible date. Did this douchebag think about someone else every once in a while? Or was he just this sexist, rich prick I got to know him as?

I made sure I had everything, before storming out of the restaurant myself, my face like thunder.

I had just passed the bathrooms, when something solid crashed into me. *Or did I crash into a wall? Whoa, this wall smelled good.* A woody, but sweet smell filled my nostrils, being a little different from the standard cologne I smelled on most men.

No, I crashed into Pretty Boy.

CHAPTER 3
Jordan

"Watch where you're going," I said agitated, trying to keep my balance. One of his hands grabbed my arm, holding me up.

"I could say the same to you," he replied and I swallowed at the deep, husky sound.

After a few seconds, I scoffed, looking up. He was even prettier up close. And he seemed somewhat familiar, but I couldn't place it.

"Please, don't," I sighed, pinching the bridge of my nose with my thumb and pointer finger. "I've had the most awful date of my life and I don't need you making my day even worse."

"I doubt I could make it worse," Pretty Boy said smugly and I rolled my eyes. "Did you just—" he added and I looked up at him, seeing something different next to the playfulness in his eyes.

"Yes, what—where's your date?" I asked, crossing my arms and changing the subject.

Pretty Boy chuckled, the low rumble not helping my mission to give him the cold shoulder. We were still standing in the middle of the restaurant, but at that point, I didn't care anymore. Not even when the hostess' smile faltered—for the first time that night—when she looked at us. *I won't lie, it scared me a little.*

"She left," Pretty Boy said and I raised a brow.

"She didn't like you?" I asked with a grin.

He smirked, looking me up and down, and rolled his lower lip between his teeth before answering. "I had my eyes on someone else."

Yeah, I was practically putty in his hands, but I wasn't about to tell *him* that.

"Is that so?"

"Hmm." His eyes scanned over my body.

We stood in a comfortable—but tension-filled—silence for a second, before he spoke again. "Well, how about I buy you another martini? To make up for bumping into you?"

As if I was going to say no to a free drink. Especially one of those amazing martinis.

"Alright then," I replied. Pretty Boy smirked before placing his hand on my back, at a more decent height than Chris' touch earlier.

We walked to the bar of the restaurant, and I climbed onto one of the stools, unfortunately, a little less elegantly than I would've liked.

Pretty Boy ordered us drinks, somehow knowing exactly how

I liked my martini. I honestly didn't mind him ordering for me—unlike with Chris. It gave me another chance to observe him.

"One martini, drop in the lemon and no olives, please, and a whiskey sour for me," he ordered, and the bartender nodded before gathering the necessities at lightning speed. I watched the bartender with great interest and admiration as he measured the ingredients and gracefully assembled our drinks.

From the corner of my eyes I noticed that Pretty Boy was watching me, and I looked up at him, cocking a brow.

"What?" I said a little harsher than I intended to.

"Nothing. Can't I admire someone pretty?" He nodded to the bartender, who handed him his drink.

You know how you talk about pick-up lines and that shit with your friends? And you say that they'll never work on you? That you find them cheesy? *Well, that's the biggest lie of the century.*

I shifted in my seat, grabbing my martini from the bartender and taking a big gulp. Pretty Boy raised his brows at me, but I ignored it.

"Of course you can," I choked out and he chuckled.

"Good."

He brought his drink to his lips and took a sip, looking over the rim of the glass with his icy eyes and making me squirm under his gaze.

Cold shoulder, Jordan. Cold shoulder.

I looked around the restaurant, my previous table clean and ready for a new batch of people, and the hostess sporting her *almost* never faltering smile, again.

"So, what did the guy do to get you so...*angry*?" Pretty Boy asked and I looked back up.

"He's a sexist piece of shit, and cheap as well. Hold on."

I placed my glass back on the bar and stood up, grabbing my last twenty out of my purse when a thought popped up in my head. I walked to the other side of the bar where Danny was waiting for drinks.

"Hi, Danny?" I said and he turned around.

"Hi, yes, how can I help you?" he asked and I handed him the twenty. He looked from the money to me with a questioning expression, waiting for me to explain.

"Your tip, I'm sorry for the rude asshole I was with." I smiled and Danny took the money.

"Thank you, ma'am." He smiled back and I nodded, my expression faltering a little when I turned around. I walked back towards Pretty Boy and sat back down, fixing my dress and brushing a strand of hair out of my face.

"What was that about?" Pretty Boy asked.

"Dickhead didn't give our waiter a tip," I replied and he frowned.

"Hmm," he hummed and I emptied my glass. "Right," he said and he did the same, handing the bartender a fifty and taking a step closer to me. I was about ninety percent sure he tipped so generously to impress me, but I would be lying if I said that I didn't like it.

I could feel his warm breath on my face and goosebumps appeared on my skin at our proximity. His scent made me feel drunker than the martinis ever could, and I closed my eyes as he brought his lips to my ear.

"Are you coming home with me or what?" he cooed as he brushed a stray curl off my shoulder. My panties were ruined, and I was in physical pain with how turned on I was. This man knew what he was doing, and I gathered all the courage I could muster to play the game with him.

"Is that a rhetorical question?" I replied, shooting him a—*I hope*—sexy smirk and lifting myself off the stool, pressing my body against his.

He chuckled and placed his hand on my lower back, guiding me out of the restaurant. He hailed a cab and opened the door for me, waiting for me to step in before he closed it and joined me on the other side. After he gave the driver his address, which I immediately recognized as the rich part of town, Pretty Boy turned to me with a smirk.

"You're a little tease," he said, placing his large hand on my leg and softly caressing it, his fingers creeping up my thigh.

Who was being the tease now?

I pressed my palms into the leather of the seats, holding my breath as Pretty Boy's hand went higher and higher. Thank God, the drive was short because I was ready to ride him in the back of the cab when we arrived at his big apartment building.

Pretty Boy paid the driver and helped me out of the car, leading me into the spacious lobby. I tried not to look around, admiring the white marble of the floor and sleek black desk the doorman sat behind, but I felt like a tourist anyway.

How rich was this guy?

He guided me to the elevator where he swiped a card across a scanner and waited until I got in when the doors slid open.

As soon as the elevator doors closed again, I pulled his face down and pressed my lips on his. He was surprised at first, but grabbed my ass and pulled me against him, wrapping my legs around his waist.

I moaned against his lips as he squeezed hard, and I dug my fingers in his back.

"What's your name?" he breathed through kisses and he pushed me harder against the elevator wall.

I hadn't even realized that we didn't know each other's names. So, my mind went a million miles per hour thinking about an answer, and I decided to go with my first instinct.

"Call me Baby," I whispered against his lips, and he took the opportunity to slide his tongue in. This was supposed to be a one-night stand, and the fact that we were complete strangers to each other was kind of thrilling.

I was so ready to get fucked in this elevator, that I was almost angry when we stopped as the doors rolled open.

"Come on," he said, putting me down and giving me a quick tap on the ass before he walked out of the elevator.

I followed him out and realized we weren't in a hallway, but already inside his lavish-looking living room with an open-plan kitchen.

Pretty Boy dropped his keys on the table next to the door, as well as his watch that he had already taken off. I placed my small purse on the same table without looking, ignoring the fact that my stuff rolled out of it because I was distracted.

I took in his spacious, modern apartment, with lots of surfaces to have the time of my life on—*and against*—as soon as possible. My heels clicked against the beautiful hardwood floor, and I let my fingers glide over the perfectly white walls as I walked inside. The apartment had an industrial look, but nothing looked uncomfortable or useless, dark steel and wood creating an almost minimalistic feel.

I hopped further into the apartment, taking my heels off and kicking them under the table, feeling the cold floor under my feet as I continued to look around.

You could look over the city through the big, floor-to-ceiling windows, and I was getting a little upset about the fact that I promised myself this would be a one-time thing. Those windows looked perfect to get fucked against.

Speaking of fucking, I wasn't here to admire his impeccable interior.

As if he read my mind, Pretty Boy grabbed me by the ass and lifted me up, my legs wrapping around his waist once again. He pressed his lips on mine and I gladly returned the favor, the kiss almost a little aggressive. My hands roamed through his hair and down his back, feeling every inch of his muscular torso.

He pulled back and I pouted.

"What's your safe word?"

I raised my brows, not expecting his question to bring so much excitement to the surface. Actually, I wasn't expecting this question at all from a one-night-stand, but I couldn't deny that I already felt comfortable enough with the guy to even discuss a safe word. Butterflies erupted in my stomach as I thought about the things he could do to me.

He noticed my hesitation, one corner of his mouth curling into a grin. "Don't worry, I'm just making sure we're not doing something you don't want."

I let out a breath and answered his question. "I—I don't have one."

"Well, pick one. But choose wisely, you only have one chance," Pretty Boy replied, pressing me into the wall and trailing kisses down my neck, my dress riding up higher and higher.

Unable to concentrate, I blurted out the first thing that came to mind. "Bubble gum!"

Pretty Boy looked up at me and showed off his dimples with a panty-dropping smile.

"I like it," he said, wiggling his brows.

A moan escaped my lips when he kissed the sweet spot under my ear, sending bolts of pleasure through my body. He walked off and I buried my face in his neck, kissing and sucking his skin. I shrieked when he threw me on his massive bed before he unbuttoned his shirt and tossed it on the floor.

Yes, it definitely looks better there.

I looked back up and swallowed hard when I saw his naked chest. Insecurity crept up on me, but there was no way I was going to let it ruin my night.

Pretty Boy smirked and walked up to me, hovering over me as he grabbed my jaw with force, and I looked into his blue eyes.

"Do you like it rough, Baby?" he asked and I nodded in response.

His grip tightened and his eyes narrowed.

"Use your words," he demanded and I took a deep breath.

"Yes," I answered confidently.

"Good." I saw a twinkle in his eyes, increasing my curiosity about the things he was going to do to me. Exactly *how* rough were we talking?

He released my jaw and started his attack on my neck, sliding the straps of my dress off as he went. The feeling of his warm lips on my skin and his hands slowly taking off my clothes had me squirming underneath him.

When the fabric got past my breasts, he pulled it off in one go, before it joined his shirt on the floor. He made quick work of my bra, having me near-naked in seconds.

I gasped when his mouth closed over my nipple, his free hand massaging the other, and I arched my back, feeling the tingle in my lower abdomen growing. I moaned louder when one of his hands grabbed the tiny bit of fabric that was my thong, and ripped it off, leaving me completely bare for him.

"Spread your legs, Baby," he commanded and I did as I was told, the cool air of the room brushing against my core as I widened my legs.

He sat back up, his eyes trailing from my face to my pussy, and I blushed. I was proud of my body, but lying there, naked, exposed to a stranger, made me want to cover up.

As if he knew what I was thinking, Pretty Boy hovered over me again and pinned my hands above my head.

"I am going to worship you tonight," he cooed and I swallowed. *I need him to do something, like, now.*

I nodded quickly and he smirked before crashing his mouth on mine, pushing his tongue past my lips and practically fucking my mouth with his. His approach was almost aggressive, and for a second I was debating if it had been a good idea to go home with him, but then he softly caressed his fingers over my naked breasts, and the thought was quickly pushed to the back of my mind.

I moaned, raising my hips, desperate for him to touch me already. One of his hands trailed down my stomach and I gasped when he pushed two fingers inside me.

"Oh, God," I cried against his lips and I closed my eyes. He moved his fingers in and out, finally giving me what I wanted.

I was vaguely aware of the fact that he was watching me,

looking at the effect his movements had on me, but I ignored it. Every thrust with his fingers was rougher and I felt the muscles in my core tighten way too fast for my liking, *but oh, well.*

"Yes! Yes!" I moaned, and I took a deep breath, preparing for the euphoric feeling to wash over me.

Just when I was about to come, he pulled his fingers out of me, and before I could protest, he shoved them deep in my mouth, almost making me gag.

"Suck," he commanded and I did, tasting myself on my tongue.

I arched my back off the bed and hummed against his fingers, the build-up to my denied orgasm rapidly fading. He pulled his fingers from my lips, but only after I pressed my teeth in them, and he chuckled before licking them himself.

"Don't move," he said and he slowly went down, sucking and biting my skin on his way. I gasped when he took a nipple in his mouth, squeezing my breasts hard and adding pleasurable pain.

"Fuck," I breathed, grabbing the pillow behind my head and balling my fists, clutching the fabric.

Pretty Boy continued his journey down, leaving a trail of open-mouth kisses as he went. He hummed against my lower stomach and stopped. I opened my eyes, frowning.

"What's this?" he chirped and he licked the 'bite me' tattoo on my groin. I chuckled as he lightly bit the skin. I got that ridiculous tattoo as a joke when I turned twenty-one.

I gasped as he kissed the inside of each thigh, bringing his lips closer to my pussy, and I arched my back slightly, getting utterly lost in this amazing feeling again.

"What do you want, Baby?" he said before blowing air against my core, shooting another bolt of pleasure through me.

"I want you to fuck me with your mouth," I said, trying to press my thighs together to release some pressure.

"No, no." He roughly pulled my legs apart and pinned them against the bed.

"I told you not to move," he said firmly.

"Are you going to punish me now?" I asked and I rolled my lower lip between my teeth. A mischievous sparkle appeared in his eyes and I hated to admit that it turned me on even more. *Was he?*

"Don't tempt me," he said and he dove in between my legs, attracting a loud gasp from my lips as he flattened his tongue over my sensitive nub.

"God, Jesus!" I moaned.

As if they were going to save me now.

His hands caressed my hip bones and moved back, grabbing my ass. His tongue dipped into me as he squeezed my ass just as hard as he did my breasts earlier, and I felt the pressure building again.

"Yes! Right there!" I moaned and I rolled my hips against his face.

I was seconds away from my release, feeling the sparks in my chest shooting in every direction.

"Please! Don't stop!" I cried, but again, he stopped right before the finale. "What the fuck?" I whined and Pretty Boy looked up. This was all a game to him, teasing me, playing with me. And I wasn't sure if I liked it.

"Patience, Baby," he said, licking his lips as he stood up, standing at the edge of the bed. "Get on your knees."

I was torn. I really wanted to lick those abs and suck his dick, but a part of me wanted to deny him *all* pleasure.

I got on my knees anyway, tucking my feet under my ass

and tilting my head a tiny bit down, remembering that video I watched last week, the random hour that I was suddenly researching everything BDSM.

"Good girl," he purred, and I had to hold in my eye roll. His fingers grazed my jaw, lifting my head. "But you can touch me."

He didn't have to tell me twice.

I grabbed the top of his slacks and pulled him closer, licking all the way from the sexy v-line, up until his chest, dipping my tongue in the grooves of his muscles.

"How long have you been wanting to do that?" he chuckled and I looked up.

"Since you took off your shirt," I admitted as I undid his belt.

He caressed the side of my face and I pushed down his slacks and boxers, gulping when I was met with his erection. Not sure how I was going to fit *that* inside me, but we'd make it work.

I looked up at him as I stuck out my tongue and licked the pre cum off his tip. He closed his eyes and hummed at the sensation. I grabbed the base with one hand, his hip with the other, closing my lips around his length, and started to suck.

This is the moment, Jordan. We haven't done this in a while, but he's extremely handsome and we need to hear that compliment we all know we want to hear.

I took him as deep as possible and moved one hand to his balls, lightly massaging them as I continued to lick and suck.

"Fuck," he breathed, and he grabbed a fistful of my hair, pushing himself in even more.

Tears appeared in my eyes but I ignored them, the gag reflex not kicking in yet.

I felt him tense, so I pulled back, trying to fuck up his orgasm as much as he had mine.

He didn't say anything, instead, he grabbed me by the waist and threw me back on the bed, my chest flush to the sheets.

"Lift your ass, Baby," he said and I got on my knees, arching my back. I was throbbing with anticipation, my fingers digging into the sheets beneath me. I heard the rip of a condom packet and a few seconds later I felt his tip was at my entrance.

"I'll let you adjust, but after that, I'm going to be a little more rough, ok?"

God yes.

"Out loud, Baby," he added.

"Yes," I moaned.

He grabbed the back of my neck with one hand, placed the other on my waist, and he slowly pushed in. "Fuck," he breathed, and I moaned when he filled me to the hilt. He gave me a second to adjust, rubbing his hands over my skin, and started to thrust into me when I began to move.

He quickly started to pick up his pace, slapping into me harder with every thrust and pushing my face into the bed.

"Oh my God!" I moaned, the angle doing everything for me. I shrieked softly when his hand made contact with my ass and arched my back even more. He repeated that a few more times, spanking me harder every time—testing how far he could go.

My orgasm was building rapidly, my body wanting a release as fast as it could, nervous that he was going to deny me again.

But he wasn't.

"Yes! Fuck!" I gasped, filling my lungs with as much air as I could. He pushed harder, reaching the right spot every time, and the best orgasm of my life washed over me—the reason he kept denying me instantly becoming *crystal* clear.

"Oh, yes!" I yelled out as he continued to thrust into me, riding out my release and chasing his own. His thrust became sloppy and after a few seconds, he tensed, filling the condom.

My legs gave out and Pretty Boy collapsed on top of me, both of us out of breath and sweaty. He was still inside me, pulsating and hot, his fingers drawing small circles on my shoulder.

After a few minutes, he got up and trashed the condom.

I flipped over, closing my eyes as I was still trying to catch my breath. The bed shifted and I could feel him beside me, wrapping an arm around my waist and pulling me against his chest.

Hesitantly, I relaxed against him, staring out of the floor-to-ceiling window until I heard light snoring come from behind me. I couldn't help but smile at how quickly Pretty Boy had fallen asleep, but I couldn't blame him.

So, now that he had drifted off to sleep, I could get out of here without awkward morning conversations and weird looks at my *I-just-woke-up*-look. And I did.

CHAPTER 4
Jordan

The next morning, the first thing I did was grab a glass and fill it with cold water from the fridge, the temperature giving me brain-freeze as I took a big gulp. Wincing at the pain in my forehead, I placed the glass down and opened my fridge again in search of something to eat.

Right, maybe it was time for some grocery shopping.

I walked to my bedroom, pulling my makeshift pajama shirt over my head and chucking it on the ever-growing pile of laundry. *Guess that was on my to-do's list too.*

Putting on a fresh thong and a sports bra, I grabbed my trusty black leggings. It wasn't like I was going to do something productive today, and the judgemental cashier at the local grocery store could go suck a dick.

The only reason I had gym wear in my possession was because it was amazing for lounging in. I tried the whole working-out thing, but soon after came to the conclusion that it was not for me.

I dragged my sore ass back to the living room, expertly avoiding the desk that was partly in my way because it wouldn't fit anywhere else in this house. *The number of bruises this piece of furniture had given me over the years...*

Grabbing the small purse I had used last night, I walked to the kitchen and emptied it over the kitchen bar, the sound of my phone hitting the counter making me flinch. I raised my brows as my eyes fell on something gold that I didn't recognize. *That wasn't there before.*

I pushed my debit card, lip balm, and coins aside and grabbed the Rolex, my eyes widening when I realized what I had done.

"Oh, fuck," I mumbled, covering my mouth with my hand and feeling the panic creep in.

Flashbacks of the night before flooded my mind, and I mentally slapped myself in the face at not being more mindful of what I shoved in my bag before I left. Though I could curse Pretty Boy for placing the piece of jewelry next to my things, too.

What if he reports me to the police? Ok, calm down, he doesn't even know your name.

"Shit, shit, shit," I cursed, carefully placing the expensive watch back on the counter before pacing around the living room, trying to think of Pretty Boy's address. The whole 'no name'-thing came to bite me in the ass, that's for sure.

I grabbed the watch, feeling a little weird that I was holding something that could pay my rent for the next two years—*at least*—and I looked at the yellow gold and back dial, getting a little lost in its richness.

What now? Hoping I was going to run into him?

I grabbed my go-to purse, putting my cards and cash in my wallet, and hesitantly placed the watch in one of the small pockets, thinking it would be wise to keep it with me in case I *did* run into him.

Or I just didn't want to leave it in my apartment—in the same building where there had been four break-ins this month alone.

I sighed as I pulled on a hoodie, deciding to put my cap on too, not feeling like talking to anyone.

"I'm sorry, Miss, but it seems that your card is being declined... again," the cashier said with an apologetic look on her face, handing me back my card, and I sucked my lower lip between my teeth in embarrassment.

I heard a scoff behind me, the line growing every minute I was standing there, unable to pay. The fact that the overall price of my groceries was around thirty dollars didn't help the awkward situation, and I decided to end my misery, fishing the fifty out of the emergency-compartment of my bag.

"I'm sorry. Here," I mumbled with crimson cheeks, wanting to get out of there as fast as I could.

"Thank you," she replied, taking the money and typing something on the screen, her acrylic nails tapping on the glass obnoxiously loud.

After she handed me my change, I started to pack up my groceries at lightning speed, tears forming in my eyes for no fucking reason. Maybe because I was embarrassed, maybe because this was literally the last money I had, and maybe, because I just hated my life altogether.

Once I was out of the store, I wiped my face and womaned the fuck up, taking a deep breath. Next week I was going to hear from Cendose Incorporated, I had two more job interviews the week after that, and five more companies who hadn't responded to my letters. *Everything was going to be fine.*

I shrieked when my phone rang, dropping my tomatoes as I grabbed the device out of my bag.

"Of *fucking* course," I huffed, pressing the green button and sandwiching my phone between my ear and shoulder.

"What?" I snapped.

"Well, good morning to you too, sunshine," Ashley chirped as I crouched down to grab my tomatoes, half of which I could throw away as soon as I got home.

"Hey, Ash." I sighed and I continued my journey home, luckily just a five-minute walk.

"So, remember yesterday, when I said, *'let's go out tomorrow'*?" she asked.

"Hmm."

"Well, change of plans," she said and I frowned, the hesitation in her voice making me uneasy. "My brother is back in town, and my parents want to have a family dinner tonight. Well, ok, he's been back for a while, but now that he's settled in they're dragging our asses to the mansion."

My face relaxed. It was a shame that we weren't going out,

but then again, I couldn't afford it anyway. Maybe next week was a better idea. Or next month, when hopefully, I had a stable income.

"Maybe we can go out another time, it's no problem," I answered, crossing the road to avoid the sketchy group of junkies on my street.

"No, erm, you're invited," she muttered, stopping me in my tracks.

"What?" I snapped. The Abbots had always hated my guts, especially Ashley's mother, and I was not ready to sit through dinner filled with nasty comments and painful questions.

"I know, but it would mean a lot to me if you were there," she pleaded. "I want to tell you something important."

I sighed. Maybe when her brother was there, her mother wouldn't pick on me as much. I didn't know the guy, but since they hadn't seen him for a while I could imagine him to be the center of attention at dinner. "Fine. Text me the time and I'll be there."

"Yes! Oh, I'm so happy, Jo. Ryan will be there too!" she beamed and I smiled. *As long as Ashley Abbot gets what she wants, I guess.* And with her boyfriend there, surely her mother would play nice?

—

"Going out, Jordy?"

I walked down the stairs, rolling my eyes at the man standing next to Mrs. Hellen. She was putting Spotty's collar on, the dalmatian excitedly wiggling his tail and trying to lick her face.

"What's it to you?" I asked and I carefully stepped off the last step of the stairs—again, wearing painful shoes. *Dinner at the*

Abbot mansion required a smarter outfit.

"Tsk tsk, Babe. Just a question."

"Eli, be nice," Mrs. Hellen warned and he crossed his arms, the muscles of his arms and shoulders straining the fabric of his sweater. God, those arms felt amazing around me when he used to slam into me from behind. *Such a shame he was such an asshole. Nothing like his mother.*

"Yes, mom," he said, pushing himself off the wall he was leaning on and giving her a kiss on the cheek. I guess he had it in him to be nice to his mother, contrary to the other people in his life. "I need to grab my phone."

"How are you doing, Jordan?" Mrs. Hellen asked, straightening up and handing her son her keys. I walked over to her, hoisting the straps of my bag higher up my shoulder.

"I'm good," I answered. *Yeah, absolutely fine.* "You?"

She looked over her shoulder, checking if Eli was out of earshot.

"I'm sorry," she said, her voice dripping with pity, and I smiled weakly at her. "I know he loved you."

I looked at Spotty, brushing a hand over his head. Early in the relationship, it became quite clear that we were not meant to be, but both of us didn't want to see it. Or, I didn't. In the end, it didn't matter.

"Just not enough."

"Hmm. I would've loved you as my daughter-in-law, but I know my Eli can be a little..." she trailed off, biting the inside of her cheek.

"It doesn't matter," I said, taking a deep breath and smiling down at the dalmatian at my feet. Eli and I were no longer a couple, and over the last couple of months, I had realized that it was definitely better this way.

"If you say so," she mumbled as Eli appeared behind her and closed the door to her apartment. He handed the keys back to his mother and shot me a grin. I diverted my eyes.

"Ready?" he asked and Mrs. Hellen nodded before her gaze fell on his pants.

"Hold on. Are you wearing ripped jeans?" she asked, grabbing Eli by his sweater.

I chuckled and walked away, leaving them to discuss Eli's bad boy's clothing style without me.

Once in my car, I rolled down the windows—as I didn't have air conditioning and the late summer nights were still hot. I put on my sunglasses and headed towards my nightmare: the Abbot's home.

I didn't need a fancy car, as long as baby Benji still worked and helped me reach my destination, I was happy. But as the houses along the streets started to resemble expensive mansions more and more the closer I got to the Abbot home, I did feel a little out of place.

I gave my name at the front gate and drove up the driveway towards the massive house when I arrived, old, happy memories coming back to the surface.

After I parked my car next to a beautiful black Camaro, I stepped out with even more nerves than before. What would Ashley want to tell us? Would her parents just be chill for once?

Taking a deep breath, I locked my door and walked up the few steps to the house, my knees wobbling and my hands clenching and unclenching with anxiousness.

"Jojo!" Ashley shouted as I walked into the hallway, and she came running down the stairs in her red, four-inch heels. *How?*

"Hey, Ash," I said as I returned her hug, grunting as she nearly squeezed the life out of me.

"Let her breathe, baby," Ryan teased as he walked down the stairs as well. He had definitely changed since he and Ashley got together. But as he came closer I noticed some of his tattoos peeking out from under his collar, reminding me that he was still a bad boy at heart.

"Hi, Ryan," I greeted, giving him a kiss on the cheek before we made our way further into the house.

Ashley suddenly pulled me aside before we could step into the dining room, and I raised my brows.

"Ok, so. I want to warn you," she said cautiously and I crossed my arms. Warn me about her parents? Too late, Ash.

"Ok..."

"Charlie is kind of... well..." she trailed off, thinking about a good way to describe her brother, and I raised my brows. *Oh, she meant her brother.* "Well, he's a playboy and treats women like trash."

Of course, he does.

"I mean, as long as he treats *you* right, right?" I asked, attempting to walk further into the house and move on from this strange conversation.

"Yeah, I adore him. But," she continued, stopping me in my tracks. "He's a ladies man and I guess I just want you to keep your distance. I don't want you to get hurt and in all honesty, I just don't really trust him with my friends. I know the way he treats girls, and..."

"Ok," I chuckled, nodding, and Ashley let out a relieved breath.

"Good, well, that's all I wanted to say."

Still a little weirded out by our conversation, I followed her into the dining room where her parents were already seated. Ashley's mother sipped her wine as her husband discussed something with her, and I swallowed hard.

"Good afternoon, Mr. and Mrs. Abbot," I tried, and I received a nod from Mr. Abbot. *Progress, I guess.*

"Ms. Sawyer," Mrs. Abbot responded coldly and I sat down as far away from Ashley's parents as I could. Ashley and Ryan sat across from me, next to Mrs. Abbot, and a weird tension filled the air.

"Erm, how are you? Thank you for inviting me," I said in an attempt to break the silence as I nervously played with the piece of string around my wrist. How I wished I was at the beach where I bought it right now.

"We didn't invite you," Mrs. Abbot retorted and I sighed, my smile faltering a little.

"Mom!" Ashley said firmly, but her mother didn't respond. *Dinner was going to be fun.*

"*I* invited her because Ryan and I have news."

"Oh God, don't tell me you're pregnant," Mrs. Abbot said and I tried to hold in a chuckle. *Wait.* My face fell and I looked at her glass of wine, frowning.

"No, no. I—"

"Hi everybody," a voice boomed through the dining room, cutting Ashley off and attracting all the attention. "I'm here."

Where have I heard that voice before?

I turned and faced the entrance, my eyes widening when I looked at the source.

Pretty boy?

CHAPTER 5
Charlie

I walked through the tall, glass doors, entering the foyer of my parents' company. I was happy to be back; after five years at Stanford and another five years of working in the city, I was finally home.

I winked at the blonde behind the front desk and walked straight to the elevators, ready to start as president under my father. I wasn't happy that I wasn't named the CEO, but that was something for the future. He'd retire one day, and I would take over for him, getting the position I deserved.

Pressing the button for the top floor and watching the doors close, I momentarily relived last night. *Fuck, that girl. No— that woman.*

Some people called me a playboy, a womanizer, but what was wrong with enjoying casual sex with women that dropped at my feet anyway?

It was a shame I wasn't seeing Baby again. I could see it in her eyes. There was something about her, and I was a little disappointed that I wasn't going to find out what it was. Maybe...

I straightened up and adjusted myself when I heard the ping of the elevator, signaling me that I had arrived at my floor. Shrugging off the dirty thoughts and memories from the night before, I stepped out. I walked through the deserted hallway with big strides, smiling when I saw my name on the frosted glass of my new office door. I eyed the empty assistant desk in front of my office, imagining various pretty girls in short skirts, and walked into my office.

"Charlie!"

I flinched when I heard my baby sister's high-pitched voice, the small woman running up to me in impossible heels before she wrapped her arms around my neck.

"Hey, Ash. I've missed you, too," I chuckled, lifting her in the air and twirling her around. It was not something we normally did, but it had been a long time since we had seen each other.

"I'm so happy you're back!" she beamed as I placed her back on the ground.

"Yes, now, let go, this is Armani." I pointed to my shirt. She rolled her eyes and playfully slapped my chest, watching me as I walked around the big, dark desk, running my fingers over the surface.

"You haven't changed a bit," Ashley sighed as she plopped down in one of the big plush chairs opposite of mine.

I looked around the room, the minimalistic and modern style

exactly how I wanted it until my eyes fell on something *not* my style.

"Ashley, what is *that*?" I asked, pointing to a green monstrosity in the corner next to the door. She turned around before looking back at me with raised brows.

"A...plant?" she mumbled, and I raised a brow.

"Yes, why is it in my office?"

"Well, you need a bit of color in here. I don't understand why everything has to be so tidy and clean," she scoffed and I crossed my arms, leaning back in the ergonomic office chair.

"I don't understand how you can be so messy," I countered with disdain, raising a brow.

"Well—No, stop. I'm not here to argue with you, you're thirty years old for Christ's sake."

I chuckled and played with one of the pens that were perfectly placed on my desk, looking at her. She looked good, her dark blond hair a little shorter than the last time I saw her, and her lips painted red, just as she always did. But this time, it fit her better.

"Anyway," Ashley chimed in, interrupting my train of thought. "I wanted to talk to you about something."

"I thought you were just happy to see me."

"I am, but this is important."

"Ok," I said, leaning forward, placing my elbows on my desk, and folding my hands together. I frowned at her expression, the way she pressed her lips together and her eyes seemed to widen, told me that it was something serious. *Did I do something already?*

"Well, now that you're back in town, I think we're going to see a lot more of each other," she said and I nodded, narrowing my eyes at her. "And, I just want to make a promise, I guess."

"What kind of promise? Where's this going, Ash?"

"I am promising you," she continued, pointing a finger at me, "that if you so much as *look* at my best friend the wrong way, I am going to cut off your dick and feed it to Percy. She has been through enough."

I raised my brows and shifted in my seat. The idea of our grandparents' dog munching on Charlie Jr. made me very uncomfortable.

Ashley had made it her mission to keep her friends away from me, and so far, she had kind of succeeded. The only thing I knew was that Jordan was her best friend and that there was a Bailey, who was married, but since I hadn't really been in town, I had never met them.

"Ok...is she hot?" I dared to ask, holding my hands up in defeat when she made a cutting gesture with her fingers. "Ok, sorry."

I cocked a brow at her. "Don't you think you're being a little bit of a hypocrite?"

She crossed her arms, her gaze avoiding mine for a second before she regained composure. "That I'm...with your best friend does not mean you can play with the heart of mine. Again, Jordan has been through enough, Charlie. I know you."

I shrugged, relaxing back into my chair. "Fine."

"Well now that that's out of the way," she said, leaning back in her chair. "Mom and Dad wanted to have a family dinner tonight."

I rolled my eyes and fiddled with my watch, sighing.

"That sounds...*fun*."

"Yes, well, do it for me. Ryan is going to be there, too, so that should make it less boring for you. And besides, you're the favorite child anyway."

"Whatever. Well, I look forward to tonight then," I retorted as I turned my computer on. "Now, get out, I need to prepare some things for Monday."

"I look forward to working with you." Ashley smiled and she walked around the desk, kissing me on the cheek. "It's good to have you back, Charlie."

—

I arrived a little early at my parents mansion and decided to sneak around the house to find my old spot. The spot where I had spent years talking with friends, smoking pot, and just escaping to have a moment to myself.

Letting my fingers glide over the weathered bench—the white paint half gone, I looked at the side table that was wiped clean. I could still make out the C and A that Ash and I scratched into the wood fifteen years ago, and smiled at the happy memories.

I brushed some dust off the bench and sat down, staring at the trees that surrounded the property. It was good to be back home.

And who knows what a new environment will bring?

Not that I had much to complain about. My life was pretty great. I had tons of money, a lot of friends, and women threw themselves at me whenever they could. Maybe there *was* something missing, but as I couldn't figure out what it was, I assumed it probably wasn't important.

I sat there for a few more minutes before it was time to go inside and get this dinner over with. Ashley had told me that Mom and Dad wanted us to have dinner with them, but as I looked in the direction of the back doors, I started to think it was more Ashley's idea.

Sighing with a smirk, I walked back to the front of the house, the spot next to my car now filled by a red mini, and I raised my brows. It looked trashed.

Shrugging, I walked into the house, hearing voices in the dining room. *Here we go.*

"No, no. I—"

"Hi everybody," I said loudly, making sure everyone could hear me, cutting my sister off. "I'm here."

"Oh, Charlie!" My mother beamed and I walked up to her, kissing her on the cheek.

"Hey, Mom. You look beautiful." I smiled and she playfully slapped me on the arm, sinking back into her chair.

"Charlie, good to have you back," my dad said, nodding. "How's the new apartment?"

"Yes, Charlie's back, yay! I have news!" Ashley whined before I could respond and I walked to the last seat available, stopping in my tracks when I saw *her*.

She looked up at me with wide, brown eyes, like a deer caught in headlights. She looked as sexy as the first time I saw her, and the blush that crept up her cheeks made every muscle in my body tingle.

"Baby?" I said without thinking, and Ashley shot up, pointing at me with a well-manicured finger. I *knew* she looked familiar.

"No! Don't, Charlie, I warned you!" she yelled and I sat down next to Ba—Jordan. I refrained from rubbing a hand over the back of my neck and looking incredibly guilty, staring my sister in the eyes.

Too late little sis.

How had I not seen it? I'd seen plenty of pictures of Ash and her best friend over the years.

"Ashley, calm down," Mom interrupted our glaring, and I felt Jordan tense next to me. Maybe the universe saw the sparkle in her eyes too. *This was going to be fun.*

"Yes, calm down, Ashley," I smirked and she rolled her eyes. I had definitely missed teasing my sister, that's for sure.

"Now, what was so important?" Mom asked and Ashley's scowl turned into a smile. She grabbed Ryan's hand and beamed with pride and happiness. "We're getting married!"

The room went silent for a minute before Mom finally spoke up. "Oh my God, honey. That's amazing! Felix, say something." She playfully slapped Dad on the arm and he smiled. "You knew, didn't you?"

"Of course, he needed my permission, didn't he?" Dad teased and Mom smiled. She made her way over to Ashley and gave her a hug.

I noticed that Jordan was still sitting next to me, the feisty woman I met yesterday nowhere to be found. *What changed?*

Once my mom sat back down, she sighed and stood up, walking around the table to give my sister a hug as well, her eyes first shifting to my mother. Something was definitely up between them, and I was very curious to find out.

"Congratulations," I said, nodding to Ryan as Ashley whispered something to Jordan. The girls chuckled, and I couldn't help but look at them.

"Thanks, man. Can I count on you to be my best man?" he asked and I smiled, diverting my gaze back to Ryan.

"Of course."

"Right, let's eat," Mom said.

"So, when's the wedding?" I asked as our dinner was served, and Jordan retook her seat next to me. The way she fiddled with her drink and shot me the occasional look made me smirk, and I knew this was going to be a fun night after all.

"Well, we actually wanted a Christmas wedding..." Ashley admitted, biting her lower lip, and Mom raised her brows. *Of course, she did.*

"You're telling me you want to have the wedding in four months?" she argued and Ashley nodded.

"Well, I don't envy your wedding planner," Dad added, diving into his dinner.

"Right. Oh! I almost forgot. Jordan, do you want to be my maid of honor?" Ashley asked, directing her attention to her best friend.

Jordan looked up, smiling. "Of course."

"Are you sure?" Mom asked Ashley and Jordan dropped her head, absentmindedly playing with a piece of meat on her plate. Did my mother have something against the girl? Because what the hell was that response?

"Yes, I'm sure. She's perfect," Ashley defended, shifting her gaze to Mom. "Please show a little more respect, Mom."

I looked from my mother, who had raised her brows, to Jordan, who gave Ashley a weak smile. Why did my mom hate Jordan so much?

I noticed the way Jordan sat back in her chair, almost as if she was trying to hide behind me. *Where was the confident woman I had amazing sex with last night?*

"Oh, Jojo, did you hear something about that job yet?" Ashley asked, changing the subject, and Jordan straightened up.

"No, but it's only been a day." She smiled, looking a little bit more comfortable. I turned slightly in my seat, grinning as Jordan jumped when our legs touched for a split second.

"What's the company?" Ryan asked and Jordan cleared her throat.

"Cendose Incorporated. It's just a front desk position, but I'm hoping to work my way up."

She seemed really proud of the position, and I kept my thoughts to myself. I needed to remind myself that not everyone had the opportunities I did.

"*Work* your way up?" Mom scoffed and I frowned. What the fuck?

I turned my head when Jordan pushed back her chair and stood up.

"Excuse me for a moment," she said calmly, even though her hands were shaking and I could almost *hear* her heartbeat.

"Jo..." Ashley mumbled, but she had already turned around and walked out of the room.

"What's wrong with you?" Ashley scolded. She stood up too, shooting Mom a dirty look before she disappeared into the hall.

"That was harsh. What's wrong with the girl?" I was curious to know why my mother was so rude to Jordan.

"What's wrong? Well—"

"Let me rephrase that," I interrupted, almost slapping myself in the face for that stupid question and sitting forward to lean my elbows on the table. "Why don't you like her?"

"Charles," my father warned, but I ignored him.

"Well?"

"She doesn't belong here," Mom finally stated a little hesitant, and I raised my brows. That much was evident, but I didn't see how that was a problem. It was definitely not a reason to make her feel unwelcome. Besides, it gave Jordan an edge, something different from the stuck-up men and women our family usually associated with.

I shared a look with Ryan, who wasn't Mom's favorite person either when he first came home with me. Taking a big sip of my wine, I tried to ignore the awkward silence that had formed around us.

"Well, dinner's nice," I added sarcastically and my mom rolled her eyes.

"She'll be here in a sec," Ashley sighed as she walked back into the dining room and took her seat. "Mom, can you at least try to be civil? She doesn't deserve this shit."

I decided that I'd rather not be involved in a heated argument between my mom and sister, so I stood up. "I'm going to the bathroom. I'll be right back."

Ryan nodded, but the rest ignored me, already fighting over this girl.

"Whatever," I mumbled as I walked out, not even sure where I was going since I didn't really *need* to go to the bathroom.

I thought I'd get some fresh air when I heard something breaking upstairs. Curiosity taking over, I ascended the stairs and walked down the hallway, following the sound of someone cursing. I ended up in my old bedroom, the doors to the balcony wide open and Jordan, in my favorite position.

Bent over.

"I'm so sorry, Ash. I'll try to replace it," she rambled, and I leaned against the wall, observing her. A half-smoked cigarette between her fingers and her skirt tightly stretched over her ass, she was carefully picking up shards of glass, the picture frame she had knocked over lying face down on the floor in front of her.

I noticed that she was barefoot, and I scanned the room, my gaze falling on her heels, chucked in the corner.

"Careful, Baby," I smirked, and she shot up.

I was a little taken aback by the anger in her face. She was definitely not sad because of my mother's behavior. Oh, no. She was *furious*.

"You," she snapped, narrowing her eyes and pointing at me with the cigarette.

"Can you take that nasty thing out of my room, please," I said, and her gaze dropped to the white stick, before she took a few drags, put it out against the doorframe, and tossed it off the balcony.

"What the fuck are you doing here?" she growled, blowing the smoke in my face. I pretended not to be fazed by it, running my tongue over my lower lip.

"I'm having dinner at my pa—"

"Oh, fuck off."

I raised my brows, watching her drop the glass back on the ground before she took a few steps in my direction, the height difference forcing her to look up to me.

She almost looked cute, all angry and tiny.

"Wipe that grin off your face, Pretty Boy," she sneered, making my grin grow wider. "Why the fuck didn't you tell me you're her brother?"

"Why would I? I didn't know you were her best friend." I shrugged with a chuckle. *At the time, anyway.*

"Ugh, shit!" she swore, throwing her arms in the air and turning around, walking onto the balcony. Of course, she knew neither one of us could've known about the other, but I was confident that it wasn't something she was admitting soon.

I pushed myself off the wall and followed her outside, where I leaned on the railing, looking her up and down from beside her.

"She can never find out," Jordan sighed, turning her head to look at me. The serious look on her face took me aback.

"Why not?" I asked, not even sure myself if it was wise to tell my sister. I respected her too much to break her trust. *Even though I already had.*

"She's my best friend, Pr— Charlie."

I stayed silent, my thoughts moving in a different direction. All I could think about was bending Jordan over that railing, and I was in the middle of imagining that I was fucking her from behind, when she slapped me hard on the chest, bringing me back to reality.

"Are you even listening?" she continued and I nodded, the corners of my mouth curling up as I looked at her.

"So what do you want to do now?" I asked, my eyes involuntarily lowering to her ass. God, it was as if I was seeing it for the first time. Which was partly true, since this was the first time I observed her from this distance, without being too busy deciding which position—

"Charlie!"

Right.

"My eyes are up here, Pretty Boy."

"Hmm," I hummed, looking back up. They were pretty to look at too, I guess. Dark and big, looking straight into your soul if you weren't careful. To be honest, they were beautiful. *Uh, ok.*

"Jesus, is sex the only thing you think about?" she asked and I nodded, shrugging when she rolled her eyes.

I took a step in her direction, bringing my face closer to hers and placing two fingers under her chin. "I'm a guy, you were amazing in bed, and frankly, I want to do it again."

CHAPTER 6
Jordan

I bit my lip, trying not to blush at his admission.
God, I really wanted to fuck him again.

It was like fate heard me when I thought it was a shame I wouldn't see him again. But Ashley's words sounded in my head as I looked at the man before me. I made her a promise, and I respected her too much to go back on it.

Even though I couldn't deny that he looked amazing in grey. The suit fit him perfectly and he radiated confidence, which was a big turn-on. As was the way he carried himself and looked at me—no, watched me—in the same fashion he had done yesterday at the restaurant. That mischievous sparkle in those icy blue eyes intrigued me.

He had definitely changed—grown up. The pictures in the Abbot mansion did him *no* justice whatsoever.

"We can't," I took a deep breath, wishing I didn't have to shut him down.

"I always get what I want," Charlie boldly responded to my rejection, taking a step closer, and I raised a brow.

"You're not even hiding the fact that you're a spoiled brat," I observed, allowing him to come closer, his scent filling my nostrils and almost making me faint. *In an annoyingly good way.*

"No. Why would I?"

I huffed in frustration. It was infuriating how he always had an answer ready. Even in the few hours that I had 'known' him, he managed to get under my skin with expert precision.

He smirked, carefully placing one hand on the small of my back, and I absentmindedly lifted my face. There was a ridiculous pull between us, forcing us together like magnets. I couldn't stop it as I looked into his eyes, a tingle going up my spine and his hand almost burning a hole in my shirt as he held me.

He watched me as his hand glided down to my ass, and I closed my eyes as his fingers played with the hem of my skirt. I was addicted to this feeling, no matter how much my mind screamed at me to stop, to leave.

"You like getting what you want, too, don't you, *Jordan*?" he cooed, the warmth of his breath fanning over my face as he spoke and sending goosebumps down my arms.

Say my name like that again.

"I—" I breathed out and a soft moan escaped me, my eyes slowly falling shut and Charlie slowly pulled me in.

"Jordan! Where are you?"

My eyes shot back open and Charlie's hand disappeared from my ass, the both of us springing apart at the sound of Ashley's voice.

"Fuck," I mumbled, my heartbeat still thumping loudly in my chest as the adrenaline from the tension-filled moment still coursed through my veins.

"It's just Ashley," Charlie stated and I scowled at him.

"Yes, the best friend that made me promise to not go near you," I hissed, pushing him to the wall beside the doors. He chuckled, his head turning to look inside the house, before he faced me again, smirking.

Of course.

"Alright, can I just..." he trailed off, grabbing my ass and giving it a little squeeze. I shrieked at the contact, playfully slapping his hand away as I grinned back.

"Stay outside," I demanded, walking into the house without giving him another look, closing the balcony doors behind me. I tried not to think about the fact that I was incredibly turned on, and took a deep breath.

"I'm here!" I yelled, and after a few seconds, Ashley walked in.

"What are you doing in here? And why do you look all flustered?" she asked, narrowing her eyes at me.

I quickly looked around the room, thinking of an excuse.

"I wanted to go to the room furthest from your parents and I accidentally dropped this," I replied, pointing to the broken picture frame on the ground as I mentally patted myself on the shoulder for the save.

"Oh, well, this is Charlie's old room," she said and I grabbed my heels, putting the horrid things back on.

"I didn't know."

Liar.

"Hmm. Well, I'll have someone clean that up. Let's go back downstairs."

I nodded, following her out of the room. Right before I shut the door behind me, I looked over my shoulder. Charlie had gotten back inside, and he shot me a wink. I quickly shut the door behind me and straightened up as I walked down the stairs.

—

After managing to sit through the rest of the evening and practically running out of the house as soon as it was over, I was back in my safe space, wearing my trusty, ripped pajama shorts and bleach-stained cami.

My music was blasting as I cleaned my bathroom the next day when my doorbell suddenly rang.

Who the fuck was disturbing my peace this morning?

I turned my music down and dropped the rag I was using in the bucket of soapy water before I walked to my front door.

"Somewhere in the near future, I need you to move to a better neighborhood. I always feel like I'm going to get robbed when I visit you."

I chuckled as Bailey barged into my apartment, her four-year-old son running up to me and holding up his little arms.

"Hi, how are you? I'm good, how nice of you to come by," I mumbled sarcastically, picking up Jayden. I gave him a kiss on the cheek, and he wiped his face in disgust. *I love kids.*

"Yeah, where do you keep your coffee?" Bailey asked from

the kitchen, and I closed the door with her son on my hip.

"Cupboard next to the stove."

"Jordan? Guess what I did yesterday?" Jayden asked and I walked to the couch, sitting down with the sweet boy on my lap. He looked at me with his big brown eyes, waiting for me to start guessing.

"You got an A in math?"

"He's four, Jordan," Bailey retorted from the kitchen, and I pressed my lips together to conceal a smirk.

"Right," I muttered, waiting for the kid to just tell me.

"I had my first day at school," he beamed and I smiled at the pride and excitement in his dark brown eyes.

"Yay! That's amazing!" I gushed, watching Jayden as he bounced up and down on my leg, his tight dark curls bouncing with him.

"Fuck, Jordan, what's this?" Bailey suddenly gasped and I covered Jayden's ears in an attempt to shield him from his mother's cursing.

"What?" I asked while Jayden jumped off my lap and grabbed a race car toy from the bag Bailey had dropped next to the couch.

"Where did you get this?" she asked and I stood up, joining her in the kitchen.

"What's wha—shit." She showed me the gold watch.

"Language," Bailey warned and I raised a brow at her. "Yeah, whatever. Where did you get the watch?"

I could slap myself in the face for not returning it to its rightful owner yesterday.

"That's a long story. The real question is, where the fuck did you find that asshole you set me up with?" I asked as Bailey crossed her arms, leaning against the counter behind her. She looked surprised at my choice of words.

"Chris? Yeah, I meant to call you about your date. How was it?"

I raised my brows, mirroring her stance. She caught the hint and shook her head. "Well, did you at least have sex?" she asked and I nodded.

"Yeah, but not with him. I wouldn't touch him with a ten-foot pole."

"That bad?"

"He practically ignored the waiter, tried to order for me, only talked about himself, talked about women as if we're less than men, and didn't give the waiter a tip. I was surprised he didn't throw a tantrum and complain about the food," I explained and Bailey chuckled.

"God, I'm sorry. He works with Theo, I thought he'd be okay."

"I need to have a talk with your husband about the men he works with."

"He's the son of one of the partners, I don't think he can do much about it," Bailey defended before she took a sip of coffee. I rolled my eyes. *Of course, he was.*

I hummed, pouring myself a cup of instant coffee too. It wasn't great, but it was cheap and I needed caffeine.

"So who did you fuck then?" Bailey continued, placing her cup on the counter.

"Mommy?" Jayden interrupted, walking up to his mother and pulling at the fabric of her slacks.

"Yes, baby?"

"What does 'fuck' mean?" he asked, and I choked on my coffee as I tried to take a sip, spraying it all over my face.

"Jesus," she mumbled under her breath and I wiped the hot liquid off my face, wondering how she was going to talk her way out of this one. "That's a grown-up word. Do you remember what mommy said about those?"

"Yes. I'm allowed to use them when I'm eighteen," he recited and I chuckled. *Interesting tactic.*

"Except..." Bailey added, waiting for her boy to finish her sentence.

"Except when I'm talking to you or daddy."

"Good boy. Now go and play with your cars, honey."

Jayden nodded and ran back to the couch, grabbing his car and running it over the edge of the coffee table.

How can kids entertain themselves with a piece of plastic for hours? *I mean, I have one particular piece of plastic I can enjoy for a while...*

"Anyway, who?" Bailey pressed, getting back on topic, and I sucked my lower lip between my teeth.

Bailey had never met Charlie either, and it wasn't like I was still sleeping with him, but it didn't feel right to tell her. Maybe it was for the best that nobody found out. Ever.

"Just some guy I met at the restaurant. He bought me a drink and we ended up going back to his place," I answered, hoping she couldn't hear my heartbeat. I was a terrible liar, even though I was technically telling the truth.

"Nice. How was it?"

I continued to tell her about the good sex I had with Charlie, leaving out the fact that it was *him*, but including every other detail. She would've gotten it out of me at some point, so I didn't bother to be vague anymore.

Especially since I knew she enjoyed living her best life through me or Ashley. Things hadn't been the same for her since Jayden came around. *Not that I was living my best life, but whatever.*

We spent the rest of the morning talking, catching up on each other's lives, and drinking more gross coffee, which, over time, tasted better and better.

"Shit, I have to be at my dad's in fifteen minutes," I suddenly realized as I poured the coffee I had left down the drain.

"Good luck with that," Bailey chuckled, downing her cup and placing it next to mine on the counter.

I ran to my bedroom and quickly threw on some decent clothes. My dad wasn't like the Abbot's, where everybody always looked like they were dining with the queen, but I wanted to at least look like I tried.

"Let's go, Jay," Bailey said and Jayden gave his mother his toy, grabbing her hand before walking to the front door.

"I'm sorry, B," I apologized as I grabbed my keys. She smiled at me as I struggled to close my door, heading for the stairs.

"It's fine. We'll set up a dinner date soon."

We went our separate ways outside, and I headed to my dad's. It wasn't a long drive to his house, but I was late nonetheless.

I parked Benji in front of my childhood home, smiling at the red roses in the yard and my mind instantly flooded with happy memories of my father working in his garden.

It was his baby; ever since I was little he was always busy taking care of the flowers. And it paid off because they truly looked beautiful.

I walked up to the house and rang the doorbell.

"Hey, Honey. I was worried you forgot about me," my dad said as he opened the door.

"I had Bailey over and we lost track of time. I could never forget you." I smiled, wrapping my arms around my dad's torso and burying my face in his chest.

"Is that Jordan?" I heard from behind my father, and I let him go to hug Eliza, his wife.

"How are you? Feeling better?" I asked, remembering the phone conversation I had with Dad a few days ago where he told me she had been feeling sick.

"Oh, it was just a cold. You know your father," she said with a nudge of her head and I chuckled.

My dad was always the type to go to the hospital for a sore throat, but I thought it made him sweet and caring.

"Well, uh, let's eat," he stammered, and he walked into the kitchen, plating the pasta he made. I inhaled the lovely smell of garlic and tomatoes, my mouth watering and my stomach rumbling.

"How've you been, Jordan?" Eliza asked, walking with me to the dinner table.

"Good. I was at the Abbots last night," I replied, taking a seat next to her.

"You ate lobster and caviar?" Dad teased from the open kitchen and I chuckled. My father was always a little bitter about the fact that I had rich friends. Not because he disliked them, but because he couldn't give me everything that they could.

It broke my heart that he felt that way, especially because he didn't need to give me everything. He was always there for me, took care of me, and though he was grieving himself at the time, he helped me cope with my mother's death.

"No, just beef," I answered softly.

"Come on, Mark," Eliza gently scolded and my dad shrugged.

"Ashley had some news, actually," I continued, taking a sip of my water while dad sat down too, placing plates of delicious food in front of us.

"Is she pregnant?" he asked.

"Jesus, no. Why does everybody think that? She's getting married," I replied, rolling my eyes. *Ok, maybe that thought had crossed my mind too.*

"Oh."

"That's amazing!" Eliza cheered, and I nodded absentmindedly. *Yes, amazing that I'll be the only unmarried friend in our little group.*

I mentally slapped myself in the face for thinking that. I was beyond happy for my friends and how they found the loves of their life, but I couldn't help being a little jealous anyway.

"And where's the princess getting married?" Dad asked.

"I don't know yet. Probably somewhere cold, with a lot of snow. She wants to get married at Christmas," I replied.

My dad hummed.

"She asked me to be her maid of honor," I added, the corners of my mouth curling up. We had been best friends since the start of college, and we had been planning our weddings ever since, so I was very excited to help her make her dream a reality.

"That's great." Eliza smiled. "You get to plan the bridal shower, go dress shopping—oh, it'll be so much fun!"

"Do *you* want to be the maid of honor?" I retorted and Eliza chuckled, grabbing her fork and taking a bite from her pasta.

"I think you'll do great," Dad reassured me, reaching over the table to give my hand a little squeeze.

"Thanks, Dad."

He let me go, smiling at me before diving into his food.

"And how's the devil woman?" Eliza asked and I chuckled. I knew she didn't like her, but also that she secretly looked up her morning routine and go-to designer when no one was watching. The woman was an icon, just not a very polite one.

"She lived up to that name yesterday," I replied, thinking about the nasty comments she made. I could pretend she didn't get to me, but my skin wasn't *that* thick. And of course, I wanted the parents of one of my closest friends to like me.

"Wasn't she on that show you watched the other day?" Dad asked and Eliza nodded.

"There was this item about Charlie Abbot, her son," she explained and I almost choked on my food.

"Are you okay?"

I swallowed hard with tears in my eyes, still trying to catch my breath. "What was it about?"

"Just that he was back in town and became president of his father's company. Then it quickly turned into an update on his love life, and I switched channels."

"He sounded like a spoiled kid who never had to work for anything in his life. I'm glad you don't associate with guys like him," dad said, smiling proudly.

"Yes..."

I fiddled with my fork, clenching my teeth together.

"Have you never met Ashley's brother?" Eliza questioned.

"I did, yesterday at dinner. But, before that he was always out of town," I explained, taking a sip of my drink and trying not to show my dad how close I was to blushing.

Disappointing my best friend by sleeping with her brother

wasn't enough, I was letting my dad down, too. Maybe even my mom, who was probably rolling in her grave and cursing at me in Thai.

"And?"

"And, nothing. I didn't really speak to him," I added, digging my hole deeper and deeper.

"Hmm. Well, good. I like Ashley, but the rest of her family..." Dad trailed off, rolling his eyes.

I'm going to hell.

CHAPTER 7
Jordan

I used the information from my Uber drive back to my apartment after the first night we...*met*, to figure out Charlie's address and return his watch.

As I looked up at the big modern building, I found the structure far more intimidating in the daylight. I felt the looks of people in my back, the jeans and sneakers I was wearing clearly not belonging in this neighborhood. *Just like I didn't.*

I could just leave it in his mailbox, *right?* Or if my aim was good, look up for an open window? Who was I kidding, my aim was terrible.

I took a deep breath, deciding to get it over with, and walked into the building. Nodding to the doorman, I walked up to the front desk.

"How can I help you, miss?" the guy behind the counter asked, sitting up straight and looking me in the eye.

"Hi, I'm looking for Charlie Abbot's apartment? I need to return something," I replied, giving the man my biggest and brightest smile. I must've looked like a lunatic, but I didn't know how this shit worked. This apartment building was different from the one where Ashley lived—fancier and bigger.

"Of course. I'll just ring Mr. Abbot."

"Sure. I'm Jordan Sawyer," I said, receiving a nod.

The man picked up the phone and brought it to his ear as I fiddled with my bracelet, actually a little nervous about Charlie's reaction. *What if he thought I stole it? On purpose?*

Maybe I should just go.

"You can go right up." He smiled, interrupting my plan to make a run for it.

"Yes. Of course. Thank you." I walked to the elevator, my legs feeling like jelly.

I tapped my foot nervously against the floor of the lift as it ascended, wanting it to reach the right apartment already so I could leave as fast as I came.

Once the doors finally rolled open, they revealed a smirking Charlie leaning against the kitchen counter. I reminded myself that I was here to return a watch, not to fantasize about him finally nailing me against the floor-to-ceiling windows, and I walked into the apartment.

"Hey, *Baby*." He smiled, and I rolled my eyes, even though I would be lying if I said that the mere sound of his voice didn't do anything to me.

I stopped a few feet from him, and he cocked a brow.

"I don't get a kiss?" he pouted, pushing himself off the counter and taking a step in my direction.

"Fuck off."

"Well, to what do I owe the pleasure?" He crossed his arms and my eyes involuntarily moved to his massive biceps that were threatening to tear the seams of his shirt. "My eyes are up here, Jordan."

I snapped out of my trance, meeting his mischievous gaze. *I hate him.*

"Well, remember that I left Friday after...?" I asked and he raised a brow.

"Vividly."

"Well," I hesitated, fishing the Rolex out of my purse with shaking hands. "I accidentally took—"

"My watch," Charlie exclaimed, closing the distance between us and grabbing the accessory out of my hands. Playfulness had disappeared from his eyes and I bit the inside of my cheek, wrapping my arms around myself.

"I didn't mean...it was an accident," I stammered, taking a step back.

He placed the watch on the kitchen counter and looked up at me, narrowing his eyes. Was he going to yell at me? Report me? Hit me? *Oh, shit, maybe I should make a run for it now.*

"Calm down, you look like you're going to faint," he smirked and I playfully slapped him on the chest in relief, shrieking internally when I was reminded of those hard muscles under the fabric of his shirt.

"You scared the crap out of me," I scolded, and he chuckled.

"Was that all you came to do?" he asked, pushing a strand

of hair behind my ear and lowering his face to mine a little. *Whoa, he's good.*

"I don't..." I muttered, practically speechless. *Why was I so attracted to this guy? Why did I miss his dick the minute I walked out of his apartment?*

Also, I don't get fucking speechless.

"Yes," I said firmly, placing a hand on his stomach with the intention of pushing him back. But, of course, that didn't happen. I just enjoyed the feeling of his toned muscles behind his crisp white button-up under my hand, his scent filling my nostrils and making me weak in the knees.

"Hmm," he hummed, brushing the tips of his fingers down my arm and giving me goosebumps. A tingle went up my spine, and I was suddenly in a trance.

"We can't, Charlie," I breathed out, looking up into his hooded eyes. It felt weird calling him by his name, especially since this wasn't really the name I had imagined him to have. "I made a promise."

"What exactly *did* you promise?" he asked, cocking his head to the side and making no move to back off or walk away.

"That I would keep my distance," I answered, *completely unintentionally* moving my hand down his stomach until my fingers rested on his belt.

I couldn't help it.

I was horny. We were alone. He had a dick.

There was something about him. Something that I couldn't resist. And the minute he opened his mouth it got worse and worse. He was able to get under my skin and make me feel like the most desirable woman in the room at the same time. It was infuriating. Frustrating.

"She kind of made me promise the same thing," he said, placing a hand on my lower back. I arched my back, pushing myself against him.

"She never said you couldn't have sex with me," I argued, earning a chuckle from Charlie.

"She didn't."

I felt his breath on my face and I pressed myself closer against him, rising to my tiptoes. My breathing became uneven and I felt all my blood rush to the junction of my legs, my entire body throbbing with anticipation.

"It's just sex," I breathed out, my lips brushing against his. The mere feeling of his warm mouth was enough to push me over the edge, and I was ready to give in.

"She doesn't have to find out," he whispered, tightening his grip on my waist and pulling me against him.

"Hmm," I hummed, closing my eyes and moving my hands to his hair.

"Oh, for fuck's sake!" Charlie exclaimed, and I sighed as we let each other go, getting interrupted *again*—this time by his apartment's buzzer. *Maybe it was a sign.*

I straightened out my shirt, trying to bring my heart rate down to a healthy speed, as Charlie stomped to the intercom and picked up the phone.

"What?" he snapped, and I smirked when I saw the tent in his slacks. It felt good to know that I had the same effect on him as he had on me. "Oh, fuck. Yes, send them up."

I raised my brows as he walked back to me, trying to adjust himself.

"Who is it?" I asked.

"I'm having dinner with a few old friends tonight, maybe some drinks after. I guess I forgot the time," he explained as he looked me up and down.

"Having drinks on a Thursday?" I frowned.

"Yeah, I have the day off tomorrow anyway. Jordan, can you stand over there, please?" Charlie pleaded, pointing to the other side of the room.

I chuckled, walking behind the counter and putting some distance between us to give him a chance to...*calm down*.

"Better?" I asked, eyeing the uncomfortable expression on his face.

"No, but give me your phone," he ordered, holding out his hand.

I looked from his face to his hand. "Excuse me?"

"I'll put my number in so we can keep in touch about..."—he briefly looked up at me— "the wedding."

"Yes, good idea," I said, grabbing my phone and unlocking it before handing the device to Charlie.

Just when he gave it back to me, the elevator doors slid open and two guys walked in. Both dressed in a perfectly fitted suit and looking like they just walked off of the cover of a magazine, they were unmistakably Charlie's friends.

"You weren't kidding when you said you chose the most expensive building in..." one of the guys trailed off as his eyes fell on me, "...town."

"Hi," I greeted, giving the men a little wave.

One of them leaned against the wall with crossed arms, watching me with his dark eyes, while the other straightened out his suit jacket and took a few steps towards us.

"Jordan, this is Ian—" Charlie said as he gestured to the guy that was leaning against the wall, who gave me a panty-dropping smile and a nod, "and this is Blake."

The other guy, who had the biggest brown eyes I had ever seen, walked up to me.

"Nice to meet you," he smiled and I shook his hand.

"Likewise," I said, smiling at his eagerness. The two of them seemed perfect friends for Charlie, one tall, dark and handsome, and the other naive and energetic, probably too kind for his own good.

"Jordan was just leaving," Charlie stated stoically, and I frowned. *He didn't have to be such an asshole about it.*

"I was," I purred, an idea popping up in my head. I walked up to him and kissed him on the cheek while grabbing his junk, feeling his cock harden again under my touch.

"You're evil," he whispered in my ear with a groan, and I smirked.

"You're an asshole. You deserve it," I cooed back before straightening up and walking to the elevators. I grabbed the card on the side table, just like the last time I was there, and swiped it against the scanner, the doors immediately rolling open.

"Have fun tonight," I said, walking in and pressing the button for the ground floor.

"Thank you, hope to see you again soon—" Blake gushed, but he was interrupted by Ian's hand making contact with the back of his head. I chuckled and gave the guys a final wave, shaking my head as the door closed.

I sighed, looking at the changing numbers on the little display. Maybe it was a better idea to avoid Charlie from now on. I seemed to get pretty comfortable with him, and it scared me. Aside from the fact that I made a promise to my best friend.

When Charlie saw sex was in his future he obviously wasn't listening to Ashley's voice in his head and neither was I, but now that I was out of the moment, I knew I dodged a bullet. Even though it was obvious that we both weren't looking for more than just sex, and we both clearly enjoyed each other's moves in the bedroom, it was still a bad idea.

I was such a bad friend.

I nodded to the guy behind the desk as I walked out of the elevator, who gave me a sweeter smile this time, and quickened my pace when I was out of the building. I didn't want to be in this neighborhood any longer.

"Hi, Mrs. Hellen," I smiled when I walked into the foyer, pocketing my keys and hoisting my bag higher on my shoulder.

"Hello, Jordan," she greeted, keeping her eyes on her groceries that were threatening to spill out of her bag. I walked up to her, grabbing one of the bags that she had placed on the floor next to her.

"Need some help?"

"Ah, thank you, dear," she replied, finally able to grab her keys. "You want to have dinner with me?"

Did I only have instant noodles and canned soup left in my apartment? "*Yes*," I answered and she smiled. "If it's not too much trouble."

"Of course not, come on in. It's nice to have some company every once in a while."

As I followed her into her apartment, a strong rosewood and

patchouli scent filled my nostrils, the fragrance instantly making me relax and feel at home. I smiled at the flowered wallpaper and followed Mrs. Hellen to her kitchen, placing the bag on the counter.

Her apartment was a little bigger than mine, and she had a small garden where I spent many summers drinking lemonade and sitting in the sun with her. After Eli and I broke up I wasn't sure where I stood with his mother, but we had developed such a strong bond, it felt as though nothing really changed. Besides, she was the one living in my building, not Eli.

We cooked dinner together and enjoyed a nice glass of wine as we ate, having me practically drunk by the time I was clearing the table.

"I think it's time for me to stop drinking now, Mrs. Hellen," I said with a little slur in my voice.

"Oh, Jordan, how many times do I need to ask you to just call me Abigail?" she replied, taking a sip of wine.

"Well, where did you even find this wine, *Abigail?*"

She smiled, giving me a wink.

It felt weird calling her by her first name. I've always known her as Mrs. Hellen and it was hard to get that out of my head.

"Eli brought it over the other day," she answered and I nodded. I didn't love him anymore, but every time I heard his name or saw his face, I still felt a little pang of hurt go through me.

I really thought he was the love of my life, and he just treated me like trash. It had been a good two years since our breakup, but I still asked myself if it was something I did. If there was something I could've done differently.

"Well, it's good wine." I watched the red liquid swirl around in my glass, saving the little bit that was left for as long as I could. Or maybe I *could* have another glass? I mean, I lived upstairs and would be home in seconds.

"I have more, take one," Abigail said, gesturing to the bottles on top of the cupboards.

Well, don't mind if I do.

I loved a good red wine and didn't have the money to buy my own. Which, of course, she knew. So, I walked to her kitchen and reached for a bottle.

"Thank you, Abigail," I smiled, placing the wine on the counter next to my keys, so I wouldn't forget to take it with me when I left.

I flipped on the kettle and grabbed two cups for some tea, deciding to quit drinking wine for the night.

"Of course." She beamed, leaning back in her chair. I watched the red cloud spread in the hot water as I poured our tea, the spicy smell hitting me in the face. I carefully walked back to the table with the two cups in my hands, retaking my seat and flowing back into easy conversation with my neighbor.

CHAPTER 8
Jordan

It was past midnight when I finally made my way up the stairs, arriving home. The effects of the alcohol I had consumed earlier that evening were almost completely gone after numerous cups of tea, and my body was ready for bed.

I quickly stripped to pull on my pajama shorts and a random cami, tying my hair up in a bun.

Yawning, I walked into my living room, double-checking if everything was locked. Unfortunately, it was something I'd gotten used to over the years—break-ins and robberies were not uncommon in this neighborhood. It was sadly the *only* neighborhood I could afford in this city, so I learned to deal with it.

After I made sure my door was locked and my windows were closed, I climbed into bed. I had closed my eyes for maybe two seconds when I heard someone bang on my front door.

I was on my feet in seconds, rummaging through my nightstand for my gun with my heart almost jumping out of my chest.

"Not today, Satan," I mumbled as I filled the magazine. I threw on a robe before I stumbled into my living room, making sure not to make too much noise.

I flinched when the intruder banged on my door again, the sound loud against the silence of the night. Sure, I was holding a loaded gun, but I couldn't deny that my heart was practically pounding out of my chest.

"Fuck off!" I yelled, aiming at the door and taking off the safety.

I heard mumbling, something falling, and then more loud banging. Surely, that woke someone up? Not that I wanted anyone to risk their lives; the intruders often carried firearms. And it wasn't like my neighbors really cared either.

I was surprised that whoever was trying to get in hadn't kicked my door in yet, but there was no way I was opening it myself and getting shot in the face.

"Go bother someone else! I don't have any money!" I shouted at the door, gripping the gun tighter in my hands.

I raised my brows when I heard someone laughing.

Breaking in wasn't enough? They wanted to laugh at me?

"Jesus Christ," I mumbled under my breath as I marched to the door, unlocking it and yanking it open.

"What do you want?" I whisper shouted, pointing my gun at the guy at my door. I gasped softly when I saw who was giving me a heart attack.

"There s—she is," Charlie slurred, and he took a step towards me, hitting the barrel of my gun with his chest. "What is this?"

I closed my eyes, taking a deep breath. My heart dropped to my stomach and it took everything in me not to slam the door in his face, but I managed to keep my cool. *Kind of.*

"What the hell are you doing here? In the middle of the night?" I hissed, lowering the gun and putting the safety back on. There was no way I was accidentally shooting myself in my foot or something like that. God knows it's a possibility with my track record.

"Can I please come in? It's scary out here," he pleaded with a pout and rolled my eyes.

"Whatever."

I stepped aside to let him in before closing the door and locking it, *again*.

"What is this place?" Charlie asked as he looked around, stumbling into my living room. "It's so small."

"Did you come here to just insult my apartment? And how did you find out where I live?"

He abruptly turned around, almost falling flat on his face, and I crossed my arms with raised brows. "Of course not," he retorted. "And I asked Ashley."

Ignoring those last words, I walked up to him and grabbed his face, slapping his cheek a few times. "How much did you have to drink?" I asked, feeling his burning skin under my fingertips.

"Just enough," he muttered, placing his hands on my hips and drawing circles over the fabric of my shorts. I could feel his breath on my face, the sour whiskey aroma strong enough to make me drunk. Taking a step back and pushing him off, I headed for the kitchen to grab a glass of water.

"Jordan."

I turned back around with a sigh, almost dropping the glass when my gaze returned to the man's torso.

"Jesus," I breathed out, trying to control myself as I stared at Charlie's undressed chest. It was as good as I remembered, and I caught myself staring a little too long. I had to remind myself that he was drunk and that no matter how much I wanted him to bury himself inside me again, there was no way I was taking advantage of him. Though he would probably still want to do that when he was sober.

"D'you know why I came here?" he asked, interrupting my train of thought, and he swayed a little.

"Please, enlighten me," I huffed, leaning against the counter behind me and keeping my distance.

"Because I want to have sex with you again. And I k-know you want it too," he slurred and I sighed—something I seemed to do a lot with him here.

I walked up to him, grabbing him by the wrist and dragging him to my bedroom.

"Ooh, I like where this is going. *Where* we are going?"
God, he's like a child.

"Charlie, I need you to drink this, and lay down on your side," I ordered, pushing him on the bed and holding out the glass of water.

He tumbled backward, spreading his arms as he landed on the mattress. "I like where this is going," he mumbled again, tugging on his slacks.

"No, no, no. Keep your pants on," I said, quickly putting his water on the bedside table before I leaped forward, placing my hand over his and stopping him from taking his pants off.

"Oh, you want to do it. Ok," he smirked and he folded his hands behind his head, giving me a perfect view of his abs as he flexed. *Fuck me.* Oh, no, that was exactly what we *didn't* want to happen.

"Charlie, stop it! I'm not going to sleep with you," I snapped in annoyance, and he sat up.

"Why not?" he pouted, grabbing my hands and pulling me closer.

"Because you're drunk."

We all know I would fuck him if he's sober at this point. Let's not deny it anymore.

"So when I'm not drunk, can we have sex then?" he asked and I rolled my eyes for the umpteenth time that night.

"Maybe. Now, go lay down."

Charlie smiled, his dimples making an unwanted appearance and almost making me regret my decision not to have sex with him right then and there.

"I don't feel so good," he grimaced suddenly, sitting up and covering his mouth with his hand.

Shit.

"Please don't throw up on my bed," I whined, pulling him on his feet and helping him to the bathroom.

We stumbled inside, just reaching the toilet before Charlie emptied his stomach. I tried pinching my nose, but he could barely stay upright without my help, so I breathed through my mouth as I held him. *Not that it made it better.*

Fortunately, it wasn't very long until he sat back and wiped his mouth, closing his eyes. I flushed the toilet and cleaned it up, grabbing a wet towel to wipe his face.

"Thank you," he whispered breathlessly, the playfulness

replaced by fatigue.

"Sure. Here," I handed him a spare toothbrush with some toothpaste and he gratefully took it.

I helped him brush his teeth and cleaned up the toothpaste stains he created in the process, trying not to get distracted as I wiped his chest. Was this behavior a turn-off? Normally, yeah. But not with him for some reason. I had to admit that I kind of liked him this vulnerable.

Once I had got him into bed, I grabbed a few painkillers and placed them on the bedside table, next to his water. *He was going to need those in the morning.*

There was no way that I was taking the couch, so I climbed into bed next to him, careful not to wake him, even though nothing probably could at that point.

—

I slowly opened my eyes the next morning, blinking against the light. I looked down, feeling a weight on me. I chuckled softly when I noticed Charlie, lightly snoring against my stomach, while he rested one hand on my left boob.

It was weird that we were so comfortable with each other, even though we'd only met a week ago. There was some sort of friendly connection between us, despite him annoying me most of the time. But I had to admit that the banter between us was something I enjoyed, and also something I never had experienced with someone else.

I carefully tried to slip out of bed, but Charlie groaned and tightened his grip on my waist, his other hand still resting on my breast.

"Charlie," I said softly, shaking his shoulder in an attempt to wake him up gently.

It didn't work though. *Time for plan B.*

I used all my strength to flip him over, pushing him back to his side of the bed.

"What?" he moaned, his brows knitting together as his eyes slowly opened. "Why's it so bright in here?"

"Good morning sunshine," I chirped extra loud, chuckling when he flinched and draped an arm over his eyes. After a few seconds, he shot up in bed, frantically looking around.

"Baby?" he frowned and I raised my brows. "What are you doing here? Oh fuck, I can't believe I don't remember that." He dropped back on the mattress, sighing disappointedly.

"Remember what? The night wasn't *that* great," I retorted, watching his expression change.

He turned his head, smirking. "A night with me is *always* great, *Jordan*."

"Not when you almost barfed all over me," I stated, cocking a brow. "And you're in *my* house, so I'll ask the same thing I asked yesterday: why did you come here?"

He frowned, looking around the room before replying. "I don't really... remember."

"Yeah, I got that."

I pushed the covers off, trying to get out of bed without Charlie's eyes on me. *Which, naturally, didn't work.*

I shrieked softly when he crawled on top of me, grabbing my wrists and pushing them into the mattress.

"I remember now," he cooed, all signs of a hangover gone.

"What are you doing?" I asked, making no attempt to wiggle out of his grasp and looking up into his blue eyes. They seemed more vibrant, almost luminous with lust.

"I'm trying to seduce you," he said, leaning down and brushing his lips against my neck. "Is it working?"

He knew damn well that it was working, and I wanted to give in, just a little.

"Hmm," I hummed, closing my eyes and arching my back slightly, pushing my body against his. He pressed his lips against the sweet spot under my ear and I let my head fall back, giving him more access. I could feel him smile against my skin as I ignored the need to push him off, surrendering to the fact that I had lost this battle.

"Charlie..." I moaned and his grip on my wrists tightened.

"God, I didn't know I could love your moaning more than I already do, but when you moan my name like that—" he paused, lowering his hips, letting me feel the effect it had on him. "It makes me want to do very dirty things to you."

I was seconds away from giving in before deciding to be smart about the situation. "Charlie, we need to talk about this."

"Then talk." He leaned down and pressed his lips against my neck once again, sucking and kissing as he listened.

"We have to keep this a secret from everyone," I breathed out, trying to think straight as Charlie continued to turn me on. If we were going to do this, and I was quite positive that we were, I needed a couple of things to be crystal clear.

"Hmm."

"I want—"

I rolled my eyes with a scoff when we got interrupted by the ear-piercing sound of my phone ringing, and Charlie let his head fall against my shoulder, releasing my wrists.

"One of these days I'm going to kill the person that dares to interrupt us," he mumbled under his breath and I chuckled, reaching for the device on the bedside table.

"Oh my God," I muttered when I recognized the caller ID, and I shot up, scooting back to sit up against the headboard.

"What?" Charlie whined, rolling off me and taking a sip of the water next to him.

I answered the call, bringing the phone to my ear with shaky hands. "Jordan Sawyer, speaking."

"Hi, Ms. Sawyer, this is Oscar from Cendose Incorporated. I'm calling you regarding your job interview from last Friday."

My eyes widened and Charlie raised a brow.

"Yes, hi."

"My apologies for the late call, but I have great news," Oscar said and I could feel my heart rate going up, butterflies storming my stomach. "I'm happy to inform you that we would like to hire you for the position."

I did a mental happy dance and without thinking, grabbed Charlie's hand, giving it a tight squeeze. He groaned, wiggling his fingers from mine, but I didn't care. My heart was beating frantically in my chest and I could almost *hear* my blood pumping through my veins.

"That's great! Thank you so much!" I answered quickly, realizing I was still on the phone, and Oscar chuckled.

"You're very welcome. We expect you in the office on Monday morning, nine a.m. sharp. We will talk over the contract and start your training."

"Yes, thank you. I'll be there."

I was bouncing up and down, almost unable to contain my happiness any longer.

"Good. Have a nice weekend and we'll see each other on Monday."

"Yes, you too."

I hung up the phone and chucked it on my bedside table, jumping up and straddling Charlie.

"What the—" He blinked in surprise as I pulled my top over my head.

"Touch me," I breathed, lifting a leg and taking my shorts off. I had a ton of adrenaline coursing through me, the amount of energy almost making me faint, and I so happened to have the perfect outlet laying beside me.

"I thought you wanted to talk?" Charlie chuckled as I undid his slacks.

I leaned forward and started to place kisses on his chest, feeling the ridges of his hard muscles under my hands and lips, my entire body buzzing with desire.

"I'm way too turned on to talk," I mumbled between kisses and he smirked, grabbing my hips with both hands.

I was ecstatic because I got the job, and I had resisted this urge to have sex with Charlie for far too long. *Ok, it had been like one week, but whatever.*

"Alright, come sit on my face," he ordered and I squealed. Eagerly, I took off my thong and moved up on the bed, letting Charlie guide me to straddle his head.

"I've missed you," he mumbled and I grabbed the headboard to steady myself, gasping when I felt his tongue against my hot core.

"Did you just talk to my pussy?" I groaned, squeezing my eyes shut with a frown, but Charlie just ignored my comment and flicked my clit with his tongue, eliciting a loud moan from my lips.

"Oh, God," I breathed out, rocking my hips back and forth to take as much pleasure as I could.

Charlie really was an expert with his tongue, dipping into me at the right moments and making me tighten my grip on the headboard.

Tingles went up my spine as he continued to pleasure me and I shrieked softly when he added two fingers to the mix. Pumping them in and out and curling to rub the right spot, he managed to bring me to the brink of my orgasm in record time. No man had ever had this effect on me in all my twenty-seven years on this earth.

"I'm coming. Please let me come," I begged, having some experience with Charlie's edging ways, but he had mercy this time.

"Hmm, I love hearing you beg," he mumbled against me before he flattened his tongue against my clit, pushing me over the edge.

"Yes, Yes! Yes! Oh, fuck," I screamed out as I rocked my hips back and forth faster and harder, riding out my orgasm.

Charlie continued the delicious strokes with his tongue until my legs were shaking, and then quickly grabbed my waist, throwing me on my back on the bed.

"Remember your safe word, *Baby*?" he asked and I opened my eyes, my vision clouded with little stars from the explosive release as I tried to catch my breath.

I pressed my teeth into my lower lip, spreading my legs. *Finally.*

"Use your words," he demanded and I was reintroduced to the playful, mischievous sparkle in his eyes.

"I do," I said firmly, and Charlie smiled. He shedded his slacks and boxers, blessing me with the sight of his big dick that was already hard and ready for me.

"One week," he pointed out, and I raised my brows. "It took you *one* week before you gave in to me."

I playfully slapped his thigh, before I wrapped my hands around his neck, intertwining my fingers and pulling him down.

"No more talking," I cooed. I wrapped my legs around his waist, feeling the tip of his cock against my entrance and rubbing the little bundle of nerves.

"Yes, ma'am," he said and he started to press in.

"Wait," I yelped, pushing him back. "Condom."

"Shit. Well, this is *your* house."

I pointed to the drawer of the bedside table, and a minute later Charlie had rolled the rubber on his length and was pushing into me.

"Jesus," I groaned, reminded that he was not normal-sized, which sounded good in my head, but felt a little less good if he went too fast.

"Oh my God," he mumbled against my skin as he distracted me with open-mouth kisses on my neck.

"Fuck," I countered, and he lifted his face, showing me his ever-so cocky smirk.

"Ready?" he asked and I nodded.

"Give it to me, big boy," I joked, gasping as he started to thrust into me with a little more force.

I moaned loudly, crossing my ankles behind his back as he

started to move, and I grabbed the sheets under my head in an attempt to steady myself.

"Fuck. Yes. Oh, God!" I gasped, throwing my head back and arching my back.

We should've just done this sooner.

Our breathless moans filled the room, the sheets half hanging off the bed as the headboard slammed against the wall with every thrust. Charlie continued to push into me as he pressed his lips on mine, shoving his tongue in. I moaned into his mouth when one of his hands glided over my chest, his fingers teasing the top of my collarbones.

But I wanted more. I *needed* more.

I shoved him off and ignored the surprised look on his face as I crawled on top of him. I rested a hand on his shoulder, using the other to align his cock with my opening before I lowered onto him.

He smiled against my skin and he took some between his teeth, biting and nibbling, as he placed both hands on my ass, pushing himself deeper into me, filling me to the hilt.

"Oh, God," I breathed out, rolling my hips on his.

"Hmm, you taste so good," Charlie mumbled, enveloping one of my nipples in his mouth and sucking, making it harder for me to concentrate on the movement of my hips.

My moans got higher and louder as I bounced up and down on him, my hips slapping faster and faster against his as I chased another orgasm.

"Yes, come for me, Baby."

I did as he said and continued moving until my walls tightened, choking Charlie's dick.

"Fuck."

As I finished, my body turned to jelly. Charlie flipped us back over and slammed into me, thrusting hard until he filled the condom, his fingers digging into my hips as he came.

Out of breath, he collapsed on top of me, and I chuckled.

"This is too good, not to do again," he panted, and I nodded in agreement, smiling at his red cheeks.

Sorry, Ashley.

"You're right. But..."

Charlie pulled out with a hiss and trashed the condom, sliding his boxers back on.

I completely lost my train of thought as I watched the muscles move in his back, sucking my bottom lip between my teeth.

"Yes?" Charlie asked, breaking me out of my trance.

"I—" I blinked a few times, trying to remember what I wanted to say. Charlie crawled back onto the bed and I rested my head on his chest.

"Lost for words, huh?" he teased and I rolled my eyes.

"So, we don't tell Ashley, or anyone, and..." I bit my lip, a little nervous about my next condition. "I want to be the *only* one you fuck."

There was no way in hell I would catch anything from this guy. And maybe, I'd admit it was good for my ego if I was enough for him. That he wouldn't *need* anyone else.

Charlie's muscles tightened underneath me, and I closed my eyes. *Did I ruin things before they even started?*

"Ok. The same goes for you," he finally said and I nodded.

"Yes."

"And, no feelings," he added and I propped onto my elbow,

turning to face him.

"What?"

"You can't catch feelings."

I forgot how conceited he was. Not that I was the love of his life or that I even wanted that, but he could at least *act* like I was in the running. Then another thought hit me.

"Who says *I'm* the one who catches feelings?" I scoffed and Charlie chuckled. Desperate not to show him that my pride was a little hurt, I shifted in my seat.

"Cute. But fine, if one of us catches feelings, we stop."

"Deal," I answered, holding up my hand for him to shake.

And he did.

After that, we went at it like rabbits.

CHAPTER 9
Jordan

"Oh, fuck." I moaned, my head jamming against the headboard as Charlie slammed into me a final few times, the tightening of my walls around his length triggering his orgasm.

Little beads of sweat had formed on my forehead and I was panting as we both tried to catch our breath. He collapsed on top of me, dropping his head on my shoulder, and held me with both arms.

It had been two weeks since we started our little arrangement, and so far, we'd fucked twenty-nine times.

I was constantly surprised by Charlie's stamina, but I wasn't complaining.

Every night, one of us would sleep over at the other's, all the while I was getting comfortable behind the front desk at Cendose Incorporated. The job was easy, I had wonderful colleagues, and the prospect of coming home and getting eaten out did wonders for my mood. *Karma was coming for me for sure.*

Charlie groaned, lifting himself off me and walking towards his bathroom to trash the condom.

I sat up on the bed, stretching my arms above my head, grunting and moaning.

"You okay, Baby?" Charlie asked as he walked back into the room.

"I'm a little sore," I admitted, resting my back against the headboard, my eyes roaming over Charlie's body.

I licked my lips as my gaze fell on his chest, his skin having a beautiful post-orgasm glow, and sighed softly when I looked at the little trail of hair going from his belly button down.

Why did this God of a man want to fuck me on repeat? He could have anyone he wanted.

"Let's take a bath."

He walked towards me and picked me up bridal style, our naked skin sticking together as we touched.

"Charlie, you wore me out. I can't—"

"Not to have sex, Jordan. To get cleaned up." He smiled as he carried me to the bathroom. I lowered my face so he couldn't see how I blushed.

"Oh."

The tub was already half-way filled and smelled strongly of something sweet, a scent I couldn't quite place but found *amazing*.

Charlie carefully placed me into the bath, the water sloshing around and nearly spilling over the top, but I was grateful. The warm water was exactly what I needed as my muscles instantly relaxed, engulfed in bubbles.

"Alright, make some room," Charlie ordered and I leaned forward, giving him space to sit behind me.

He started rubbing soapy water over my shoulders, but I stopped him, leaning back against his chest.

"But—" he protested, but I interrupted him.

"I just want to sit like this for a moment," I mumbled, closing my eyes.

I had learned over the last few weeks that Charlie was a very physical person—not just in a sexual way. He tried to hold himself back, probably afraid to give off the wrong signals, but I knew it was just sex between us and I was perfectly fine with that.

Lucky for him, I was a physical person, too.

We sat in silence for a while, the only sound being our breathing and the moving water. I could've easily fallen asleep right then and there, but Charlie rudely awakened me from my slumber by speaking up.

"What is your wildest fantasy, Baby?" he asked, and I bit the inside of my cheek, thinking through my answer.

In all honesty, I had a lot.

Over the years I had seen and read about some, but I had never felt comfortable enough with Eli or hook-ups to suggest them. *Maybe...*

"Mhm, I have a few, actually," I answered, and Charlie straightened up behind me. I turned around and scooted to the other side of the tub, leaning against the porcelain and sending more water over the edge.

"Please, do tell."

"Well," I looked into Charlie's eyes, still a little hesitant to tell him the dirty things I dreamed about doing. "There's a threesome, of course—"

"You never had a threesome?" Charlie cut me off and I shot him a scowl. "Sorry, continue."

"I really want to have sex outside at least once, I don't know." *Can't believe I just admitted that.*

Charlie narrowed his eyes as he leaned back, running a finger over his lower lip. *Was that too weird for this playboy?*

"Hmm, what else?" he pressed on.

"Oh! Sex against that window in the living room," I exclaimed, remembering the first thing I wanted to do when I stepped foot into his apartment.

Charlie chuckled. "Damn, Baby, I might have to write this down."

I rolled my eyes.

"Whatever. What about you?"

"How do you feel about anal?" he asked softly and I raised my brows.

How *did* I feel about anal?

I would be lying if I said that I never thought about it. The plugs with a big diamond on them that all the girls in porn wore intrigued me, but maybe I was too scared to actually try it out. *The few times guys 'accidentally' put it in the back didn't exactly feel amazing.*

"I'm...intrigued," I admitted and I giggled when I saw Charlie's eyes light up.

"Really? Damn. What about handcuffs? Or let me tie you up?"

He named a few of my other fantasies and I felt my core

tingle at the thought of actually experiencing them. Maybe this was an opportunity.

"Yes."

"Spanking?"

"Didn't you already bruise my ass last week?" I frowned and Charlie shrugged.

"Sex with food? Role-play? Striptease?"

"You know what, we might have to write this shit down after all," I said as I lifted myself and climbed out of the tub.

"Like a list?" Charlie suggested as he got out as well, grabbing a towel and drying himself off. I couldn't quite visualize it yet, but the idea sounded very interesting in my head.

"Yeah, that could be fun, right?"

"I'll get my laptop. Meet you in the living room."

I chuckled as Charlie headed towards his walk-in closet, and I moved to my bag in the bedroom, grabbing the fresh pair of panties I brought with me. I pulled on one of Charlie's shirts and made my way to the living room.

Half an hour later, we found ourselves sitting at the kitchen bar, eating Chinese take-out and discussing more sex-related fantasies.

"Ok, number one—" Charlie said as he grabbed his laptop and opened a new document.

"Threesome," I replied and he started typing with a giant devilish grin on his face. I mirrored his expression when I thought about one of his friends joining us in the bedroom, especially Ian. *Sorry, Blake.*

"How long do we want this list to be?" he interrupted my dirty thoughts, and it took me a couple of seconds before I realized that he was asking me a question.

"Like fifty things?" I suggested.

"Let's do a hundred. It'll be like a challenge."

I raised my brows. *How long did he think we would keep screwing each other?*

"But isn't that going to take a long time? Like, don't you think we'll get bored of each other?" I argued and Charlie crossed his arms. "I mean, you probably love a new girl in your bed every week."

"Are you slut-shaming me, Baby?" He smirked, cocking his head to the side.

"No, I'm just stating facts."

"Well, if we make this list interesting enough, you might keep me satisfied until it's done." He shot me a wink.

God. I forgot how much of an asshole he was.

"Are you fucking serious? Satisfy you until it's done?" I scoffed, getting angrier than I should've. "What makes you think I won't get sick of *you*?"

"Fine. Let's just make this list and not fight about the details." He huffed, quickly focussing back on his laptop.

"Hmm. Ok...one hundred things."

"Good. Second one. Edging," he said, shooting me a grin before he started typing.

"Yes, but we can cross that off."

Charlie cocked a brow. "You didn't like it when I did that?"

"Well, it was worth it, I guess, but not if you haven't had—" I stopped myself, almost spilling the beans on my non-existent sex life prior to Charlie. There was no need for him to know that I hadn't had many sexual partners in a while.

"Next," he continued, and I nodded, thankful that he moved on.

"Well, tying up, handcuffs, blindfolding..."

"Good one."

"...vibrator, nipple clamps, hair pulling—you don't do that enough," I added, pointing an accusing finger at him.

Charlie chuckled. "I'll keep that in mind. What else?"

"Uhm, like that hot wax thing?" I suggested and Charlie nodded. "Yes, and we can also do ice and a tickler. I think I have one of those."

I looked at him in disgust. "Yeah, we're going to have to buy a couple of things. I don't want to use anything you've used on someone else."

"Why not?" Charlie frowned. "I clean my shit. I'm not *that* nasty."

I've noticed.

Charlie's apartment was always squeaky clean, unlike mine. He had taken it upon himself to casually clean up my apartment when we were there, and I continued to act like I didn't notice. Whatever he did, I didn't have to do anymore.

Not that we were at mine often.

His apartment was bigger, better, *cleaner*, and we didn't have to worry about junkies or robbers roaming the streets and hallway.

"We'll buy new ones," I stated, sounding more confident than I should be. The money at Cendose was good, but not amazingly good, so I still had to think about everything I bought. "Or, *you'll* buy new ones?" I batted my eyelashes, giving him my sweetest smile. I didn't like asking others to buy stuff for me, but this was something we'd *both* use.

"Whatever, next," he mumbled, though I could tell that he was amused.

"Uhm, so we have a tickler, maybe we could also use a whip or flogger or something?"

"Let's just put them all together." Charlie started typing away on his laptop.

We continued to name all the things we could use, including anal beads—*whatever those do*—which lead to anal making the list.

"So we're only at twenty-two and it's already harder to come up with things," I said, leaning on the counter with my elbows, my chin in my hands.

"Hmm, maybe like phone sex?" Charlie asked and I nodded.

"Yeah. And sexting—nudes?"

Charlie's eyes widened. "You would?"

I chuckled. "Sure, but I only want sexy photos of you in good lighting, and tasteful ones of your ass and dick," I stressed, the unsolicited dick-pics I had gotten in the past reappearing in my memories. "And your body, after working out or something."

"Alright, alright." Charlie grinned, holding up his hands in defense.

"Good. Oh! I want to go down on you when you're on an important phone call," I added, wiggling my brows.

"Noted, but I get to do the same to you."

"I don't get important phone calls." I scoffed, but Charlie shrugged.

"Well, what about a quickie in the office?" He suggested, smirking, and my smile disappeared.

"I don't want to lose my job, Charlie."

"I meant *my* office. I could sneak you in one day."

I shook my head, grinning. The thought turned me on and I shifted in my seat, rubbing my thighs together.

"Are you turned on, right now?"

"We've been talking about sex for the past half hour, of course

I am," I admitted, slapping him playfully on his bicep. Maybe it was just an excuse to touch him, but I wouldn't tell him that.

"Alright, let's finish this list, then we can fuck," Charlie said and I nodded.

"So, your office," I continued, thinking of other places. It would definitely fill up the list pretty quickly, and it was easy to cross off. "The car, a pool, a hot tub?"

"That's kinda like a pool right?"

"Whatever. Add it in."

"Alright, what about your outdoor fantasy?" Charlie asked and I nodded. All hesitations about my fantasies had vanished, and I was getting pretty excited about this.

"Sex outside, sex while we're being watched, sex in a public place..." I listed, adding every place I could think of. I wasn't sure if we would be able to do them all, but getting to a hundred items proved to be difficult, so I just suggested everything I could come up with.

We added a few of the classics, like vibrating panties and sex involving food, but we had to get more creative after that. We consulted a few websites for ideas, and eventually managed to fill the list up with ninety items.

"Ten more." I sighed, standing behind Charlie to look at the screen over his shoulder, my brain ready to turn off for the night. I paced behind him as I tried to think about more, rubbing my fingers over my temples.

"What about a ceiling mirror?" he suggested and I frowned.

"Where are we going to find that?"

Charlie turned his head to look at me and shrugged. "Maybe we could find a hotel room with one."

"Ok. Ninety-two," I said.

"What about this one? *Answer the door naked.* You could do that."

I raised my brows at his hopeful expression but had to admit that it could be fun. Ideas started to fill my mind and the corners of my mouth curled up into a grin. I honestly couldn't wait to get started.

"Sure. How about you try to make me squirt?" I suggested.

"Baby, *please.*"

"I'd like to see you try," I teased.

"Challenge accepted." Charlie turned to the screen, adding it to the list.

We came up with a few bullshit ones, like sex under the full moon and having five orgasms in under sixty minutes, until we reached number one hundred.

"I'm out of ideas," I admitted, walking to the couch and plopping onto the comfortable cushions.

"We only need one more," Charlie stated, standing up and throwing away the empty take-out boxes.

I sighed, fiddling with the corner of one of the plush pillows. "I don't know. Honestly, my brain is mush at this point."

"Wait! Having sex a hundred times," Charlie suddenly yelled and I turned around, leaning over the back of the couch.

"You want to have sex a hundred times?"

"Don't suddenly act like a prude, Baby. We already did it about thirty times in the last few weeks."

"Ok. Add it in."

Charlie walked around the couch and took a seat next to me, adding the last item to the list.

"We *actually* came up with a hundred sexy things to do,"

he said and I grabbed his laptop, placing it on the coffee table. "What are you doing?"

I crawled towards him, unbuttoning a few buttons of the shirt I was wearing, and pushed him back on the couch. "I'm just looking forward to all the pleasure."

Charlie chuckled and placed both hands on my ass.

"We could start right now?" he cooed, and I smiled, bringing my lips closer to his.

"The Pleasure List!" I suddenly exclaimed.

"Eh..."

I sat back, tucking my feet under my ass. "We can call it *The Pleasure List.*"

Charlie looked at me with raised brows for a few seconds, before he grabbed the laptop and added the title.

"I love it," he said as he pressed print.

We both looked up, surprised by the sound of the buzzer going off, and my eyes lowered to my chest where the shirt I was wearing still stood half-open.

"Are you expecting anyone?" I asked as Charlie stood up.

"No. Let's see who it is," he said as he walked to the intercom. "Hello?"

I watched as his expression slowly morphed into stress, and I started to get worried. If it was his mother I would probably go and try to drown myself in the bathtub. She didn't like me, and would probably have me arrested for something if she found out I was screwing her son.

"Give me five minutes before you send her up," he said before placing the phone back on the wall. Oh, God. It's a she. It really *was* his mom.

"What's wrong?"

"It's Ashley."

I immediately jumped off the couch and buttoned the shirt back up, my heart beating loud in my chest and threatening to burst out. That was even worse than his mom. "Fuck. Shit."

"We have five minutes," Charlie stated as I nodded, not registering what he said.

My mind was going a million miles per hour, playing every scenario in my mind as the guilt crushed me. This was going to be the end of our friendship for sure. I knew it was hard for Ashley to trust someone, and betraying her like this...*oh, what was I doing?*

I hadn't noticed that Charlie had walked up to me until he grabbed my arms, bringing me back to reality.

"Baby?" he asked, concerned.

"She can't find me here, Charlie."

"I agree, but you kinda have to hide if you want to avoid that."

I rolled my eyes at his smirk, even though he was right.

"She doesn't go into your bedroom right?" I asked, grabbing my phone from the coffee table, heading in that direction.

"No..." He frowned as I took one last look around the room, seeing if any of my stuff could give me away before I pecked Charlie on the cheek and turned to leave. I shrieked when he grabbed me by my wrist, twirling me around and pulling me against him, capturing my lips with his.

"Hmm." I moaned into the kiss as he placed both hands on my ass, squeezing, and pulling me closer. I almost got caught up in the moment, but reluctantly pushed him off. "I need to hide, Charlie," I breathed out, and he nodded.

"I'll make sure she doesn't stay too long," he said with a wink, giving me a tap on the ass as I walked away.

I chuckled as I closed the bedroom door behind me, quickly grabbing my things and stuffing them in my bag. Sitting down next to Charlie's dresser, beside the door and out of sight, I heard Ashley's voice. The sound was muffled but clear enough for me to follow the conversation.

"Why did you need five…oh. Yikes," she said and I pressed my back harder against the wall, closing my eyes. *Please leave.*

"It's a natural thing, Ash," Charlie retorted and I had to suppress a scoff. "You should try it sometime."

"Whatever, I need a favor," Ashley continued.

"Yes?"

"Are you still friends with that hotel owner in Canada?"

Canada?

"Canada is a pretty big country, Ash. You need to be more specific."

"Alright, are you still friends with Perry, the owner of the Plaza?"

Who the fuck is Perry? I scoffed, scolding myself, because I knew the kind of man Charlie was, and being jealous of this 'Perry' was no use.

"I don't know if she'll listen to me. I think you're better off asking her yourself."

He probably fucked her and left.

"I *want* the plaza," Ashley whined and I could hear Charlie sigh.

"I'll see what I can do. If you're lucky, she might still be in love with me."

Charlie's arrogance surprised me sometimes, but I would be lying if I said it wasn't something I found incredibly hot about him.

Ashley scoffed. "Not everyone is in love with you, Charlie."

I could almost *hear* his lips parting for a comeback, but Ashley quickly resumed before he could. "Whatever. Please do this for me."

"I just said I will, didn't I?"

What Ashley wants, Ashley gets.

"Yes!" she shrieked. "Thank you! Thank you!"

"Of course, anything for my baby sister," Charlie responded, and a small smile danced on my lips. I listened to their sibling banter for a while and with every minute that passed, I got less and less comfortable. After what felt like at *least* half an hour, I had enough and tried to stretch my legs.

Big mistake.

I lost my footing—*of course*—and fell face-first on the floor, my cheek slapping hard against the ground and making lots of noise in the process. I stayed perfectly still, not daring to move a finger, even though I was sure I had been discovered.

"Is she still here?" Ashley asked.

"Yes," Charlie admitted and I sat back up. "Do you want to meet her?"

I swore that my heart *literally* skipped a beat hearing his bluff and held my breath as I waited for Ashley to respond.

She hesitated before answering. "Ew, no."

"Your loss," Charlie teased.

"Well, don't let me hold you up. I should get going anyway." Ashley's heels clicked against the hardwood floor as she left, and I exhaled as the nerves in my stomach finally calmed down a little.

CHAPTER 10
Jordan

I had insisted on not staying over, even though Charlie hit me with the *'it's not safe out there so late at night'*- bullshit.

As much as I enjoyed sex with Charlie, I just wanted some time on my own, especially since we'd spent two weeks together. The list was a nice addition to our sex life, giving me a chance to explore and experiment, but I really craved a little time alone.

I parked Benji in its usual spot, turning the engine off and waiting in the dark for a few seconds to see if there were any nut jobs on the loose. The parking lot was quiet and deserted, as to be expected at this time of night, but I had to be cautious.

I never got as scared as I probably should've, but my heart *did* beat a little faster as I made my way home through the pitch black.

Walking around the other side of the building so I didn't have to pass the group of junkies that were always stationed in my street, I quickly made my way inside. It was just as dark and quiet as outside, but once I made sure the door to the foyer of my building was correctly pulled shut, I felt a little safer.

I shrieked when my phone rang—the sound of my ringtone startling me—and answered the call as fast as I could so I wouldn't wake the neighbors.

"Hey, Ash." I tried to keep my voice down as I made my way up the stairs, avoiding attracting unwanted attention.

"Hi, Jo. Why are you whispering?" she asked as I ran up the last few steps, taking my keys out. Running up the stairs wasn't the smartest thing to do, because now I was out of breath, but I managed to squeak out an answer anyway.

"I just got home and I don't want to wake my neighbors up. Give me a second."

Ashely hummed and I unlocked my front door, quickly getting in and shutting it behind me. "I'm back."

"Good. Well, I won't ask you where you came from so late on a Friday, but I wanted to see if you were free tomorrow night?" I listened as I locked my door and kicked off my shoes. "Bailey and I thought it'd be fun to have dinner together."

"Sure, that sounds like fun." I smiled, dropping my bag on my bed as I walked into my bedroom.

"Good. Let's meet at our usual spot at seven p.m.? I'll make sure we have a table."

"It's a date," I replied, rolling my eyes at Ashley's last words. The restaurant Bailey and she always dragged me to was fully booked every time, but Ms. Abbot could get herself into the most exclusive parties, so a restaurant was child's play. Sometimes I wished I had her charm and charisma, but I just didn't.

"See you then!"

I ended the call and threw my phone on my bed, shedding my clothes, ready to take a nice, long shower. I sighed as the warm water hit my shoulders, easing my sore muscles, and I tilted my head back, soaking my hair.

I felt like I had lived in a bubble for the last couple of days, almost the same routine every day; work, fuck, eat, shower, sleep, and repeat.

It was nice to do something else for a change, especially when the dinner was long overdue. It had been a while since Ashley, Bailey, and I did something together, and with everything going on with Charlie, I felt like I had neglected them a little.

—

"Can I have a dry white wine, please?"

The waiter nodded at me and started tapping on his little device, shifting his attention to my friends when he looked back up.

"Make that a bottle." Ashley smiled.

"Ash!" I hissed, thinking that one glass would probably be cheaper than a whole bottle, which would most likely turn into two.

She ignored me, widening her smile at the waiter and earning a nervous grin from the guy.

Ashley was definitely Charlie's sister—able to seduce anyone with just a smile.

"I'll be back with your drinks shortly."

"Thank you, Jake."

Crossing my arms, I sat back, raising a brow at her.

"I thought you were engaged?" I questioned sarcastically, knowing that she wouldn't cheat if her life depended on it.

"I thought smiling at someone was still legal," she countered, and Bailey rolled her eyes, raising the menu in her hands.

"Sure."

Reading through the items on the menu, I tried not to look at the prices, and I practically flinched when Jake placed a wine cooler next to our table.

"I have an *Alsatian Riesling*, a crisp white wine with floral notes," he recited, and both my friends nodded, all the while he had already lost me at *Alsatian*.

I drink wine like lemonade—it'll be fine.

Jake poured a sip for Ashley, who professionally swirled the wine around before she brought the glass to her nose, smelling it. I was used to this kind of behavior, and Ashley *did* know a lot about wine, but I just really wanted my drink now.

She took a sip and sloshed it around in her mouth before she let out an approving hum, swallowing and placing the glass back on the table.

"Delicious, thank you." She beamed and I impatiently slid my glass to the edge of the table, smiling up at Jake as he poured.

"Are you ready to order?" he asked as he carefully placed the bottle in the cooler, grabbing the tablet out of his apron. *You bet your ass I was ready to order.*

I had my eye on that risotto, and I couldn't wait to take in the cheesy goodness.

After we had ordered, and Jake had blushed two more times, Ashley focused her energy on me.

"So, we haven't seen you in weeks," she retorted, leaning back in the plush chair.

"Don't be so dramatic, it's only been two," I bit back, getting a little *too* defensive.

"Ah, so you're aware then."

"Whatever."

"My point is," Ashley continued. "Who have you been fucking?"

I expected this question at some point, but maybe further into the future when I had a better response prepared. *But no.* Instead, I was slowly downing my—*way too expensive to down—* wine, trying to come up with an answer.

"You ok there, Jo?" Bailey asked as I placed my now empty glass back on the table, feeling the alcohol burn slightly in my throat.

"Yes," I answered a little raspy, shifting in my seat.

"Well?" Ashley pressed on.

"It's the same guy from the night of my date—just twice. I've been busy...with my new job."

Yes, very nice. Change the topic to the important shit in your life.

"I still don't know—"

"How *is* your new job?" Bailey interrupted, and I gratefully took the chance to change the subject.

"Amazing, really. It's fairly easy work and I have amazing colleagues." I gushed, smiling from ear to ear.

My first day at Cendose Incorporated had been a challenging one, but I was a fast learner, and within a couple of days, I had mastered all of the basics.

Nadine, the girl that occupied the second seat at the front

desk, had quickly become a friend, and my favorite part of the day was judging the assistants of the executives, who always entered the building with the smuggest of expression on their faces.

Although they were always dressed to the nines, and probably had personal stylists helping them in the morning, their behavior in the office wasn't always as perfect.

Various rumors kept the staff busy on their breaks, and I was happy to join the little gossip group that had formed.

"I'm so glad it's working out, Jordan. You deserve it." Bailey smiled.

"Thank you. I will keep an eye out for better opportunities, but I'm just relieved I have a job."

"Well, me too. And I'm sure something better will come along soon, you're far too smart for a simple desk job," Ashley chimed in, giving my hand sitting on the table a squeeze. I loved how caring she was, supporting me every step of the way.

"We'll see."

I looked up when I spotted Jake coming our way, carrying three plates with delicious food.

"I have the salmon," he offered, walking towards Ashley.

"Thank you." She smirked, and Jake placed her order in front of her.

Never in my life have I ever liked salmon.

"Ma'am," Jake said as he delicately placed my dish in front of me. My mouth watered as the beautiful smell filled my nostrils. I half-shouted my *thank you* after our waiter as he walked away, distracted by my creamy risotto.

We dove into our dinner, enjoying each other's company, and another bottle of wine later we were ready for dessert. Well, *I* was.

"I'm stuffed." Bailey huffed, sitting back in her chair and taking a sip of her wine.

"I think I saw something about chocolate cake on the menu," I mumbled and Ashley chuckled.

"Of course, you checked the desserts first," she retorted but I ignored her. *She didn't get it.* "I'm just getting a tea."

"Would you like some dessert? Tea? Coffee?" Jake asked, appearing next to our table.

"I'd like a tea please." Ashley smiled, folding her hands together on the table and sitting back.

"Me too," Bailey added.

"I would like the chocolate lava cake." I beamed, and I earned an approving nod from Jake.

"Excellent choice."

He gave me another smile before he walked away, and I couldn't help but smile back. He was quite handsome. Dark lashes framing emerald green eyes, a sharp jawline, and beautiful brown curls laying messy on his head.

"Jordan," Ashley interrupted my train of thought, looking at me with her brows raised.

"Sorry, what?"

"I thought you had a boyfriend?" Bailey asked and I chuckled.

"I don't have a *boyfriend*," I stated indignantly. Charlie had been very clear from the start that this was just sex, and besides, I wasn't in love with him either.

"Oh."

"Doesn't matter," I said, playing with my napkin. I was definitely ready to change the subject, *again*. "How is everything going with the wedding, Ash?"

Bailey and I frowned when she let out a sharp breath and leaned forward, burying her face in her hands.

"Not...good?"

"I want a Christmas wedding *this year*, but—" She sighed again, looking up and pausing when Jake returned with our orders.

"Thank you," I said, my mouth watering once again.

God, I love food.

"There's just so many things I need to arrange." Ashley continued as I took a bite, grinning at my friends' jealous faces. I straightened out my expression when I received a look from Bailey. *Right.*

"It's going to be okay, Ash," she comforted our friend, reaching over the table to grab her hand. "Jordan and I will arrange the shower and the bachelorette party, make an appointment to go dress shopping...it'll be okay."

"Ashley!" We heard, and I turned my head to see who it was, probably with chocolate all over my face.

I recognized the guy but didn't know where from. His crisp white shirt brought out the darkness of his skin, and it seemed to glow as he approached our table. He was really handsome and I was sure I had met him before. But where?

He gave Ashley a hug before his gaze went from Bailey to me.

"Hey! Jordan, right?" he questioned, narrowing his eyes ever so slightly.

"Eh, yeah..." I trailed off, waiting for the guy to tell me who he was, and how he knew my name.

"You know Ian?" Ashley asked, confused, and I swallowed hard. *Oh, no.* That's where I met him before. At Charlie's apartment.

"You know? Charlie's friend," he continued and I felt my

heart race, getting so loud I swore they could hear it. *How was I going to talk myself out of this one?*

"I...Charlie?" I stammered, trying to play dumb. According to Ashley, I had only met her brother once, so I could have easily forgotten him and his connection to my best friend. *Right?*

"Yes, we met—"

Panicking, I reached for my drink, spilling it all over the table. "Oh, no!" I exclaimed, jumping up and grabbing all the napkins on the table.

"Jordan," Ashley scoffed, standing as well and picking at her soaked shirt.

"I'm sorry." I frantically rubbed the tablecloth, probably ruining it in the process, but I would do about anything not to look Ian or Ashley in the eye at that moment.

"I'll just...leave you to it then," Ian said softly, and I let out a breath when I heard him walk away.

"What was that?" Bailey asked, placing a hand on my shoulder and forcing me to sink back into my seat.

Ashley left her shirt alone, sitting back down as well and looking at me with a frown. My eyes shot from one to the other, and I smiled weakly, trying to come up with an excuse.

"I think," I started, shifting in my seat and noticing the empty wine bottle on the table. "I think I had a little bit too much to drink."

Both women looked at me with a brow cocked, but they dropped the subject, making my heart sink in my chest. *What am I doing?*

CHAPTER 11
Charlie

"What's next?" Ian asked as I pulled the heavy weights off the Olympic barbell, putting them back on the racks where they were stored.

"Cardio," I panted, still out of breath from the set of squats I'd just finished.

"Are you sure?"

I chuckled. "I don't like it either, but you know it's good for you."

"I'm surprised you still know what cardio is," Ian countered softly, wiping the sweat from his forehead with his towel.

I crossed my arms and raised a brow. "What's that supposed to mean?"

"We used to work out at least three times a week together, Charlie."

"So?"

"Where the fuck have you been?" he asked, mirroring my stance.

Ah, yes. I was wondering when I would get this question. *I've been getting my dick sucked by a tattooed goddess.*

"We see each other at work," I said, avoiding giving him a direct answer. I let my mind drift back to yesterday morning when Jordan—

"Yeah, and you leave the minute the clock strikes six," he continued and I grabbed my water bottle, taking a big gulp. Ian narrowed his eyes, staring at me. "You were always the last to leave. Are you seeing someone?"

I lowered the bottle and chuckled, trying not to choke on the sip I had just taken. "Me? Seeing someone? Not in a *million* years."

"Whatever," he mumbled, picking up his phone and getting ready to move. "As long as you don't end up in jail again, I guess."

I looked up, furrowing my brows, though a small smirk danced on my lips. "That was *one* time, and you know damn well that I was *very* drunk," I defended, pointing an accusing finger at my friend.

"I told you." He shrugged. "You should've taken a leak when we were still at the bar."

"Mistakes are made to learn," I mumbled as my eyes caught a brunette walking by, giving me a perfect view of her round ass.

I sighed as I watched her leave, shaking my head.

"Hmm," Ian hummed, grabbing his towel and drink, heading for the treadmills.

—

Once I got home, I thought about my promise to Ashley, and my decision to keep it. Ok, one of the promises.

Picking up my phone, I forced myself to get it over with and call Perry—even though it was pretty late in the evening. I hadn't spoken to the woman in a while, better yet, it was a miracle I still had her number.

Dropping my gym bag next to the kitchen bar, I took a seat, tapping the *call* icon next to her name. I put the phone on speaker and placed it on the counter, actually a little nervous about the call.

I hated letting my sister down, and if I wasn't able to convince Perry to do me this favor, I would for sure. *We'll just forget about the whole me-having-sex-with-Jordan-thing for a second.*

"Well, well, well. Charlie Abbot is *actually* calling me," Perry sneered sarcastically as she picked up.

This was why I didn't date.

"Hi, Perry."

"What do *you* want?" she snapped. *This was clearly going to be harder than I thought.*

"How are you doing?" I asked, trying to get her to warm up to me before I started asking for favors.

"Like you care. I'm good, actually—happy."

Whatever.

"That's good to hear. You know, I never forgot about that weekend," I said in a low tone, trying to sound sincere. And I wasn't lying; I never forgot anything.

"Right. And I'm supposed to believe that."

Of course, it didn't work.

I brushed my fingers through my hair, a few damp strands

reminding me I needed a shower after my workout at the gym. Plus, it gave me an excuse to end this call as soon as possible.

"I'm really—"

"I don't care. I'm happy now. What do you need?" she interrupted, and I grinned. *I knew she still had a soft spot for me.*

"Well, maybe you've heard, but my sister is engaged," I said, knowing how much she loved gossip, following all of the talk shows and reading every tabloid. Sure, she wouldn't admit it to anyone, but it definitely came in handy right now.

"Yes, I heard."

"Well, she wants the Plaza as the venue. She really loved it there when we—" I stopped myself, afraid I was going to say something wrong.

Hearing a sigh on the other end gave me a little hope.

"*Maybe*, I could rent you the hotel for a weekend, but it won't be cheap."

Please, I'm rich. And so is my family.

"Don't worry about the money," I smirked. "The problem is, she wants to have a Christmas wedding."

I bit my lower lip, crossing my fingers that she could make it happen.

"Jesus, Charlie. That's the busiest time of the year. I can't possibly do that."

I clenched my jaw, my mind going a million miles an hour to think about ways I could persuade her.

"We'll cover any lost revenues and more."

She remained silent for a while, and I was honestly ready to give up.

"I'm still not sure—"

"Think about the publicity," I continued thinking of ways to convince her when I heard the hesitation in her voice. "Her wedding is going to be one of the biggest weddings of the year and the press will definitely cover it, writing your Plaza's name in every magazine and mentioning it on every show."

"Fine. I'll make it happen," she sighed defeatedly. "Have your sister call me and we'll talk specifics then. This is going to cost you, Charlie."

Sure.

"Thank you, Perry."

"Yeah. I gotta go."

The line went dead and I picked up my phone, quickly texting my sister the good news before sending Jordan a dirty line, making sure not to mess the two up. I connected with my Bluetooth speakers, blasting a jazzy beat through my apartment as I took my shower.

This was probably the first night that Jordan and I were apart, and it felt a little weird.

Aside from the fact that she could give head like no other, I actually kind of liked having her around. It was fun teasing her, and even more fun when I got my desired reaction from her. *But maybe it was a good thing that she wasn't here—people would get the wrong idea.*

Once I finished washing my hair, I turned off the water and stepped out of the shower, grabbing a towel and wrapping it around my waist.

"Charlie Abbot!"

My hand stopped mid-air as I reached for my toothbrush, not expecting to hear Jordan in my apartment. *When did she get here?*

I smiled to myself, giving myself a last look in the mirror and sucking my lower lip between my teeth before making my way to my living room.

"Baby, what's all the shouting for?" I asked, casually flexing as I walked over to her.

I smirked when I saw her eyes lower to my abs, her angry expression momentarily fading. Her head snapped back up, eyes shooting daggers at me when she caught herself staring.

"You need to keep your friends in check," she hissed, pointing a finger at me.

"What did I do?" I asked, holding up my hands in defense and trying, but failing to keep myself from smiling.

"I was out to dinner with *your* sister, and what do you know—*Ian* shows up," she explained, throwing her hands in the air before placing the bag on the counter and leaning against it.

It was then that I noticed what she was wearing, a little, red dress tightly hugging her soft curves, short enough to give me a full view of her beautiful legs.

She wasn't the tallest, but the heels she was wearing gave the perfect illusion that she was, elongating her legs in the most amazing way.

"Are you wearing underwear under that dress?" I asked, running my tongue over my lower lip as my eyes stayed glued to Jordan's hips.

"Charlie!" she scolded, and my eyes shot up to hers, a little taken aback by the fire in them.

"What?"

"Ian recognized me, acted as if he knew me," she said, placing one hand on her hip. "Did you tell him something?"

I crossed my arms, frowning. "No? He only saw you here when he and Blake came by."

Jordan sighed, letting herself fall back on one of the stools at the kitchen bar before grabbing her phone. "Well, can you make sure he doesn't speak of that again? Blake, too. Ashley knew something was up for sure."

"Sure."

I walked up to her as she checked her messages, watching her grin as she read mine.

"Did you really have to text me *that* while I was out to dinner with your sister?"

"Of course, I did. Don't think that just because we've completed number twenty-five on the list that I'll suddenly stop sexting you," I replied, placing a hand on her hip.

"I wouldn't want you to."

"Hmm."

I drew circles on her skin with my thumb, letting my free hand run up her leg as I stood between them. She relaxed under my touch and her eyes closed as I continued to touch her.

"Well, are you going to do what you promised me in the text?" she cooed, her eyes shooting back open and meeting mine with a mischievous sparkle.

"That depends," I smiled sinfully, bringing my face closer to hers. "Have you been a bad girl, Ms. Sawyer?"

The air was suddenly filled with sexual tension, and as usual, the only thing I could think about was *her*. Her beautiful dark hair that flowed down her back in waves, covering her tattoos. Her skin that I *knew* would feel silky smooth under my fingers. Her big, brown eyes that looked innocent and up to no good at the same time.

"Maybe," she teasingly smiled, tilting her head up and running her tongue over her lower lip.

"You know what happens to bad girls," I grabbed her jaw with a little force, eliciting a small gasp from her and her eyes widened ever so slightly as she looked up to me. I loved getting this reaction, and by now, I knew exactly what to do to get it.

"*Show me*," she whispered, and I licked my lips before bending down and throwing her over my shoulder, earning a cute shriek from her.

She giggled as she grabbed the towel around my waist and jerked it loose, the fabric falling on the ground as I walked. "Oops."

I chuckled, walking around the couch and dropping her on it, taking a seat next to her.

"Come here," I ordered, tapping my lap, and Jordan got on all fours, crawling her way up to me.

She stopped next to me and pulled the dress over her head, revealing her beautiful tits, bouncing a little as she threw the fabric behind the couch. *God, she was the hottest woman I had ever met.*

I got the answer to my question, too. The only thing she had on was a black, lace thong, perfect for what I planned to do.

She bent over my lap, her warm skin against my thighs and her ass up in the air, Charlie Jr. instantly awake and ready as she hummed.

"Remember your safe word?" I whispered in her ear, noticing the hairs on the back of her neck rising at my voice.

"Yes," she answered confidently, and I smiled.

I caressed my palm over her soft skin, grabbing one ass cheek in my hand before I pulled back and slapped, the sound resonating through the apartment as Jordan arched her back.

"Harder," she mumbled almost inaudibly, but I could hear her loud and clear.

A feeling of pure satisfaction rushed through me as I landed my palm harder on her ass, hearing her whimper and moan. I had all the power and honestly, doing this had always been top of my list.

I repeated the action a few times, until red streaks covered her beautifully tanned skin, practically branding her as mine. I had no desire to turn our little arrangement into a dominant-submissive one, but I understood why people found satisfaction in seeing someone experiencing pleasure from the pain they inflicted, and especially the power it provided.

I saw Jordan as my equal, but I knew she enjoyed giving me a little more control in the bedroom, and I, of course, loved having it.

"How are you doing?" I asked, softly brushing my fingers over the red marks, my other hand moving a few hairs out of her face.

"I am—" she breathed out, lifting herself off my lap and moving to straddle me as I smirked, "—so turned on, right now."

"Let's do something about that then, shall we?"

She giggled as I threw her down, back to the couch. I pulled off her thong, spread her legs, and positioned my face between them.

Eating Jordan out really was my favorite thing to do, the look on her face and the sounds she made was almost enough to push me over the edge.

"Number fifty-eight?" I asked, my hands caressing over her hips to her thighs.

"What's that?" she sighed, propping up on her elbows to

look at me.

I held her gaze as I moved my lips closer to her core, sticking my tongue out to quickly dip between her folds. She moaned softly, falling back and grabbing the edge of the couch with one hand, the other sliding up to her breasts, touching herself.

"Only oral," I said, blowing a little air against her pussy before I dove in, burying my face between her legs. I watched her gasp and bite her lip as I worked my tongue around her clit, her perfectly smooth pussy being my favorite meal these days.

Her grip on the couch tightened and her knuckles turned white as she tensed under me. She squirmed in my hands, her hips bucking and her back arching as I quickly brought her closer to her release.

"Oh, Charlie!" she moaned as her legs started to shake, and I flattened my tongue over her clit before sucking on the little bundle of nerves, giving her as much stimulation as I could while she came.

I continued my movements until she pushed me away, closing her legs and opening her eyes, still panting as she slipped into a state of bliss.

I smirked proudly, leaning against the back of the couch as I observed her.

"Jesus," she panted, slowly sitting up and brushing a hand through her hair.

"No, *Charlie*," I retorted, earning an eye roll.

We sat in silence for a minute, all the while I tried to ignore my painful erection, Jordan's pleasure and the sounds she let out because of it making me rock hard. I drew circles on her knee with my fingers, but she surprised me when she suddenly stood up and kneeled in front of me, nudging my knees apart with her arms.

"Your turn, *Pretty Boy*," she cooed, gathering her hair and guiding my hand to grab it.

Oh, was I fucking ready.

I watched the little minx lower her head, her eyes still on mine as she licked my tip, shooting a first bolt of pleasure through my body.

She wrapped her lips around my length, taking me as far as she could before hollowing her cheeks, sucking as she moved.

I grabbed her hair tighter in my fist, moving with her as her head bobbed up and down on me. Closing my eyes, I let my head fall back on the couch, moaning softly as she brought me closer and closer to my orgasm.

Jordan always told me that she had no idea what she was doing, but the way she ran her tongue along the underside of my dick and the way she gave my balls the right amount of attention, showed the exact opposite.

"Fuck, I love your mouth," I groaned, bucking my hips a little, fucking her face as I dangled on the edge, ready for her to push me over.

She hummed against me, moving faster and faster until I came, sucking down every bit of me until I was clean.

I pulled her head up and she licked her lips as she sat down next to me, cross-legged.

"Number fifty-eight, done," she smiled as she drew a check sign in the air, making me chuckle as I tried to catch my breath.

CHAPTER 12
Jordan

A week later, on Monday morning, I walked out of my bathroom with my freshly washed hair up in a towel and some black lace underwear on. Not that I really had any other colors in my drawer, but I did have a favorite pair.

I changed into my trusty black pencil skirt and paired it with a white blouse, smiling to myself in the mirror as I observed my outfit. I looked like a proper businesswoman, and you know what they say: *dress for the job you want.*

I took a cab to work, stepping into the building twenty minutes later with nerves in my stomach, the environment still new.

"Hey, Oscar," I greeted the guy who stood behind my colleague, Nadine, wearing a perfect blue suit.

"Morning Jordan," he smiled, his sparkling grey eyes standing out against his dark skin.

"Jordan!" Nadine shrieked, jumping off her chair and rounding the front desk.

I chuckled as she wrapped her arms around me, the platinum blonde always greeting everyone with the same enthusiasm.

Especially on a Monday.

"Good morning, how was your weekend?" I asked, walking with her around the counter after she finally released me. *Ok, maybe I was in a good mood too.* I wouldn't admit it to anyone, but spending time with Charlie did have a positive effect on my mood.

"I had a date," she beamed, plopping back in her seat and twirling around to face me.

"Oh?" I smirked, turning on my computer.

"He was amazing." She sighed, leaning with her chin on her palm, her elbow resting on her desk, and Oscar and I shared a look. We had a feeling she wasn't talking about his cooking skills, especially since we were familiar with Nadine's definition of 'dating'.

"Are you going to see him again?" Oscar asked, crossing his arms.

"Hmm...no."

Oscar and I chuckled, not expecting anything else. Nadine was living her best life and I was happy for her.

"Oh look, here they come." I straightened in my seat, flipping my hair over my shoulder as two women entered the building, the foyer immediately turning silent, apart from the clicking of their heels against the marble.

We watched them as they strutted towards the elevators,

their perfect hair neatly tied up in identical buns and flawless outfits hugging their fantastic curves.

They radiated confidence and arrogance, the redhead—Gail Carmichael—giving us a nasty look, her chin slightly tilted up in disdain. *Yeah, look down on me Gail. I know you're screwing the COO's husband.*

Focusing on the brunette, I felt a little jealous of her as she seemed to glide over the floor. Not just her position, *because God knew I wanted it*, but the way she looked as well. Her hair seemed inhumanly shiny, and I sighed softly as they reached the elevators.

I mocked them as they giggled, my imitation a little loud, making them look back.

"Fuck." I quickly looked away, scowling at Oscar as he tried to contain his laughter.

He chuckled loudly when the two assistants disappeared behind the elevator doors, and I couldn't help but smile.

"Thank you, for that, Jordan," he said, rounding the counter and making his way to his office.

—

I grabbed my phone as the screen lit up, narrowing my eyes when I read the text message.

Jesus.

As much as I enjoyed Charlie's naked chest, it was not something suitable for work, hence why I was cursing Face ID for unlocking my phone and bringing up the photo.

I tried to contain my smirk as I took a peek, sighing softly as I took in the hard ridges, remembering how they felt under my fingers.

"Excuse me?"

My head shot up and my phone dropped with a loud bang on my desk as I was pulled back to reality, internally flinching when I saw the disapproving look on the face of the man before me.

"Yes. My apologies. Welcome to Cendose Incorporated, how can I help you?" I smiled, clenching my jaw.

I directed the client to the right floor, my cheeks probably resembling two tomatoes by the time I excused myself to the bathroom.

The day was almost over anyway, with only five minutes left until Monday was done.

Sighing, I closed the door to one of the toilets, sitting down on top of it and taking my phone back out.

I was aware that I wasn't exactly winning employee of the month with my evasive work behavior, but this particular day, I was just really tired. And besides, the day was almost over anyway.

"Oh my God," I breathed out, shaking my head at an explicit text from Charlie, watching the three dots as he typed.

My eyes widened when I received the next text, telling me that he was picking me up from work. *People can't see him here.*

Tripping over my heels, I stormed out of the restroom and made my way back to the foyer. I didn't see Charlie yet, but he could appear at any second and I was far from ready.

"Are you ok?" Nadine asked as I began to pack my bag and log off my computer.

"Yeah, I just remembered, uh—" I stuttered, checking my desk one last time before throwing my coat on. "I need to go."

"Sure." She smiled up at me. "See you tomorrow."

I turned to place a few documents back in the assigned

cabinets, freezing when I heard a familiar voice.

"Hey, Jordan. Ready to go?"

I turned to see Charlie, leaning with one arm on the front desk, his grey suit jacket stretching tightly over his bicep in the process.

"I didn't know you were dating Charlie Abbot?" Nadine chirped, looking from Charlie to me.

Shit.

"We're not dating," I quickly replied, walking around the counter and tugging on Charlie's sleeve to signal to him that I wanted to leave the damn building already.

He smirked down at me instead, before turning back to Nadine.

"We're not." He winked, and I rolled my eyes.

"Let's go, Charlie."

He pulled his eyes off my coworker, placing his hand on the small of my back as we walked out of the building. I resisted the urge to slap it away, secretly enjoying the gesture. Until I saw a couple of people on the street look our way.

"People will see," I hissed, but Charlie just hummed, sliding his hand down to my ass and completely ignoring the attention we were getting.

I could finally breathe when I sat safely behind the tinted windows of Charlie's Camaro, waiting for him to round the car and get behind the wheel.

"Are you ok?" he asked, turning in his seat.

"What part of *'we have to keep it a secret from everyone'* do you not understand?" I scolded, my heart thumping loudly in my chest as I looked at his stupidly handsome face.

"Jordan," he said calmly, his tone annoying *the fuck* out of me. "Calm down."

"Char—"

"Jordan." He cupped my face with both hands, rubbing his thumbs over my cheeks.

I took a deep breath, closing my eyes as I focused on Charlie's touch.

Was I overreacting? Probably.

"I'm ok." I sighed, and Charlie released me, facing the wheel and turning on the engine.

"Good, because nobody cared. It's going to be fine."

Leaning back in my seat, I let my head roll to the side, watching the tall buildings move as Charlie pulled out of the parking spot.

"Why did you come to pick me up?" I asked softly, continuing to stare out of the window.

I jumped slightly in my seat when I felt his hand on my thigh, his fingers sliding under the fabric of my skirt.

"I got you a little something."

"What?" I questioned.

"It's a surprise," he added, and I turned to face him. I rolled my eyes when he didn't elaborate, and shifted in my seat when my stomach rumbled, making me realize that I hadn't eaten anything since lunch.

"Ok, but can we get something to eat first?"

"We can order something," Charlie offered, but I had a different idea.

"Can we go to the diner on my street? Nobody will recognize you there," I pleaded, grabbing his hand with both of mine, the diner's strawberry milkshake appearing before my eyes.

He frowned, giving me a quick look before he focused on the

road. "That diner looks...not safe."

I rolled my eyes. "But I want their homemade milkshake," I whined, pouting like a child.

"Fine."

Twenty minutes later, Charlie parked his car in the *secure* parking lot behind my building, the both of us thinking it would be best to walk from there.

I had a small skip in my step as we made our way to the diner, ready to enjoy a strawberry shake—*the best on the planet*.

Sometimes the best food comes from the shabbiest of restaurants.

"Hey, Larissa," I greeted the lady behind the counter as Charlie and I walked into the diner, the place surprisingly full for a Monday night.

"Hi, Jordan. Long time no see." She smiled, crossing her arms.

I glanced over my shoulder, chuckling and rolling my eyes as I watched Charlie look around with a disgusted expression on his face.

"Who's this princess?" Larissa asked, nodding to Charlie.

"He's—" I actually didn't have a good answer to that question. "It's complicated?"

She shrugged, accepting my answer as she moved behind the outdated register. *It added to the authentic vibe, I guess.*

"What can I get you?"

"Of course, I'm going to need a strawberry milkshake," I beamed, "And a cheeseburger with fries."

Larissa nodded approvingly, typing away on the register, knowing all the prices by heart.

"Charlie?" I called over my shoulder and he walked up to us, tucking his hands in his pockets as he stopped next to me.

"Do you have white wine?" he asked with raised brows, and I snorted. I knew Charlie was a smart guy, but asking a question like that at a place like this showed quite the opposite.

"I don't, actually. But I can lace your milkshakes with vodka if you want?" Larissa retorted and Charlie and I shared a look before we shrugged.

"Sure," we said in unison, and Larissa shook her head, grinning as she typed.

"What milkshake do you want?" she asked Charlie and he shifted his eyes to mine.

"Strawberry," I whispered.

"Strawberry," he told Larissa, and she looked from him to me with a raised brow. I tried to ignore her gaze, my cheeks undoubtedly heating up under her gaze.

"Anything else?"

"Actually, I'll just have whatever she's having," Charlie said, and Larissa nodded.

I led Charlie to one of the last tables available when we were done ordering, a small booth by one of the windows—even though it was beyond me why anyone would want to look at the dirty street and scruffy-looking people.

The sun began to set, and it created a gorgeous warm glow, the last rays of sunshine fighting through the trees to bathe the restaurant in its beautiful radiance. I smiled at the number plates that covered the entire wall behind the counter, at least *one* from every state.

"This table is dirty," Charlie complained, running a finger over the surface before rubbing his thumb and pointer finger together.

I ignored his comment, narrowing my eyes at him as he looked around.

"Your milkshakes." Larissa appeared next to our table, placing two tall glasses in front of us. "With a little extra on the house," she whispered, grinning as she walked back to the register, the empty tray now flush against her side.

"Yes, thank you," I exclaimed, grabbing the red and white straw and placing it between my lips, moaning softly when I tasted the sweet drink on my tongue. This really *was* the best milkshake in town.

"Stop that," Charlie stated, sitting back in his seat, apparently giving up on the hygiene.

"Stop what?" I asked innocently, looking at him over the rim of my glass and gliding the straw a little deeper in my mouth.

"Moaning and stuff," he explained, shifting in his seat. "You're making me hard."

I almost choked on my next sip, the milkshake nearly coming out of my nose as I tried to catch my breath. "Charlie!" I scolded, wiping my mouth with my napkin.

He just shrugged as Larissa returned with our food.

"Thank you," I beamed, my stomach audibly growling as I smelled the fries.

"If you need anything, just give me a wave." Larissa smiled, nodding to Charlie before she walked away.

As much as I wanted to dive into my dinner, I held back, staring expectantly at Charlie, excited for him to taste the food.

"What?" he asked, taking one of the fries and bringing it to his nose.

"Charlie!"

I grabbed his hand and pulled it down, looking over at Larissa to see if she noticed him freaking *smelling* his food with a disgusted look on his face.

"Just put it in your mouth."

"That's what she said," he smirked before he ate the fry, his eyes widening slightly as he chewed.

I sighed at his immature remark and mirrored him as he started to stuff his face with food, noticeably surprised by the quality.

"Good, right?" I asked with my mouth full cheeseburger, the juices of the patty dripping down my chin and on my plate.

"Hmm," he just hummed, closing his eyes as he took in the food.

We finished our dinner with lightning speed, leaning back in our seats once we were done.

"Jordan." Charlie cleared his throat as he wiped his mouth with his napkin. "I hate to be proven wrong." I smiled. "But you did it."

I shrieked, throwing my napkin on my plate and making Charlie chuckle. I knew it was difficult for him to admit that he was wrong, or rather, that someone else was right, so I felt amazing.

My phone vibrated against the table, and I picked it up to look at the text. My hands instantly got clammy and a sudden surge of adrenaline went through me when I read Ashley's 'SOS'. I quickly slid off the bench.

"I need to make a call," I said, not waiting for Charlie's nod as I turned to the restrooms.

I immediately dialed Ashley's number when I closed the door behind me, bringing the phone to my ear with shaking hands.

"Jordan?" she answered, and I scoffed at her calm tone.

"Are you ok?" I asked, my heart no longer in my throat.

"No! I'm not ok," she whined and I sighed. "I have to go to this charity gala on Friday and Ryan can't come with me and I don't want to go alone and—"

"Ashley," I interrupted her. "Breathe."

I heard her take a deep breath before she continued. "Ryan has some dinner with his boss, so he can't come with me to the charity gala."

"Ok..."

"So I need *you* to come with me."

I rolled my eyes, looking up at the ceiling as I mouthed *oh my God*, scolding myself for expecting Ashley to not make a big deal out of something minor and using the emergency signal for it.

"Ash, I don't think—"

"I *need* you," she pleaded softly, and I bit the inside of my cheek as I thought about my reply. Honestly, a gala is something I secretly really liked—or rather the *idea*—but it was that world that I didn't fit in. Those people. There was no doubt that Ashley's parents were going to be there, and I couldn't see myself socializing with other snobby rich people.

"I don't—"

"Please, Jordan. I don't want Charlie to keep me company the whole time," she added, and I shook my head in defeat. Ashley had done a lot for me over the years, and I knew she could get anxious when she didn't have someone from her circle with her at these things.

"Ok, but you're paying for my ticket."

"God, I love you."

I chuckled, absentmindedly kicking a bottle cap away. It clattered against the tiled wall, creating a track into the dust under the sink.

"I love you, too." I smiled.

"Oh! The theme is *Hollywood* by the way," she said, her voice dripping with excitement.

Great.

"Sounds expe—good."

I really needed to stop thinking about money so much. Ashely was paying for my ticket, and I was sure I had something in my closet that would fit the theme. It wouldn't be *Versace* or *Dior*, but I had a certain red dress in mind that I never got to wear, and it would be perfect.

"You're the best, Jojo. We're *so* going to enjoy that open bar," she chirped, making me scoff. Open bar?

"You should've led with that," I retorted, and she chuckled.

"I wanted to see if I could convince you this way."

"Hmm, well, I have to go."

We said our goodbyes and I hung up the phone. Charlie would probably have insulted half the staff by now, so I quickly walked out of the restrooms.

"Took you awhile," Charlie stated as I walked up to the table, raising my brows when I noticed a third milkshake glass.

"Looks like you didn't mind," I retorted, sliding into the booth and pointing at his empty glass.

"I'll go pay," he said, avoiding my eyes and ignoring my question.

I watched him walk to Larissa, radiating confidence and grabbing everyone's attention. Not just the women, but the men too. It made sense since he clearly didn't come from this neighborhood with his tailored suit and perfect haircut, but I didn't expect him to turn *this* many heads. I couldn't deny that he was very easy on the eyes—one of the reasons I wanted to keep him around—plus he just oozed sophistication and, well... *money*.

"Ready?" he asked when he returned.

"Yes."

I rolled my eyes at the waitress clearing our table who was bending a little *too* far over for it to be natural, but surprisingly enough, Charlie didn't even look at her.

It made me question his true intentions with me, a weird feeling creeping up on me as we walked home. I tried to shrug off the thought, thinking about the gala instead, but it was no use. *For some reason, I needed to know.*

"Why didn't you look at her ass?"

Charlie stopped in front of the door to my apartment building, his hand resting on the handle as he froze, watching me with one brow raised. "What kind of question is that?"

"The girl. Her ass was almost in your face," I explained, attempting to take a step towards the entrance, Charlie's hand still gripping the handle. He studied me for a second, his icy eyes boring into mine with a mysterious glimmer in them as if he was trying to figure me out. He kept me from walking into the building, cocking his head to the side.

"Should I have looked?"

"I—no. That's up to you," I rambled, a little taken aback by the intensity of his gaze.

He didn't say anything, instead, he opened the door, letting me step inside first before he closed it behind him. We made it up to my apartment in silence, the air feeling weirdly thick with something unfamiliar, but I ignored it.

"I think that it would've been disrespectful," he spoke when we went inside.

I took off my coat, walking into the kitchen to make some tea. "Why?"

Charlie followed, leaning against the counter next to me with his hands in his pockets.

"What would people think if I was staring at someone else when I was already out with a beautiful woman?" he elaborated, surprising me for the millionth time this evening.

"Thank you."

"I'm not *that* much of a dick, Baby," he smirked, grabbing a glass of water and walking to the couch.

I refrained from contradicting him, making my tea and joining him on the sofa.

"Well, what did you get me?" I asked, referring back to Charlie's justification for picking me up.

His eyes lit up like a Christmas tree, the mischievous sparkle appearing back in them as he fished something out of his pocket.

My eyes widened as I looked at the shiny toy, the big red diamond on the end glittering at me as he held it up.

"You got the one I wanted." I beamed, taking the tiny butt plug from him.

"It's part of a set. We're going to have to stretch you out." He grinned, tingles going up my spine at the suggestive wiggle of his brows.

"It's so pretty."

"Wanna try it out?"

CHAPTER 13
Jordan

I turned the toy in my hand, studying it. "You know how this works?" I asked, regretting the question as soon as it left my lips. *I didn't want him to know how inexperienced I actually was.*

He lifted himself off the couch, holding out his hand for me to take, but I jumped up, eagerly running to the bedroom instead. Hearing Charlie chuckle, I surprised myself by how excited I felt for some anal play. I was getting out of my comfort zone, but I found myself trusting Charlie with my body.

"Baby?" he asked, walking into the room, leaning against the door frame.

"Tell me what to do," I purred, kicking off my shoes.

Charlie ran his tongue over his bottom lip, raking his eyes over my body before he spoke. "Alright. Strip and get on the bed."

Desire and arousal coursed through me, my panties undoubtedly already soaking wet by the sound of his demanding voice alone. I did as he said, quickly shedding my clothes before I crawled onto the bed, my eyes on Charlie as I laid down on my stomach.

"I have something else in mind first, so you can get used to the feeling, and we'll go from there," he explained as he took off his tie, placing it carefully on my dresser.

Fully clothed, he walked up to me, unbuttoning the top buttons of his white shirt as he stood at the foot of the bed. My eyes roamed down his chest, following the buttons until I reached his belt, licking my lips as my eyes shot up to Charlie's. I liked this dominant side of him, just like I did the first time we met.

I didn't hesitate as I got on all fours, looking up at him and awaiting his next command. Charlie quickly picked up on my enthusiasm, rolling his bottom lip between his teeth and combing one of his hands through my hair.

"You like to be told what to do, huh?" he asked, hooded eyes dropping to my chest as I grabbed his belt.

"I do."

He hummed. I rolled my shoulders back, exposing my chest a little more and grinned at the attention I was getting.

"Well," he cooed, pushing a stray curl behind my ear. "Undress me."

I obeyed, eagerly undoing his belt and unzipping his slacks. The bulge in his boxers stared at me, ready to be touched—pleased.

"Go ahead," Charlie mumbled, and I took off his underwear, rubbing my hands over his hips as I smiled up at him.

Leaning closer, I licked his tip, watching his eyes close slightly, his lower lip between his teeth again.

"Hmm." He grabbed a fistful of my hair and pulled my head back, just before I was about to take him fully into my mouth.

"What?" I pouted.

"Turn around," he replied, nodding to the headboard.

I did as he said, anticipation making the nerves in my stomach flutter, arousal still pooling between my legs. Waiting for the next command, I closed my eyes and burried my fingers in the sheets.

Feeling the bed dip behind me, I gasped when his fingers crept between my folds.

"Charlie..." I moaned, tilting my head back as he expertly swirled his fingers over my clit, his other hand grabbing a breast, massaging it.

"I love it when you moan my name." I felt his hot breath against my neck as he spoke, goosebumps covering my arms from the sensation.

"You can make me moan it louder," I smirked over my shoulder, catching a glimpse of Charlie's eyes, the icy blues a great contrast to the obvious fire in them.

"I know," he groaned as he thrusted his cock into me with expert precision, completely taking me off guard and almost making me fall forward.

"Charlie!" I half scolded, half chuckled, grabbing the headboard as he started to pump into me.

We didn't bother with condoms anymore since a couple of days, and Charlie's face had lit up when I told him I was on birth control.

I couldn't contain my moans, probably waking the neighbors as I cried out louder and louder. Charlie's hips slapped against my ass, his fingers grabbing onto my shoulders and waist. He let out the occasional raspy groan, telling me he was enjoying it, too, and it turned me on even more.

"Yes," I breathed out, tightening my grip on the headboard. I shrieked when Charlie's hand made painful contact with my ass.

Our pants and moans quickened, the two of us coming closer to our release, but Charlie had other plans, slowing down his movements. I frowned when he moved one finger over my core, coating it in my arousal, but not actually rubbing my clit.

"Char—ah!" I bit my lower lip hard as he pushed the finger in my ass, the sensation foreign, but not unpleasant.

"How does that feel? Be honest," he asked, still slightly moving his dick in and out of me, waiting for me to answer.

"Good," I breathed out, dropping my head and closing my eyes, pushing my ass against him, to let him know that he could go faster.

He grabbed my hair with his free hand and pulled hard, eliciting a gasp from my lips and forcing me to arch my back. "Words, Baby."

"Faster! I'm sorry, faster."

Charlie hummed in satisfaction, releasing my hair and brushing his fingers over my scalp. "Your wish is my command," he cooed against my ear before he steadied himself again and quickened his pace.

He continued to press his finger in my ass as he slammed into me harder, confusing the fuck out of me—in a good way.

Why did this actually feel good?

"Come on, Baby," Charlie rasped, his voice strained from our workout, as he sped up even more, pushing me over the edge, into paradise.

"Charlie!" I moaned loudly, squeezing my eyes shut.

"That's more like it!" he said, removing his finger from my behind and grabbing both hips to thrust into me a few final times before filling me. The grunt that he let out as he came was almost enough to give me another orgasm.

He wrapped his arms around my waist when he was done, the both of us dropping onto the bed.

"Step...one," Charlie mumbled between breaths, his chest rising and falling quickly against my back.

I hummed, my eyes still closed, not really paying attention.

We stayed in that position for a few minutes, feeling each other's heartbeat, before Charlie let me go.

He lifted himself from the bed, walked to his folded clothes, and grabbed the tiny butt plug out of his pants pocket, turning to me with a smirk. "You didn't think I was done with you yet, did you?"

I turned onto my back, leaning on my elbows as I stared up at Charlie's naked chest. He smirked and flexed, his eyes roaming my body as mine roamed his. Rolling the plug through his hands, he walked up to me and grabbed the bottle of lube from my nightstand.

"Are you ready?" he asked, kneeling on the bed in front of me.

Was I?

"Hell yes."

I got on all fours, pushing my ass in Charlie's face and he chuckled.

"Ok, Baby. Relax."

I heard the cap of the lube bottle and flinched when I felt Charlie rub some around my ass before I felt the cold tip of the plug against me.

"Relax," he breathed into my ear, his free hand sliding over my stomach to my core.

Moaning softly as Charlie began to rub my clit, I tried not to focus on the foreign object being pressed into my ass.

A few minutes later, the plug was in and I was laying on my back with my legs spread, Charlie's fingers playing with the sensitive nub at the apex of my thighs. He watched me as I groaned and gasped, the strange sensation of the toy only adding to the pleasure.

"Oh, Charlie," I moaned, my eyes rolling back and my hands grabbing the sheets tightly.

"Hmm, you like that?"

He quickened his pace with his fingers, still applying the right amount of pressure on the little bundle of nerves as he brought me closer to my orgasm. This was something I've *never* felt before, and I was pleasantly surprised that a little ass play would have such a good effect, contrary to what I initially thought.

"Yes!" I gasped, my eyes squeezing shut as Charlie made me come, every single muscle in my body tightening and my toes curling.

Rolling onto my back once more, I took a second, my chest rising and falling quickly as I tried to catch my breath.

"And?" Charlie asked as he slowly removed the plug to roll it in some toilet paper and place it on the bedside table.

He expected me to talk after that?

"Hmm," I hummed, grabbing his face and pulling his lips to mine, feeling like a good make-out session would complete this day.

Charlie eagerly moved his tongue into my mouth, smiling against my lips as he deepened the kiss. We got lost in each other again as I rolled on top of him, tangling our legs together and caressing his tongue with mine.

I pulled back to catch my breath, studying Charlie's face. From his slightly swollen pink lips, the stubble that always tickled me, to his blue eyes, shocking me every time with their paleness. You could get a lot of information from them, the light orbs often telling you more about the man than he did himself. Yet right now, they were affirming what I already knew,

"What do you wear to a gala?" I asked, Charlie's hand stopping mid-air as he attempted to tuck a strand of hair behind my ear.

"What?"

I got off the bed, opening my closet.

"Ashley invited me to the charity gala on Friday," I explained, turning and resting a hand on my hip.

"This will be fun," Charlie smirked devilishly, his eyes lowering ever so slightly to my naked chest.

"Charlie. I'm serious!" I threw a shirt at his face.

"Well." He scooted back to sit up against the headboard and crossed his arms over his chest, flexing his muscles. "It's for the World Wildlife Fund, and I believe the theme is *Hollywood* this year."

I nodded, gesturing for him to go on.

"Just wear something long, classy,"—he wiggled his brows—" and a little sexy."

I rolled my eyes. *What did I expect? This was Charlie.*

"Fine, but any suggestions?" I asked, sliding a few hangers over the bar, searching for a particular red number that I had in mind.

"I'm not helping you pick," Charlie retorted.

"This one?"

"Jordan!" he scolded, covering his eyes with both hands when I held out the dress.

"What?" I asked, genuinely confused.

"I want it to be a surprise," he explained, and I chuckled, placing the dress back in my closet before closing it and walking back to the bed.

"It's not a wedding dress, Charlie."

He dropped his hands, revealing raised brows. "That's not what I meant."

An awkward silence settled between us and we both avoided each other's eyes.

I knew he didn't plan on getting married—*especially not to me*—and it was also something I didn't see us doing, but the mere mention of a *wedding dress* made the air in the room suddenly feel very uncomfortable. Almost unbearable so.

Maybe, over the last couple of weeks, the lines had become a little blurred, even though we both knew there were no feelings involved.

I quickly threw on a robe and walked into my tiny bathroom to brush my teeth. I stared at myself in the mirror, not daring to let my eyes wander to the man in my bedroom. I washed my hands, put on some face cream, and tied my hair in a bun, flinching when I heard the front door close.

Did I already fuck things up?

CHAPTER 14
Jordan

"Just two more days," Nadine mumbled, her eyes narrowing onto her computer screen.

"And...?"

"Then it's the weekend again," she explained, giving up on the document she was reading and focussing her attention on me.

I nodded, taking a sip of my tea.

It was Wednesday, and we were ready for this week to be over after another busy day.

"Any plans this weekend?" Nadine asked, and my face dropped.

Charlie and I hadn't seen each other since Monday, which didn't sound like a long time, but after spending almost every day together for a month, it was to me.

Maybe that was the problem.

I had mixed feelings about the gala on Friday. I looked forward to spending some time with Ashley and dressing up, but I was nervous about seeing Charlie. And let's not forget that their parents were going to be there, along with a bunch of other rich assholes looking down on me like I was some charity case.

"Jordan?" Nadine interrupted my train of thought. "Are you okay?"

"Yes," I answered quickly, trying to avoid her further prying. She seemed to understand my answer, turning to me in her chair.

"If you don't want to talk about it, that's fine," she added, smiling reassuringly.

"No, that's ok," I replied, mirroring her expression. Maybe it was good to talk about it after all. And maybe she could give me some advice or ease my mind. "I'm going to this charity gala on Friday, and I guess I have mixed feelings about it."

"That's so exciting!" Nadine shrieked, making a passing client jump. "I want to hear everything about it after," she continued, leaning forward in her chair.

"You do?"

"Yes! Want to come over for lunch on Sunday?" she asked, taking me by surprise. Nadine and I got along really well but never talked outside of work. I realized that I actually didn't know her at all.

"Sure."

"Ms. Sawyer?"

Nadine and I looked up as an older, *clearly* more important man appeared at our desk.

"Yes?"

"Do you have a minute?" he asked.

I jumped off my chair, nerves swarming my stomach as I rounded the front desk. "Yes, sir."

Taking a quick look over my shoulder, I watched Nadine mouth *good luck* as I followed the man to the elevators.

"I'm Henry Grimaldi. I don't believe we've met before," he said as we entered the elevator. After he pressed the button to one of the top floors, he held out his hand to greet me. *Am I in trouble? Why is Mr. Grimaldi—the Vice President of this company—bringing me to his office?*

"We haven't," I replied, shaking his hand. "Nice to meet you."

We made small talk as the elevator ascended, but I felt more at ease when the doors finally rolled open and Mr. Grimaldi beckoned me to follow.

"Now, Ms. Sawyer," he said, circling his desk to sit down in the big, plush chair across from me. "I understand that you've been working here for over a month now."

"Yes, sir," I answered, feeling equally nervous and curious to see where this was going.

"Well," he continued, grabbing a few pieces of paper from the corner of his desk, stacking them in front of him. "Let me get straight to the point."

I nodded slowly, looking at the man in front of me. I noticed a little grey on the sides of his hair, his dark eyes reading over the papers from behind his glasses. I had seen him in the building before, all tall and important, but I never dreamed of sitting in his office.

"Mrs. Perez just handed in her resignation, leaving me without an assistant starting next month," he explained. I tried to not get my hopes up, even though I had a feeling I knew where this was going. Surely not, right?

"Instead of searching for an external candidate and dealing with the lengthy interview process, I've looked into promoting one of the fine employees that we already have."

My heartbeat was definitely speeding up.

"You probably have an idea where I'm going with this," he said, peering over his glasses. "I'd like to offer *you* the position."

"What?" I exclaimed, cupping my palm over my mouth as soon as the word left my lips.

Mr. Grimaldi chuckled as he slid a piece of paper towards me. "I took the liberty of looking over some of the resumes of our employees, especially those who have a supporting position," he elaborated, and I nodded. "Yours stood out to me."

I didn't say anything, momentarily frozen in place as Mr. Grimaldi waited for me to answer. This kind of thing didn't happen to people like me. Things didn't just fall into my lap—luck was never on my side.

"I don't know what to say," I replied.

"Yes?" he suggested, and I smiled at him.

"Can I think about it?" I asked, hoping my question wouldn't make him second guess his decision to give me a chance. This was way too good to be true, and I needed to let it sink in for a second before I agreed to anything.

"Of course. Everything you need to know about the position is written here," he pointed to the piece of paper in front of me. "And if you have any questions, you can ask Mrs. Perez."

Staring at the job requirements in my hand, I shuffled back to the front desk, ignoring Nadine's puzzled expression as I sat down. *Was someone finally giving me a position that was more in line with my education?*

"Jo?" Nadine asked, placing a hand on my wrist and making me look up at her. "Is everything okay?"

"Yes, I—"

I was speechless, my eyes racing over the words in my hand but not really registering them.

"Did something happen?" she pressed, rolling her chair closer to mine.

"I'm sorry. He...offered me the position of his assistant," I finally answered, still not quite believing what just happened.

"Oh, I knew you'd leave at some point, but I never expected it to be so soon," she scoffed, crossing her arms and pouting. *She expected me to leave?*

"You didn't think I would stay?"

Nadine turned her head back to me with a smile. "Have you *seen* your resume?"

I chuckled softly. "Thank you." I smiled up to her, grateful for her faith in me.

"Well, ladies." Oscar sighed as he walked up to the front desk, leaning on the surface as he looked at us. "Time to go home."

"I have to make a quick call," I said, standing up and walking into one of the corners of the foyer. Ashley picked up after one ring.

"Jojo! How've you been! Haven't talked to you in ages!" she chirped, and I shook my head.

"You texted me this morning," I retorted, looking down at my high heels and wiggling my toes to relieve some of the pain.

"You know what I mean," she replied. "What can I do for you?"

"I need an *ice cream night.*"

"Tomorrow?" Ashley offered.

"I have to get my birth control shot tomorrow after work," I explained, chewing on my cheek. "Can you do tonight?"

I held my breath as I waited on Ashley's answer—such a spontaneous idea was often her worst nightmare. She was just as much of a control freak as her brother sometimes.

"Ok, yeah. Sounds fun!"

"Yes! I'll ask Bailey if she's in and text you the details in a sec," I said, ending the call and skipping back to my desk.

—

"Oh, come on Benji!" I exclaimed, slamming the steering wheel when my car wouldn't start later that evening. I turned the key in the ignition again, dropping my head when it didn't work. Bailey and I had promised to be at Ashley's at seven, and I was already running late, so my car finally giving up on me didn't really brighten my mood.

"Baby, please," I pleaded, caressing the steering wheel. "I need you."

I closed my eyes for a second, taking a deep breath, before I turned the key in the ignition one more time, finally bringing the engine to life.

"Yes! God, I love you!" I cheered, quickly pulling out of the parking lot and making my way to Ashley's apartment. I ended up being only ten minutes late, right as Bailey was taking the ice cream out of her bag.

"Finally," she said as Ashley let me in, closing the door behind me and following me into the kitchen.

"Hey, Bailey." I smiled up at her.

"Alright," she started, ignoring me. "I have *Strawberry Cheesecake* for Ashley."

"Thank you," Ashely said, taking the tub of ice cream from Bailey and grabbing three spoons.

"*Cookie Dough* for me," Bailey continued, taking two more tubs out of the bag. "And plain *Vanilla* for Jordan."

The only time I love vanilla.

I squealed as I took the tub from Bailey, grabbed a spoon from Ashley, and walked to the couch as I popped off the lid.

"I have a question," Ashely asked, sitting down behind the coffee table on the floor.

"Hmm," I hummed, already stuffing my face with ice cream.

"Not that I didn't miss our *ice cream nights*," she continued. "But, why now?"

"Well,"—I placed my tub on the coffee table and straightened up on the couch—"I was offered a promotion!"

Both Ashley and Bailey gasped, setting their ice cream on the table next to mine before jumping on top of me.

"Ouch!" I grunted when Ashley's elbow made contact with my ribs, but still pulled them in tighter.

"Sorry," Ashley breathed out.

"That's amazing, Jordan!" Bailey cheered as she sat up, straightening out her shirt.

"It's not final yet, but I'm pretty excited," I admitted, grabbing my ice cream again when Ashley let me go. "I still have to accept, but I wanted to tell you guys first, get your opinions on the details."

"What's the position?" Bailey asked.

"The Vice President's assistant." I beamed, bringing another spoonful of ice cream to my lips.

"Nice!" Ashley said, smiling at me. "I knew it was only a matter of time before you would get promoted."

"Thank you, Ash."

"Well..." Bailey stood up, walked to the kitchen, and grabbed a bottle of wine. "This calls for more than just ice cream."

Ash and I chuckled, following her and grabbing our own glasses. We enjoyed our ice cream and wine as both girls asked me more questions about my new job offer. And an hour later we were back on the couch, eating pizza this time.

"Can I ask you guys something?" Ashley questioned, placing the slice that she picked up back in the box.

"What's up?" I replied, taking in more cheesy goodness.

"Well," she hesitated, biting her lower lip. "Have you guys ever..." she trailed off. I put down my pizza, taking a sip of my drink as we waited for Ashley to go on.

"What's wrong?" Bailey asked.

"No, nothing is wrong." Ashley took a deep breath. "Have you guys ever done, like...anal?"

I raised my brows at her question, the subject being quite the opposite from what we discussed earlier.

"Sure," Bailey admitted before she grabbed the last slice of her pizza, surprising us with her quick and honest answer.

"How was it?" Ashley pressed on.

"You want to try it, don't you?" I crossed my arms, sitting back on the couch as I watched her.

"Maybe," she said, avoiding both our eyes. *I mean, me too.*

"Well, just make sure you're relaxed, and maybe try some plugs first," Bailey explained, confirming that Charlie really knew what he was doing. *Ok, I need to stop thinking about him.*

A weird feeling had crept up on me in the last couple of days, and I knew that the space we silently agreed on giving each other, was much needed. I was all for completing the list, but maybe we underestimated the amount of time we had to spend together to do that.

The only thing I knew for sure, was that I didn't really miss him in the time we spent apart. Sure, I missed his dick, but it was comforting to know that I hadn't developed some type of feelings for the man. *Right?*

Maybe everything would get back to normal when we'd see each other on Friday, and maybe we could find a quiet corner to—

"Jordan?" Ashley interrupted my wandering thoughts.

"Sorry, what were you saying?" I asked, grabbing my last slice of pizza, despite it now being a little cold.

CHAPTER 15
Charlie

"Do you have a date for tonight?" Ian asked as he leaned back in the plush chair across from me, looking around my office as I stood from my seat.

"No," I replied, pouring us both a glass of whiskey.

The charity gala had been the last thing on my mind these past few days, a certain brunette overshadowing all my other thoughts. It was a foreign feeling. *And it scared me.*

"What about that sexy girl with all the tattoos? You've been spending a lot of time with her," he said, and I looked up, nearly dropping the bottle out of my hands.

"What did you just say?"

"Please don't act like I'm stupid. You've been different since

I saw you two a month ago."

"Different?" I questioned, clearing my throat and handing him his drink.

"Yeah, more...cheerful, I guess. And a little distant."

I opened my mouth to respond, but for the first time in my life, I had nothing to say—*he knew*. And honestly, it didn't bother me. I was more scared of Jordan's reaction, the feisty brunette dead set on keeping whatever was going on between us a secret.

I hadn't talked to her since I left her apartment earlier this week and it felt...weird.

"Whatever," I mumbled, swirling the amber liquid around in my glass. "She's going to be there anyway. My sister invited her."

"Interesting," he said, raising his brows. I ignored him, taking a sip of my drink and enjoying the burn of the alcohol as it seeped down my throat.

"I have to leave in a few minutes to get dressed," I sighed, watching Ian nod slowly as he looked at his drink.

"Well, I don't want to keep—"

Interrupted mid-sentence, Ian and I looked up as one of the double doors to my office opened, my assistant, Laura, appearing.

"Sir, I have Mrs. Abbot for you," she stated, and I beckoned her to let her in.

"I'll be going then," Ian smirked, downing his glass and walking out of my office.

I sighed, sitting back in my chair as I watched my mother stride into the office. With her head held high, her perfectly made up, light, blue eyes scanned the room until she reached my desk.

"Hi, honey," she greeted as she sat down, carefully placing her designer bag on the seat next to hers and straightening out her skirt.

"Hi, Mom," I said, frowning slightly.

My mother never came to the office, let alone visit me or Ashley while we were working.

"What can I do for you?" I asked, narrowing my eyes at her.

"Are you ready for tonight?" she asked, evading my question and giving me a sweet smile.

"I am. What's going on?"

"Well." She folded her hands together on her lap. "Do you have a date?"

I rolled my eyes. *Why is everybody suddenly so interested in my love life?*

"I don't need one."

My mother scoffed, checking her watch. "I thought you'd say that."

I crossed my arms, not liking where this was going. I thought I was old enough to pick a date for myself, and besides, I didn't want to bring anyone anyway.

"What are you up to?"

"You can't turn up to this event without a date, Charles. Think about your reputation," she warned, straightening up in her seat.

"*My* reputation," I repeated softly, but she ignored me.

"So I've arranged something for you," she continued, smiling brightly. *There it is.*

"And?" I sighed.

She rose from her seat, grabbing her bag and hanging it on her arm before she turned her attention back to me.

"Luna Radcliffe expects you to pick her up at eight," she said, walking out of my office before I could react.

The Radcliffes were close friends of my parents, and for the past decade, they had tried to set me up with their only daughter. It had been a while since I saw Luna, and I was kind of hoping she had found someone else by now.

Guess not.

—

Sighing, I walked up to Luna's apartment, knocking three times before tucking my hands in my pockets. I was not looking forward to spending the night with her. Not because I didn't like her, but because there was someone else I wanted to mess around with at the gala.

"Just a sec!" I heard Luna yell, the sound muffled by the door.

I leaned against the wall behind me, waiting for her to come out. Looking at my reflection in the window, I nodded in satisfaction.

"I'm ready," Luna said as she pulled the door open, stepping out in a sleek, light blue dress, the small train dragging slightly across the floor behind her.

"You look good," I smirked, holding up my arm for her to take.

She rolled her eyes, locking the door behind her before wrapping her arm around mine.

"How've you been?" she asked as we waited for the elevator.

"Good, how about you?"

"You know, same shit, different day."

I chuckled, holding the elevator doors open for her to walk in before I followed her and pressed the button for the ground floor.

"Your parents still trying to push you into the family business?" I asked, looking at her bright blue eyes. They were almost a perfect match to her dress and gave her something mysterious.

"Yeah," she sighed, dropping her head and looking at her feet. Even with these high heels on, she was at least a foot shorter than me. Still taller than Jordan, though. *Why did I—*

"But, I took matters into my own hands," Luna continued, looking up at me with a bright smile. "I actually signed with *Elite*."

I raised my brows—not surprised that she was modeling for one of the biggest agencies in the world, though.

"Congratulations," I said, following her out of the elevator.

We made more small talk as I drove us to the venue of the gala, and I realized that spending most of the night with her wouldn't be too bad.

"Charlie, darling," Mrs. Radcliffe exclaimed as soon as Luna and I walked into the main room where the gala took place.

I was momentarily distracted by the beauty of the great hall in the *Natural History Museum*, especially the large marble stairs and massive chandelier that hung from the ceiling.

"Hello, Mrs. Radcliffe and Mr. Radcliffe," I greeted Luna's parents as we walked up to them, joining them at one of the red velvet-covered high-top tables.

"Good to see you, Charles," Mr. Radcliffe said as he patted me on the shoulder, hard. He was always a little rough with everybody, crushing your hand as he shook it and almost beating your heart out of your chest as he patted you on the back.

"Likewise," I croaked out, scanning the room for...*someone*.

"I believe your parents are over there," Mrs. Radcliffe offered, nodding to another room behind them. I couldn't care less why they weren't all standing together, and excused myself to go talk to my parents.

"Wait for me," Luna whispered, grabbing my arm as we walked to the other side of the hall.

"Luna, I know our parents want us to be together, but—"

She interrupted me by chuckling, stopping mid-step to stare at me with a frown.

"Oh, Charlie, you're not my type," she explained, and I cocked a brow.

"I'm everybody's type," I retorted, and she laughed harder, making several people turn their heads in our direction.

"You're cute and all, but your *sister* is more my type."

I watched her walk away, processing what she just said for a second before jogging after her.

"Since when?" I asked and she slowed her walk with a smile on her face.

"Did I hurt your feelings?" She smirked. *Feelings? Pride, maybe.*

I ignored her teasing. "Do your parents know?"

"Not yet," she replied, looking over her shoulder for a second.

"Charlie! There you are," Mom exclaimed in the same fashion as Mrs. Radcliffe had earlier, walking from behind the table and pulling me against her chest.

"Hi, Mom," I said, but her attention was already on Luna.

"You look amazing," she gushed, holding the girl at arm's length as she looked her up and down. I nodded to my father, grabbing a flute of champagne from a passing waiter and taking a big gulp. My eyes were on the doorway, even though I couldn't see the dance floor, nor the entrance of the building.

"Has Ashley arrived yet?" I asked, casually leaning against

the table next to me.

Just as Mom was opening her mouth to answer, my gorgeous sister came striding through the hall, a fuchsia-colored, blindingly pink dress grabbing everyone's attention. Her wavy hair was styled to perfection, and she looked like she was made for this theme, radiating sophistication and glamour. *That was my sister, alright.*

"Hi, honey," Mom greeted her, and Ashley returned her hug before turning to me and Luna. I tried to be subtle, checking behind her, but there was no sign of Jordan.

"Luna! Long time no see," Ashley smiled, and they started catching up while my eyes stared at the doorway. *What's up with me today?*

"Where's Ryan?" Mom asked, sparing me from creating any suspicion.

"He couldn't come," Ashley explained, also grabbing a drink from one of the passing waiters, downing half in one go.

"You came alone?" Mom didn't even hide the judgment in her voice, always scared to have her precious *reputation* tarnished.

"No, Jordan's at the bar," Ashley said, and I shifted my gaze to the entrance of the room once more, desperate to catch a glimpse of—

"Hmm," Mom hummed disapprovingly, making the reason why Jordan was avoiding our parents very clear. I ignored her, even though I probably should've spoken up about her idiotic behavior.

"I'm going to the bathroom," I told Luna, leaving her with my family after she nodded and I made my way to the main hall. I scanned the room until my eyes caught something red. Smirking as I recognized her tattoos, I made my way up to Jordan. I was only a few steps away when she turned, her long dark ponytail swaying from side to side as she did.

"Charlie," she breathed out, looking up at me with those beautiful brown eyes, seeming surprised to see me.

"Jordan," I smirked, my eyes trailing over her body, the tight, red dress showing off her killer figure, and putting her tattoos rebelliously on display. "You look hot," I said, sucking my bottom lip between my teeth as I continued to study her. She looked a little tense, awkwardly avoiding my eyes as she stood before me.

My smile faded the longer she stayed silent until she sighed and finally spoke up. "I'm sorry about Monday."

I peeked over my shoulder, checking that no familiar faces were looking our way before I held out my hand to her. She dropped her eyes with a puzzled look on her face before she finally looked back at me.

"May I have this dance?" I grinned, watching a little red spread over Jordan's cheeks.

"Oh, shut up," she said shyly, taking my hand and following me to a corner of the room, out of my family's sight.

I pulled her against me, one hand gliding over the small of her back as she looked up at me, hesitantly placing her hand on my shoulder.

"How've you been?" I smirked, and she rolled her eyes.

"I'm sorry things were weird Monday," she said again, watching her hand on my shoulder. Honestly, I had already forgotten about it, and I really didn't want to talk about it either.

"Let's just forget about it," I offered, and she nodded.

"Did you miss me?" I continued, trying to get her to loosen up a little.

She sighed, closing her eyes for a second, undoubtedly

rolling them before she looked back up. I was intrigued by her reaction, her eyes darkening and the corners of her lips curling up ever so slightly.

"I couldn't stop thinking about you," she teased after quickly looking around, her hand gliding down my chest before she grabbed my junk. My teeth bore into my lower lip as I tried not to flinch, my heart rate speeding up and the air around us suddenly feeling thick with desire.

"Is that right?" I countered, my hand sliding down to sit on her ass, the both of us trapped in our own little bubble, teasing each other.

"Hmm," she hummed, stroking me through my dress pants, and I tightened my jaw, pulling her closer.

"You're playing with fire, Baby."

I watched her tongue run over her lips with hooded eyes, the arousing sight enough to bring any man to his knees.

"Wanna play with *me* in the bathroom?"

CHAPTER 16
Jordan

I never got enough of seeing Charlie in a suit. Especially this black one, the contrast between the fabric and the white shirt underneath bringing out the vibrant blue in his eyes. His hair was styled perfectly—*as always*—but the most attractive thing about him was his unwavering confidence.

The smirk on his lips as his eyes roamed my body ignited something inside me, reminding me of the reason we started our little arrangement in the first place.

"Charlie," I breathed out, still feeling a little awkward about the last time we were together.

"Jordan. You look hot."

I avoided his eyes as he rolled his bottom lip between his teeth, feeling weird and uncomfortable in his presence. *What was I supposed to say?*

I sighed. "I'm sorry about Monday."

Charlie peeked over his shoulder before he held out his hand. "May I have this dance?" He grinned, and I blushed. *Nobody had ever asked me to dance.*

"Oh, shut up," I said, taking his hand and following him to a corner of the room, presumably to avoid his family's field of view.

He pulled me against him, his fingers gliding over the small of my back as I looked up, hesitatingly placing one hand on his shoulder. "How've you been?"

"I'm sorry things were weird Monday," I said again, watching my hand on his shoulder.

"Let's just forget about it," he replied, and I nodded slowly. "Did you miss me?" he continued, that mischievous sparkle in his eyes returning.

I sighed in annoyance, closing my eyes for a brief second, even though I actually liked this playful side of him. To be honest, there were a couple of things I liked about him.

"I couldn't stop thinking about you," I teased after taking a quick look around, letting my hand travel down his chest before I cupped his dick through his pants. I watched how his teeth bore into his lower lip and adrenaline coursed through my veins, the sight one of the most erotic things I'd ever seen.

"Is that right?" he countered, his hand sliding down to sit on my ass, trapping us both in our own little bubble.

"Hmm," I hummed, stroking him through his dress pants, and watched as his jaw tightened.

"You're playing with fire, Baby."

I ran my tongue over my lips, hoping he would catch on and bring me somewhere quiet.

"Wanna play with *me* in the bathroom?" I purred, and his eyes widened.

He didn't say anything. Instead, he just grabbed my hand and made his way through the crowd, heading for the restrooms.

I squealed as he pushed me into the men's room, locking the door behind him and gathering my dress to grab the back of my legs, lifting me. Wrapping my legs around his hips, I crashed my lips on his, moaning into the kiss as Charlie instantly deepened it.

He walked to the vanity, dropping me on the counter before he pushed my dress higher up my legs, his tongue still battling with mine.

"Charlie," I moaned as his lips trailed down my neck, sucking and biting his way to my chest.

"God, I missed you, Baby," he mumbled against my skin, his hands disappearing under my dress to take off my thong.

I lifted my hips to help him get it off before I quickly undid his belt.

"I need you," I breathed out, scooting to the edge of the counter and pushing his boxers down.

"Are you ready for me?" he asked, looking up at me as one of his hands cupped my pussy, his fingers spreading my lips, dipping in.

"Do what you want to me."

"Be careful what you wish for, Baby."

I let out something between a gasp and a moan when he grabbed me by my throat, pushing my shoulders and head against the mirror behind me and slamming his cock into me at the same time.

He applied perfect pressure with his fingers, thrusting me against the vanity and using me in a way I didn't know I wanted to be used.

"Fuck, yes," I moaned, my eyes rolling back as he filled me to the hilt every time, pleasure spreading through my whole being.

One of the straps of my dress fell off my shoulder, and Charlie saw it as an opportunity to grab my breast, taking the nipple between his fingers. How he was able to pinch the little nub with so much control when his thrusts showed me he was slowly losing it, was beyond me, but I wasn't complaining.

I never imagined that I would miss sex this much, but as Charlie slammed into me harder, banging against the vanity and making a couple of towels fall to the ground, it became clear to me that I could.

"Oh, yes!" I gasped loudly, steadying myself by leaning a hand on the wall beside me.

"Come on, Baby," Charlie panted, his fingers tightening around my throat.

It only took me a few seconds before my eyes widened, my walls and muscles tightened as my orgasm washed over me, triggering his.

"Fuck," he breathed out, thrusting into me a final few times before he filled me.

My chest rose and fell quickly as I continued to lean against the mirror behind me, closing my eyes and catching my breath. Charlie rested his head against my breasts, his breath fanning over my skin in quick bursts.

"Let's get back," I suggested, running my fingers through the short hairs on the back of his head. He hummed, straightening up and pulling out of me before he silently began to clean me up.

A few minutes later, we walked out of the restroom with our heads down, ignoring the people that were waiting in line and smirking at their judgmental expressions.

"Charlie, there you are," Mrs. Abbot said as we joined the family, her face slightly falling as her eyes caught me.

I smiled weakly at her, grateful that Ashley was too busy chatting to notice me and her brother walking up to them together.

"Mom." Charlie nodded, grabbing a drink from a passing waiter.

"Jordan," his mother continued, focusing her attention on me. "You look—" her eyes trailed down my body, "—simple."

I looked down at my long red dress, admitting that the design was a little plain, but knowing it was actually what had drawn me in the most when I bought it. I loved myself in this dress.

"You look amazing, Mrs. Abbot," I tried, taking in the glittery black dress she was wearing. And I meant it. Of course, she probably had an entire team help her with her hair and makeup, but still.

"Hmm."

Grabbing my own glass of champagne, I quickly downed half, the alcohol burning in my throat and making me feel a little more at ease.

"Should you be drinking so much?" Mrs. Abbot asked bluntly and I frowned at her.

"Excuse me?"

"Maybe it's wise to switch to water," she added with a little smile and I looked at Charlie.

"Mom," Charlie warned, but I saw the way his father looked at him. It gave me the chills, so I understood why Charlie didn't continue. Mr. Abbot never really said much, but he definitely had a way to control his family.

"I'll be fine," I said, emptying my glass as I continued to look into Mrs. Abbot's eyes over the rim. She scoffed, turning to her husband and going back to ignoring me.

"Jojo!" Ashley waved me over, and I gladly took the opportunity to put some distance between me and her mom.

"I want you to meet Luna," she said as I joined her and the unfamiliar girl.

"Hi," the woman smiled as she held out her hand.

"I'm Jordan," I greeted as we shook hands.

I was a little taken aback by her beauty. Her light blond hair was tied back in a perfect bun, exposing her small face and long neck, and a baby blue dress showed off her killer body. I was immediately intimidated by her. She and Ashley belonged in magazines and runway shows, whereas I should've just gone back to the dodgy side of town where I wouldn't embarrass myself.

"Nice to meet you, Jordan," she smirked before rolling her lower lip between her teeth, looking me up and down. *Was she checking me out?*

I blushed under her gaze and shot Charlie a quick look over my shoulder. He cocked his head to the side as he studied us, his brows slowly furrowing. I loved to tease him like this, and I knew exactly what he was thinking.

Though I would never admit it, it felt good to be desired by someone. To have someone be jealous because of me.

Before I could respond, I felt something ice-cold run down my back. I gasped, turning to see who spilled their drink on me.

"Oh my goodness," Mrs. Abbot exclaimed, feigning shock. *This bitch.*

Charlie stood behind her, frowning at the scene before he opened his mouth to say something.

"Don't worry about it," I hissed through clenched teeth, trying to contain my anger.

"Jo..." Ashley reached for me, but I avoided her hand, forcing a smile at her and Luna as they looked at me with pity in their eyes. *I was done with this family for tonight.*

"I'm just going to go."

Without waiting for anyone to react, I made my way to the exit, ignoring the other rich assholes that were staring.

"Mom!" I heard Ashley scold behind me, but I continued to make my way outside.

Finally standing on the curb in front of the museum, I took a deep breath. The cool evening air instantly cleared my mind, and I managed to feel a little bit better. Charlie and I could cross 'sex in a public bathroom' off our list, and I had an opportunity to wear this dress, so if you just ignored Mrs. Abbot and her behavior, it had been a decent night.

"Jordan," Ashley said as she joined me outside, placing a scarf over my shoulders. "I'm so sorry."

I looked up at her, taking her hand and giving it a little squeeze. "It's ok."

"Come on," she mumbled, nudging my shoulder. "I'll call us a cab. The party's dead anyway."

Wrapping her arm around my waist, she pulled me against her, and I returned her hug, grateful to have her as a friend.

—

The address Nadine had given me at work led to the cutest little house, just outside of the city. I made my way up to her front door that Sunday, a bottle of wine in my hand.

"Jordan!" Nadine greeted me with a smile as the door swung open, even before I could raise my hand to ring the bell.

"Hey. Nice place," I said chuckling, following her inside as she beckoned me to come in. The interior was cozy. The walls were painted a dark red, and a beautiful, colorful rug covered the tiled floor.

"Thank you!" She beamed as she closed the door behind us and walked around me, taking my coat before leading me into the next room.

We walked into a surprisingly spacious living room, the walls white, covered with bright paintings. *She loved color, that's for sure.*

I sat down on the navy couch, studying the throw pillows that were just as colorful as the rug in the hall.

"Have you traveled a lot?" I asked, imagining her decor to be from various foreign countries.

"I have," she replied, walking into the small open-plan kitchen.

"What's your favorite place?"

She contemplated her answer as she put the kettle on, opening and closing various cupboards. "Gosh, that's a hard question."

I smiled at her as she returned to the couch and sat next to me, placing a plate with chocolate chip cookies on the coffee table. I attempted to keep my eyes from lighting up at the sight, but a small chuckle from Nadine told me I had failed miserably.

"I think I would go with Italy. But I *loved* Tanzania!" she spoke, ignoring my obvious love for chocolate chip cookies.

I nodded in agreement, though I'd barely been outside of the US.

"That's so cool," I said, my eyes still roaming her living room. I could sit there for days looking around and I still wouldn't have seen everything.

"So what are your roots?" Nadine asked as she walked back to the kitchen, pouring us both a cup of tea.

"My mom was from Thailand, my dad's American," I replied, a little taken aback by her question.

"Hmm."

I smiled at her as she placed a cup of tea in front of me and retook her seat, grabbing her own cup with both hands as she sat back.

"If you don't mind me asking," she continued. "Your mother *was* from Thailand?"

Nodding as I looked at my hands in my lap, I sighed and grabbed my tea.

"She passed away when I was fifteen. Car accident."

"I'm sorry," Nadine gave me a weak smile. Her expression was surprisingly comforting, and I was grateful the air around us didn't turn very awkward. "Do you want to talk about her?"

"Thank you, but I wouldn't know what to say."

"How did your parents meet?"

I looked up at her, appreciating the way she wasn't jumping around the subject or ignoring it completely. "My dad was in

Thailand with my grandparents and my mom was working at the hotel they were staying at." I rubbed a hand over the back of my neck. "They had a one-night stand and my mother got pregnant."

Nadine gasped softly. "And then?"

"They tried the long-distance thing, but eventually my mom moved to the states and they got married."

"Ah, true love."

I chuckled, nodding at myself. Yes, the love between my parents had been something most people could only dream of.

"So do you speak Thai?" she asked, blowing some steam off of her tea.

"I can understand it, but don't ask me to read or speak it." I chuckled softly, regretting that I didn't improve my language skills. It was hard for me to keep learning the language after my mother passed, mainly because it reminded me too much of her and that she wasn't there to teach me anymore.

I got the *sak yant* tattoos when I was traveling to Thailand with my dad at twenty-three, carrying part of my culture now permanently with me.

"Ah, ok." Nadine nodded, taking a sip from her tea.

"What are *your* roots?"

"My parents live in Sweden," she answered with a smile, her eyes traveling to one of the picture frames on the wall next to us.

"You were born there?"

"Yes, I came to the states for a boy when I was eighteen. The relationship didn't last long but I kinda liked it here," she explained, turning in her seat and curling her legs on the couch.

"Do you miss them?"

"I do. But they visit at least once a month and I go home

whenever I can."

I wish I had the means to travel internationally monthly.

"Jordan," she started, placing her cup on the table and folding her hands on her lap. "How was the gala?"

Sighing, I mirrored her actions. Running a hand through my hair, I thought about the best way to explain.

"Well, it was...*something*."

"What do you mean?"

I thought about the best way to approach this.

"So I had sex in the bathroom and the devil herself threw her drink on me." I blurted out, quickly pressing my lips together to prevent myself from laughing.

Nadine stared at me for a second, before she chuckled. "That definitely sounds like *something*." I nodded softly. "So who were you fucking? He's gotta be rich, right?"

"Well, I have to tell you something," I said, avoiding her gaze. "Something you can't tell anyone."

"Sure. What's up?"

"Well." I finally looked her in the eye, having a hard time getting the words out, even though I knew what I wanted to say. Would she keep it to herself? Was I stupid for trusting someone with this secret that had been eating away at me for over a month now? *Rip off the band-aid.*

"Charlie Abbot and I are sleeping together," I stated, holding my breath as I waited for her to react. She didn't, though. Instead, she kept looking at me, as if she waited for me to go on.

"You know, the guy you saw me with on Friday?"

"I know who Charlie Abbot is," she finally said. "But I already had a feeling something was going on between you two. This is so exciting!"

I frowned as I looked at her bouncing slightly in her seat.

"Well, I mean...He's my best friend's brother."

"Oh," she breathed out, and I nodded.

I continued to explain how Charlie and I met, how we had sex before I learned that he was Ashley's brother and how I tried to resist him. Nadine just listened as I explained how I eventually gave in, starting our little agreement, coming up with a list in the process.

"Can you send it to me?" she asked and I chuckled.

"Of course."

It felt good to have told someone. Keeping this to myself for weeks had been exhausting, and I had to admit that I was more excited about it all than I would let on.

CHAPTER 17
Jordan

"Well, ordering a wedding dress usually takes months—"

"I'm sure we can figure something out," Ashley interrupted the bridal consultant, Cora, smiling at the older lady. I watched the scene unfold, leaning against the wall with my arms crossed.

"I'm just not sure—"

"Can we have a moment?" Mrs. Abbot asked, cutting the woman off and gesturing towards the hall. It was clear that the consultant's patience was wearing thin, but she nodded and walked off with Ashley's mother.

"Why do you insist on getting married in December?" Bailey

asked, plopping down on one of the plush couches and placing her bag between her legs.

"Because, Christmas!" Ashley exclaimed.

"Let me rephrase that," Bailey replied. "Why do you insist on getting married *this* December?"

Bailey and Ash continued to debate the rushed wedding, as I focused my attention on someone else. It had been a week since I had seen Charlie, mostly because I was avoiding him. We hadn't properly talked about the weird energy between us, instead, we went straight to fucking. *Having sex instead of figuring shit out. Nothing wrong with that, right?*

My thumb hovered over the unread message from Charlie, asking me what I was doing this weekend. Sure, I've been missing the sex like crazy, and to be honest, him teasing me as well. Maybe I started to develop—

"Jordan?" Ashley appeared in front of me. I quickly locked my phone, almost dropping it out of my hands. "Are you ok?"

"Yes! Yes," I said a little too fast, but apart from raising a brow, she didn't react.

"Let's go." She beckoned me to follow her, leading us to another fancy couch, a bottle of champagne sitting on the little side table. I went straight for the alcohol, sat down as close to the bottle as I could, and started to open it.

All the women stared at me and I shrugged. "What? Is this just for show?"

"No, please, help yourself," Cora said with a hint of sarcasm in her voice.

"Well, Ashley," she continued, "please follow me to the dressing rooms."

Ashley squealed excitedly and I joined her as I finally got the bottle open. Ignoring Mrs. Abbot's judgmental gaze, I poured all of us a glass.

By the time I was on my second glass of bubbly, Ashley reappeared with the bridal consultant, walking up to us with her head held high and holding up the front of a beautiful white dress. Bailey and I gasped as we took in the glittery, lacy, tight, mermaid-style dress showing off Ashley's curves.

"So, how do you feel?" The bridal consultant asked her, finally, with somewhat of a smile on her face. I was starting to think she wasn't capable of showing any sign of joy in general.

"I don't know," Ashley answered, cocking her head to the side as she looked in the mirror.

We got a better look at the dress when she turned, her eyes going from her mother to Bailey, to me, waiting for us to say something.

Ashley could pull off anything, so it was hard for me to determine what didn't look right about the dress, but I did know what she wanted.

"I thought you didn't want sparkle?" I questioned, and Ashley slowly nodded in agreement.

I ignored Mrs. Abbot's scoff, keeping my eyes on the blonde in front of me.

"You're right," Ashley said, turning to Cora.

The two women walked back to the dressing rooms, and I looked anywhere but at Mrs. Abbot, sipping my champagne.

"She's going to look beautiful," Bailey mumbled in my direction, and I shot her a smile.

"I remember someone else who looked absolutely beautiful on her wedding day," I replied, grabbing Bailey's hand and giving it a little squeeze. I knew she had always been insecure about her curves, especially when Jayden was born, but I was never going to stop telling her that she was perfect. No matter what.

The sound of someone's phone filled the store, and I jumped in my seat. "Jesus."

"Sorry, I have to get this," Bailey said, picking up the device and walking away.

So, I was left with Mrs. Abbot. Alone.

The silence was killing me, but what kind of subject could I bring up without her cutting me off or judging me? Hell, maybe she would even ignore me.

Since I became friends with Ashley all those years ago, I had desperately tried to get her parents to like me. But, I guess it was time to stop forcing something that was never going to happen.

Ashley and Cora continued to show us two more dresses until Ashley walked up to us in a strapless mermaid dress that was all lace, sporting a big smile as she stepped on the plateau in front of us. I knew by the look on her face that this was her dress, and I was beyond happy for her that she had found it.

"I can already tell by your expression, but how do you feel about this dress?" the bridal consultant asked, placing the train of the dress neatly behind Ashley on the floor.

"I love it." Ashley grinned, her eyes watering.

Both Bailey and I smiled brightly at her as she turned around, definitely looking ready for the walk down the aisle.

"Mom?" Wiping her eyes carefully, she faced her mother.

Mrs. Abbot looked her daughter up and down, and I was ready to fight her before her frown turned to a smile. "You look beautiful, honey," she squealed, jumping from the couch in her four-inch heels and hugging Ashley. *So she was capable of being nice.*

"I'm so happy!" Ashley shrieked.

After all of us had quieted down, Cora stepped in to talk about the price, something that made me choke on my freshly filled glass of bubbles. The same thing happened when Ashley mentioned the bridal shower that I was supposed to organize, and I shared a look with Bailey, who clearly forgot about it too.

—

"No, Baby, please!" I exclaimed, grabbing the wheel of my car tighter in my hands as the engine quit in the middle of the road. I had just enough time to steer Benji to the side of the deserted street and made sure to stop in a safe spot.

"Couldn't you break down a little closer to home?" I sighed before I stepped out of the car, walking around to check for anything out of the ordinary. *Yeah, professional mechanic over here.*

Naturally, I couldn't find anything, and quickly sat back behind the wheel as it started to rain. "Great," I mumbled, grabbing my phone and scrolling through my contacts.

The sound of the rain against the hood of my car was deafening, but also calming, the rhythmic noise providing me with some comfort as I tried to find the number I was looking for.

I was about to tap *call* when the screen went black. "Fuck, really?"

Banging my head back against the headrest of my seat, I closed my eyes. *Why did this fairly good day need to take such a bad turn?*

Looking out the window, I watched a couple of cars drive by, my vision blurred by the rain. I usually loved the rain, but only when I was at home and didn't need to go outside—not when I was stranded on the side of the road with a dead phone.

I shrieked when I heard a knock on the passenger door, gasping softly when I saw who it was.

"Charlie," I breathed out as I opened my door for him to get in, his suit jacked half soaked, dripping all over my seat as he sat down.

"Hey, Baby." He smirked, closing the door behind him.

"How did you know it was me? What...?" I asked, studying his face.

He combed a hand through his wet hair, trying to adjust the blond mess that the weather created on his head. "I'd recognize this car anywhere."

I smiled softly as I dropped my head, rubbing one hand over the wheel. An uncomfortable silence settled between us, and I took the opportunity to clear the air. The weird feeling I got when I thought about Charlie was probably just because I missed the sex.

"I—"

"Before you say anything," he interrupted me. "There's something that has been bugging me for days." I nodded for him to continue, interested to see where he was going with this. "I don't like to say that I was wrong—or *in* the wrong—but I should've done something when my mother was..." he trailed off.

"Being a bitch?"

Charlie rubbed the back of his neck, nodding softly.

"You did enough. I know you couldn't exactly let everyone know you knew me a little better than they think," I said, folding my hands together in my lap.

Charlie nodded, waiting for me to continue.

"I have a proposal," I continued, lightly clearing my throat.

He turned slightly in his seat, waiting for me to continue.

"What if we just forget about it? The weird stuff. Everything."

He licked his lips, contemplating his answer.

"Just sex," he stated, though it sounded more like a question, and I nodded. "I'm down. We have a list to complete, Baby." He wiggled his brows suggestively, and I felt myself getting turned on by the thought. My breathing quickened as I felt the adrenaline course through me, my body heating up due to the look in Charlie's eyes alone.

It had only been a week, *but boy*, did I crave him right now. It was as if I was addicted to some type of drug, and only he could give me my fix.

Driven by lust, I startled Charlie by unbuttoning my pants and kicking my shoes off, taking off my panties after pushing my jeans down my legs.

"What are you—" he asked, but I interrupted him by climbing over the center console, straddling his thighs.

"Car sex is on the list, right?" I mentioned breathlessly as I brought my lips to his neck, fumbling with his belt.

"Fuck, yeah," Charlie replied, and I smiled against his skin.

His hands slid under my shirt, dipping into my bra and grabbing my breasts, making me moan as he rubbed his fingers over my nipples. I continued to cover his neck in open-mouth kisses, the warmth of his skin against my tongue mixed with the rainwater heating me up even more.

"Oh, God," I breathed out, getting distracted by Charlie who had moved one hand to my bare ass, and the other to my pussy.

He was already rock hard, and his length jumped out of his briefs as I pushed them down.

Our quick breaths fogged up the windows, but we couldn't care less, the need to feel each other and to get our releases gave us tunnel vision. I let out a loud moan as I lowered myself onto Charlie, before crushing my lips onto his and rocking my hips back and forth.

"You're so fucking hot," he mumbled between kisses before he pushed his tongue into my mouth and started to play with mine. I hummed against him as I quickened my pace, changing up my movements and riding him like there was no tomorrow.

Unable to focus, I disconnected our lips and threw my head back with closed eyes, the sound of my thighs slapping against Charlie's now overpowering that of the rain.

"Fuck." I felt Charlie's tongue against my neck, leaving a wet trail as he made his way down.

"Come on, Baby," he said, placing his hands on my hips and guiding me harder and faster up and down his shaft.

"Yes!" I gasped, feeling the pressure build, and I squeezed my eyes tightly shut as I came. My pussy clenched and I dug my fingers into Charlie's shoulders as I let out a high-pitched moan, having trouble continuing my movements.

"A little more," Charlie grunted, forcing my hips harder onto him and meeting my thrust with his until he filled me.

"Fuck," he breathed out, his fingers digging into my ass.

I rested my head against his chest, wrapping my arms around his shoulders. His hands moved up, pulling me closer against him and caressing my back as we sat there for a moment and tried to catch our breath.

"Want me to call for a tow?" he asked softly, and I nodded against his chest. "Alright."

I managed to climb off Charlie's lap, redressing myself as quickly as I could. The rain was still slamming against the windshield, and I was grateful that nobody could've seen what'd just transpired inside.

After Charlie called for some help, I turned on the radio, and we listened to some crappy music while we waited.

CHAPTER 18
Jordan

"Charlie. Babe," I breathed out, attempting to grab his wrist as his fingers moved over my pussy.

"I can do it," he exclaimed, gently rubbing my clit, determination written over his face as he stared at my core with his brows furrowed.

"But I don't know if I—ah!"

I moaned as he expertly pleasured me, managing to quickly bring me to the brink of orgasming, even though my body was spent after this morning.

"Come on, Baby," he mumbled, using his free hand to work my nipples and giving them both equal attention as he attempted for the sixth time to finally make me squirt.

"Charlie," I moaned, curling my toes and grabbing the sheets beneath me, a loud gasp escaping my lips as I came. *Again.*

"Yes!" He fisted the air like he won the lottery when I squirted over his hand, and I covered my eyes with my own, embarrassed about the mess, but breathlessly chuckling at the same time. I didn't see the benefit from squirting—it only created a mess and ruined the bed that I'd just made with clean sheets—but Charlie thoroughly enjoyed it.

"Told you I could do it," he bragged, rubbing the palms of his hands over my hips.

"Hmm." I closed my eyes, bathing in the blissful state of my six orgasms. It was a good thing it worked this time because my body couldn't handle any more pleasure after all the attention.

"Baby?" Charlie had gotten off the bed and stood at the end with a pair of low-hanging sweats on. I couldn't help but sigh as I took in his muscular chest, immediately distracted. *Would this feeling ever go away?*

"Jordan, focus," Charlie scolded, snapping his fingers in front of my face.

I propped up on my elbows, focusing my eyes on his. "Yes, my dear?" I replied sarcastically, and Charlie rolled his eyes.

"Don't we have a bridal shower to get ready for?"

My eyes widened and my stomach dropped as I frantically searched for my phone.

"Shit!" I exclaimed when I saw the time, only having an hour left before Ashley would arrive home and we were supposed to scare the crap out of her with her party.

"On the dresser, Baby," Charlie said, looking at me with his arms crossed as I searched for my underwear.

"What should I wear? Fuck, fuck, fuck!"

Charlie chuckled, annoying the shit out of me, and held up his hands as I scowled at him.

"You brought the black dress right?" Charlie offered, nodding to my bag. "By the way, that's not really—"

"Yes, it's a little short and dark, but what else do they expect?"

He shook his head, disappearing into his closet to get dressed, as I tried to apply mascara with shaking hands.

"Ouch!" I flinched when I stabbed myself in the eye with the wand, feeling myself tearing up.

"Are you ok?" Charlie shouted from his closet, but I ignored him. Though I loved some morning sex, I felt stupid for not saying no this time. I knew we had to leave early, and Charlie knew, too. To be honest, at this moment I was rolling my eyes at Ashley for insisting her hot and sexy brother needed to keep Ryan company and be at the party as well.

"Jordan?" Charlie walked back into the room, and I blinked rapidly, convinced my eyes were deceiving me as he stood there in his suit, perfectly styled. *I hate him.*

"What?" I ran to the bathroom, trying to save my makeup and do something about the bird's nest on my head.

"Please calm down, you're scaring me," he whined, and I managed to force out a hum in response. *This was a great start to the day. What more could go wrong?*

—

We arrived fifteen minutes before Ashley was supposed to be home, and Charlie and I agreed that I would go in first, and he would follow five minutes later.

"Finally," Bailey said when I walked into Ashley's apartment, smiling at the gold and white decorations. "Thanks for helping me set everything up."

"Sorry," I replied softly, feeling guilty about being late.

"Honestly, I loved doing it. And I had *some* help."

She closed the door behind me, gesturing to the group of friends who were preparing drinks and bites in the open kitchen.

As I looked at the guests Ashley had requested we invite, I grinned. Whatever Ashley wants, she gets. Bailey and I did a pretty decent job of keeping the date and location a secret, but Ashley had an idea of what she wanted and how she wanted it since college.

As my heels clicked against the beautiful hardwood floor, I was reminded of how jealous I was of Ashley's apartment—especially the view. Because we were higher up, she had the same gorgeous view as Charlie, but with the sun basking the spacious living room in warm light.

We were lucky the weather was a little warm for the middle of October, and we took advantage of that by decorating and setting the balcony up, too. That, and we needed the extra space for all the people Ashley wanted us to invite.

"I'm just going to...check out the balcony," I stated, and Bailey nodded.

I let out a breath when I stepped outside and I quickly fished a stray cigarette out of my purse, ready to calm my nerves. I brought it to my lips and lit the end, inhaling the nicotine that instantly put me more at ease. I had no idea why I was this nervous. Maybe it was because of the bridal shower, about

Ashley's reaction, or just being with Charlie and his sister in the same room for an entire day.

A little before one p.m., everyone that was in the house found a hiding spot and waited until the bride-to-be would walk in. Charlie had arrived as well and shot me a cocky smirk as he dragged me behind the couch.

"What are you doing?" I whispered, looking around to see if anyone was looking our way.

"I love annoying you." Charlie shrugged, leaning with one hand on my leg as we crouched behind the couch.

"Somebody will see." I hissed, but I didn't remove his fingers that were creeping under my dress. Instead, Charlie ignored me, staring at the front door over the back of the couch with a grin on his face.

I rolled my bottom lip between my teeth, focusing on the hall and smiling when I heard keys in the lock.

"Surprise!" Everyone yelled in unison, jumping up and out from their hiding places, some throwing white confetti over the bride-to-be. Ashley's hand shot to her chest and a big smile spread over her face as she stopped just past the threshold.

"Oh my God," she squealed, turning to Ryan, who stepped in behind her. "You knew about this?"

He closed the front door and wrapped an arm around her waist, bringing his lips to hers. "Do you like it?"

"I do. Thank you."

"I love you," Ryan added before he pecked her one more time on the lips.

They shared a moment, looking into each other's eyes and smiling at one another, showing off the love that was evident between the two.

"And thank *you*, guys!" Ashley turned her attention to us, hugging Bailey before she ran up to me, pulling me against her chest.

We started the first round of drinks as Ashley greeted everyone, bringing around the virgin and liquor-filled cocktails of the guest's choosing. Bailey and I had racked our brains on Ashley's favorite drinks and appetizers, hopefully giving her the bridal shower of her dreams.

Charlie was mainly invited to keep Ryan company, especially when the women engaged in a little game of '*fuck, marry, kill*.'

Some of Ashley's work friends felt the need to stare at me judgmentally, so I readjusted my breasts and flipped my hair over my shoulder, giving them just enough cleavage to gawk at. I was proud of my tattoos and gladly showed them off.

"I'll be right back," I said an hour later, and stood from the couch, carefully stepping around the legs in my path as I made my way to the bathroom. I set myself up for a lot of bathroom visits today with downing all my drinks.

Ashley was by far my best friend, but I was forever on edge in the presence of her stuck-up friends.

"Ah!" I shrieked when I walked out of the restroom a few minutes later, running straight into Charlie.

"If you want people to stay in the dark about us, you need to save your screams for the bedroom, Baby," he retorted, pushing me against the now-closed door.

"Fuck off," I bit back, grabbing him by his belt and pulling him against me. *Just one kiss couldn't hurt, right?*

I kept my ears open as Charlie pressed his lips on mine for a sensual and toe-curling kiss, making me forget about the pain in my feet from these damn heels.

"Hmm," I moaned as he took my bottom lip between his teeth and pulled, before releasing, letting it pop back in place.

"Go to dinner with me tonight," he offered, licking his lips. I looked down the hall, trying to ignore the tingle in my stomach as the words left his lips. *Stop this crap, Jordan!*

"Sure."

Quickly pecking him on the lips, I tried to go back to the living room, but Charlie stopped me. "What?" I asked as I looked at his hold on my wrist to his face.

He bent down to bring his lips to my ear, his hot breath fanning over my neck as he spoke. "Take off your panties."

I frowned but did as he said with a grin, taking off my thong and handing it to him.

"Thank you," he said, stuffing the piece of lace in his pocket before he gave me a tap on the ass. "Let's go back."

I squealed softly at the contact, shooting him a look over my shoulder before I quickly made my way back to the living room, hyper-aware of the fact that I wasn't wearing any underwear anymore.

"Are you ok?" Ashley asked when I sat down next to her on the couch. I kept my eyes on my drink as I picked it back up.

"Yes, of course," I answered, smiling as I adjusted my skirt.

"So, *Jordan*," one of the blondes across from us started, tilting her chin up as she looked at me. "What do you do?"

Ha, I just got promoted.

"I'm an executive assistant at Cendose Incorporated." I beamed, proud of my new job. I had officially taken the offer earlier this week, and I was glad I had the opportunity to show it off.

"I see," she replied, clearly not satisfied with my answer.

"Yeah, but she deserves so much more," Ashley piped in before taking a sip from her cosmopolitan. "I wish I was as smart as her."

I looked at my best friend, tears almost appearing in my eyes. *I love her so much.*

We both knew that Ashley was ten times smarter than me—not just book-smart—but I really appreciated her standing up for me.

"Thank you," I said softly, giving her free hand a little squeeze.

"Anyway," the blond bitch continued, scrolling through her phone. "Jamie Dornan, Chris Hemsworth, or...Ryan Reynolds?"

Around five p.m., the guests headed home, but Bailey, Charlie, and I stayed behind to clean up.

"Jordan?" Bailey asked as I dried off a couple of glasses.

"Hmm?"

She joined me in the kitchen, leaning against the counter next to me and cocking her head to the side as she looked at me. "Is there something going on between you and Charlie?"

The glass I was cleaning almost clattered out of my hands, but I managed to remain somewhat calm. "What? No."

"Just asking," she replied, looking me up and down. *Oh, God.*

"Charlie isn't really my type anyway," I added, probably raising more suspicion than I would've when I just kept my mouth shut. I was usually a pretty good liar, but whenever someone asked about Charlie, I just didn't know how to behave anymore.

She let it go, though, and I was able to breathe again when she walked over to Ashley to help her with taking down some of the decorations. I saw Charlie coming my way from my peripheral vision, and I shot him a frown. He frowned back but continued to approach me.

"Go away," I hissed softly, my eyes shooting from him to Bailey and Ashley.

He quickly turned on his heels and walked up to Ryan instead.

An hour later, Charlie, Bailey, and I took the elevator down and made our way out of the building. Just when we were about to enter the street, I froze. I had totally forgotten that Charlie and I had arrived together and that I had no car to walk up to.

"What's wrong?" Bailey asked, placing a hand on my shoulder and looking at me with a worried expression.

"Nothing!"

She stared at me with wide eyes and her brows raised, obviously confused by the way I was acting. *Hell, I was confused too.*

My mind went a million miles per hour, trying to come up with literally anything to say, and I blurted out the first thing I could come up with. "I forgot that I took a cab here. My car's at the mechanic."

"Oh, I can bring you—" Bailey started, but Charlie interrupted her.

"I'll drive you home."

I shot him a look and he shrugged, fishing his car keys out of his pocket.

"Ok..." Bailey trailed off, looking from Charlie to me, and I felt the blood rush to my cheeks. "Are you ok with that?"

"Hmm." I nodded, keeping my lips firmly pressed together, my heart almost jumping out of my chest when she narrowed her eyes at me. *She knew.*

"If you're sure," she mumbled, now watching Charlie.

"It'll be fine."

"Ok, well, I'll see you later then."

I exhaled once she got into her car and waved as she drove off, quickly turning to the man beside me once she was out of sight.

"Char—"

"Yeah, yeah. I know. Shall we get dinner?"

—

"Really? Here?" I stared up at the building, getting flashbacks of the first time I saw Charlie.

"The food that you ordered looked really good," he said, nodding to the big sign. I rolled my eyes with a slight smile, nudging his arm before walking into the building.

We were greeted by the same blonde as the first night. "Welcome to *Latmeyer*, do you have a reservation?"

"We don't, unfortunately," Charlie stated confidently, smirking at the hostess. He probably thought he could get her to do anything for him with that smile, and honestly, that wasn't very far from the truth. *I wish I could do that.*

"Oh, I'm sorry but—"

"Charlie!" A big, bulky man who clearly loved good food came over, holding out his hand. "Good to see you."

The hostess and I both observed the conversation between the two men as they were catching up like old friends. *Which, let's be honest, they probably were.*

"Who did you bring *today*?" The stranger teasingly asked.

"Excuse me?" I cocked a brow as I looked at him. I wasn't one of the desperate women with boobs hanging out that Charlie usually associated with. I knew he was a playboy, and to be completely honest, that's also kind of why I liked him, but I wasn't just another gold digger.

"She's feisty," the guy continued, running his tongue over his bottom lip as he looked me up and down.

"Damn right she is," Charlie shot back, not an ounce of playfulness in his voice as he pulled me against his side, wrapping his arm possessively around my waist. He startled me with his actions, showing me a side of himself I hadn't seen before, but one I was all too eager to explore.

"Alicia, I'm sure we have a table for two?" The guy focused his attention on the hostess, who nodded as she searched the tablet in front of her.

Only when we arrived at our table, did Charlie remove his hand, flipping through the menu as if nothing happened. I opened my mouth to say something, but decided against it, not wanting another fiasco like the Monday before.

"What are you doing?" I asked when he scooted his chair around the table until he was next to me, smirking mischievously.

"You were so far away," he cooed, sliding his fingers towards my inner thigh. *I see.*

Looking around the restaurant, I noticed that we were in the corner of the room, the perfect place for Charlie to misbehave. I leaned forward with my elbows on the table and my face in my hands, watching one of the waiters walk our way as Charlie's fingers crept between my legs.

"Welcome to *Latmeyer*, my name is Diana and I will be your waiter for the evening. Can I get you something to drink?" the brunette asked as she handed us our menus.

"Can I have a martini? No olives and the lemon dropped in." I replied, smiling at her.

She nodded, tapping away on her tablet before she shifted her attention to my table partner. "And for you, sir?"

"A whiskey sour. And can we have some water as well, please?" Charlie asked, giving my thigh a little squeeze under the table. "I'm a little *thirsty*."

I scoffed softly, trying not to roll my eyes.

"What are you playing at?" I asked Charlie when Diana walked away.

"I just want to see you squirm and shake under my touch while we're in public," he replied, nudging my legs a little wider, walking his fingers up my thigh.

"Charlie," I warned, taking a sharp breath when the tips of his fingers brushed against my naked core. The reason he wanted me to take off my panties earlier became abundantly clear when he slowly started to tease me under the table.

"Shh, Baby."

"I have a martini?" Diana offered when she returned with our drinks, completely unaware of what Charlie was doing as she placed the glass in front of me.

"Thank you," I choked out, grabbing the edge of the table as I sat back and attempting to maintain my composure as Charlie slowly drew circles over my core. I couldn't focus on anything else as he quickened his pace, rubbing the right spot and making it very difficult for me not to moan. Fortunately for me, Diana had already left. Charlie casually sipped his drink as if he wasn't bringing me to the brink of orgasming.

I felt conflicted—like I wanted to let go and give into the pleasure, but at the same time, I was hyper-aware of the fact that everyone could see us.

"Come on," I breathed out softly, pushing my teeth into my lower lip to contain any sounds that wanted to escape. A tingle went up my spine and I forced my hips against Charlie's hand when I felt that I was about to come undone, but he had other plans.

"Ma'am? Are you ok?"

My head shot up when I heard Diana's voice again, and I swallowed hard, both of Charlie's hands now above the table.

"Yes, what were you saying?"

"What do you want to eat?" Charlie replied, slowly bringing his glass to his lips as he watched me with a devilish smirk on his face.

Shit, I hadn't even looked yet. *Same as last time it is.*

"The fillet steak with brussels sprouts, please," I said quickly, handing Diana my menu.

I watched her as she walked away, facing Charlie when she disappeared into the kitchen. "I thought we were done with the edging, *Pretty Boy*," I sneered, still feeling flustered from his touch.

"Of course not," he answered. "It's way too much fun."

You'll change your mind when you're the one on the receiving end.

"Whatever." I took a big gulp of my drink, ignoring the ache between my legs. *Or as much as I could.*

"Don't be mad, Baby," Charlie cooed, rubbing his hand over the inside of my thigh, making the throbbing of my core reach a very uncomfortable point. I took a sharp breath when he lightly scratched his nails over my skin, clearly enjoying the effect he had on me.

"Please, Charlie," I whined, placing a hand on his arm and holding it down.

"Hmm, we're in public."

"But—"

He shut me up by pushing two fingers into me, eliciting a gasp from my lips in the process.

"God dammit," I cursed under my breath, turning a little towards Charlie to give him better access. I was already desperate for a release, but he wasn't giving it to me anytime soon.

CHAPTER 19
Jordan

During dinner, Charlie continued to tease me, and by the time he had paid and we were out front, I still hadn't had a single orgasm.

"Oh my God, Charlie!" I exclaimed, stomping my foot down like a child and stopping in the middle of the street. It wasn't too busy tonight, so it was easier for me to be openly dramatic, even though I usually despised people like that.

"What?" He turned around, crossing his arms and looking at me with a smirk. That damn smirk always made my insides stir, and I wasn't sure if it angered me at this moment, or turned me on even more.

"I need you to fuck me," I whined, ignoring the people that

were passing us and giving me a weird look as they did. My body was on fire and there was only one thing I wanted at that moment.

"You want to do this now?" Charlie teased, running a hand through his hair. His expression faltered, and his eyes seemed to darken with desire. I had him right where I wanted him.

"Mhmm," I moaned, shifting on my feet.

"Right now?" He took a step in my direction, and immediately, a surge of adrenaline spread through me, excitement and nerves swarming my stomach.

"Yes, Goddammit!"

Before I could say anything else, he grabbed me by the back of my neck and crashed his lips on mine. I moaned into the kiss, pulling his hips closer to me by his belt and completely forgetting we were standing in the middle of the street. *Shit, we were really doing this.*

We sprinted to an abandoned alley, and the sewer smell, fortunately, was not as much of a turn-off as I would've expected.

"Take me, come on," I breathed out, turning to the brick wall and pushing my ass up.

The three martinis I had during dinner made me ignore the footsteps we heard, along with the other sounds of traffic coming from the street. Everything about this excited me.

It didn't take long before Charlie had entered me, and it was the easiest thing in the world to do because I was beyond soaking wet from all his teasing and edging during dinner. I moaned loudly, a sense of freedom coming over me as I squeezed my eyes shut and just enjoyed the ride.

"This what you want? Huh?" Charlie said in a strained voice, pounding into me and grabbing my throat with one hand to bring his lips closer to my ear.

"Yes!"

Digging my fingers into the brick wall in front of me, I tried to arch my back further, feeling him fill me to the hilt every time. My eyes rolled back in my head and my legs slowly turned numb—*in the best way*.

"Whoa!" I heard somewhere in the distance, and I looked at the end of the alley, seeing a group of drunk people stumbling by. Smiling as I heard the intoxicated group cheer, I squeezed my eyes shut, the feeling I had been craving all night finally getting its chance to shoot through every inch of my body.

I didn't pay attention to the flash of a camera as I was too busy focusing on my climax, the feeling of euphoria finally washing over me. Charlie followed quickly behind—just as oblivious—and we stayed in the compromising position for a few seconds to catch our breath.

"Happy now?" he breathed into my ear before pulling out and putting his pants back on. My heart was still beating frantically in my chest as I readjusted my dress before I turned around.

"Very," I choked out, my cheeks burning up when I noticed that the group of guys was still watching us from the end of the alley.

"That was hot," Charlie smirked, clearly just as perverted as me, if not more. "Sex outside, *check*."

"Sex with people watching, *check*." I chuckled, drawing the symbol on his chest.

We didn't have much time to further catch our breath before two men in blue appeared, heading straight for us. They made their way through the group that had gathered at the end of the alley, and I watched the drunk men and women run off. *Did someone call the cops on us?*

"We have to go," I told Charlie, grabbing his hand and walking in the opposite direction, putting some distance between us and the officers.

"Shit," he exclaimed when he saw them too, and I yelped when he started to pick up his pace.

"Hey!" one of the officers yelled.

And that was our cue to run, though I was still wearing four-inch heels.

Honestly, we didn't even make it halfway to Charlie's apartment before we stopped. We had managed to shake off the officers, and I covered my side with my hand when I felt a sharp pain.

"Damn," I cursed out of breath, shooting a quick look over my shoulder before I slowly continued walking.

"Are you ok?" Charlie asked, not as out-of-breath as I would've liked.

I wiped a little sweat from my forehead and nodded. "I'm just really out of shape."

He chuckled, shielding his ribs as I pulled my hand back.

"We'll work on that," he said, wrapping his arm around my shoulders and pulling me against his side as we walked to his place.

———

Ashley looked at me over the rim of her wine glass when she was over at my place the next day, her eyebrows raising slightly.

"Really, who are you fucking? You're glowing," she said, putting her drink back on the coffee table.

I chuckled softly, shrugging her question off like I had

done every time she asked since Charlie and I started sleeping together. Luckily for me, she shook her head before she turned her attention back to the movie we were watching. I got up to grab another bottle of wine, desperate to refill Ashley's glass and make sure she wouldn't start about my sex life again.

Ryan agreed to pick her up later this evening, so she could help me empty this next bottle and I didn't have to feel guilty about it.

She had convinced me to let her order some sushi for dinner, and I had insisted on sharing the costs, proudly showing off the fact that I had a little more to spend than before.

"Jojo?" Ashley asked from the couch, leaning over the back to look at me.

"Yes?" I pulled the cork out of the bottle with a grunt, feeling like a sommelier as I did. Maybe this was what I was supposed to be doing, pouring expensive wine for snobby rich people instead of—

"Thank you, for yesterday," she interrupted my train of thought, smiling softly.

I frowned. "For what?"

All I could think about was dinner with Charlie and our little moment of 'fun' after.

"The bridal shower," Ashley reminded me with a giggle, shaking her head at my memory. I still felt bad about the fact that we took our sweet ass time to plan the bridal shower, but I was beyond happy that she enjoyed it.

"Oh. You're welcome. Though you deserved more."

Ashley waved my statement away, turning back in her seat when I joined her on the couch.

"Anyway, Ryan and I are going to Canada tomorrow," she said, totally taking me by surprise. It wasn't strange or uncommon for her to go on a trip, but usually, she wouldn't shut up about it for weeks.

"Since when?" I asked, pouring her another glass of wine and placing the bottle on the coffee table. We were probably finishing this one as well so I might as well keep it close.

"It was kind of a spontaneous thing..." she trailed off, tapping away on her phone before holding it up to me, showing a picture of a beautiful hotel that was surrounded by an abundance of greenery. "We're going to check out the venue for the wedding!"

"Oh! You got the venue you wanted?" I regretted my question as soon as it left my lips, realizing that I wasn't supposed to know what her venue was going to be yet. "But, Canada?" I quickly added, hoping she didn't notice the little tremble in my voice. *Smooth*.

"Yes, but don't worry, all travel expenses are going to be taken care of." She beamed, bouncing in her seat and fortunately ignoring my slip up.

"Well, ok," I replied, smiling at her excitement. "How long will you be gone?"

"We're making a trip out of it, so about two weeks," she replied, locking her phone and throwing it on the couch next to her. *Two weeks without Ashley around?*

I mentally slapped myself in the face for thinking that, trying to pull my mind out of the gutter. "Well, it sounds amazing," I replied, curling up on the couch with my glass in my hands.

"It is! I'll miss Charlie's birthday, though. But hopefully, he will let me make it up to him when I get back."

I looked up at the mention of his birthday, quickly taking a sip to keep me from blurting something out. But, before Ashley continued, I spoke up anyway. "It's his birthday soon?" I choked out, trying to sound casual.

Why didn't he say something? To be honest, I would've expected him to mention his birthday every time he possibly could.

"Yeah, Wednesday, actually."

"Hmm."

"But I'll take him out to dinner when I'm back or something," she continued, and I bit my tongue. Asking more questions about her brother would raise suspicion, but there was still so much I wanted to know. *Why? Unclear.*

"Ah," I said softly, not really knowing what to say and feeling guilty. Why did it have to be Charlie at the restaurant those months ago? Maybe I should've fucked Chris.

I chuckled, almost choking on more wine as Ashley raised a questioning brow.

"Sorry, I zoned out for a bit," I explained, nudging my head back to the movie before pretending to watch it intently.

CHAPTER 20
Jordan

My finger hovered above the call button for Mr. Grimaldi, as all the ways he could deny my request flashed through my head. I had thought about Charlie's birthday all of Monday morning, my mind overflowing with ideas, but all of them required me to take a day off of work.

Deciding to get it over with, I pressed the button and brought the phone to my ear with shaking hands.

"Yes, Jordan?" he answered almost immediately, and I took a deep breath.

"Hi. I was wondering if I could ask you for a favor," I said, drumming the fingers of my free hand on my desk as I nervously waited for him to reply. I didn't know my new boss very well yet, so I had no idea what to expect from this conversation.

"That depends on the favor," he said, and I let out a breath when I heard the playfulness in his voice.

"Can I have Wednesday off?"

I didn't mean to just blurt it out like that, but at the same time, I knew Mr. Grimaldi was very straight to the point and he would appreciate it. I held my breath as I waited, the silence on the other side of the call making me anxious.

After a few seconds, Mr. Grimaldi chuckled.

"This was what you were so nervous about?" he replied, and I felt my body relax.

"I—yes, sir."

"You've done some amazing work these last couple of weeks, you deserve it." My eyes widened and I was ready to end the call before a thought shot into my head.

"So..." I trailed off, making sure to get a direct and clear answer. I knew Mr. Grimaldi was fair, but better safe than sorry, *right*?

"Yes, you can have Wednesday off. Make sure you leave the documents for my appointments on my desk tomorrow, and I'll be fine," he added.

"Thank you so much, sir!" I exclaimed, feeling excited.

"You're welcome, Jordan."

I hung up the phone and headed to my browser. I needed a few things for my surprise, and I hoped they would arrive in time.

It was the first time I was this thrilled about someone else's birthday and what I could do for them to make them feel special, but I ignored the feeling. I was just excited because it would probably end in sex.

The mountain of unclosed client files on my desk was staring at me as I looked up the best sushi place to order from, and after about five minutes, I couldn't ignore it anymore. So, I tried to finish all my tasks at lightning speed, ready to get home and continue brainstorming.

Five o'clock sharp I made my way out of the building, my mind going a million miles an hour trying to think about things I could do for Charlie's birthday. I was so caught up in my own thoughts, that I almost crossed the street without looking.

"Jordan!" I heard behind me, a familiar voice stopping me in my tracks. My hair swayed up by the wind caused by a passing truck, and my heart beat in my throat when I realized I nearly got into an accident.

Still a little in shock, I turned around. "Bailey? What are you doing here?"

"Saving you from an early death, I guess," my friend smirked as she walked up to me, her beautiful dark curls bouncing up and down as she moved.

We gave each other a hug, and I waited for her to give me a serious answer.

"I was visiting Theo at work," she added, pointing to one of the skyscrapers behind her. "Then I saw you almost killing yourself there."

I chuckled softly, rubbing the back of my neck. "Yeah, I was thinking about..."

Bailey raised her brows and I quickly closed my mouth before I could finish that sentence. She crossed her arms and cocked her head before she spoke. "About Ashley's brother?"

The blood drained from my face and I swallowed hard. *Oh, God.*

"I'm...I don't..." I stammered, my cheeks heating up and my palms getting sweaty.

"You don't have to deny it," Bailey said, nudging her head to the parking lot and placing her hand on my shoulder as we walked to our cars.

Bailey had always been very good at reading people, and to be honest, Charlie and I hadn't exactly done everything in our power to hide it from her. I should've just taken her offer to drive me home after Ashley's bridal shower.

Since she had Jayden, we didn't see each other as much, but still in these few moments, she had figured it out. What if Ashey knew too?

"How long has this been going on?" Bailey asked me, and I bit my lower lip as I contemplated my reply.

"Remember when I told you about my date? And that I left with a guy that wasn't Chris?" I said, avoiding her eyes.

She gasped softly, playfully punching me in the arm. "That was weeks ago, months even."

I nodded, fishing my keys from my pocket when we reached my car.

"Please don't tell Ashley," I pleaded, feeling like I was asking her to give me a false alibi for some murder I had committed.

My face fell when Bailey shot me a look of disapproval. "Jordan..."

"I know," I interrupted her, placing my hand on the handle of my car door, turning to face her. "It just happened and I don't want to hurt her."

"And by keeping this from her you aren't doing just that?" she responded, telling me exactly what I didn't want to hear. But it was the truth.

I *was* hurting her. With everything I knew about her, what we experienced together, I still betrayed her trust.

"You're right," I said, running a hand through my hair.

Bailey looked at me with a slight frown, her expression softening. "You do seem happier."

"Right, I gotta go," I exclaimed quickly, pecking her on the cheek before I unlocked my car and got in, trying to avoid more of this conversation. It was probably not the best move, nor a very nice one, but it was all I could think of at that moment.

Bailey rolled her eyes and walked past my car to her own.

—

Stepping out of my car on Wednesday morning, I looked up at the tall building, my heart almost bursting out of my chest as I closed my door. What if he wasn't in the office today? What if he took a day off? What if he was busy? *Stop it!*

I locked my car with fresh determination, striding into the foyer with newfound confidence. No, this was a great idea and Charlie was going to love it.

The grand, marble space distracted me for a second, even though I've been here a couple of times before, visiting Ashley.

"Ma'am?" I shifted my gaze to the woman behind the front desk, already failing in my attempt to look like I belonged here.

"Yes, sorry. Hi," I greeted her, wrapping my long coat tighter around me as I walked up to the counter. "I'm looking for Charlie Abbot."

"Do you have an appointment?" She asked, typing away on

her keyboard and not giving me a single look.

I shifted my weight from one leg to the other, giving the woman a painful smile as I replied. "No..."

"Then I'm afraid that you can't see him today."

Could've expected that.

"Well, it's really urgent," I pleaded, racking my brain for excuses or ways to persuade her to let me in. She didn't even flinch looking at me with her perfectly made-up eyes.

"Look lady, it's always u—"

"Jordan!" A voice boomed through the foyer, and I turned to see Ian walking my way. I didn't know the guy well, but this was my shot, and I was beyond happy to see him.

"Ian!"

The girl behind the front desk rolled her eyes and went back to work as I walked up to him, shaking his hand. He smirked at my enthusiasm, looking equally as handsome as Charlie as he did.

"What are you doing here?" he asked, leading me to one of the plush seats next to the floor-to-ceiling windows, swiping his card over the gates that separated us from the foyer.

"I'm...Uhm..." I stuttered, not sure how to approach this. How much did Ian know anyway? Would it be so bad if he knew?

"You can tell me. I know that you and Charlie have something going on." He surprised me with his words, and I fumbled with the strap of my bag as I contemplated my reply. Well, that made this a whole lot easier for sure, but it felt weird to talk so openly about Charlie and me to someone. As if I was doing something illegal.

"I heard that it's his birthday today," I explained, looking up into Ian's dark eyes.

"Hmm."

"And I wanted to surprise him," I sighed before I firmly grabbed my bag, changing my mind. "This was a bad idea."

Quickly lifting from the chair, I straightened out my skirt and fished my car keys out of my bag. Charlie probably didn't want to see me. Or he would think it was weird for me to come here while we were *technically* just two people who enjoyed having sex together.

"Thank you for letting me in, but—"

"No, wait," Ian stopped me, grabbing my wrist and twirling me back around. "It's not a bad idea."

I pushed a few strands of hair behind my ear, looking up. "It's not?"

"Look at it this way," he added, the corners of his mouth curling up into another smirk. "Charlie is the type of guy who wants a pretty girl like you in his office, *if you catch my drift*."

I had my scoff ready, but then I realized that what he was implying wasn't very far from the truth, so I shrugged instead. That was kind of exactly what I came to do. It did sting when the thought that Charlie had girls in his office before shot through my head, but I tried to push it out of my mind.

"Well, where am I supposed to go?" I grinned, hoisting my bag higher up my shoulder and making sure my coat was still properly closed. I wanted what I was wearing to remain a surprise, and it wasn't exactly appropriate for the office.

Ian beckoned me to follow him, walking towards the elevators and pressing the button for one of the top floors when we stepped in.

"What do you have planned anyway?" he asked when we ascended, and I felt my cheeks heat up a little. I had never done anything like this in my life, and I felt like everyone that we passed could see right through me.

"Maybe a little sexy surprise," I mumbled, the corners of my mouth curling up into a grin as I looked up at Ian.

He nodded with a knowing smile, gesturing for me to walk into the hallway when we reached the right floor. He pointed to the office I sought before he walked the opposite way, entering an office of his own. *Here we go.*

I stopped in front of the double doors and listened, making sure I wouldn't walk in on something important. Maybe he was in a meeting. If that was the case, I would've been mortified if I had just walked in, in this...*outfit.*

"I just wanted to say happy birthday, sir." The voice of a woman sounded through the frosted glass, and I frowned. *Uhm, ok.* That didn't sound like an important meeting.

"Laura..." Charlie said, and my curiosity was piqued. This was not what I thought it was, *right?*

"Do you want to unwrap your present?"

This motherfucker.

The nerves I felt earlier vanished into thin air and were replaced by pure anger. Maybe it was stupid of me to jump to conclusions, but my pride was hurt and it was suddenly all I could think about.

Swinging one of the doors open, I saw Charlie in his chair, slouched back and looking up at the blonde in front of him, her shirt half-open.

CHAPTER 21
Charlie

I looked up from the file on my desk when I heard a knock on my door. I had asked my assistant not to disturb me until lunch, but apparently, that was a difficult task. "Yes?"

"Can I come in, sir?" Laura appeared in my office, closing the door behind her and I placed my pen back on my desk.

"What is it?" I asked, gathering the pages of the file and closing the folder. I sat back in my chair, frowning when she walked up to me and stopped a little too close, the door swinging closed behind her.

"What are you doing, Laura?"

My frown deepened as I watched her shift from one foot to

the other. She was nervous about something, and the way she was slowly getting closer and closer didn't sit right with me.

"I just wanted to say happy birthday, sir," she said, and I knew where this was going when she started to unbutton her shirt.

"Laura..." I warned, hopefully letting her know that I wasn't interested.

"Do you want to unwrap your present?" she continued, completely ignoring my uncomfortable state.

I was about to give her another warning when the door to my office opened again and Jordan appeared. *Of course.*

"Baby!" My veins turned to ice when her face fell, clearly getting the wrong idea.

"What the fuck?" she shrieked, and I jumped from my chair, running a hand through my hair.

"It's not what it looks like," I defended, completely ignoring Laura as I rounded my desk and ran up to Jordan. She looked beautiful as ever, but the pissed-off look on her face scared the crap out of me. She was getting the wrong idea and at that moment, I had no idea how to fix it.

"I don't care," she said softly, turning to leave. *No!* This wasn't going to end because my assistant couldn't be professional.

"Wait..." I grabbed her arm but she pulled herself from my grip, shooting me a last look of hurt before she walked out of my office.

"Baby, please!" I shouted, but she quickened her pace. Was I supposed to go after her? Did I need to give her space?

I watched her walk away, her head lowered as she swiftly made her way to the elevator. Ian's office door opened and the man peeked around it, raising his brows at me before his gaze shifted to Jordan, who disappeared behind the elevator doors.

"I didn't know..." Laura said behind me and I slowly turned, trying to refrain from punching a hole in the wall. Of course, I was no saint, and I messed around at the office before but she just crossed a line.

"You're fired," I hissed through my teeth, holding the door open for her to leave, my knuckles turning white with how tight my grip on the handle was.

"Sir?"

"Don't make me repeat myself."

She quickly shook her head and redressed herself, making her way out of my office. The tears in her eyes as she looked at me didn't faze me. I had to hold myself back, not to slam the door or put my fist through it.

"Shit," I breathed out, leaning against the door. How was I going to fix this? Did I want to fix this? Wasn't this the perfect opportunity to show her that I didn't have feelings for her?

I close my eyes in frustration, hearing another knock on my door. I really hoped it wasn't Laura again, begging for a second chance.

"What?" I snapped, yanking it open.

I sighed when it was my *father's* eyes staring back at me, and I let him in. He didn't say anything, giving me a bad feeling as he walked up to my desk, clearly angry about something.

"What can I do for you?" I asked as I followed him and sat down in my chair, running a hand through my hair for the umpteenth time that day.

The silence in the room was broken by the sound of a tabloid magazine slapping on my desk. I looked at the cover, all the blood draining out of my face when I saw a familiar head of hair.

"What *the fuck* is this?" Dad finally said—the fact that he was cursing scaring me more than his expression ever could.

"That's...me," I said softly, looking at the headline. *'Charlie Abbot arrested?'*

"We weren't arrested," I defended, flinching when my father exhaled sharply through his nose, threatening to breathe fire any second now.

I had to say that Jordan and I looked *very* good in the image that was plastered over the cover, but my dad obviously didn't agree. It was good that you couldn't recognize the brunette, since our little plan to stay under the radar would fail miserably if you could.

"I knew you were screwing around with a lot of different girls, and I allowed that, but having sex in the middle of the street? And getting caught while doing so? You're walking on thin ice, Charles."

I nodded slowly with my lower lip between my teeth, hearing him but also really grateful he couldn't recognize Jordan.

Jordan.

Happy birthday, Charlie.

"The board is furious. And I have to use everything in my power to make sure they don't get rid of you."

He sounded calm, but the vein on his forehead told a different story. Did I regret our little rendezvous after dinner? Not a chance. But maybe getting caught wasn't the best.

"I'm sorry, Dad."

He scoffed, grabbed the magazine, and walked away.

—

The day dragged on, and I couldn't focus on anything I had to do. I almost missed a vital piece of information during one of my meetings, and I was drowning in phone calls and emails because Laura had packed her shit the minute she'd walked out of my office this morning.

I decided to leave a little early—*the day had already gone to shit anyway*—and took a deep breath when I sat behind the wheel of my car in the parking lot. My birthday was always like any other day to me, and besides going out to dinner with Ashley every year, I didn't really care. But this year, somehow, I thought could be different.

And the only person I wanted to spend the day with had seen me with another woman.

Determined to make it right, I drove off in the direction of Jordan's apartment.

I parked behind the apartment complex, wanting to save my windows from this neighborhood, and made my way into the building. The front door was still broken, so it just took an extra pull to get it open.

"Hello," an older woman greeted me as she watered the plants in the foyer, placing the watering can on a nearby table. "You're Charlie?"

"I am. How did you—"

"Jordan can be quite loud," she interrupted me, smiling. Memories started to flood my mind, and I placed my hands in my pockets, smirking to the floor before I looked back up.

"Yes, but that makes it more fun." I gave the lady a wink before I walked to the stairs.

"She's not home," she called after me, placing her water can on the floor and wiping her hands on her apron.

I stopped at the bottom of the stairs, walking back to the woman. "What?"

"She left in a hurry about an hour ago."

My shoulders dropped and my smirk faltered. *Now what?*

"Do you know where she went?" I asked, fishing my car keys out of my pocket and shooting a last look to the stairs.

She shook her head. "I'm afraid not."

"Hmm." I attempted to walk out of the building but the lady placed a hand on my arm. I looked up to her, taking a step back.

"Be good to her," she said, pleading with her eyes. I sighed. *Too late.*

"I will," I lied, nodding to her and walking off.

Back in my car, I contemplated driving around to see if I could find her, but I knew it wouldn't be any use. So I drove home instead.

I nodded to Jerry behind the front desk when I walked into my building, swiping my card before I could step into the elevator. Maybe I could see her tomorrow? Make things right? *Why did I want to make things right so bad?*

I shook the thought out of my head, walking into my apartment as the doors of the lift rolled open. Freezing in place, I noticed all the lights were on.

Did I get robbed or something?

"Happy birthday, Pretty Boy." There she was. Sitting on a chair that she had placed in the middle of the living room, dressed in a skimpy maids outfit with a lollipop between her lips.

I stared at her with my jaw on the floor, turned on and confused at the same time. "What...how?"

She jumped from the chair, striding up to me in high heels, the skirt of her outfit barely covering her ass and her breasts almost pouring out of her top. *Hello.*

"I knew she was just coming onto you" she explained, slowly placing the red candy back in her mouth, her lips glistening with sugar.

"But...You're not mad?" I asked, still gawking at her like a horny, love-sick teenager.

"No. I just wanted to mess with you a little, so I could surprise you," she explained, and she took a few steps in my direction. I licked my lips and looked her up and down.

"So, we're good?"

"Yes, Charlie," she cooed, placing a hand on my chest and walking her fingers towards my throat. "Happy birthday."

I smiled, taking the lollipop from her before bending down and giving her a sloppy kiss, tasting the cherry-flavored candy on my tongue. Her warm mouth felt amazing against mine and if this was all I got today, it was the best present.

"Hmm." She moaned into the kiss, taking my bottom lip between her teeth.

"This is the best present I've ever had," I said when she pulled back, closing her lips seductively around the piece of candy in my hand and hollowing her cheeks.

"So," she started, popping the lollipop out of her mouth and walking away from me. "First, we have dinner."

I crossed my arms, watching her as she sat down on the chair. "Hmm."

"But, you decide *how* we'll eat dinner," she added, giving me a seductive look and flipping her dark hair over her shoulder.

A grin spread over my face as various scenarios flashed before my eyes. "Go on."

"Then, you can do whatever you want to me, and order me to do whatever you want." *Maybe this day wasn't so bad.*

"And then?"

She spread her legs and sat back, licking the lollipop with one stroke of her tongue. "You can *continue* to tell me what to do, all day, tomorrow."

I bit my lip, feeling my cock twitch in my slacks as I thought of all the things I could make her do. How was it possible for her to get even hotter? Everyone else in the world was bland and boring in comparison to her.

"And what's with the outfit?" I asked, gesturing to the little dress she was wearing.

"I've always wanted to wear something like this." She shrugged, picking at the lace underskirt. "Do you like it?"

"You look hot."

She jumped up with a grin, turning and flashing her beautiful round ass before she walked into the kitchen. I followed, stopping right behind her to grab her by her hips and nip her neck as she unpacked our dinner.

"I got you some sushi," she said, placing two pairs of chopsticks next to the food, crumpling up the paper bag it came in.

"I want to eat it off of you," I mumbled, running my tongue over the edge of her ear. I felt her shiver under my touch, and I slowly pushed one of the straps of the dress off her shoulder.

"Your wish is my command," she replied, sliding the other strap off before letting it fall to the ground, revealing that she wasn't wearing any underwear underneath.

I let out a breath, my eyes roaming over her body and taking every inch of her in. "You're killing me, Baby."

She shot me a smirk over her shoulder and walked to the dinner table, lifting herself on top. "Well?" she questioned impatiently, and I pulled my eyes off her naked chest, grabbing the sushi.

"Right."

A few minutes later, Jordan was laying on the table with a few pieces of food on her body, soft music playing in the background and the lights a little dimmed. Setting everything up hadn't been as sexy and easy as we initially thought, but as she laid there I once again couldn't keep my eyes off her.

I crawled on the table, straddling her hips and bringing my mouth to a piece of sushi on her stomach. Her breathing sounded erratic as I placed my lips around it, making sure to suck some of her skin into my mouth as well.

"Hmm," she hummed, arching her back ever so slightly.

"Are you hungry?" I asked, picking up a piece from her chest with my teeth and bringing it to her mouth.

"Always," she replied, chuckling as she bit into the sushi, sharing half with me. I shifted on top of her as we chewed, but her grin changed into a frown.

"Ouch! What's that?" she suddenly exclaimed and I stopped, hovering over her chest and looking into her eyes. "It burns!"

Scanning her body, I discovered the culprit that was causing her...displeasure.

"Fuck," I said, quickly grabbing the sushi and licking the wasabi off her pubic bone, my tongue instantly on fire. I ignored the feeling, imagining that she was in way more pain, and straightened up.

"Oh my God, make it stop!"

I tried to contain my smile as I quickly jumped off the table, picking Jordan up bridal style and hurrying to the bathroom, leaving a trail of food behind us.

"I might have spilled a little wasabi on you," I admitted, placing her in the shower before I turned the water on. She grabbed the showerhead and placed it over her core, washing away the spicy condiment as she scowled at me.

We stayed there for a few minutes, her shooting daggers at me, and me trying not to burst out laughing before she beat me to it. "This is hilarious!" she yelled, tears of laughter streaming down her face as she continued to wash the wasabi off.

Relieved, I joined her, my stomach hurting as we sat in the shower, shaking with laughter.

We decided to order McDonald's when Jordan was free from the spicy substance, trashing the sushi that had dropped to the floor. It was a waste, but she probably didn't feel like eating sushi after that little incident anyway.

"I'm going to be honest with you, Charlie," she said, swallowing a handful of fries. "I prefer McDonald's over sushi."

I gasped, though I secretly agreed.

Jordan looked at her phone when she got a message, and she quickly picked up the device, scrolling through her messages.

"What's wrong?" I asked, slowly chewing on my own fries.

She held up the phone, one brow cocked and her face *not amused*, showing me a message from Ashley, containing the same image as on the cover of the tabloid my father threw on my desk this morning.

CHAPTER 22
Jordan

"I'm going to be honest with you, Pretty Boy," I said, swallowing a handful of fries and sitting back in my chair. "I prefer McDonald's over sushi."

Charlie gasped, but there was no way I was going to change my opinion any time soon.

I looked at my phone when the screen lit up, reading a message from Ashley. Even though I knew she wasn't in the states, my stomach dropped. I quickly picked it up and opened the message, my smile turning into a frown.

"What's wrong?" Charlie asked, and I held up the phone, showing him the message from Ashley, and the image attached.

"What the *fuck*," I cursed, even though it was as much my fault as his. How was I ever going to explain this?

"Yeah..." he trailed off, rubbing the back of his neck. "But at least no one recognizes you?"

I looked from him to the image. He was right. It was clear that Charlie was having sex with someone on the street, but at the moment the picture was taken, I had dropped my head and my hair had fallen like a curtain over my face. It was too dark to be able to distinguish my tattoos or see my outfit, which Ashley would've recognized for sure.

Just like with the wasabi situation, I realized that it was kind of funny, so I chuckled.

"What a mess," I mumbled as I retracted my hand, looking at the message Ashley had sent with the image. "Do you know what the message said?"

Charlie sat back, shaking his head.

"*See, this is what my brother is like.*"

He grinned, finishing his cheeseburger, and I sent a quick reply before doing the same.

"You know," I said, wiping my mouth and swallowing my last bite, an idea popping into my head. "I do wonder what her brother is like."

Charlie's eyes instantly darkened, and within seconds I was thrown over his shoulder, the slutty maid dress completely exposing my bare ass in the process. I didn't know why I had put it back on in the first place. Maybe because I didn't want any mustard near my core too.

I giggled as he carried me to the bedroom, throwing me on the bed.

"First things first," he said, walking to his dresser and pulling the top drawer open.

"Hmm?" I quickly took off my dress as I kept looking at him. When he turned, my eyes were instantly drawn to the plug in his hands, this one a little bigger than the last, but with the same red diamond on the end.

"I know what I want to do to you tonight," he continued, taking off his shirt and placing it over the back of a chair in the corner.

"Is that so?" I purred, propping up on my elbows and watching him as he walked around the bed. My entire body seemed to be buzzing with anticipation, the nerves in my stomach going wild.

"First, let's get this into you."

I smiled nervously, rolling onto my stomach and pushing my ass in the air. Once the plug was in, I was ordered to get on my back, and Charlie disappeared into the hallway. I shifted on the bed, trying to get comfortable with this foreign object inside my body.

"I thought we could combine a couple of things today," he said as he walked back in, carrying a bowl.

"Ok..." I trailed off, lifting myself to see what was inside, even though I already had an idea because of the condensation on the outside of the bowl.

Ice.

"Can you lay back for me, please, Baby?" Charlie asked, and I did as he said. "Spread your legs."

Butterflies swarmed my stomach as he took out a silk ribbon, grabbing both of my hands and tying them together.

"Next time we have to do this at yours," he mentioned, standing back up and undoing his belt. I swallowed as I looked at his groin when he lowered his slacks, my mind still processing what he'd just said.

"Why?"

"Because you have a wire bed frame." He stripped down to his boxers, his length already creating a beautiful tent in his underwear. "I can tie you up better."

I hummed softly, too excited for what was to come to be able to respond.

"Safe word, Baby?"

"Bubble Gum," I replied quickly, my core already throbbing with anticipation, the sensation almost painful.

"I'm not going to blindfold you, we'll save that for another day. Besides, I want to see every single part of your face while I pleasure you," he added, shooting me a wink. I rolled my eyes. *Fucking do it already, Pretty Boy.*

As if he read my mind, Charlie fished an ice cube out of the bowl and placed it in the valley between my breasts, making me gasp. He crawled on top of me, closing his lips around the cube, and slowly ran it down my chest.

I moaned and arched my back, the cold feeling against my skin sending bolts of pleasure and adrenaline through my body, the plug in my ass only making the sensation more explosive.

"Charlie..." I groaned when he slid the cube back up, circling it around my hard nipples and leaving a wet trail behind.

My hands instinctively wanted to grab his hair, but he pushed them back on the bed, looking up. "Tsk tsk, Baby."

He kept his eyes on me as he licked the wet trail up my stomach, searing my nipples with his warm mouth.

Rubbing my legs together to create some kind of friction, I moaned louder, realizing that it was going to be a very long night.

"No, no. Keep those legs spread," Charlie warned, nudging them back open, and I pushed my head back on the mattress, trying to ignore the ache in my core.

"Please, touch me," I begged, balling my hands into fists and fighting slightly against the ribbon around my wrists.

"You want me to touch you?" Charlie teased, taking the cube—*or what was left of it*—back into his mouth.

"God, yes!"

He moved the cube around again, this time going lower and lower, brushing the ice over my slit and down my thighs. I sucked in a deep breath when the cube passed my clit, and I took my lower lip between my teeth, trying to cope with every sensation.

"Where?" he asked once the cube had completely melted, and he positioned himself between my legs, licking his lips.

"Here?" he added, bringing his face to my chest and sucking on the skin right under my left breast.

"Higher," I breathed out, pushing my chest up, my hands gripping the edge of his headboard with all my force.

"Hmm, here?" He licked the spot right next to my nipple.

"Charlie!" I whined, pulling my legs up and curling my toes into the sheets.

"Yes, Baby?"

"Fuck me!"

I gasped when he patted my pussy, grabbing me gently by the throat and pushing me further into the mattress, bringing his lips to my ear. "Patience, Jordan."

"Please..." I whispered, looking into his eyes and squirming under his grip, my wrists once again fighting against the ribbon. His grip around my throat tightened, and I was convinced that my orgasm could wash over me as soon as he pressed one single finger against my pussy.

"I love it when you beg," he said, grinning mischievously before he trailed kisses down my stomach.

"Yes!" I exclaimed when he suddenly spread my folds and sucked on my clit. His hands slid to my chest and he took my nipples between his fingers, giving me more stimulation than I thought humanly possible. I tightened my muscles, taking as much as I could.

"Hmm," Charlie hummed against my pussy as he dipped his tongue in, the vibrations adding more pleasure.

"Shit, Charlie..." I groaned, squeezing my eyes shut as I already felt my orgasm approaching.

"Don't come yet, Baby," he ordered, pulling back and taking his hands off me. The rush stopped and simmered down when my core lost contact with Charlie's mouth, and I sighed.

"You're torturing me," I whined as he stood from the bed, walking around and taking off his boxers. I couldn't help but let my eyes fall to his length, the tip glistening.

"No, I want you to come when I'm inside you, pounding into you until you're sore for days."

I licked my lips as his rock-hard length stared me in the face, and I spread my legs as wide as I could. "Take me then. Please."

Charlie crawled back onto me, positioning his head at my entrance, even the smallest contact sending bolts of pleasure up my spine.

"Remember to stop me if it's too much," he mentioned, waiting for me to give some kind of confirmation before he pushed in. I frantically nodded, balling my fists to get ready for the ride of my life.

"Oh my, *Jesus*!" I gasped, arching my back and pushing my bound hands against the headboard. The feeling of his cock and the plug inside of me created the perfect amount of pressure I didn't even know I wanted.

"That's right," Charlie grunted as he started to move, quickly thrusting in and out, watching my face as I moaned and gasped, every nerve in my body exploding.

"Ah! Charlie! I can't hold back!"

"Then don't."

At that, I let go, letting the euphoric feeling wash over me, replacing my growing ache with pure bliss.

Charlie continued to pound into me, chasing his own release as he rode out mine, prolonging my orgasm as long as he could.

"Fuck, fuck, fuck," he panted, clenching his jaw as he filled me, his movements slowing down until he collapsed on top of me. We caught our breath together, our chests rising and falling in sync and beads of sweat covering our faces.

"I thought it was *your* birthday," I mumbled softly, little stars still dancing in front of my eyes.

"Watching you come like that," he replied, leaning onto one hand and untying mine with the other, throwing the ribbon on the bed next to him, "is all I could wish for."

"Hmm." I closed my eyes, smiling, pulling Charlie back against my chest and brushing my fingers through his hair as we lay there.

At some point, I remembered the plug, so I carefully stood from the bed and walked to the bathroom. I felt Charlie's eyes burn a hole in my back, so I decided to exaggerate the swaying of my hips.

"Do your tattoos have meaning?" Charlie asked from the bed, and I gave him a quick look over my shoulder before I took out the plug and washed it.

"What?" I replied, walking back into the room and placing the plug on one of the nightstands before I crawled back onto bed.

Charlie ran a finger over my back when I relaxed against him. "For example. This tiger?"

"Well," I said, placing my hands under my chin as I looked up at him. "The tiger is a sign of strength and power in Thailand, and this particular tattoo is believed to help a person's life change from bad to good."

"Hmm," he hummed, nodding.

"My mother was from Thailand, as you may have guessed." I closed my eyes for a second, thinking about her, but opened them again when Charlie brushed a strand of hair out of my face. "And I wanted to honor her and my heritage."

"That's beautiful."

I smiled, a sigh leaving my lips.

"Have you ever visited Thailand?" Charlie asked, his hand returning to my back.

I nodded against his chest. "Yes. It's where I got the tiger and the other tattoos on my back. It's part of the tradition to get them there."

"Go away with me," he stated, surprising me with his words. I pushed myself off him and leaned on my hands as I looked into his eyes.

"What?"

He looked back at me, cocking his head a little to the side. "Where have you always wanted to go?"

"I've never been to Los Angeles," I replied, falling back at his side and drawing circles on Charlie's chest.

"No, I meant outside the US."

"Charlie, I don't—" I knew what he meant, but this conversation felt weird. And, I didn't want to get my hopes up. It wasn't like going on trips was something *people-who-just-have-sex* did anyway.

"Humor me," Charlie pushed and I sighed, looking at his chest as I contemplated my answer. Where *did* I want to go? I had never traveled much, since we didn't have much money when I was growing up, and now that I was older, I didn't have time. Nor money.

"I've always wanted to go to Italy," I answered eventually, thinking back to my conversation with Nadine about her travels.

"Can you get a week off work next month?"

I almost choked on my saliva, my eyes widening. "Char—"

"Can you?" he pressed, running his finger over my side and following the curve of my waist, instantly distracting me.

"I can try." I sighed, curling up against his chest with no intention of actually asking for the time off. But he didn't need to know that.

Charlie wrapped his arms around me, pulling me tighter against him, and I fell asleep listening to his steady heartbeat.

—

"You can go right in, ma'am," the guy in front of Charlie's office said, invitingly. I tried to hide my smile as I nodded to the new assistant. Trusting Charlie had been a good call.

I closed the door and leaned against it, biting my lower lip as I looked at him, all sexy and professional sitting behind his desk. Honestly, the way he was frowning at the papers in front of him was a huge turn-on alone.

"I'm sorry to disturb you, sir," I purred, grabbing his attention. His frown instantly turned into a grin when he looked up.

"Come here, Baby."

I walked up to him, stopping between his legs. "You summoned me?" I stated, grabbing the hem of my skirt and pulling it up a little.

"How long until you have to be back?" he asked, slipping his hands under my skirt and playing with the lace of my thong. "Tsk tsk, Jordan. Didn't I tell you not to wear underwear?"

I smirked, pushing my skirt all the way up and sitting down on his lap, straddling his thighs. "Are you going to punish me?"

"Of course." His hands brushed over my thighs before he grabbed my ass with force, pushing my hips closer onto his.

"Hmm, we have fifteen minutes." I grabbed his face with both hands and pressed my lips on his, instantly deepening the kiss when our mouths touched.

"I'm sorry, sir. Mr. Abbot is busy!" We heard his assistant shout, and my heart dropped.

"Shit," I breathed out before I jumped up, looking around to find some kind of hiding spot, but of course, the modern furniture offered no such thing. We heard footsteps outside the door, and I felt the blood drain from my face as I looked at the frosted glass.

"Under here," Charlie suggested, patting me on my ass as I crouched down and crawled under his desk. I was still a little out of breath when I sat down, my face almost hitting the top.

Just as Charlie scooted his chair closer to the table—*almost kicking me in the face*—I heard the door to his office open followed by the sound of footsteps.

"Two times in one week," Charlie retorted, his knees spreading a little under the table.

"I see that you already have a new assistant?"

More blood drained from my face as I recognized Charlie's father's voice. Of course, it was my luck that none other than Mr. Abbot came to disturb our little moment, and I held my breath as I listened to the rest of the conversation.

"I do."

"You can't just go around firing people, Charlie."

I rolled my eyes. *He could fire that bitch though.*

"She came onto me and I won't allow that level of unprofessionalism."

I ran my hands over Charlie's legs when I felt a little more at ease, reminding him that I was still here, having only ten minutes to be fucked before I had to go back to my own office.

"What did you need?" Charlie asked, and I rubbed my palm over his bulge. Maybe I could use this moment to give him a little payback.

My fingers moved to his belt, and I undid it as quietly as I could, continuing to open up his slacks as Charlie cleared his throat.

"Are you ok?" his father asked, and a smirk appeared on my face. I tried not to chuckle as I managed to grab his length from his boxers, spitting on my hand and slowly starting to pull him off under the table. I wish I could take him in my mouth, but there was simply not enough room.

"I really have to get back to this," Charlie replied, placing his hand over mine and forcing me to stop.

His father huffed. "We'll talk this weekend."

My grin grew wider when I heard footsteps followed by the door closing. I pushed Charlie back, quickly rising to my knees and taking his dick in my mouth.

"Oh my God, Jordan," he breathed out, grabbing the armrests of his chair with force and throwing his head back as I bobbed my head up and down. I quickened my pace, using one hand to work the base of his shaft.

Just when I thought he was going to come undone in my mouth, I pulled back.

"What?" he asked, a deep frown on his forehead and his head snapping back in my direction.

I licked my lips and got on my feet, pulling my thong to the side before I lowered on his hard cock, straddling his thighs. "We, oh..." I moaned, taking a deep breath before I looked him in the eye. "We have seven minutes."

CHAPTER 23
Jordan

"Thank you!" Ashley said to the delivery man, closing the door to her apartment and turning towards me with a big box in her hands, an equally big smile on her face.

"What's that?" I asked, cocking my head at the big, fancy-looking box.

"The invitations!"

"With forty days to go?" I questioned, placing my tea back on the table.

"It'll be fine," she replied, setting the box in the middle of the table and grabbing a pair of scissors from the kitchen. Bouncing on her feet, she ran the scissors over the tape and opened the box, taking out one of the invitations.

"And?" I asked, watching her smile slowly fade into a frown.

I grabbed one of the invitations when Ashley slumped onto her chair, staring at the card in her hand. *Oh, shit.*

"No one will notice right?" I tried to comfort her, carefully placing the invitation on the table and a hand on her arm.

"No one will notice that they spelled my name wrong?" Ashley exclaimed, throwing the card on the table as she scowled at me.

I quickly retracted my hand, trying to think of things to make her feel better or to help her, but was coming up empty. I had no experience with weddings, or with everything around it.

"We'll just send them back and demand they get corrected," I suggested, checking the return address on the box.

She sighed, rubbing her hands over her face. "I just hope everything else goes right."

"I'm sure it will," I said softly, grabbing Ashley's cup and walking to the kitchen to make her more tea. We had been talking about the bachelorette party she didn't want to have and other wedding-related things before the doorbell rang, but it was safe to say that Ashley's mood was ruined.

"Did you get your dress yet?" she asked over her shoulder, running a hand through her blonde locks.

I nodded. "I did, it's safely put away in my closet, cover and all."

"Good." She sighed, crossing her arms and looking up at me when I put a fresh cup of tea in front of her. "Thank you."

"Everything's going to be okay," I reassured her, putting the invitations we took out back into the box and closing it up. I placed it on the ground beside me, out of sight.

"I love you, Jordan." Ashley placed her hand over mine on

the table, giving me a watery smile.

I knew Ashley always struggled with friendships in the past, and I was grateful that she had let me in. We were very different, but very close since we met six years ago. She had my back and I had hers.

When she had told me about her time in high school and the people she had met there, I nearly exploded, especially when she told me there was this one bitch who only wanted to befriend her to get with her brother...*oh, God*. What was I doing?

"Are you sure you can't stay for dinner?" she asked, interrupting my train of thought, and she looked up when Ryan came home.

"I promised Mrs. Hellen I'd have dinner with her tonight." I stood up and put on my coat, fishing my keys from the pocket.

"Alright."

"Hey, baby," Ryan greeted Ashley, giving her a kiss on the forehead. "Hi, Jordan. Did you guys have a fun day?"

"Yes, we did," I replied, opening the front door. *Kinda*. "I'll see you guys later!"

Ashley began telling him about the invitations, and the last thing I saw before I closed the door was Ryan crouching down in front of his fiancé, caressing her cheek. *Sometimes I was really jealous of their relationship.*

—

Just before I was able to press the doorbell, the door to Mrs. H— *Abigail's* apartment swung open, and Eli appeared in front of me.

"Bye, Mom!" he yelled over his shoulder, freezing when he

saw me, my finger still hovering over the button on the wall.

"Hi," I said, expecting to feel some kind of way as I stared into his eyes, but I felt nothing. All I could think about was that the blue looked muddy and boring compared to the bright ice in Charlie's.

"Hey, Jordy," he cooed, smirking as he looked me up and down. "You look good."

Dream on, boy.

"Thanks," I replied, pushing past him into the apartment and greeting Abigail when I saw her sitting at the dinner table. I ignored Eli's eyes on my back, yet feeling powerful under his gaze.

"Hey, Jordan. How've you been?" she asked, rising from her seat and giving me a hug as I heard the front door close behind me. My body relaxed and I placed my phone and keys on the table.

"Good, you?"

"Good, good." She shuffled to the kitchen, taking out the supplies for our dinner.

"Need some help?" I asked, following her.

"Could you cut the vegetables?"

I nodded, taking the cutting board from her and grabbing a knife, starting with an onion. Fighting against the tears that appeared in my eyes as the strong smell hit my face, I looked up at Abigail when I felt her eyes on me. "What?"

"You look happy," she explained, smiling.

I went back to cutting, grinning to myself. "I guess I am."

My mind went to a certain someone when I said that, and I casually shook him out of my head, trying to conceal the blush that had crept onto my face. *Just sex. Just sex.*

"He's handsome," she added, turning on the stove and putting some water on. I looked up at her, but I wasn't surprised.

"Of course, you know." I chuckled softly, wiping my eyes. "A guy like that stands out around here."

I had to agree, especially since Charlie only wore tailored suits and expensive, Italian shoes. It was one of the things that really drew me in and attracted me to him. Not only the way he carried himself or how charismatic he was but how he always dressed to impress.

"He does," I replied, handing her the diced onion.

"I'm glad you found someone," she said, and I frowned.

"Oh, we're not together."

Abigail turned to me with a brow raised, the onion sizzling in the pan next to her, releasing that amazing smell. *Focus, Jordan.*

"Are you sure?"

Deciding to change the subject, I started talking about work as we finished making dinner, having a glass of wine as we ate.

"How is the wedding planning going?" she asked, finishing her pasta and putting her fork back on her plate.

"Ashley went to Canada to check out the venue a week ago," I replied, sitting back in my chair and finishing my wine. "She has her dress, but the invitations..."

Abigail chuckled, taking another sip herself. I flipped my hair over my shoulder. "Her name is spelled wrong on them, so she has to send them back."

"Poor thing."

"It'll be fine." I smiled.

"It's been a while since I've seen her," Abigail added.

Had I been deliberately keeping Ashley at arm's length because I was having sex with her brother on the regular? *Yes.*

Looking up at the blonde before me, I studied the grey streaks in her hair and her comforting green eyes. *Should I tell her?*

"Charlie is Ashley's brother," I said, and Abigail nodded. No going back now.

"I thought he looked familiar."

"Yeah, and she's kind of against him and me—together."

I could see the lightbulb appearing in her eyes, realizing why I was sneaking around and keeping him and me a secret from everyone. "If she doesn't want you to be together, why don't you just...stop?"

How was I going to explain that it was physically difficult for me to stay away from Charlie, without making it seem like I had feelings for him? Because I didn't. It was just lust and my high sex drive.

"Because...we...have fun." *Nailed it.*

With a shrug of her shoulders, she let the subject go, accepting my answer—for now.

—

"Yes, Mr. Hensley's appointment was scheduled for next Thursday, but he called to ask if he could move it to Friday instead," I requested, going through some important calendar items this morning with my boss.

"I'll give him a call after my four o'clock appointment," Mr. Grimaldi replied, nodding softly.

"So I'll just have to clear your schedule for next Tuesday, and make some calls to find out who we need to contact from the tax administration about the Asina file."

He sat back in his chair and placed his phone on his desk.

"I'll do that myself, you can go."

I blinked rapidly in confusion, wondering if I did something wrong. Though there was no hint of annoyance or anger in his voice, his choice of words concerned me. "Sir?"

"Go on," he pressed, and I hesitantly rose from the chair I was sitting in, looking over my shoulder one last time before I walked out of his office.

"Hey, Baby." I froze when I saw Charlie sitting in my desk chair, playing with a stapler. He looked as handsome as ever, but the thing that infuriated me the most was the way he didn't care about being subtle.

"What are you doing here?" I hissed as I looked around, making sure no one was around to see us together.

"I'm picking you up," he stated, grabbing the picture frame with an old photo of my mom and dad, smiling at the couple.

I raised a brow. "It's not even two p.m.."

"I know, let's go. Our plane leaves at six."

My eyes closed for a second before I took a step in his direction. "Our *plane* leaves at six," I repeated, crossing my arms and raising a brow.

"Yup. Let's go, Baby," he replied, putting the picture frame back and jumping from the chair.

"Charlie Abbot, I swear to God..." I warned, pressing an accusing finger into his chest.

"Oh, we're using my full name now?"

I rolled my eyes as he stuck the stapled piece of paper on my whiteboard before he turned back around, grabbing me by the hips. Looking over my shoulder, I pushed him off. "I can't just leave for God knows how long," I hissed, walking around him and sitting down behind my desk, logging into my computer.

"You're not. Henry agreed to give you a week off," he mentioned, leaning casually against the wall. The fact that he and my boss were on a first-name basis didn't sit right with me, but that he asked him for time off was worse.

I froze in my seat, slowly turning to him. "You asked him to— Charlie! You can't just do that! Oh, God. What must he think of me?"

"That you're a hard worker." My boss responded as he exited his office, carrying a stack of files in his arms.

"Sir?" I questioned. *Hard worker my ass, more like Charlie Abbot asked.*

"I had a nice chat with Mr. Abbot yesterday over the phone, and he told me about his plans. He's quite convincing," Mr. Grimaldi explained, and I sighed. He really *was* convincing, and it annoyed the fuck out of me.

"I'm so sorry, sir. I don't want you to think that I'm slacking," I replied, realizing that this was the second time within a month that he gave me time off.

"I know you're not. Besides, Mr. Abbot arranged for a temporary replacement."

"Sorry I'm late," Nadine chirped as she walked over to us, my jaw dropping to the floor. *What the fuck was happening? She was in on it too?*

"You're free to go, Jordan," Mr. Grimaldi smiled, and I slowly rose from my seat, taking my bag from Charlie.

"Are you sure?" I questioned again as the man started to push me towards the exit.

"Have a nice trip, Jordan!" Nadine waved goodbye before she bounced towards the desk, sitting down and nodding to Mr.

Grimaldi as he explained a couple of things to her.

Once the doors to the elevators closed, I took a moment to fully comprehend what just happened.

"Fucking rich, spoiled, idiotically handsome, dick!" I yelled as I playfully hit him everywhere I could, my bag swinging on my arm.

"Save it for the bedroom, Baby," he chuckled, shielding his face with his arms.

"What's happening?" I stopped slapping him, leaning against the back of the elevator.

Charlie straightened out his suit jacket, running a hand through his hair before he took a step in my direction. "Jordan..."

"Why are you doing this? Where are we going? How long will we—"

He shut me up by pressing a finger against my lips, waiting for me to calm down.

"I'm cool," I mumbled. "I'm cool."

We heard the ping for the ground floor, and I followed him out when the doors of the elevator rolled open.

"In my defense," Charlie said as we walked to his car, and I shot the building a last look over my shoulder as if I was expecting my boss to hang out of a window and yell at me to get back in. "It was meant to be a surprise."

I scoffed. "Well, it worked. That's for sure."

He held my door open, waiting for me to step in before he rounded the vehicle, sitting down behind the wheel.

"Look, I'm sorry," he said as he started the car and drove off. "But I just want to be able to kiss you in public without the fear of someone snapping a photo or my sister turning up."

I stared at him in response. *That was actually kind of...sweet.*

"Where are we going?"

"It's a surprise," he replied, and I rolled my eyes, leaning my head against the window as I watched the city flash by.

Four hours later, we were sitting in our way too expensive, first-class seats, getting served a glass of bubbly before take off. I had put up a fight when I first read our boarding passes, but Charlie knew exactly how to handle me, so here we were. On our way to *Florance, Italy*.

"Relax, Baby," he cooed as the plane traveled to the runway. He grabbed my hand, letting out a high-pitched shriek when I nearly crushed his fingers.

"Have I ever told you that I'm not too fond of flying," I muttered, and closed my eyes when the plane started to pick up speed, pushing me back into my seat.

I loved fast cars and an adrenaline rush, but taking off in an airplane was a whole different story.

"It'll be over soon," Charlie groaned, trying to pull his hand from my grip, but I wasn't letting go any time soon.

"It's a nine-hour flight, Pretty Boy," I hissed, my eyes shooting open as I turned to him.

"Alright." He surprised me by pressing his lips on mine, distracting me with a kiss until the plane slowly leveled in the air.

The soft strokes of his tongue against mine and the warmth of his lips definitely helped with the nerves, and I was ready to let him take me right then and there.

It took me an hour to fully calm down, but when I did, I couldn't help but appreciate the spacious seats and other perks of flying first class. We had dinner, got some snacks, and were offered plenty of drinks until the lights dimmed, and everyone went to sleep.

Listening to the engines, I looked out of the small window to my left before closing my eyes and drifting into slumber.

Maybe this wasn't going to be so bad.

CHAPTER 24
Jordan

After checking into our hotel and *exploring* our room, Charlie and I roamed the city for a bit. The beautiful architecture caused us to pause, several times, accompanied by an occasional sigh from Charlie.

On the first night, he took me out to dinner, and I decided to surrender to the butterflies in my stomach and fully enjoy our week together.

"So, I don't speak Italian," I mentioned as I attempted to read the menu, the entree names and listed ingredients making *zero* sense to me.

"Hold on," Charlie smiled, scooting onto the bench next to me. "Let's see."

I stared at him as he explained and translated the menu, surprising me with the amount of knowledge he had about the Italian language and cuisine.

"So my personal favorite," he said, pointing to one of the dishes, "is actually the simplest thing."

I narrowed my eyes at the words. "*Prosciutto e melone.*"

He tried to hold in a chuckle, and I shot him a pained look when I realized how stupid I must've sounded.

"You have any idea what that is?" he asked, crossing his arms and sitting back.

"Well, *melone* looks like melon." Charlie nodded. "And *Prosciutto* is a type of ham right?"

He nodded again.

"You know what,"—I closed the menu—"I'm just going to have whatever you're having."

That ended up being a wise decision.

The combination of the ham and melon was one of the best things I'd ever tasted, and the pasta dish we had as our main course was putting my own cooking to shame. *Not that that's hard to do, but still.*

"I still can't believe we're here," I said, looking around the square we were dining at, studying the Roman sculptures and the big, beautiful fountain, carved into marble.

"You said you've always wanted to go to Italy," Charlie answered, swirling his wine around in his glass, one arm draped over the back of the bench. I looked at my hands, smiling at the view as I answered.

"I did, but I didn't expect you to actually take me here." Was I going to mention that I thought he was acting more like a boyfriend than a fuck-buddy? *Definitely not.*

"You underestimate me, Baby."

I scoffed. "Clearly."

My eyes traveled over the orange turning sky, the evening sun fighting the buildings to bathe us in its last rays. Street lights were turning on, but the square was still packed with people taking photos or looking for a place to eat.

I broke from my trance when I felt an arm on my shoulders, and I realized that Charlie had scooted a little closer to me, *subtly* pulling me against his chest.

His woody, yet sweet cologne filled my nostrils as I let myself fall back against him, watching our magical surroundings with somewhat of a smile on my face. I felt my heartbeat in my throat, nervous to move a muscle and do something that would pull us out of the moment we were having.

Charlie noticed. "Relax," he cooed in my ear, and I dropped my head back on his shoulder, shifting in my seat to get even more comfortable.

"Can I get you anything else?" Our waiter appeared next to our table, startling both of us.

"The check, *per favore*," Charlie replied, giving the man a nod and pulling me even closer. The waiter took our empty plates before walking off, and I sunk back into my new favorite place. *It's just comfortable, that's all.*

"Want to take the long way back to the hotel? Do some window shopping with me?" he said softly.

"Sure," I replied, sitting up as his arm left my shoulder. He took care of the bill when the waiter reappeared, and I grabbed my purse.

The streets were surprisingly busy as we walked back, various couples and groups of people roaming the ancient paving, peeking into shop windows, or chatting at dinner tables. It created a perfect ambiance, the light of the stores now turned on, illuminating centuries-old buildings and making our walk almost seem...*romantic.*

I heard music and smiled when we came across a man with a guitar, playing beautifully and singing something in Italian.

"This is amazing," I whispered, my eyes glued on the performer, joining the audience he had attracted. People were dropping coins in his guitar case, and I fished a couple of euros out of my wallet, throwing them on the growing pile. The man winked and I tried to conceal my blush, quickly moving back to my spot, looking around for Charlie.

I came up empty.

"Charlie?" I shouted somewhat panicked. Today was not a good day to become stranded in an unknown city where I didn't know anyone or speak the language. "Fuck," I cursed under my breath, scanning the crowd.

I had been so mesmerized by the street performer that I hadn't noticed that Charlie had walked off. For whatever reason.

"Are you ok?" I quickly turned and almost lost my footing, falling right into Charlie's arms. "Oh, hello, Baby."

When I found my balance, I pushed him off, straightening out my dress and shooting him an angry look. "Where were you?"

I shouldn't have reacted the way I did, especially considering we weren't a real couple, but he scared me.

"I was looking at some watches," he explained, pointing over his shoulder to one of the shops. *Of course.*

I rolled my eyes, looking up at him with a smirk. "Don't you have enough?"

He grinned, snaking his arm around my waist as we continued our walk back to the hotel. "I thought I'd buy a new one for you to *accidentally* steal."

I slapped him playfully on his chest before I wrapped my arm around his waist, matching my step to his.

—

The next morning, I awoke to a warm light on my face, accompanied by the chirping of birds and the sound of the already busy street below us. I rolled onto my side, hugging the amazing smelling sheets, and looked out the open window, enjoying the soft breeze on my face.

This was by far, one of the best feelings I've ever felt in my life.

Patting my hand behind me to feel for Charlie, I frowned when I came up empty, and turned around.

"Charlie?" I asked, sitting up. *Where did he go now?*

"Good morning, Baby," he said as he walked into the bedroom of our suite, carrying a white tray.

"What's this?" I scooted back against the headboard as he sat on the edge of the bed, placing it in front of me. My mouth instantly watered at the lush breakfast that stared me in the face.

"I thought we could eat in bed. You know, our favorite place to be," Charlie responded, giving me a wink before he carefully laid down next to me, propping up on an elbow.

"Hmm." I scanned his body. "Usually, you're wearing *fewer* clothes."

He chuckled softly before he grabbed the back of his shirt, pulling it over his head and throwing it on his suitcase. I raised my brows at his carelessness but got distracted by one of the strawberries he was pushing in my face. "Eat."

"Excuse me?" I pulled up a brow.

Charlie sat up, biting into the fruit himself. "Let's eat."

Shaking my head, I took a sip from the cup of coffee, thoroughly enjoying the amazingly rich flavor.

"They make some good coffee here," I mentioned, pushing a strand of hair behind my ear before I dug into the pancakes.

"Hmm," Charlie hummed, shoving a pancake in his mouth, too.

"What's a typical Italian breakfast?"

Charlie took the coffee from me, taking a sip himself before answering. "Italians don't really have breakfast."

I flushed the bite of pancake down with some orange juice, giving him a questioning look. "What?"

"It's true, at least from what I've seen." He chucked another strawberry into his mouth, jumping from the bed and almost spilling coffee on the white sheets.

"What the fuck?" I exclaimed as I was trying to keep all the orange juice in the glass, and I watched Charlie walk out of the bedroom. I scoffed, taking a sip from my drink before placing it on my nightstand.

"So," he said when he came back in, both of his hands behind his back. "I got you a little something."

I cleared my throat, carefully scooting it to the end of the bed as Charlie sat next to me, smirking. "I'm still sore from yesterday," I replied, gathering my hair into a ponytail. "But I'll give you some head."

"No, no," he chuckled, adjusting himself in his slacks.

"What?" Releasing my hair, I cocked my head to the side, my eyes moving to his hands when he removed them from behind his back. I gasped softly when I saw a sleek, square box, recognizing the gold lettering from the shop Charlie was looking at yesterday.

"You didn't," I breathed out, brushing my fingers over my lips. *What the hell was he playing at?*

"Open it."

I took the box from him with shaking hands and slowly lifted the lid.

"Charlie..." I trailed off when I laid my eyes on a gold necklace, a sparkling pink stone hanging from the delicate chain.

"It's *bubble gum* pink," he beamed, his eyes wide and the corners of his mouth curled into a bright smile.

I chuckled softly before I came to my senses. "I can't possibly accept this."

Charlie took the box from me, taking out the piece of jewelry and gesturing for me to come closer. "Come here."

"But—"

"Just do it," he pressed with a roll of his eyes, and I turned, holding my hair up as he placed the stunning necklace around my neck. I brushed my fingers over the stone, still in shock.

"Go, have a look in the mirror," Charlie said, sitting back.

Still not saying anything, I stood from the bed and walked over to the full-length mirror, staring at my reflection. *I couldn't possibly accept this kind of gift.*

For the last couple of days, I had already felt conflicted—confused about my feelings—and for him to buy me such an expensive gift... What was I supposed to do now?

I loved the pink—*choosing it to match my safe word*—and the emerald-cut stone looked beautiful against the gold chain, but it was way too expensive.

"I can *hear* you overthinking from here," Charlie interrupted my train of thought, walking up behind me.

"What's the meaning of this?" I asked, looking at his reflection.

He rolled his lower lip between his teeth before answering. "I noticed it in the window yesterday and thought of you."

I was surprised by his confession, not expecting such an honest answer—*especially to this question.*

"But it's—"

"Shh." He brought his lips to my shoulder, distracting me by trailing kisses to my neck. "Do you like it?"

I felt my body burning up from his touch, the feeling of his lips against my skin always had the desired effect. Honestly, one single look at half-naked Charlie was more than enough to have me on my knees.

"Baby?"

"It's beautiful," I replied, letting my head fall back to expose more of my neck and hopefully receive more intoxicating kisses.

"Just like you."

That's it. I startled Charlie by swiftly turning, pushing his back flush against the wall and attacking his lips, feeling like I needed to be closer to him, even though my pussy needed a break.

"Hmm," he hummed into the kiss, grabbing my ass with both hands and digging his fingers in.

"Fuck!" I cursed loudly when the ear-piercing sound of my phone filled the room, making the two of us immediately spring apart.

"If that's my sister, you can tell her to fuck off," Charlie yelled, pointing to the device on my nightstand.

I rolled my eyes, grabbing my phone to look at the caller ID. "It's my dad."

Charlie sighed, shuffling into the bathroom and leaving me alone in the room.

"Hey, Dad," I chirped, plopping onto the bed and grabbing the glass of leftover orange juice as I listened. Before he could say anything I pulled the device from my ear, looking if he was calling through FaceTime or not. *He's going to have one hell of a scare when he sees his phone bill.*

"How are you doing, sweetie?" he asked, and I smiled.

"I'm good, you?"

"Good, good..." he trailed off. *Did he see the tabloid? Did he hear something from someone?*

"What's up?"

"Well, I haven't seen you in a while." I let out a breath at his words, playing with the hem of my pajama shorts.

"I'm sorry about that. What about a game night when I—" I quickly cut myself off, realizing what I was about to say.

"You what?"

"When I get off work on Monday." *Smooth.*

The silence on the other end was killing me. I looked up when Charlie walked back into the room, a towel wrapped around his waist and a few drops of water running down his chest.

"Jordan?" I jumped slightly as my dad refocused me.

"Sorry, what were you saying?"

Charlie smirked, and I threw a pillow at him.

"That sounds good, darling," Dad repeated.

I sighed, quickly finishing the call.

We had a lot to catch up on; I hadn't even told him I got promoted yet. I had been so busy with this adonis—who was currently pulling a clean shirt over his head—that I completely forgot about everyone else around me.

"Charlie?" I asked, placing my phone back on my nightstand and folding my hands together in my lap.

"Yes, Baby?" He ran a hand through his damp hair, sitting down next to me.

"Can we do a day at the pool today?"

Though we had lots to explore in the city, I suddenly felt nauseous and on edge. The conversation with my dad had pulled me back to reality, and the guilt was crushing me.

"Are you ok?" Charlie frowned, crawling up to me and pushing a strand of hair behind my ear.

I sighed, nodding before I looked into his eyes. "I just need a day at the pool I think." I smiled, pecking him on the lips before jumping up and rummaging through my suitcase for my suit. He didn't push further, and we both changed, getting ready for a day at the infinity pool on the roof of this luxurious hotel.

CHAPTER 25
Jordan

The following days I was able to push the guilt I felt to the back of my mind, and enjoy our time in Florence. Charlie took me to various hot spots like the *Duomo* and the *Ponte Vecchio*, nice restaurants, and I finally let him spoil me for the remainder of the week.

We enjoyed numerous cups of coffee back at the *Piazza della Signoria* in the mornings, and every night, Charlie suggested we try something new on the menu. I dragged him into many shops to find cute souvenirs to get for...ourselves, and occasionally, he let me buy us a cup of delicious Italian *gelato*.

We were having such a good time, that it was over before I knew it.

The last evening, we decided to get some drinks at the hotel bar after another wonderful dinner, and he even got me to try something else other than my usual drink.

"This is actually really good," I said as I put my *pornstar martini* back on the bar.

Ok—I wasn't being too adventurous. It was still a martini.

"Right?" Charlie agreed, sipping his own and watching me over the rim. I looked at my drink, swirling my finger through the condensation on the glass.

"Can I ask you a question?"

He shifted in his seat, placing his drink next to mine. "Depends on the question." What kind of answer was that? Were there things he didn't want me to know? *Probably.* We weren't a couple.

"I'm going to ask you anyway," I continued, straightening up. "Can I pay for something?"

I saw his jaw tense, undoubtedly from his teeth clenching together. "What?"

"Charlie..." I rolled my eyes. "I want to contribute to this amazing trip."

He sighed, taking his time as he brought his drink to his lips. "It was *my* surprise."

I crossed my arms over my chest, raising a brow. I did desperately want to chip in, at least a little bit. I knew this trip was expensive and that I probably couldn't *afford* to contribute, but my pride told me at least to try.

"Really. Jordan," he added. "It's fine."

"At least let me pay for something," I said, brushing my finger up and down the stem of my glass.

"You can pay for these drinks," he offered, emptying his and beckoning the bartender for another round.

"Alright." I was already feeling the first cocktail, the alcohol making my cheeks flush and giving me the feeling that I was floating. *What did they put in their drinks here?*

"Want to try something else?" Charlie asked as the handsome Italian bartender made his way over. I quickly scanned the menu—*thanking the lord that everything was in English*—but decided to just stick with what I knew.

"Just a martini please, you know how I like it," I replied as I handed him some money. He nodded, quietly passing our order onto the bartender and slipping him the money as he did.

I felt myself heating up even more as I watched Charlie move, talk, do anything.

"Baby?"

"What?" He caught me staring as I was imagining all the dirty things that I wanted him to do to me.

The corners of his lips curled up into a smirk, and he looked me up and down. "What were you thinking?"

"Hmm?" I tried to act like I had no idea what he was talking about, but after the last couple of months, we kind of got to know each other, so of course, he looked right through me. He let it go, for now, though, nodding to the bartender when he placed two fresh drinks in front of us.

"So," I continued, avoiding his eyes and brushing my fingertips over the stone from my new necklace. "I wanted to thank you for this week."

Charlie put two fingers under my chin, lifting my face to look at him. "It was my pleasure."

Without thinking, I leaned forward, softly placing my lips on his and moving one of my hands to his face, cupping his jaw as he kissed me back.

A comfortable silence surrounded us before we flowed back into light conversation, ordering drink after drink until we were both heavily intoxicated. I didn't quite remember how many drinks it took, but not nearly as many as I would've liked.

"Babe..." I cooed, leaning on Charlie and caressing his thighs. Ok, *maybe* I was a bit drunker than Charlie.

"Yes, Baby?" he replied, looking at me with hooded eyes.

"I wanna go."

Slipping off my barstool, I stumbled forward and almost fell to the floor, but Charlie grabbed me just in time. I could smell the whiskey on his breath, but something about it made him even more desirable.

"Ok, let's go." He chuckled, finishing his drink and standing up. He looked pretty sober, but the way he lightly swayed from one foot to the other told me otherwise.

"I want to do the sex!" I exclaimed, tugging at the hem of my dress, and a couple of people turned their heads in our direction. I was too drunk to care and walked up to Charlie to place my hands around his waist, sliding them down to his ass.

"Alright," Charlie mumbled before he grabbed me by the waist and threw me over his shoulder.

I giggled as we swayed to the elevator, not a single part of me worried that he'd drop me even though he had as much to drink as I did, if not more.

"You're insatiable, Baby." He patted me on the ass before walking into the lift, pressing the button for our floor.

"Don't pre—pretend that you don't like it."

Once we made it to our hotel room—*which turned out to be more difficult than we remembered*—Charlie threw me on the bed. I propped myself up on my elbows, running my tongue over my bottom lip as he stood at the foot of the bed, watching me with equal desire.

"You like what you see?" he asked, fumbling with his belt as he tried to stay on his feet.

"I'd like it better when—if you're not wearing clothes," I slurred, the world spinning around me but my mind set on only one thing.

"Ok." He roughly pulled his shirt out of his pants after another failed attempt to undo his slacks and dropped it on the floor. I loved it when he was being messy, and I guess getting him drunk was the way to get him there.

"Let me." I crawled up to him and grabbed his belt, almost falling over as I took off his pants and briefs.

He pushed me back on the bed and I tried to take off my dress, but honestly, I just couldn't be bothered. "Charlie," I whined, pouting at him.

"Right, hold on," he crawled on top of me, grabbing the fabric with both hands and tugging it up. "Can you hold your butt in?"

I chuckled, letting myself fall back like a rag doll, my limbs feeling heavy. "*Hold my butt in.*" I laughed, placing an arm over my face, the skin hot under my touch.

"Can we try this?" I lifted my arms in the air and waited for him to catch onto my idea. He grabbed my dress and tried to roll the fabric up, but to no avail.

"How did you get this on? It's so tight." He jerked the dress harder up, but it was no use.

How *did* I get the dress on?

"Oh!" I exclaimed, rolling onto my stomach. "Try the zipper."

Once we finally managed to get each other naked, we fell onto the bed, dozing off to sleep.

—

"Baby?"

I groaned, opening my eyes ever so slightly—my head pounding.

"What?" I moaned, turning to face Charlie who was poking me in the back. It was exceptionally annoying since I was super hungover.

"Do you still want to have sex?" he asked with closed eyes, his face half-buried into his pillow. *I feel like shit.*

"Part of me does," I admitted, flinching as I sat up and rubbed my eyes. I looked down, noticing that we were both still naked, laying on top of the covers.

"What time do we need to be at the airport?" I asked, swinging my legs over the edge of the bed and thinking about the pros and cons of a little sex session.

"Four."

Rolling my lower lip between my teeth, I decided that an orgasm never hurt anybody. Maybe I could even let him do all the work. And maybe it would even aid my hangover. "Hmm, we can do some shower stuff."

At that, Charlie was suddenly wide awake, quickly turning to jump out of the bed. "Let's go, Baby. We're on the clock."

Rolling my eyes, I quickly downed a glass of water with some painkillers, grabbing clean underwear before following him into the bathroom. He had already turned on the shower, the glass door fogging up and getting ready for my handprints.

Images started to shoot through my head, and I felt my arousal between my legs growing, begging me for some release. *Hungover, but still in the mood for sex. This was a new one for me.*

I squealed when Charlie pulled me under the water, my hair immediately soaked and sticking to my skin.

"What about number sixty-two?" he suggested and I raised my brows. I was constantly surprised by how well he knew the list by heart. Was it something he recited before bed, or...

"Super loud sex," he continued, filling in the blank I drew. Honestly, the sex was the best when you could completely let go of yourself, so why the hell not.

"Alright—ah!"

Charlie pressed himself against me, his rock-hard length pushing into my stomach and his fingers creeping between my legs.

"How'd you want to do this?" he asked and I moaned loudly as he rubbed my clit, my fingers digging into his biceps. It had become nearly impossible for me to answer at that point.

"I don't care," I managed to breathe out, and he swiftly turned me around, bending me against the glass.

I closed my eyes, my legs already shaking in anticipation before I gasped when he entered me.

"Let me hear you, Jordan."

He didn't have to tell me twice. I completely lost myself in him and the moment, the hot water mixed with the pleasure that shot through me making my cheeks flush.

"Yes!" I moaned, my heart pounding against Charlie's hand

as his fingers wrapped around my throat, making me arch my back even further. The angle caused him to hit the perfect spot deep inside me in the best way, and it didn't take long for me to feel my orgasm coming.

"Charlie!"

"Fuck, Baby," he groaned, tightening his hand around my throat.

The both of us came undone at roughly the same time, our headaches completely forgotten as we attempted to catch our breath. As I continued to bathe in the state of bliss Charlie had brought me in, I thought about the fact that we would be back in the states tomorrow. *And how I wished we could stay here forever.*

—

With only one month to go until her wedding, Ashley had frowned when I asked her to come to game night with my dad. Yet here we were. At the dinner table in the small home filled with both happy and unhappy memories.

"It's so good to see you, Ashley," Dad said, shuffling the deck of cards like a true croupier, something he never forgot how to do ever since he worked at a casino when he was younger.

"Likewise, Mr. Sawyer," Ashley replied, sipping the cheap rosé like it was her favorite drink.

"Please, call me Mark," Dad replied, gathering the cards in a perfect stack, ready to deal.

"Never." She smiled.

We all chuckled softly, and I took the cards Dad handed me, checking out my chances. *I hate Blackjack.*

Thank God that Eliza put the cards away after a couple of rounds, ignoring my dad's pout. "So, Ashley," she said, pouring us another glass of wine. "How are the preparations for the wedding going?"

I expected Ashley to sigh, but for the first time in months, she beamed with happiness. "We have everything ordered and planned, including *correct* invitations." She gave me a quick look.

"Yes, they turned out very pretty," Eliza replied, grabbing the card from the edge of the table.

"We're afraid we won't be able to go, though," Dad added, and I cocked my head to the side.

"Why not?" *And why didn't he tell me?*

He took a deep breath, grabbing Eliza's free hand, and I suddenly got very uncomfortable. "We wanted to tell you another time, but—"

"What?" I interrupted him, my heart beating loudly in my chest. *Did someone die? Lose their job? Got sick?*

"They found a lump in my mother's breast," Eliza choked out, digging her teeth into her lower lip to hold in her tears.

"I'm so sorry!" Ashley exclaimed, jumping from her seat and rounding the table to give her a hug. I did the same, wrapping my arms around both women.

Though Eliza's mother was already over eighty, it was still her mom. And I knew all too well what it was like to miss a parent.

"Thank you, girls," Eliza said as Ashley and I returned to our seats.

"Yes, so that week the doctor's determining how bad it is, but based on her scans we fear the worst," Dad continued, rubbing Eliza's back. "That's why we want to be near her around that time."

I nodded, my eyes on my wine as I swirled it around in my glass. "I'll pay her a visit when I get back."

"That's sweet of you, darling." Eliza gave me a watery smile before she changed the subject, clearly desperate to talk about something happier. "Anyway, are you going to have the rehearsal dinner on location?"

Ashley hesitated to answer, but a nod from Eliza encouraged her to respond. "Yes, we have the hotel for the weekend."

"Can I have a room as far away from yours as possible? I don't want you guys keeping me up all night." I asked.

Ashley laughed, acknowledging that she could be really loud during sex, and nodded. "I'll make sure to keep that in mind."

"I don't get it," Dad said, looking from Ash to me. I pressed my lips together trying to hide my grin, and I quickly took a sip of my drink instead.

"Maybe it's better that you don't." Eliza placed a hand on his arm.

All of us jumped slightly in our seats when Ashley's phone rang loudly, her volume once again as high as possible. "Oh, it's my brother, Charlie," she noted, grabbing the device and standing to leave the room. *Why was my stomach reacting so weird at the mention of his name?*

I tried not to listen as she picked up, and after a questioning look from my father, I quickly took another couple of gulps of wine to distract myself.

"Everything ok?" I casually asked when she sat back down beside me.

"Yeah, he just wanted to tell me that we're having dinner at my parents' tomorrow." She rolled her eyes, placing her phone facedown on the table and grabbing her drink.

She continued to tell us more and more about the wedding, and as the evening progressed, I was able to push Charlie to the back of my mind. Because we had been drinking, Ashley and I had prepared to stay the night, sharing the bed in the guest room my dad had created when I moved out. We listened to the rain as we lay under the covers, staring out of the small window.

"Jordan," Ashley started, propping up on her elbow to see me, the light of the moon shining on her face.

"Hmm," I hummed in response, absentmindedly running my fingers over the stone around my neck. I was nervous about her tone, but I tried to stay calm.

"Do you..." she hesitated, her eyes momentarily moving to my fingers. "Are we still best friends?"

I quickly sat up, my heart aching. Realization suddenly hit me, and I swallowed the lump in my throat. Ashley was far from insecure, and the fact that she was about our friendship, crushed me.

"Of course. Why do you ask?" I replied, grabbing her hand laying on the sheets between us, and giving it a little squeeze.

"I just feel like,"—she took a deep breath—"like you don't tell me everything anymore."

I chewed on the inside of my cheek, thinking about her brother and everything that had been going on. Of course, I wanted to tell her. I wanted to share this with her.

But I also didn't want to hurt her. Was I hurting her more by not telling her?

"I'm sorry," I choked out, pulling her against me. "I never meant to make you feel this way." She nodded against my chest, but I was going to dig my hole deeper. "I think maybe my new job has taken a toll on me."

Closing my eyes for a second, I felt physically sick for lying to her, but I didn't want to put our friendship in jeopardy. Or end whatever Charlie and I had going on. I felt like I was trapped in my own lies and it was terrifying.

"I'm so proud of you," she softly mumbled, and I smiled weakly. *I am so selfish.*

"Thank you, Ash. I love you."

"I've been wondering something all night though." She lifted herself, pointing at my necklace. "Where did you get this?"

Shit.

"I—" The words got stuck in my throat, even though I didn't even know what words I was searching for.

"Is that a hard question?" Ashley pressed, raising her brows and curling her mouth into a small grin.

"I saw it at an antique shop, after work." Was there such a shop near my office? *No.* But would she know?

"It looks really nice, how much did you pay for it?"

"Twenty dollars."

My heart almost skipped a beat when she frowned. "I bet it's worth a lot more. You got a good deal, Jo."

I chuckled nervously, turning to look at the ceiling. Thinking about my arrangement with Charlie, I wondered, *did* I get a good deal?

—

Logging off my computer, I still couldn't shake that terrible feeling from yesterday after my conversation with Ashley. I was totally letting her down, and the worst part was, it was completely my own fault.

After I said goodbye to Mr. Grimaldi, I took the elevator down, my eyes immediately going to the front desk when the doors rolled open. "Hey, Jordan!" Nadine exclaimed, packing her bag.

"Hi," I replied, walking over and leaning on the counter.

"How was your trip?" she asked in a low voice, bringing her face closer to mine. I chuckled softly at her attempt at secrecy.

"I wanted to talk to you about it yesterday, but you weren't here?"

She blushed, and the smile that spread over her lips almost didn't fit on her face before she answered. "I had a date."

"Oh?" I wiggled my brows, waiting for her to continue.

"Well, he was only in town for a day, before he had to go back to Sweden."

"Go on."

"Maybe it wasn't a date, but I hadn't seen him in years and—"

"Who's this mystery man?" I interrupted her, curiously following her to the door. she avoided my eyes, closing her coat and hoisting the strap of her bag higher up her shoulder.

"A friend," she answered, biting her lower lip. "Who I dated in high school."

There it is.

"Do you...still have feelings for him?"

Her face fell and I regretted the question as soon as it left my lips. *What's it with me and making my friends sad?*

"I don't know..."

"Have you ever been in love?" I walked with her to the parking lot, waiting by her car for a second to finish our conversation.

"I think so. At least I think that's what I feel—*felt*, for Mikael is—*was*, love. Shit."

"I think it's obvious what's going on here," I teased, nudging her arm with my elbow. She looked up at me, shrugging.

"It doesn't matter anyway." She sighed, grabbing her keys from her bag. "There are five thousand miles between us."

I watched her open her car, and I turned to leave, but one more question popped into my head. "Ever thought of moving back home?"

She looked at me with a stoic expression, a sign that I had caught her off guard. The usual bubbly and optimistic Nadine seemed gone for a minute as she thought about her response. "I never..."

"Maybe you should," I interrupted her.

Begging that I didn't come off as rude—like I wanted to get rid of her—I walked to my car, leaving Nadine alone with her thoughts. It was clear to me that she was in love with this Mikael, and here, she only had a few flings since her relationship ended, so why *wasn't* she thinking about trying things back home? *If you love someone, you have to go for it, right?*

My train of thought was rudely interrupted by the ringing of my phone, and I almost dropped my keys. *Who the fuck...?*

My annoyance disappeared into thin air when I saw Charlie's name, and I picked up. "Hey."

"Can you come over?" he asked and I ignored the butterflies in my stomach.

"Why?" I said, already sitting down behind the wheel with the intention of driving to his place.

"I just need to see you."

CHAPTER 26
Charlie

"Ready to go?" Ryan asked when he appeared in my office at exactly five o'clock. Ever since he had been with my sister he never failed to be on time.

"Do I look like I'm ready?" I retorted, gesturing to the open files scattered in front of me. He rolled his eyes and sunk into one of the chairs, looking around my office as I cleared my desk.

"Where'd you want to—"

My phone interrupted, loudly ringing and vibrating against my desk. Sighing when I saw that it was my mother, I picked up the device and sat back down. "Hey, Mom."

"Hey, honey," she replied sweetly, instantly making me suspicious of this conversation. I raised my brows at Ryan, who looked back at me with a frown before he grabbed my half-empty glass of liquor and took a sip. I rolled my eyes at him, sitting back in my chair.

"I'm about to head out. What's up?" I replied, playing with a pen on my desk.

"Your father and I wanted to have dinner with you and your sister together, and this time, you can't get out of it." *Of course, she caught on.* "You've been avoiding us for weeks, but we really need you here tomorrow."

It was true. I *was* avoiding them. These last couple of weeks, I'd seen their true colors, and they weren't pretty. Sure, they were rich and really loved showing that off, but I never expected them to treat another person as awful as they did Jordan.

"Fine." I let out a harsh breath, realizing that she was probably bringing dinner to me if I didn't go to her.

"Can you call your sister to let her know?"

Refraining from rolling my eyes, I quickly answered. "Sure. Bye, Mom."

She tried to keep the conversation going, but I ended the call.

"Everything ok?" Ryan asked, following me out of the office.

"Yes, remind me to call Ash later tonight."

We made our way to our regular bar—something we hadn't done in ages—and walked straight to one of the window tables. Though we parted ways after Stanford, we always stayed in touch, and even when he started dating my sister, I still saw him as one of my best friends.

"Charlie," Ryan started after we received our drinks, sitting back in his chair. "Don't you think it's time for you to find someone to share your life with?"

I frowned at his question, especially because I never imagined *fuck-boy-Ryan* to ask it. He had been notorious for sleeping with everything that moved in college, and only when he met my sister, did he change his ways.

"Why?"

He took a sip before shrugging. "You're getting old, man." *Dick*.

I chuckled, crumpling a napkin into a ball and throwing it at him. "I hear the ladies like older men," I retorted, crossing my arms. *Did Jordan—*

"Whatever helps you sleep at night, buddy."

—

Sitting in my car in front of my childhood home the next day, I stalled, thinking of ways to avoid going inside. *What was I even expecting from this dinner?*

It wasn't normal to eat with just the four of us, especially after Ashley started dating Ryan, and the fact that we were tonight, did nothing for the uneasy feeling in my stomach. I just wanted to go home to—

Checking my watch one last time, I finally stepped out of my car, walking into the house. "There you are," Mom huffed when I entered the dining room, food already on the table.

"Nice to see you too, Mom," I replied sarcastically, taking a seat next to Ashley. She looked just as anxious, if not more.

"What's this all about?" she asked before Mom could say anything else.

"Well, I'll just get straight to the point," Dad began, sitting back in his chair. "It's been a couple of months since you've been back, Charles, and the board and I have been talking."

My interest was officially piqued as I shared a look with Ashley, the both of us starting to get excited—a feeling opposite of the one I expected to have.

"Now, despite your little...mistake," Dad continued, and I couldn't help but smile at the memory. "We've decided to move forward with the preparations for you to take my place."

Finally.

Ashley squealed, grabbing my bicep with force and shaking me around. I chuckled, turning back to my parents. "You won't regret this, Dad."

He nodded softly, diving into his plate of food before Mom shifted her attention to my sister. "Ashley, darling," she said, folding her hands together and resting her elbows on the table. "We've been talking about your position in the company, too."

"You have?" Ashley beamed, eager to hear more. She was a very hard worker, and if I wasn't perfect for the position of CEO myself, she would be the one to take over from Dad for sure.

"Yes, and your hard work has not gone unnoticed. We've been looking into appointing you as CFO."

My eyes widened, and I did the same to Ashley, grabbing her arm and shaking her around. She didn't say anything, probably still a little shocked by the announcement—something neither of us saw coming. I looked back at my mother when she spoke again.

"We do have something to add," Mom added, and Ashley frowned, waiting for her to continue. "With the position comes a lot of responsibility, and you'll be even more in the spotlight than you already are."

I let out a frustrated sigh when I started to suspect where

she was going with this, affirming the reasons I didn't want to be here in the first place.

Dad shot me a look, but Mom ignored it.

"Sure," Ashley replied, oblivious to what Mom was implying. "Anything."

"In order for you to get taken seriously, you'll have to be more careful with the company you keep," Dad added, and the lightbulb above Ashley's head flicked on.

"Excuse me?" she exclaimed, jumping from her seat and pushing her chair over in the process. The piece of furniture clattered on the floor, and it was the only sound in the room as my sister shot daggers at our parents.

"Ashley!" Dad scolded, but she didn't even flinch.

"You want me to cut Jordan off, don't you?" she continued, her face turning a little red.

"Cut off, that's not—"

"What the fuck do you guys have against my best friend? You've known her for over six years!"

I felt scared for my parents, Ashley's blood undoubtedly boiling as she was close to breathing fire.

"She's not a good influence. With her run-down apartment and tattoos. Don't think we haven't noticed that you've been talking back more since you've met the girl," Dad added, the calmth of his voice making my face pale.

I balled my hands into fists, trying to stop myself from doing something I would regret.

"I'm not a child anymore, Dad. And you know what," Ashley grabbed her phone from the table, turning to leave. "Talk to me when you've apologized to Jordan and come to terms with our friendship because she is not leaving anytime soon."

She stormed out of the room, slamming the front door on her way out. Mom scoffed as she sat back in her seat, her eyes looking in the direction Ashley had disappeared in.

"Are you going to ask me to stay away from my friends as well?" I hissed, desperately trying not to give them the wrong impression.

"No. I'm happy you don't associate with women like her," Mom sneered and I snapped, not bothered by my reputation or about what they would think after all. Putting them in their place was long overdue, family or not.

"What the fuck is wrong with you?"

Getting me angry was not an easy task, but my parents finally managed to get under my skin.

"Charles!" Dad warned, but I stood from my seat, almost kicking my chair over like Ash did a minute ago.

"Jordan has done nothing but be polite, despite the rude and disrespectful way you've been treating her."

I ignored my mother as she narrowed her eyes on me, finally speaking up about what had been on my mind for weeks.

"I'm with Ashley on this one." I shook my head, walking out of the house with confident strides, my heart rate still uncomfortably fast. I knew this *family dinner* was going to be a disaster.

It was still quite early in the evening, and after pacing around my living room for half an hour, I picked up my phone to call Jordan. I had argued the decision in my mind for a while, but sometimes you just had to trust your gut.

"Hey." I felt myself instantly calm down when I heard her voice, ignoring the confusing feelings that surfaced.

"Can you come over?" I asked, pacing again.

"Why?"

I hesitated before answering but decided to just tell her. "I just need to see you."

Closing my eyes as I waited for her to respond, I almost slapped myself in the face for how stupid I was acting. Why was I so Goddamn nervous?

"I'll be there in twenty minutes."

Quickly hanging up the phone, I made my way to the kitchen and rummaged through the cupboards to find something edible. Cooking was not my thing, but it couldn't hurt to try. *Right?*

I managed to find a couple of things for a plate of pasta and had dinner ready when the elevator doors rolled open.

"Hi." She smiled when she walked in, all dressed up in her work clothes.

She shrieked softly as I pulled her against me, cupping her face in my hands and brushing my lips against hers. "Everything ok?" she asked, softly pushing against my chest and looking up at me.

"Hmm," I hummed, walking to the kitchen and grabbing two plates.

"You...cooked?"

"Don't be so surprised, Baby," I smirked, plating the food and placing it in front of her.

She looked at the pasta with raised brows, slowly grabbing her fork. "We'll see."

I watched her take a bite, nervously rubbing the back of my

neck when she tried to keep her poker face—but failed.

"Not good?"

She smiled painfully, and I dropped my head. "You can go spit it out."

I chuckled when she did just that, downing a glass of water right after. "How much salt did you use?" she choked out, filling up another glass.

I looked at my plate, pricking a piece of pasta with my fork and bringing it to my lips. "I...don't know."

Clearly too much.

Quickly taking a sip of my drink, I grabbed both our plates and trashed the food, noticing that Jordan had already taken out her phone and was looking up what to order.

I sighed when I sat back down, running a hand through my hair.

"What?" Jordan questioned, placing her phone on the table.

"Nothing," I replied, looking anywhere but at her.

"Charlie?"

I rolled my eyes, crossing my arms. "Fine, I just wanted to make you dinner." She cocked her head to the side, smiling sweetly, and I scoffed. "It's not what you think."

"Weren't you supposed to have a family dinner?" she asked, and I rolled my bottom lip between my teeth, thinking about my answer. Was I going to tell her the truth? Did I want to?

"We...got into a fight," I admitted, leaving out the subject of said fight. I wasn't going to make her feel miserable like my parents liked to do.

"Oh, I'm sorry," Jordan comforted, grabbing her phone again. "Do you want to talk about it?"

Talk about it...

"No, it's fine, let's order some proper dinner."

We ended up getting McDonald's again, and I finally admitted that I, too, preferred it over sushi. Of course, she was pleased with that, but I honestly just enjoyed being the reason she had a smile on her face.

"What are you grinning at?" she asked, stuffing more fries into her mouth.

"Nothing."

I continued to look at her like a creep as she shamelessly devoured her dinner.

CHAPTER 27
Jordan

"What are you doing tonight?" Nadine asked, playing with a strand of her platinum blond hair while turning her computer off.

"I'm...I—" How was I subtly going to tell her that I had planned a movie night with Charlie?

"You can say it."

"Did you just read my mind?" I questioned, still waiting for her to pack her bag. She chuckled, finally standing from her chair.

"I wanted to go out tonight, but I guess you have other plans." She gave me a wink, swinging her purse over her shoulder and rounding the front desk.

"We're just having a movie night," I admitted, avoiding her eyes. She wiggled her brows but didn't say anything, though I knew what she wanted to say based on her expression.

"Did you tell Ashley yet?" she asked, and I sighed. I'd been thinking a lot about telling her lately, especially because I usually shared everything with her.

"No, I guess I'm scared."

Nadine hummed understandingly, beckoning for us to leave. "You got time for one drink?"

I checked my phone, deciding that being half an hour late couldn't hurt. "*One*."

We went to the overpriced bar next door, sticking to the cheapest white wine, and continued our conversation. *Or, Nadine did.*

"Jordan, I'm going to be honest with you," she said, smiling at the waiter when he placed our drinks on our table. "I think you're head over heels in love with him."

I choked on my sip, quickly setting the glass back down before wiping my face. "What? No." I scoffed, looking at my friend with a frown.

"Jordan."

"I'm not in love." She cocked her brow at me. "Can we talk about something else?"

She ignored my question. "*Have* you ever been in love before?"

I stayed quiet for a minute, studying my wine. Honestly, I had no idea. Maybe I had been with Eli, or maybe not. I had no idea what love felt like at this point.

"I think so," I replied, looking up at my blonde friend.

She nodded. "What happened with you and your ex?

The... Eli guy."

"Nothing much." I sighed. It was true, and maybe that had been the problem. "At one point we just decided it was better to split up. He couldn't give me what I wanted and I was tired of asking for it, I think."

"Hmm. Well, good riddance."

I smiled at Nadine, taking another sip from my wine before chuckling awkwardly. "Let's change the subject."

"Sure. Oh! I heard from Brian that Jessy heard from Kells that Harry, you know, from HR," she rambled, already losing me at Brian. "Allegedly, he asked Gail out, but she turned him down because she's obviously screwing her boss' husband."

"Eh..." I trailed off, but she just told me more and more rumors she'd heard today, in and out of the office.

I really enjoyed having drinks—or, having *a* drink—with her after work, and we decided to try and do it every Friday instead of hanging around with the other colleagues after work, who we honestly didn't like. *Except for Oscar.*

"Well, I'll see you on Monday," she said when we exited the bar, shooting me a wink before we parted ways in the company parking lot.

"See you Monday!"

—

"Hey, babe," I called out when I entered Charlie's apartment, going straight to the kitchen to get dinner ready. It had become somewhat of a routine, especially because Charlie couldn't cook to save his life.

I jumped when *Ian* appeared before me, smirking as he leaned on the kitchen counter. "Hey, babe."

"Yeah, he was just leaving," Charlie said as he walked up to me, giving me a quick kiss on the forehead.

"I was. No part of me wants to see what you two are up to at night," Ian retorted, grabbing his keys from the counter.

"Just at night? You underestimate me, Ian," I replied, pouring myself a drink and unpacking the groceries I had gotten.

He rolled his eyes, turning to leave. "You two are perfect for each other."

When he was gone, Charlie put on some music as I cooked, and we ate dinner on the couch. I wasn't a great cook either, but it was decent, and Charlie seemed to enjoy it, so that was good enough for me.

"I'm going to take a quick shower," I said when we were done, and I walked to the bathroom.

He nodded, keeping his eyes on his phone screen. "Half an hour?"

"Hmm." I closed the door to his bedroom behind me, stripped, and walked into the bathroom.

I washed with Charlie's body wash, even though he had offered to buy me my own to keep at his place. Rinsing it off, I just stood there under the hot water. With closed eyes, I leaned back under the stream, letting the water bounce from shoulder to shoulder, until it suddenly went dark.

My eyes shot open when I realized we probably lost power, and I blinked to get used to the night, the small window in the bathroom just giving enough light to make me see some shadows.

"What the hell?" I mumbled, tapping the counter for my towel. I dried myself off and wrapped it around me, walking into the bedroom in search of clean underwear from my bag. The large windows allowed more moonlight into the room, and I put on my panties, almost tripping in the process before I pulled the elastic from my hair. *So much for movie night.*

Irritated by the lack of electricity in the house, I grabbed a shirt from Charlie, and buttoned it halfway up, before I walked out of the room.

"Char—" The words got stuck in my throat when I noticed the living room was bathing in candlelight, numerous tea lights littering almost every surface. My eyes traveled to Charlie, who was checking the battery on a small speaker, turning when the soft music began to play.

He smiled, placing the speaker on the TV cabinet and walking up to me.

"Wha—" Once again, I was unable to finish my sentence, but this time because of a finger that Charlie softly pressed against my lips.

The air felt thick with something I couldn't place, and I blushed, avoiding his eyes as he tucked a strand of hair behind my ear.

His thumb brushed over my jaw until he reached my chin, and he slowly tilted my face up. My heart beat frantically in my chest as he slowly brought his lips to mine, gently kissing me. Letting my hand slide to the back of his neck, I caressed his short hair and pulled him closer.

We parted our lips in sync, deepening the kiss and getting further lost in each other.

No words were spoken or needed as he led me to the couch, sitting down in front of me and sliding his hands up the back of my legs to my thong. I kept my palms on his face and he continued to look at me as he slid it off, before he guided me onto his lap.

My breathing was uneven, but I noticed that Charlie's was too, proving that we were both a little overwhelmed by the moment.

Everything was slow, yet perfectly timed, as we tenderly undressed each other. The energy between us was different, both unable to look away, or stop. *And I didn't want to.*

I let myself drown in his eyes, resting my forehead against his as I slowly lifted, and he lined himself up with my entrance. A soft moan escaped my lips when I sunk onto him, taking my time to adjust before moving up and down.

Somehow, I needed him closer. Closer than humanly possible. It almost physically hurt when we weren't together.

I was finally able to place this feeling I had but had no idea what it meant.

His hands moved over my back and I leaned forward, capturing his lips for another kiss and deepening the connection that I craved. He handled me with care, unlike all the other times we'd had sex, and this time, it felt right. Like this was how it was supposed to be.

It was a scary feeling.

"Charlie..." I breathed out, closing my eyes as I moved quicker, rolling my hips onto his.

He just hummed, using his hands to guide me up and down his length.

Noses touching, breaths hitching, we came closer and closer to our release, something that meant so much more at that moment than ever before. I was almost scared to look back into Charlie's eyes, seeing the opposite of what I was feeling, but instead, I felt at ease. Comfortable.

"Oh, Baby," he groaned, his fingers digging into my skin, and my walls tightened around him, pushing both of us over the edge.

My toes curled as bolts of pleasure shot through me, mixed with something else. Something I was terrified of.

At that moment I knew. I knew what I had been feeling for all these weeks. How I felt empty and alone without him near me. Or how warmth spread throughout me as he laughed.

I knew and so did Nadine. She was right.

I am in love with Charlie Abbot.

CHAPTER 28
Jordan

For three weeks, I had been keeping my thoughts and feelings to myself. Something I was used to doing, but this time, it took more of me than expected. I had come to the conclusion that all I wanted was to be around Charlie. But at the same time, I didn't.

Fear of uttering the words that had been swirling in my head caused me to avoid him at times, and I had reached the point where I just didn't know what to do anymore. *Do I tell him? But what if he doesn't feel the same way about me?*

"Jo?"

I looked up when Nadine snapped her fingers in front of my face, bringing me back to reality.

"Sorry, what?"

"We're here," she said, paying the driver of the cab and opening her door. I nodded, following her onto the street and sighing at the company building I thought I'd left for the weekend.

"Why are we going to the party again?" I asked, taking in the decorated hall as we walked in.

She abruptly turned and stared at me with her brows furrowed. "Because, *Jordan*," she replied, crossing her arms. "It's Christmas."

I rolled my eyes. "Why is everybody so in love with Christmas?"

"I'll just ignore that. Come on."

She pulled me further into the building, almost making me trip on the black, floor-length dress that I was wearing. I had decided to put my hair up as I did for the gala with the Abbots, and my makeup wasn't more than winged eyeliner and a red lip, but it was all I could do, to be honest.

The foyer of the building was decorated with hundreds of Christmas lights, and tasteful music was playing in the background as numerous waiters in suits carried trays of drinks around. The front desk was turned into a makeshift bar, and I couldn't help but smile at Mr. Grimaldi as he casually swirled the candy cane in his drink.

"Let's find Oscar," Nadine suggested and we each grabbed a glass of bubbly. I was definitely going to need all the alcohol I could get tonight.

"How long are we planning on staying here?" I whispered, holding up my hands in defeat when she scowled at me and almost spilling my drink on one of my colleagues from the marketing department.

I kept my head down as we weaved through the crowd, something Nadine was obviously better at than me. After a few apologies for bumping into people, we finally found Oscar.

"Hey, girls," he greeted as we joined him at the high-top table he was standing at.

"Thank God," I breathed out, downing my drink and grabbing a new one from a passing waiter.

"Are you okay?" He chuckled, raising a brow.

"Parties like this aren't really my scene." I quickly shook the memory of the last gala out of my head.

"Well, who is this?" Nadine chirped, holding out her hand to the gentleman that had one arm wrapped around Oscar.

"This is Gabe, my husband," Oscar introduced us, and Nadine and I both shook his hand. "Babe, these are a couple of my favorite coworkers, Jordan and Nadine."

"Nice to meet you," the tall brunette replied, giving the both of us a bright smile.

"I didn't know you were married?" Nadine questioned, leaning on the table.

"You never asked. And besides," Oscar held out his hand, showing a sparkling gold band. "You could've just paid attention."

I chuckled, playfully tapping Nadine on the shoulder.

"Ah, I guess...I guess you're right."

"So, what I'm getting from this is that you never talk about me?" Gabe retorted, cocking a brow. We watched Oscar squirm under his husband's gaze, seeing that he had found his match.

"I...do," he hesitated, smiling sweetly at Gabe, and Nadine and I chuckled softly.

"Jordan?" I suddenly heard behind me, and I turned, seeing a man with big brown eyes walk up to me.

"Yes?"

He stopped before me, waiting for me to recognize him, but I really had no idea. Yes, he looked familiar, but that was about it.

"Blake," he finally said after a couple of seconds, and I racked my brain. "Charlie's friend." *There it is.*

"Oh! I'm so sorry!" I exclaimed, shaking his hand.

"No worries." He chuckled, joining me at the table. "It's been a while since we saw each other."

I had a hard time coming up with something to say since we barely knew each other. I had seen him on one occasion, and at the time, there was only one man on my mind. Maybe there still was...

"Yes."

Luckily for me, he was all too eager to keep the conversation going. "How's everything between you and Charlie?"

I sucked my lower lip between my teeth, the question way more loaded than it should've felt. How *were* things between me and Charlie?

I still hadn't told him about my true feelings, or the desire to 'make it official.' Yes, we weren't sleeping with anyone else, but I wanted more. I wanted to show the world that we belonged together. Show him off everywhere I went, and just be able to touch him in public without creating a scandal or becoming front-page news.

All that, and I wanted to be seen as more than just *another girl he fucked*.

"Jordan?"

I straightened up when Blake refocused my confused

thoughts—something a lot of people had to do lately.

"I'm sorry," I replied, taking a quick sip of my drink. "Charlie and I aren't together."

Was the slight pain I felt in my heart part of this whole love thing now?

I thought I was in love when I was with Eli. Shit, I thought he was the love of my life. But the more I let these feelings in, let them guide me, I started to understand that what Eli and I had wasn't necessarily love. *Maybe I was heartbroken when he left because I didn't want to be alone?*

"Are you sure?" Blake questioned with a slight raise of his brows.

"I..." *Secret, Jordan. Secret.* "Yes, I'm sure."

"If you say so." He shrugged, smiling sweetly and taking a step into my personal space. I got a feeling about what he was trying, the same as the first time we met, but I needed him to know I wasn't interested.

"What are you doing here?" I asked, taking a step back. He leaned on the table—*luckily taking the hint*—and looked around for someone. "A friend of mine works here, and he asked me to come with him."

I hummed, shifting my weight from one leg to the other, trying to stretch my foot in the painful shoe.

"Who's your friend?" Nadine joined my side, looking Blake up and down.

"This is Blake, a friend of Charlie's," I replied, lowering my voice as the words left my lips.

"Oh, he knows! I have a question then," she went on, and I tried to elbow her in the side, but I missed as she leaned in to shake his hand.

"Shoot."

"Did Charlie change at all, since he started seeing Jordan?"

I flinched, closing my eyes for a second before I dared to look Blake back in the eye. "So there *is* something going on," he smirked, nodding softly.

"No, she—" I tried to talk my way out of it, but the damage had been done.

"Jordan is dating someone?" Oscar asked, both him and his husband now looking at me.

"I'm not—"

"Ever heard of Charlie Abbot?" Blake said, turning to the couple, even though they weren't introduced to each other yet.

"Hell yeah, he's..." Oscar started, but Gabe raised a brow at him. "He's....rich."

"Nice save, dude," I mentioned before making another attempt to clear the air. "Guys, I'm not dating Charlie Abbot."

All four of them stared at me, and it was obvious that they didn't believe me, but I ignored it, grabbing a new drink.

How long was I going to be able to keep up this lie? We weren't officially together, no. But I knew that I wanted us to be, and we were spending a lot of time together, so it would be easy for people to assume that we were.

"Look." I pointed to the corner of the hall, changing the subject.

"Is that..." Nadine narrowed her eyes at two people that were sneaking off before she grinned at the scene.

"Yep," Oscar confirmed, rolling his eyes. "She really needs to learn to be more discreet. Her boss is right there."

I moved my eyes to the right, noticing Mrs. Hearst, the always well-dressed COO, talking with some colleagues.

"Do you think she knows her husband is cheating on her?" Nadine asked, turning back to the table when Gail and Mr. Hearst disappeared down the hall towards the restrooms.

"I think so," I replied. "She's incredibly smart."

Would Charlie—

"I'm sorry for Mrs. Hearst, but I really want to see Gail get fired, though," Nadine continued before downing her glass.

I chuckled, nodding in agreement.

—

I managed to avoid the topic of Charlie for the rest of the night. We stayed longer than expected, really enjoying the open bar and drunk higher-ups. Around midnight, Nadine and I stumbled out of the building, giggling about...*who the fuck knows.*

"But, Jordan," she slurred, stepping into the cab that had appeared in front of us.

"Hmm?"

"How long are you going to deny your feelings?"

I stepped in behind her, greeting the driver and putting on my seatbelt before I answered. "I'm not denying them anymore. You were right."

Nadine squealed, playfully slapping me on my thigh. "I knew it!"

"But," I added, making sure I had her attention before I continued. "I don't know if he feels the same."

She scoffed. "Of course he does."

I ignored the butterflies that fluttered in my stomach when she said that, contemplating getting it over with and just calling him. *No! No drunk calling people!*

"Ok, but it's still supposed to be a secret," I continued, attempting to cross my legs without kicking the driver in the back. "Especially because I haven't told Ashley yet."

"What?" Nadine exclaimed, making said driver jump and yank the wheel to the right.

"Miss!" he scolded, and she pressed her lips together, blood rushing to her cheeks.

"Sorry, sir."

"I know," I replied, rubbing my hands together.

Telling Ashley made me more nervous than telling Charlie, and based on his history and our agreement, that was saying something. Nadine responded by placing a comforting hand on mine, not saying anything else. I smiled at her before I turned to the window, watching the dark city flash by.

"Text me when you get home," I stated as we pulled up in front of my apartment building, and I handed her some money for the cab.

"Only if you text me when you get inside," Nadine shot back, mockingly.

I chuckled, saying goodbye to the driver and closing the door of the car behind me, giving them a little wave as they drove off.

It was a cold night, so I wrapped my coat tighter around me, quickly making my way inside. Only when I closed the door to the foyer of the building, was I able to let out a breath. I wasn't safe yet, but a step closer.

I tried to walk on my toes and not wake up the neighbors as I made my way up the stairs, and took off my shoes as soon as I entered my apartment.

The alcohol in my system was slowly wearing off, but the thought of getting into bed, all cozy and comfortable, warmed me right back up inside.

I couldn't be bothered to take a shower, so I just stripped to my underwear, brushed my teeth, and laid down under the covers. I enjoyed the smell of the clean sheets filling my nostrils as I wrapped myself up in a little cocoon.

Just when I was about to drift off to sleep, I heard a knock on my door. *Charlie?*

Trying to contain my smile, I was suddenly wide awake, pulling on my robe. "I'm coming," I chuckled when he knocked again, a little louder this time.

I struggled as I tried to open the door, the keys slipping through my fingers numerous times.

"Charlie..." I shook my head at his impatience and sighed when I was finally able to pull the door open.

But it wasn't Charlie. Instead, I was met with three men in black masks and the barrel of a gun against my forehead.

"Please," I whispered, slowly walking back into my apartment with my arms raised.

"Where are your valuables?" one of the intruders asked, and I quickly pointed to my bedroom, stopping in my tracks when my back hit the kitchen counter.

I prayed that they wouldn't find my mother's ring—something I had been keeping separate from my other jewelry. I was happy that I didn't own any expensive items.

Shit, the necklace.

Two of the men moved to my bedroom, making a mess as they searched my place for anything valuable, while the one holding me at gunpoint kept staring. I needed him to look away so I could make sure they wouldn't find my necklace, but he kept a close eye on me.

Nerves swarmed in my stomach as I looked at the metal barrel in front of my face. "Please, don't kill me."

The guy stayed silent, looking in the direction of his buddies when we heard a loud bang. "Do you guys want to wake up the entire building?" he hissed, and I took the opportunity to rip off my necklace and stuff it in my underwear.

I held my breath as the shooter snapped his head back in my direction, praying they would leave soon. His eyes looked me up and down from behind his mask, and I felt my heart beat harder in my chest.

Why was I so stupid? I knew the kind of neighborhood I lived in—hell, this wasn't my first armed robbery, and I still carelessly opened the door, not even attempting to take my gun with me. *Charlie had made me weak. He made me lower my guard.*

"There's nothing here man," one of the intruders whispered, and I swallowed hard.

"Were you lying to me?" the man in front of me asked, pushing the gun against my forehead.

"No, please," I pleaded, squeezing my eyes shut and trying to hold back tears as I frantically shook my head.

"It's not worth it," the third man warned.

"Fuck it. Let's go."

They walked out of my apartment with big strides, keeping the gun pointed at me until they were out of sight.

I dropped to my knees, breathing heavily as I pushed a hand against my chest. "Oh my God," I breathed out, trying to calm down before I quickly closed my front door.

It wasn't even the things they took I was worried about, more so the knowledge that strangers went through my stuff and invaded my space, my privacy.

I slowly walked to my wrecked bedroom, taking the necklace out of my underwear and placing it on my nightstand.

Dropping on my bed, I grabbed my phone with shaking hands and dialed 911. After I ended the call, making sure the police were on their way, I phoned the only person I wanted to see right now.

"Pick up, pick up, pick up," I mumbled as I waited for him to answer, my leg bouncing nervously up and down.

"Baby?" I finally heard, his voice groggy.

"Charlie." It was more a squeak than a word. "Can you come over?"

"Are you okay?" he asked.

"I don't know."

Half an hour later, I gave the police a statement, which ended up being pretty useless because I had no idea what the intruders looked like. A few minutes after they had left, I heard another knock on my door. I knew it was Charlie this time, but I didn't take any chances.

I opened the door with my gun raised this time, my fingers trembling around the cold metal.

"Hey, hey..." Charlie said softly when he saw me, quickly closing the door behind him and folding his hands over mine and the gun. He took the weapon from me and placed it on the kitchen counter before he wrapped his arms around me. "What happened here? And did I see the police outside?"

Closing my eyes as I leaned my head against his chest, I breathed in his scent, calming me down instantly. He softly brushed his fingers over my hair, waiting for me to explain.

"I don't know what they took," I mumbled against his shirt, and he pushed me back.

"Wait, were you just robbed?"

I looked up at him, nodding softly, and he walked past me, further into my apartment. Following him into my bedroom, I grabbed the necklace from my nightstand. "I managed to keep this, but I had to break it," I explained as I held it out, biting my lower lip as Charlie slowly turned.

"I couldn't care less about some jewelry, Jordan."

Trying to contain the butterflies in my stomach, I gave him a small smile, placing the necklace back on the table.

"Come on," he said, beckoning me to help him as he started to clean up the mess the intruders had made.

Once everything looked somewhat tidied up again, we went to bed, and I hoped he couldn't hear my heart that was still frantically beating in my chest.

CHAPTER 29
Jordan

"What do you want to do today?" Charlie asked as he drew circles on my shoulder, scrolling through his phone. I had a hard time coming up with a response because I was thinking about something completely different.

Ever since he'd came to my rescue last night, and I stared death in the eyes, I had been thinking about telling him how I felt, and now that we were laying here, all curled up against each other, I felt like I couldn't hold it anymore.

"Just a lazy day?" I suggested, kissing him on the chest before I got out of bed.

"That sounds like a good idea." He followed me to the kitchen where we made ourselves some coffee and rummaged the cupboards for some breakfast.

"Charlie?" I started, looking at my feet and fumbling with the belt of my robe.

"Yes, Baby?"

Was I really going to do this?

"I—"

Looking up into his eyes, the words got stuck in my throat. *Guess not.*

"What?" he asked, leaning against the counter behind him, sipping his piping hot coffee.

"It's not important."

He hummed but dropped the subject, and we went to have breakfast at the kitchen table. We spent the day watching movies and just cuddling up with each other, all the while the thought of telling him kept swirling in my head.

"Are you ok, Baby?" he asked from the couch. I instantly stopped pouring myself a cup of tea and walked up to him. He raised his brows. "What's wrong?"

"I have to tell you something."

I cleared my throat as he sat up and placed his phone on the coffee table. "Is it bad?"

"I don't think so." My hands were sweaty and shaking. I quickly tucked them into the pockets of my joggers, hoping I wouldn't seem too nervous. Not that it really mattered, I guess.

"Alright, let's hear it."

I took a deep breath, hesitating before I finally spoke. "I...I broke our rule."

He frowned, crossing his arms. "Which one?"

Observing his beautiful blue eyes, the light stubble on his

sharp jaw, and the cute dimples that occasionally made an appearance, I continued. "The...*feelings* one."

It remained silent for a second. I didn't know what to expect. I had no idea how he would react, or if he felt the same. I would've liked to think so, especially because of the way he acted around me, and how he immediately came running yesterday.

"What?" he said softly, his voice calm but emotionless.

Did I fuck up now? Maybe it wasn't the best decision to tell him. We could've just continued whatever we had going on as is, *right?* Nope, I had to make it worse.

"I think I love you," I mumbled, tucking a strand of hair behind my ear. I gasped when he jumped up, looking at me like he was going to charge at me.

There were a lot of reactions I had anticipated, but this wasn't one of them. "Jesus, I told you not to do it!" he yelled.

I flinched.

"You don't...feel the same?"

It hurt to ask the question, but I wanted—no, *needed*—to know.

"Of course not!"

The way he acted showed me he felt something and it angered me that he just couldn't admit it. "Charlie! You're lying," I bit back, my chest rising and falling at an alarming pace.

He rolled his eyes.

"I can't help it that I am the way that I am, Jordan," he continued, and I got more upset by the second. "That doesn't mean I fell in love with you."

I narrowed my eyes at him, trying to figure him out. What was holding him back? I was almost certain he was lying his ass off, but why?

"Oh my God, couldn't you just control your feelings?" he scoffed, and it clicked. There *was* something holding him back.

"You're so desperate for control, you can't even see what's right in front of you!" I yelled, tears springing in my eyes. This was not how it was supposed to go.

"I can see what's in front of me," he said calmly, though his chest rose and fell at a rapid pace. He looked me up and down before he spoke again. "A girl I fucked."

I swallowed hard at his comment, my heart breaking into a million pieces. Did I read the signals wrong? Was he really this selfish prick who treated women like trash, like Ashley had warned me about?

The pain in my chest was foreign, and it really hurt.

"What the fuck is this then?" I whispered, grabbing the necklace from my bedroom and pushing it into his chest.

He caught the jewelry, tucking it in the pocket of his pants. "Don't read too much into it, Jordan."

This was it. No Baby. No 'I love you, too.'

"Get out," I said softly, looking at my feet.

He didn't say anything, as if he was thinking about the entire situation, contemplating our time together. I wanted him gone. I didn't want to see his perfect face anymore. *He broke me.*

"Get out!" I screamed, pushing him towards the door, tears finally streaming down my face. I kept shoving him until he bumped against my front door. "Get out, get out, get out!"

"I..." He gave me one final look before he grabbed his keys and left my apartment. He closed the door behind him, slamming it shut, and I, once again, dropped to my knees.

Tears dropped on my cheeks and I tried to wipe them away,

but it was in vain. I hadn't cried since my mother died. Not even when Eli and I broke up, or when I had a tough time with keeping my shit together.

But he really broke me. *How could I ever let it get this far?*

I cradled my face in my hands, feeling the wetness of my tears on my palms, but it didn't matter.

In order to let myself go for a minute, I quickly stripped and stepped under the shower. The tears mixed with the water washed down the drain but left the pain in my chest behind. He had warned me not to catch feelings, but I thought that maybe after all the time we spent together, he would change his mind.

Maybe he would want to make an exception for me in his whole *no-strings-attached* ideology?

My fingers brushed over my collarbones, feeling how empty the spot was. Maybe I had grown a little too attached to the necklace, too. Something I received in one of the happiest times of my life.

Why does it hurt so Goddamn much?

All the things he did for me, the small displays of affection—*at least, that's what I thought they were*—made me wonder.

Deciding that this wasn't working, I quickly turned off the shower and walked to my bedroom. I put on my fluffiest, comfiest pair of pajamas, and went to bed, not even bothering to lock the front door.

Then I cried myself to sleep.

CHAPTER 30
Jordan

"Oh, I'm so excited, Jo," Ashley exclaimed as she pulled various items of clothing out of her closet to determine which she would be taking with her to Canada. I was sitting on her bed, supposed to be helping her pick out items, even though it had become clear to me I was just there for show.

I was thinking about something else anyway.

"Hmm," I hummed, staring at my phone.

Not a single message.

It had been almost a week—and nothing. *Did I read the signs wrong?* I made such a fool out of myself, crying over this...boy.

"Jojo?"

"Yeah, sorry." I put my phone away, looking up at her. "What were you saying?"

She cocked her head to the side, placing the top she was holding on the bed beside her as she sat down. "What's going on with you this week?"

"It's nothing."

She raised her brows, waiting for me to give her an honest answer. *Which I couldn't.* Besides, there wasn't really much to tell anyway.

"I think I'm just a little overwhelmed," I lied, looking at my hands in my lap.

"How come?"

I sighed, various excuses running through my mind until I found the most believable one. "Everything is going so right," — *what a joke*— "I wonder when shit will hit the fan."

She smiled softly at me, pulling me against her chest. I wanted to burst out crying—*again*—but that was another thing I couldn't explain.

"I'm so proud of you, Jo," she mumbled against my hair, and I closed my eyes. Was I going to tell her? Right before one of the happiest moments of her life? I knew it was the right thing to do. Besides, it was over now anyway, so might as well.

"Ash?" I straightened up from our hug, taking a deep breath before continuing. "I need to tell you something."

She waited for me to go on, staring at me with those big brown eyes. Was she going to yell at me? Would I put our friendship in jeopardy? *Who am I kidding, I already had.*

"I..."

The words got stuck in my throat, and I was taken back to the last time I confessed something. This was probably not going to go any better.

"Never mind," I said, shaking my head. "I already forgot."

"Ok." She jumped up, going back to stuffing her suitcase and giving me the space I honestly didn't deserve from her.

"Did you have a good Christmas?" she asked, neatly placing her clothes on the bed in perfect stacks before figuring out the best way to bring *everything*.

"Yeah, we just had a family dinner. Went to see Eliza's mom after."

Ashley paused. "How is she?"

"She's ok. She's trying to be, anyway." I brushed my fingers over one of the tops on the bed, nodding softly.

"I never met her, but she sounds hella strong."

I chuckled softly. "I don't know her that well either, but she is."

Ashley continued packing her bags, only a *few* items she hadn't already sent to Canada along with her wedding dress.

"How was your Christmas?" I countered, definitely not with the intent to hear how Charlie was doing.

"Please don't remind me," she replied, plopping back on the bed.

I sat up against the headboard, eagerly waiting for her to continue. God, I needed to forget about him already.

"We had a little...argument a couple of weeks ago," she elaborated, and I had to act as if I didn't already know this from her brother. "So there was already some tension between me and them."

I hummed, mentally slapping myself for wanting to hear about Charlie.

"And Charlie was in an awful mood. No idea what the fuck's up with him these days." It was hard to ignore the little spark of hope I felt at those words, but I tried to push it away. It was no use anyway. "We had dinner together but when we talked about the wedding Charlie stormed out. I've actually never really seen him annoyed, or angry."

I felt the urge to change the subject, partly because it hurt to talk about him, and partly because I didn't want Ashley to suspect something. "So, what time are we leaving?"

My suitcase was sitting in her living room, and Ryan had packed his stuff before he went to work, so we were practically ready to go.

"Ryan's supposed to be home any minute."

I raised my brows at her. "That's not an answer to my question."

She huffed, placing the last items into her suitcase. "Well, let's say half an hour?"

Nodding, I stood from her bed and walked towards the living room. I stopped when another question popped into my head. "Ash?"

"Hmm."

"Is...is it just going to be the three of us? On this flight?"

Her suitcase landed with a loud thud on the floor, and she looked up to me as she grabbed the handle. "Bailey's coming Saturday morning." *Come on, Ashley, that's not what I meant.* "And Charlie's coming straight after work. Apparently, that's all he cares about." She let out a harsh breath. "Sorry, I'm only talking about him."

I gave her a soft smile. *Yeah...*

"Babe?" Ashley and I turned to the hall when Ryan's voice boomed through the apartment.

We gathered in the living room, packed and ready before we

left for the airport.

Here we go.

—

The plane ride went well, especially considering it wasn't as long as the last one I—

"Mr. and Mrs. Thompson?"

A short man in a blue suit greeted us at arrivals, locking his iPad which had Ryan's surname on its display.

"Not yet," Ashley chirped enthusiastically, and I rolled my eyes.

"I'm Stephan, your driver for the weekend." I almost choked on my saliva at his words. Clearly, I had underestimated the amount of money Ash and Ryan had spent on their wedding.

We shook hands before we followed Stephan to the black Mercedes, handing him our luggage.

I looked out the window from the passenger seat, watching our industrial and modern surroundings turn into breathtaking views of nature until my eyes caught the hotel Ashley had desperately wanted for her big day. The white blanket of snow covered every surface and the branches of numerous pine trees, sparkling from the light of the sun.

It was a very secluded and exclusive spot, perfect for a somewhat intimate wedding.

"Just as beautiful as last time, right, babe?" Ryan mentioned to Ashley.

"But now there's snow," she replied, almost jumping out of the car as soon as we stopped at the edge of a red carpet. Lights covered the rim of the short canopy, drizzling down like diamonds.

"Whoa," I breathed out when I stepped out of the vehicle, following the bride towards the building.

"Right?" She squealed to the doorman, leaving Ryan forgotten behind with the suitcases. A porter with a cart rushed over to him, and I tried to catch up with Ashley. "Ash!"

Quickening my step, but refusing to run, I was relieved when I saw her at the front desk, chatting with a busty brunette. "Ashley, I get that you're excited but—"

"You must be the maid of honor," the woman said, grabbing my attention and I shifted my eyes to her.

"I am," I replied as we shook hands. "I'm Jordan."

She smiled at me, revealing her perfect, white teeth, and I tried to conceal the fact that I was insanely jealous of this woman, who *obviously,* had her shit together. Unlike me.

"My name is Perry, and I'm the owner of this hotel. Nice to meet you." *Oh, the one Charlie had to ask for a favor.*

"And where's your brother?" she asked Ashley, and I couldn't help but clench my jaw. *Oh God,* what if he fucks her this weekend? After the way he acted, I didn't know what to think anymore.

—

The following day I woke up early, my mind set on taking a dive into that massive pool on the rooftop of the hotel. The sun wasn't up yet, and the hotel was quiet.

With one more day to go until the wedding, I felt like this was my only opportunity to enjoy some of the facilities at this fine establishment in peace, even though the pool wasn't officially open yet.

Dressed in a simple red bathing suit, I snuck over the little gates with my towel draped over my shoulders, trying not to slip and break something. Which, wasn't unlikely to happen with my luck.

As I tiptoed into the giant space, I gasped when my eyes fell on the colorfully lit pool, the water appearing dark purple, pink, and blue, it being the only light in the room.

"Whoa," I said softly, dropping my towel on one of the lounge chairs. Tying my hair into a bun, I was eager to slide in. The water was the perfect temperature, and I instantly relaxed as I let myself sink into it. *This is exactly what I need.*

I wanted to collect myself before the busy weekend ahead, especially with the prospect of seeing Ashley's parents—and Charlie. I sighed, closing my eyes as I leaned against the far corner of the pool, moving my arms from side to side and feeling the calm water brush against my skin.

It had been a week since we...*broke up?*

I frowned slightly at my hands as I watched them, thinking about the moment I got my heart broken. Just like every other day, different scenarios ran through my mind, none of them making me feel any better. Except for the very optimistic ones, but I knew that Charlie wasn't that kind of man.

Behind the sadness, there was another emotion. I was so angry at him for leading me on. And angry at myself for falling into his trap.

A soft gasp left my lips when I heard the door to the pool open.

I tried to ignore my frantically beating heart, knowing I wasn't allowed to be in here. The room was still pretty dark, so I tried to remain very still as I listened to the approaching footsteps.

I held in a whimper when I saw who was walking in, his blue swimming shorts hanging low on his waist, accentuating the v-shaped muscle below his abdomen. What did I ever do to the universe to deserve this? *And when did he get here?*

Observing him as he dropped his towel on one of the chairs, I sunk deeper into the water. My chest tightened at the sight of him, but I couldn't look away. It was going to take a long time to get over him.

I started to panic when he turned in my direction, before diving into the water. *Where was I going to go?*

He waded to the edge of the pool when he surfaced, running his hands through his wet hair as he leaned against the wall. "I think this is the first time you've been this quiet since we've met."

I let out a breath, rolling my eyes. Of course, he knew I was here. *Nothing gets past him.*

Deciding that I didn't want to spend more time with him than absolutely necessary, I swam to the stairs, ignoring Charlie's gaze.

I quickly got out of the water and wrapped my towel around my waist, feeling exposed in the skimpy bikini. The look on his face gave me a boost I desperately wanted to ignore, though. Maybe I had imagined it like I did many things. It was dark in here after all.

"Asshole," I mumbled under my breath as I hurried out of the tension-filled space, not giving him another look. Only when I closed the door to my hotel room behind me, did the adrenaline wear off, and I was able to let everything else out.

"Shit," I groaned, breathing heavily and feeling tears behind my lids. *I hate him.*

I thought I was more prepared to see his handsome face, but apparently not. Roughly wiping away the water that dared to escape my eyes, I made my way to the en suite bathroom to get ready for the day.

We spent that Friday checking if everything was set up and ready to go for the big day, as well as rehearsing the wedding, and I hid in my room for an hour when Ashley's parents arrived.

Unfortunately for me, I was forced to face them at the rehearsal dinner that night, which I was currently getting ready for.

I had taken two evening dresses with me and was staring at the red one I had already worn multiple times, debating if it was too much to wear again. Deciding to go for the navy blue gown, I tried my best to piss off Ashley's parents as much as I could while still staying classy. This one was risky, considering the slit on the side was *very* high, but fuck them.

I nodded at my reflection in the full-length mirror, twirling in my heels. I had taken a pair with me that weren't as high, so I was confident I wouldn't embarrass myself tonight. *Too much, anyway.*

With a few nerves swirling around in my stomach, I made my way to the hotel restaurant, where Ashley and Ryan were already waiting for me.

"Oh, Jordan," Ashley cooed. "You look fantastic!"

I smiled at her, giving her a quick hug. "You too!" I looked her up and down. The shorter white dress hugged her curves in all the right places and really made her tan stand out.

"Thank you." She beamed, resting her head against Ryan's shoulder. Her happiness made my anger and annoyance from earlier that day completely wash away, and all I could think about was that enormous smile Ashley had on her face.

"You've done an amazing job, darling," Mrs. Abbot said as she walked in, stopping right next to her daughter and gesturing to the decorated restaurant.

"*Jordan* did, yeah." Ashley nudged my shoulder, and I gave her a smile.

"We did it together, Ash."

She gave me a wink. "Oh, can I do your hair?"

I frowned as I ran a hand through my styled curls, wondering what she was on about. "What?"

She ignored my confusion, walking up behind me and gathering my hair as I shot Ryan a questioning look.

"I want to see your tattoos, they're so beautiful," she said when she finished the low bun, securing it with an elastic. I loved how she always encouraged me to be myself, even around her judgmental family.

"Oh, ok."

"Right, Mom?" she added, looking at her mother before crossing her arms. I almost felt sorry for Mrs. Abbot but waited for her to reply.

"Yes...y-you look nice, Jordan," she managed to force out a compliment, smiling sweetly. I knew it was a fake smile, but I was taking what I could get.

"Right, Charlie's here," Ashley interrupted the awkward silence, beckoning for us to take our seats. "Let's do this!"

I turned to the table, clenching my jaw when I noticed which seat was mine. Charlie looked me up and down with his arms crossed over his chest, the fabric of his suit stretching dangerously tight over his biceps. But instead of smirking, he just looked away, ignoring my presence. *This is how it's going to be, huh?*

"Sorry I'm late, everyone!" All of us turned to the entrance of the restaurant, and I let out a breath when I saw Ian. *Thank God.*

"Ian, you made it!" Ryan exclaimed, sitting back in his chair, one arm draped over the back of Ashley's.

"Wouldn't want to miss this for the world."

I gave him a little wave as he took a seat next to me, feeling a little more at ease with him there, even though he was closer with Charlie than me.

"Right, before we start eating," Ryan announced, standing from his seat with his drink in his hand. "We want to say a few words."

I chuckled softly, the memory of Ashley saying they were never going to be *that* couple coming to the surface.

"First of all, a huge thank you to my mom and dad, as well as Mr. and Mrs. Abbot, who generously contributed to making this weekend possible and giving my beautiful bride the wedding of her dreams."

Smiling at the couple, I watched Ashley as she cocked her head to the side, caressing a hand over Ryan's arm.

"Secondly, thank you, Jordan and Charlie, for your efforts and support, not only with regards to the wedding but by being great friends in general, too."

I raised my glass at the groom, ignoring Charlie who did the same. *This was going to be harder than I thought.*

"We're thrilled to have you all here tonight, and couldn't think of a better group of people to celebrate our union with," Ryan added before sitting back down.

Dinner was served, and I refrained from raising my brows at

the lack of food in front of me, the elegant plating clearly more important than the amount.

"For the first course, we have grilled trout on a bed of pickled quinoa, with a raspberry coulis and caramelized onion," one of the waiters recited, nodding before walking away.

Ian and I looked at our food, before looking up at each other. "What the fuck did he just say?" I whispered, and he smirked at me.

"I hate fish," he replied, and I chuckled. Feeling Charlie's eyes burn a hole in my back, a little idea popped up in my head. *If he was only fucking me, it wouldn't be possible to make him jealous, right?*

During the rest of the dinner, I actually had a great time, joking with Ian and getting to know Ryan's parents, who I had never met before tonight.

After dessert we retired to the bar, having a couple of drinks before we went to bed. At some point, I went to get a drink for me and Ian, but when I returned, he was nowhere to be seen. "Ash, have you seen Ian?"

She turned her head to me with a smirk. "Ian, huh?"

You have no idea.

I rolled my eyes. "Did you see him?"

"Yeah he left with Charlie, don't know where to though."

I placed the drinks on one of the empty tables, thanking Ashley before I walked out of the restaurant, too curious for my own good to know why they suddenly left.

"Ian?" I called out, walking down one of the hallways. This hotel was massive so finding them was going to be a pain. *Why was I so determined to find them, anyway?*

"Really, I'm warning you." I suddenly heard and I walked in

the direction of the voice.

"Relax, man. We're just having fun." Rounding the corner, I was met with the pair, Charlie looking ready to charge at Ian.

"What's going on?" I asked, slowly approaching.

"Nothing," Charlie barked, storming past me. I shot Ian a questioning look.

"I didn't know you guys broke up?" He said, and I sighed.

"I guess we were never a couple to begin with."

CHAPTER 31
Jordan

I had gone back to my room almost immediately after Charlie's little outburst. He made me feel like I was losing my mind. If he didn't feel the same about me, why would he warn Ian to stay away from me?

My thoughts kept me up deep into the night, and around about two in the morning, I decided to take a walk, trying to clear my head.

As I was about to put my shoes on, I caught a glimpse of myself in the mirror, noticing the outfit I was about to roam the hotel in. Or rather, the lack thereof. Shaking my head, I rummaged through my suitcase until I found a pair of joggers, quickly pulling them on before I stepped into my sneakers.

With my keycard in one hand and a pack of cigarettes in the other, I made my way to the main entrance, quickening my step until I felt the cold, winter air against my face. Closing my coat, I walked towards the frozen-over pond on the side of the hotel, taking a seat on the freezing bench that stood opposite of it.

Releasing a sigh, I lit a cigarette, enjoying the instant effect the nicotine had on my nerves. I was surprised it took me this long to snap and finally smoke one, especially since I had been on edge for days. *I'll quit next week.*

"Ma'am?" I heard from behind me, and I slightly jumped in my seat. The employee from the front desk was walking up to me, trying to keep the biggest smile on, even though he was probably freezing his balls off.

"Yes?" I replied, taking another drag from my cigarette.

"You can't smoke here."

Great.

"Oh, I'm sorry." I put the bud out on the bench, earning a frown from the guy, and followed him back inside, throwing it in the bin.

A little annoyed that my breath of fresh air—*so to speak*—was cut short, I huffed and said good night before making my way back up to my room.

What's Charlie doing right now?

I rolled my eyes at the thought, scolding myself for thinking about him, *again*. I probably wasn't even on his mind. Plus, he shattered my heart into a million pieces, so I shouldn't be thinking about him in the first place. Unfortunately, it was one of the things I had no control over. And maybe somewhere in my mind, I held on to the idea that he had been lying.

Stuck in my own head, I wasn't paying attention to where I was going, and I shrieked softly when I made contact with something hard.

"What the fuck?" I breathed out, looking up as strong arms wrapped around me, keeping me from falling backward. *Of course, it was him. It had to be him.*

"Careful, Jordan. Wouldn't want you falling for me again," he chuckled, getting me back on my feet.

Tears sprung to my eyes, a sharp pain shooting through my chest at those words, and I pushed Charlie off when I regained my balance.

"You're a fucking dick, Charlie," I shot back, desperately trying not to let him see me cry.

"It was a joke!" he called after me as I raced to my room, my breathing uneven and everything hurting. *How did I ever fall for that asshole?*

—

"Jordan!"

I slowly opened my eyes, getting used to the light on my face as the pounding on my door continued. I knew it was her wedding day, but couldn't she leave me alone for a couple more minutes?

"Jordan!" Ashley yelled again, knocking so loud I swear she would put her hand through the door.

"Yeah, yeah," I mumbled, rubbing the sleep from my eyes and swinging my legs over the edge of my bed. I hadn't bothered to take my joggers off yesterday, and my hair was an absolute mess, but *let's be honest*, she had seen worse.

"Good morning!" she chirped when I opened my door, her hair already in curlers and nails done perfectly. *What time is it?*

"Morning," I groaned back, closing the door behind her and walking to my bed, ready to go back in for a nap.

"No, no." Ashley pulled the covers off me, turning me on my back and straddling me. "It's my wedding day!"

I squeezed my eyes shut at her loud voice, not even having a hangover to blame this time. She bounced up and down on the bed, shaking me around as I just laid there. "As much as I could use a good fuck right now, I don't think your fiancé would appreciate you humping me like this."

Ashley rolled her eyes, jumping off the bed and making her way to my closet. "We've only got a couple of hours until the ceremony!"

I yawned, stretching my arms above my head and arching my back, before stumbling towards the bathroom.

An hour later, I was sipping my second glass of champagne as Ashley rambled on about the reaction of her coworkers when she explained she wouldn't be having a bachelorette party while getting her makeup done by the makeup artist she had flown in.

All the bridesmaids had gathered in the bridal suite, helping each other with the finishing touches to their looks, and a little before three, it was time for Ashley to put her dress on.

"Deep breaths, Ash," I said as she stood before the mirror, looking at herself.

The usually stoic and reserved Mrs. Abbot was sitting in the corner of the room, trying to dry her eyes with a soaked handkerchief. Ashley grabbed my hand and I felt tears from behind my lids too.

"I love you, Jordan," she whispered, bending down slightly to tell me.

"I love you, too. You look absolutely stunning."

After another deep breath, Ashley turned, and her eyes watered even more when she saw her mother. "Oh, baby," Mrs. Abbot cooed, walking up to her daughter and carefully taking her into her arms.

I dug my teeth in my lower lip, trying not to fully burst out crying, jealousy overtaking me when they shared a moment. It wasn't my day, and I should be happy, but as I watched Mrs. Abbot caress a thumb over Ash's face, my chest tightened. *I would never have this moment with my mother.*

To my utter surprise, I felt a hand on my forearm, pulling me closer towards them. I watched wide-eyed as Mrs. Abbot smiled weakly at me, pulling me into their embrace. *There goes the waterworks.*

"You're ok," Ashley said against my ear, rubbing her palm over my back as I desperately tried not to smudge mascara into her white dress.

"Shit," I breathed out, releasing both women and taking a step back, trying to save my makeup. "This is your day, Ash."

Mrs. Abbot gave me a pitiful look, turning to the other bridesmaids.

"Jojo," Ash said softly, placing one hand on my shoulder. "It's ok. I'm so sorry your mom had to miss and will miss all the milestones in your life. I'll try to be there for you as much as I can."

I looked up at her, smiling, grateful for such an amazing friend. "Thank you."

We stood there in comfortable silence for a minute when a

thought popped up in my head. "Was your mother...*nice* to me just now?"

Ashley chuckled softly, her eyes shooting to her mom before she looked back at me. "She lost her mom, too, when she was younger. I never knew my grandma."

"Oh."

I still thought Mrs. Abbot was a bitch, but I understood her pain. I wouldn't wish that upon anyone.

"Alright ladies!" the wedding planner announced, clipboard clutched tightly against her chest. "Showtime."

The ceremony was beautiful. Intimate and small, but absolutely perfect. Walking down the aisle next to Charlie was very awkward, but I had managed to keep my attention on the beautiful couple this day was all about. There was one window for the reporters who had eagerly waited outside to snap a few photos and ask a couple of questions before they were asked to leave the property.

Ashley and Ryan were over the moon, unable to keep their hands off each other as we finished dinner.

Of course, the food was beyond delicious, and instead of getting a single serving of dessert, the couple had chosen a sweets bar, which included the wedding cake. They didn't have to tell me twice when we were told to dive in, and my mood was immediately lifted as I stuffed my face with sugar.

"I would ask if you're enjoying yourself," Ian said as he sank into the chair next to me, a cup of black coffee in his hand. I was relieved it wasn't Blake, since I always got a weird vibe from him, especially after the Christmas party.

"I am. Thank you," I replied with my mouth full of cake. He chuckled softly, placing a hand on my arm.

"What are you doing?" I questioned, looking from his hand to his face.

"Trying to see if I can get a rise out of Charlie."

I let out a breath of relief, leaning closer to act the part. He broke my heart, but I wanted to know if he cared just a little bit.

"Here he comes," Ian mumbled, abruptly sitting back. I swallowed hard when Charlie appeared next to us, his suit perfectly hugging his muscular frame and his hair done as neat as ever, though I could tell he'd run his hands through it a couple of times.

"Can we talk?" he asked, and I rolled my eyes.

"I'm busy."

I scoffed when he grabbed me by the arm and guided me out of the main room, though I was secretly loving his persistence. "What?" I snapped, tugging my arm out of his grip.

"I..."

Just like *that* night, he had nothing to say. No, *I'm sorry*. No, *I love you, too*.

I gave him a couple more seconds, feeling the urge to kiss him and slap him at the same time before deciding to walk away.

"Wait." He stopped me, pulling me back and into his arms. Before I could register what was happening, he pressed his lips on mine, almost as if I was his oxygen, the thing that kept him going.

I gave in at first, but the hurt and anger came bubbling to the surface almost immediately.

"No!" I exclaimed, pushing him back and slapping him across

the face. "One, you can't just kiss someone. Two, you broke my heart, put it in a blender, and made a Goddamn smoothie!"

Poor choice of words, because I almost burst out laughing, but I wouldn't give him that.

"Jo—"

Shit, the tears have arrived at the party.

"No," I repeated softly, my bottom lip trembling. "I won't let you mess with me again."

He opened his mouth to say something but decided against it. And it was all I needed. I turned on my heels, quickly wiping my eyes and making my way back to the party. *Asshole.*

"Oh!" I shrieked when I bumped into someone, and to my horror, it was Mr. Abbot. "I'm sorry, sir."

He looked unimpressed by my apology, giving me a stern nod before walking past me to the restrooms. Why did I have to feel like shit on the happiest day of my best friend's life? No, I just needed to focus on what was really important, not Charlie-fucking-Abbot.

"There you are!" Ashley called me over, still stuck to Ryan's side and clearly a little tipsy. I smiled, seeing her like this made me feel instantly better—*jealous, but better*.

"Are you enjoying yourself, Jordan?" Ryan asked, clearly more capable of holding his liquor than his new wife.

"I am."

"We wanted to party all night, but...but there's only one thing I want to do right now," Ashley added, and I smirked. She started to tug at Ryan's slacks, and that was his cue to speak up. Bailey rolled her eyes, giving Ashley a peck on the cheek before walking off with her husband.

"Alright, babe, let's say goodbye to everyone." He tried to hold her hands away from his dick, turning her in the direction of both their parents.

It took us about half an hour to get the couple sorted and ready to go, and we waved them goodbye from the front door, watching them drive off to the airport. I had no desire to stick around near every single person I didn't want to see, so I decided to get an early night.

Ignoring Charlie's looks and attempts to talk to me, I said goodbye to Bailey and walked towards the elevator. *He won't have the chance to hurt me again.*

CHAPTER 32
Charlie

It had been weeks since the wedding. I had buried myself in work, making longer days than ever. Partly because I wanted to prove myself to my dad, but also because it was a distraction.

My mind had been a mess since Jordan expressed her true feelings towards me, especially because for the last couple of days, I've been doubting everything that I thought I knew about love.

I remember feeling warmth and some sort of happiness spread through me when she told me, but almost immediately after, I didn't want anything to do with her. I called it panic or just the way I was.

Either way, I had no idea what to do with myself.

"Hey, Charlie," Ashley greeted when the elevator doors rolled open and she walked into my apartment.

"Hmm," I hummed, still deep in thought.

Did I make a mistake? *Probably.* Was it something I needed to fix? Or better yet, *wanted* to fix?

"Charlie."

Rapidly blinking, I looked up at my sister, who was unpacking the groceries for tonight. We had set a date to have dinner together after she got back from her honeymoon and to be completely honest, I needed it. My sister and I always had been close, no matter if we were separated or not, and she always knew the right things to say. Even though I couldn't exactly tell her what was really going on.

"Yes, sorry." I stood from the couch and walked up to her, sliding onto one of the barstools.

"What's up with you?" she asked, stopping mid-action and leaning on the counter. *No fucking clue.*

"Can I ask you something?" I countered, letting out a breath. Ashley crossed her arms in front of her chest, one brow cocked.

"Sure."

My eyes fell on the giant rock on her finger. "How did you know it was love?"

At first, she laughed at me. "Jesus, Charlie. Good one."

I kept my eyes on her, with no hint of humor in my expression as I waited for her to take me seriously. I knew it was a weird question coming from me, but ever since everything happened between Jordan and me, I had been questioning my entire life and determination to never fall in love.

"Oh, you're not messing with me," she admitted, her smile

faltering for a second before her entire face lit up. "Are you in love?"

"Jesus." I covered my ears when she screamed that last bit, running around the kitchen island to hug me.

"Get off," I scoffed, frowning at her. "I'm not in love. Well...I don't know."

After she had calmed down, she took a seat next to me. "Who is she? What's her name? Or his? Their? Shit, tell me!"

I rolled my lower lip between my teeth, studying her face. "Can you just answer my question?" I asked instead, definitely not ready to enlighten Ashley about Jordan and me. *If there even was an us in the first place.*

"Well, what do you feel when you look at her? When you're not near her?" Ashley questioned, finally with a serious expression on her face.

I contemplated my answer for a few seconds, still a little hesitant to finally admit my feelings to myself or anyone for that matter. Would Ashley think differently of me once I told her? Would everyone see me as a pussy? Someone who isn't in control of his life, or himself?

"Charlie?"

"Right." I shifted in my seat, taking a breath. "I feel lonely if she's not here, like I'm missing a limb, even though that's such bull—"

Ashley raised her brows.

I cleared my throat before I continued. "I'm at my happiest when I'm with her, and I've come to like the few flaws she supposedly has maybe better than everything else. She's beautiful, smart, and has a sharp tongue. That, and she's amazing in—"

"Charlie!"

I chuckled softly. How could I not make a joke out of this?

"I know what's going on," Ashley said, having an annoyingly smug smile on her face. I had an idea of what she was thinking, and I didn't like it one bit. Yet I asked anyway.

"Do you?" I raised a brow.

"You *are* in love."

I expected myself to burst out laughing, or scoff, walk away, yell at her. But I didn't. I hated to admit it, but she was right. I had no idea what love was, how it felt, but somehow, I believed her instantly.

"But...oh, fuck."

Dropping my head in my hands, and leaned on the kitchen counter in front of me.

"What?"

I looked up at her, giving her a painful smile. *I fucked up.*

Ashley cocked her head to the side with a frown. She was going to murder me. And murder me again when she would find out who I was talking about.

"What did you do?" she pressed, narrowing her eyes at me.

I sighed. "I broke her heart."

She jumped up, slapping me with unfamiliar force and bruising me as I tried to shield my head from her attack. "I fucking knew you would mess up one day! I knew if you found someone, you would fuck up!"

"Yeah, yeah. I panicked ok?" I explained, trying to get her to stop. It was a lame excuse, but it was all I had.

She slouched back in her chair, closing her eyes for a moment. "What did you say?"

My mind took me back to the awful day; one I would remember for a long time. "She told me she loved me and

I flipped her off. I told her it was just sex. God, I was such an asshole to her."

Ashley stared at me wide-eyed, waiting for me to continue explaining.

"I just..." I trailed off, giving up on trying to sound tough and put together. I wasn't without Jordan anyway. "What if she left me? What if she got bored, found someone else? I don't like things I don't have control over."

"Charlie..." she placed a hand on my arm, scooting her stool a little closer. "Some people are worth losing control for. And I've never seen you like this, so she must be the one."

Then it dawned on me. *She is the one.*

"I need to go."

"What? We haven't even eaten yet."

I jumped from my chair, searching my living room for my keys. "Ashley, *I need to go.*"

Her face lit up, and she mirrored my actions. "Oh my God, this is so exciting! I can take you!"

"No!"

We both froze. There was no fucking way she was finding out before I could even make it right. "I need to do this myself."

She shrugged, quickly packing the groceries she brought before she hurried out of my apartment. "Good luck!"

I nodded to myself, taking a deep breath before I made my way to Jordan's apartment.

—

I should've known that she wouldn't open the door for me. Even after I practically kept the entire building up all night—*apologizing again and again*—begging for her to let me in and explain.

It took me hours before I finally managed to get up from her doorstep and make my way home, my heart hurting after I had indirectly broken it myself.

The next day at work, I was in the worst mood. Angry at myself, the world, that stupid four-letter word, I flipped everyone off and had smacked my door in numerous faces.

"What?" I barked when I heard *another* knock on my door, wondering who dared to interrupt me this time. It was my father who was going to test my patience. He didn't say anything as he walked up to my desk and took a seat in front of me, his expression making me wonder what I had done now.

"What can I do for you?" I sighed, placing my pen down and crossing my arms. I really tried not to sound snappy or short, but I wasn't sure if I cared anyway.

"I had been suspecting something since the first night you got home, but of course, I hoped that I was wrong."

I cocked a brow, biting my lower lip. *Did he—*

"Then, I saw you two at the wedding..."

The color drained from my face, and I got a nasty feeling in my stomach. *I don't like where this is going.*

"I don't know what you're talking about," I said hesitantly, knowing that lying to my father was not even remotely possible.

"I have a proposition for you," he continued, ignoring my uneasy state. "Either you forget about the girl, or you will never be CEO."

What the fuck?

"Are you kidding me right now?" I didn't mean to raise my

voice, but he was asking for it. "You're giving me an ultimatum?"

He didn't seem fazed by my outburst, keeping his eyes on me and showing me that he was dead serious.

"Your choice."

Jordan probably didn't want me, but if I had even the slightest chance of having her in my life, I'd give up this stupid position for her any day. Yes, I had been working up to this for my entire life, following my father's plan so I would grow up to be his perfect successor, but the respect I had for him at the time was slowly fading. And I simply didn't care anymore.

My blood was boiling and I leaned forward, making sure I was being crystal clear. "Without her, I don't even *want* to be CEO of this company."

It was obvious that this was the last answer he expected, and he jumped to his feet. "Charles, I'm warning you," he hissed, losing his reserved and stern facade. "You stay away from Jordan Sawyer."

The both of us looked up when the door to my office swung open, almost shattering in the process. Ashley stormed in, her face red with rage. "You're asking *Charlie* to stay away from my best friend now, too?"

Oh, shit. How much did she hear?

"Ashley," Dad breathed out, clearly startled by her appearance as I was.

"I am so done with this crap!" she exclaimed, her eyes getting watery as she looked at our dad. "I'm ashamed to call you my father."

I couldn't agree more, standing from my chair and leaning my palms on my desk as I brought my face closer to my father's. "Please get out of my office, Dad."

He could shove this entire company up his ass for all I cared.

I was going to do everything in my power to make things right with Jordan, and if that meant leaving this job, so be it.

—

Every day for a week I went straight to Jordan's after work, begging her for forgiveness and sending her an abundance of messages. One time, I could hear a soft sob on the other side of the door, and I slapped myself in the face on every other occasion. There was no bigger idiot than yours truly, who fucked up the only thing that mattered.

"Baby, please let me in," I pleaded on a Friday, resting my head back against the door, my ass hurting from sitting on the concrete.

I made an utter fool out of myself in front of her neighbors, but they could shoot me any look they wanted. Maybe I was acting like a stalker, harassing this poor girl, but I was selfish. I needed her. And I just really hoped that there was a part of her that, perhaps, needed me too.

"Jordan, I'm so sorry about the things I said, the things I did."

I heard a muffled sigh and I got on my feet, turning to her apartment. She was probably within reach if this door wasn't between us, and my hands burned against the wood as I leaned against it, desperate to be closer. "Please, Baby, I love you."

It was the first time I said it out loud, and hope coursed through me when I heard a gasp. But that happiness was short-lived when a familiar voice sounded behind me.

"Charlie? What did you just say?"

Ashley.

CHAPTER 33
Jordan

Charlie had been calling and messaging me all week. Showing up at my door right after I got home from work, begging me to let him in. *I wasn't falling for another one of his tricks.*

Listening to his pleas, I couldn't help but shed a tear every once in a while, wishing everything had gone differently. That he'd reciprocated my feelings the first time I admitted them. That he would've wrapped his arms around me and kissed me, whispering *I love you*'s in my ear. I should've known that wasn't the case.

"Baby, please let me in," he said through the door.

I continued pacing, wondering if I should just open it.

"Jordan, I'm so sorry about the things I said, the things I did."

Was he really sorry? Should I believe him? I sighed, feeling incredibly conflicted. I hated the hope he gave me acting like this after everything, but a little voice in my head reminded me of his nature.

"Please, Baby, I love you," he mumbled, and my breath hitched in my throat, making me gasp.

What?

I froze, watching the door with wide eyes.

I had no chance of asking him to repeat it, though, because Ashley's voice was the next thing I heard and I felt all the blood drain from my face.

"Charlie? What did you just say?"

Fuck, fuck, fuck. This is not how I wanted her to find out.

"Ash," Charlie said breathlessly, and I quickly wiped my face, walking to the door and opening it. She stood there, shopping bag in hand as her expression slowly morphed into anger.

My stomach dropped and my hands got shaky, watching her eyes go from my tear-stained face to Charlie's, who looked just as sick as I must've looked.

"This is...no," she said softly, angry tears springing in her eyes. I kept my gaze on the floor, unable to look at her as she spoke. "You were talking about *her*?"

Charlie took a step in her direction but she backed away. "Tell me it's not true. That I'm dreaming."

"Ash," I squeaked out, anxiously wrapping my arms around myself and attempting to take a step in her direction.

"We need to talk." She ignored Charlie, walking up to me and pushing me back into my apartment before closing the door behind her. "Go home, Charlie!" she yelled over her shoulder, turning back to me.

I kept my eyes on my hands, digging my teeth so hard into my lip I tasted blood. Guilt overtook me, even more than before, and I wished I had never met Charlie.

"Jordan," she spoke, her voice sounding hoarse, and she threw the bag she was holding on the kitchen counter. "I warned you! And you went behind my back anyway!" Her voice broke, and with that my heart. *Again.*

"Ashley, let me explain," I sobbed, stepping closer.

She let out a harsh breath, running her hands through her blonde locks as she turned. "How could you?" Her voice was soft, but I could hear the underlying rage and hurt.

"I..." I couldn't get the words out. What could I even say to make it better? *Nothing.* Nothing could make this better. I should've told her the first time his name came up. Right when I realized what I had done.

Now I had betrayed her trust, just like all the other girls.

"It just happened."

She snapped her head in my direction, slapping her palm on the counter. "I don't care that it happened, Jordan. I mean...I do. But what hurts the most is that you kept it from me."

I nodded to the floor, tears now freely running down my face. "You told me he would break my heart."

Her expression softened slightly at my tears, and she beckoned me to continue. "Go on, tell me."

"I'm so sorry, Ash," I cried, sinking into the couch. "It got out of hand and I didn't want to hurt you. I thought it was best that I didn't tell you."

She sighed, rounding the kitchen counter and taking a seat opposite of me, crossing her arms over her chest. "You *did* hurt me."

I rolled my bottom lip between my teeth again, taking a deep breath. Now that she knew, it was time to be completely honest with her. "I met him the night before dinner at your parents' house."

"What?" she exclaimed, furrowing her brows together. "You kept this from me for over four months?"

I buried my face in my hands, shaking uncontrollably and bawling my eyes out. "I'm so, so sorry."

She let out a long sigh, trying to compose herself before she spoke again. "What happened?"

I looked back up, watery eyes staring back at me. How the fuck was I supposed to fix this? *Am I as much of a disappointment as her parents thought I was?*

"I went home with him that night. We didn't share names or any other information. It was only meant to be a one-night stand."

Her face still looking like thunder, she listened.

"I tried to stay away, I did. But it was almost impossible. So, I gave in."

I told her everything that had happened after that. *Well almost.* I told her about the list, his birthday, nights out, lazy mornings in bed, and how he shattered me when I finally admitted my true feelings. I left out some details, stuff she definitely didn't want to hear about her brother, but tried to tell her as much as possible.

She seemed conflicted, deep in thought after I finished and probably thinking about the best way to cut me off. *Her parents will get their wish after all.*

"*That's* why my dad asked Charlie to stay away from you. He knew," she spoke, though probably more to herself.

I frowned but didn't dare to ask her to elaborate, so I just waited.

"You really hurt me, Jordan." She stood up and walked back to the kitchen, grabbing the shopping bag from the counter. "But you making it up to me will have to wait."

Hopeful, I looked up, watching her grab two spoons.

"I knew something was up with you, even before the wedding." She opened the bag and took out two tubs of ice cream. "So I thought..."

I broke down again, hating myself for how I had treated my best friend. The one person that despite our differences, had always been there for me.

"I'm so sorry, Ash," I sobbed, crying uncontrollably now.

To my surprise, she placed the ice cream on the coffee table and sat next to me, wrapping her arms around me. "Shh, I'm not going to leave you."

I clawed at her blouse, smearing mascara all over her, but she hugged me tighter and pulled me closer. "For now, I'm just sorry about my brother."

"I love him, Ash. But all I am to him is a good fuck." I sat back up, trying to wipe the water from under my eyes. She looked at me, deep in thought, but again, I didn't dare to ask what she was thinking.

A lonely tear fell down her cheek, and I placed my hand on hers. "I'm sad you didn't get to share your happy moments with me. Even though it was your own decision," she mumbled.

"I knew you wouldn't approve, and I should've never given in, but..." I sighed. If I could go back in time, I would do it all differently. Would I avoid Charlie at all costs and not get sucked in like I did? *Probably not.* But I would tell Ashley from the start what happened, hoping she would understand.

"I suspected it wasn't just your job that made you so happy. Tell me all the good things."

I looked up at her, smiling to myself when I thought about all the happy moments Charlie and I had experienced together. "He, uh...he always calls me Baby, because that's what I said he could call me the first night we—"

I stopped when Ashley got a slight look of disgust on her face. *Ok, leave the sex out.*

"He tried cooking for me once, and it was absolutely horrific."

"He *cooked* for you?" She raised her brows, more surprised than I would've guessed. "Like, made something on the stove other than pancakes?"

"He tried," I said with a chuckle. "*And* he made me a lot of pancakes." I smiled at the thought, thinking back to the times he even brought me breakfast in bed.

Ashley didn't respond, she just kept looking at me with a pained expression. "What else?"

"He..." Was I really going to tell her? *Yes! No more secrets!* "He took me to Italy."

She gasped, furrowing her eyebrows even more, but her expression looked more on the happy side than on the angry side, so I let out a breath. "Oh my God. How was it?"

I was happy she reacted all giddy and excited because honestly, that's how I felt about the trip. Italy had always been on my bucket list, and making the trip with someone I was this comfortable with made it even better. But, comfortable was probably 'in love with', even though I didn't know it at the time.

"That's actually where—" I stopped talking when I brushed my fingers over my naked neck, remembering that I shoved the necklace in his hands when...

Ashley's eyes went to my hand, realization hitting her a few seconds after. "He bought you the necklace."

I nodded, shifting my eyes to my lap.

"Jordan," she said sternly, grabbing me by my shoulders and forcing me to look back up to her. "As much as I don't like the idea of you and my brother together, and even though you really hurt me by not telling me, I think...I think he really is in love with you, too."

Snapping my head up, I almost strained my neck. "Why do you think that? He made it very clear that it was *just* sex," I said quickly and my face fell once again at the thought.

"He's been...different since he met you."

I rolled my eyes, scoffing. "He had no problem breaking my heart and stepping on it."

Ashley slowly shook her head, biting on her lower lip. "A couple of days ago, I was supposed to have dinner at his place," she started, grabbing one of the tubs of ice cream and opening it. "He asked me how I knew I was in love, and I asked some questions."

I grabbed the second tub, acting like her words didn't faze me when in reality, I couldn't wait to hear more.

"He told me that he felt lonely without her, I quote"—she added air quotes—"like I'm missing a limb."

"I—"

"I'm not done," she interrupted me, shifting in her seat and swirling her spoon absentmindedly in her half-melted ice cream. "He said that he was only really happy when he was with her, said she's beautiful, smart and that she has a sharp tongue."

"But you don't know it's me," I countered, quickly stuffing a big chunk of ice cream into my mouth.

"Jordan." She nudged my knee with hers, looking me in the eyes. "After what I saw today, I *know* it's you."

I couldn't help but smile ever so slightly, my cheeks warming up.

"And no matter how much the idea of you two freaks me out—*because I know my brother*—you're actually kind of perfect for each other."

A comfortable silence settled between us, both of us trying to spoon as much ice cream into our mouths before it turned into liquid. Could any of what she said be true? Was there a tiny chance Charlie didn't lie earlier? When he *actually* told me that he loved me?

"How will I know that I'm not falling for another one of his tricks?" I questioned, wiping my lips with the back of my hand.

Ashley put her tub back on the coffee table. "Jordan, the guy is head over heels in love with you. Ugh, how did I not see it sooner?" I watched her as she let out another frustrated sigh, slapping her palm against her forehead. "He turned down becoming CEO for crying out loud."

"He did what?" I questioned softly, placing my tub on the coffee table and wondering if I had heard her correctly.

She looked back up at me, smirking. "My dad gave him an ultimatum. You, or becoming CEO. Charlie chose *you*."

Fireworks exploded in my chest, and I couldn't contain my smile. I knew how much the position meant to him. We never really talked much about work, but I was aware that he had been working really hard to prove himself to his dad and earn the title. *He gave that up for...me?*

My smile faltered. "What do I do?"

There was no way in hell that I was going to forgive him just like that. Though it was still a little weird to be talking about this with Ashley, she gave me an idea.

"You're going to make him work for *you*. Make him sweat."

CHAPTER 34
Jordan

After another week of unanswered phone calls, Charlie decided on a different approach.

Rubbing the sleep from my eyes as my doorbell rang for a second time, I stumbled to the front door, not even bothering to get properly dressed. Sure, it was almost noon on a Saturday and I just got out of bed, but whatever.

"Yes?" I croaked out as I opened the door, gasping when I was met with a sea of flowers.

"Miss Sawyer?" the delivery guy droned, tapping away on his tablet. *Wait, how did he get into the building?* Ok, I guess that wasn't the hardest thing to do.

I stared at the array of red roses and white peonies, little bits of green completing the bouquets. "Ma'am?"

"Yes, sorry. That's me," I replied, still a little stunned as I signed for the flowers. *Accepting flowers wasn't a sign that I had forgiven him, right?*

It took me a while before I had carried everything inside, unable to avoid a few confused looks from neighbors, and after I had managed to fill every surface of my apartment with flowers, I searched for the card.

Refraining from ripping it to pieces before I had a chance to read it, I opened the envelope. I sighed at the words *I'm sorry* and *I love you*, feeling my determination to give him the cold shoulder for a while slip away.

To be honest, I missed him. I missed the mornings we would wake up in bed and just curl up against each other, I missed him teasing me even though it could drive me insane sometimes, and I missed just *him*, his presence, making me glow with happiness.

Yes, he had been an absolute dick, and his words hurt me more than anything else ever could, but did he really mean them? I didn't think he was the type to do the *love* thing, and hearing him mumble the words against my door, really changed something for me.

Letting out a breath, I dropped the card on the coffee table between two bouquets that barely fitted on there and decided to get dressed. I ignored the ten-thousandth voicemail Charlie had left me, and quickly put on a pair of leggings. It wasn't like I was going out anyway.

Just when I pulled a sweater over my head, the doorbell rang again. "I swear to God," I mumbled under my breath, walking back to my front door.

But it wasn't flowers, chocolate, or the man himself.

"Mrs. Abbot?"

There she stood, on my doorstep, her hair in a perfect blonde bun, a streak of grey giving away her age. She looked uncomfortable in the poorly lit hallway, both hands clutching her handbag tightly.

"Jordan," she breathed out, her eyes shifting over my outfit for a second before she looked up. Where Charlie's icy eyes always looked beautiful and inviting to me, the same color in his mother's had always scared me. *Could be the woman herself, though.*

"What brings you here?" I took a step back, gesturing for her to come in.

"I..." She cut herself off when she saw the flowers, one of her perfectly made-up brows rising slightly.

I closed the door behind her, clearing the coffee table. "Sorry for the mess, these just arrived and I didn't have time to clean up yet."

She nodded, taking a seat on the couch and placing her bag next to her before she looked around. "They're beautiful."

I smiled in agreement, watching her eyes shift to her hands, a pained expression on her face. I would ask her what's wrong, but that was definitely not the kind of relationship I had with her.

"Ma'am, what are you doing here?" I bluntly asked, done with her bullshit.

"I know I'm not your favorite person," she started, looking over. "And I know that it's not something that's going to change overnight, but..."

She took another breath, making sure she had my attention.

"I wish to try."

Eh...what?

I blinked rapidly and pinched myself to see if I was dreaming. "Ouch." *Ok, I wasn't.*

"Would you like something to drink?" I asked, deciding to be the bigger person and giving her the opportunity to explain herself instead of throwing her out. Even though that might have been a wiser move.

"A cup of tea, please."

We didn't speak as I made the drinks, the tension in the room almost tangible. I had no idea what to expect from this visit but secretly hoped that she would ease up on me. Honestly, I really wanted Ashley's parents to like me.

I sat down on the opposite side of the couch, placing our tea on the table.

"I've been meaning to apologize," she said, turning slightly towards me. I waited for her to continue and trying not to show what her apology did to me. I never expected her to admit that she was wrong, let alone apologize. "Ever since Ashley brought you home, I've treated you unfairly."

I blinked rapidly, pinching myself once again to make sure I wasn't dreaming. There was just one question on my mind, something I have been asking myself ever since I first met Ashley's family. "Why?"

She pouted her lips, probably contemplating her next move. Was she going to change her mind? Was I going to feel worse because of her answer?

"I...I was jealous."

It took everything in me not to burst out laughing. Was she

messing with me?

"Excuse me? What are you jealous of? You have everything," I replied, unable to stop myself. "You never have to worry about money, you have an amazing family, a loving husband."

She shifted in her seat, folding her hands on her lap and giving me a quick reply. "Yes, I had everything handed to me when I was young."

I heard sadness in her statement, and couldn't help but wonder. Why *was* she this way?

"So why were you jealous?" I asked. It was clear that the subject was touchy, but explaining why she was such a bitch to me all this time was the least she could do.

"Because you have the life I wanted."

I choked on my tea, quickly placing the cup back on the coffee table and wiping my mouth. Looking around my dodgy apartment in the sketchy neighborhood, I wondered, what was she jealous of? "I don't understand."

She sighed, taking a sophisticated sip of her tea, unlike me. "My father was strict, to say the least," she explained. "Especially after my mother passed away, money and a good reputation were all he cared for."

Realization hit me, and I started to feel bad.

"You're able to make your own decisions, do whatever you want, and...*be* whoever you want. My father arranged the marriage between Felix and myself when I turned twenty-one, and I just..."

I hung on to every word she said, curious to hear more. These were things not a lot of people knew, and it made me understand her a little more. Not enough to forgive her for the way she's been treating me, though.

"I'm sorry for the lack of freedom you had all your life, Mrs. Abbot, but that doesn't excuse the way you've been talking to me," I said, crossing my arms. *Yes, stand your ground, Jordan.*

"You're right. I will do everything in my power to make it up to you, hoping you can forgive me one day. I see how happy Ashley is with you, and how much my son—"

"What?" I interrupted her, my eyes widening. How much did she know?

"He's been in love with you for a while."

I swallowed hard, my eyes trailing over the flowers. "I'm not sure..."

"Please, believe me, Jordan. I know my son very well, and this is the first time I've seen him like this. That's part of the reason I came here today."

We looked up when my phone rang, and I rolled my eyes when I saw that it was Charlie. Did I feel good about him stalking me? *Yes.* Was I going to forgive him just like that? *Hell no.*

"Sorry, what were you saying?" I ignored the call, noticing that Mrs. Abbot's eyes had found the card.

"I hope you'll accept my apology. You're a wonderful girl, Jordan, and I feel ashamed for the way I've treated you."

Still a little stunned by our conversation, I stared at her as she stood up. I had no idea what to expect when she had turned up at my door, but certainly not this.

—

Monday, after work, I told Nadine what happened during the

weekend. The flowers, but most of all, my conversation with Mrs. Abbot.

"Whoa, that's...surprising," she said when I was done, both of us sipping our white wine in the overpriced bar next to the office. I had been in desperate need of some alcohol that entire day, and when Nadine had invited me for a drink, I had taken her offer with the biggest smile.

"I'm mad at myself because all I want is to get along with Charlie's—Ashley's parents." Nadine raised her brows at me.

"I get what you mean." She snuck another chocolate into her mouth, one of the many Charlie had sent to me today. "I'd say just give it time. Don't suddenly act like it's all ok, but I think it's important to give her a chance to make it right. In the end, as long as you're friends with Ashley and potentially dating—*sorry, I won't go there*—she's going to be in your life."

I downed my wine to buy myself some time to think, hating how right she was. Sure, I wasn't the pettiest person anyway, but I could already feel the satisfaction I would hopefully get by giving Mrs. Abbot what she deserved.

"Why are you so smart?" I asked, though it was more of a rhetorical question.

She chuckled softly, rising from her seat to pay. "Oh, by the way, I'm moving back to Sweden."

I almost dropped my glass on the table, watching her walk away. Who the fuck drops a bomb like that and just walks off?

"Wait!" I stumbled after her, following her outside after she had settled the bill. She was already halfway to our cars when I finally caught up with her.

"What?"

I stopped in my tracks, crossing my arms. "You're leaving me?"

She turned on her giant heels, looking at me with a big smile. "I'm going after the love of my life."

Fair.

"But I'll miss you," I pouted as I walked up to her, wrapping my arms around the tall blonde. And I really was. She was the first friend I had made when I started working here, and over the last couple of months, we had become really close.

"I'll miss you, too." She returned the hug, pulling me closer.

We talked about Mikael—said *love-of-her-life*—as we made our way to our cars, giving each other a last hug before we parted ways.

I waved to Mrs. Hellen as I walked into my apartment building half an hour later, and looked through my mail, trying not to trip on the stairs. Bills still scared the shit out of me, but after a few seconds I realized that I could pay them. *Maybe I should think about moving?*

"Baby?"

I gasped when I heard his voice, freezing in place.

There he was. In a perfectly fitted suit, his hair on point, but with dark circles under his eyes. I frowned when I smelled the alcohol, watching him as he pushed himself off the wall, almost falling over.

"Charlie?"

"Baby, please," he pleaded, falling to his knees in front of me. "I'm so sorry."

I looked at him as he grabbed my hips, leaning his forehead against my stomach. I had never seen him like this, nor expected him to get like this. Did I take it too far? "What are you..."

"I need you." He pulled me closer before looking up. "I—I

can't live without you. Life doesn't make sense anymore. I love you so much and I *need* you back. Please."

I was at a loss for words, just staring at his watery eyes. His hands gripped me tighter and I softly lifted his chin, rubbing my thumb over his cheek. "You're drunk, Charlie."

"I'll do anything," he continued, begging me with his eyes. The smell of whiskey hit me in the face as he spoke up, and I suddenly felt super guilty. "*Anything.*"

"I..."

Was I really supposed to trust his pleas in this drunken state? I wanted to. My heart ached when I wasn't near him and I thought of him every minute of every day. *But would it be worth the risk?*

"Give me a week," I said, helping him up. "One week without flowers, calls, or visits. I need to think."

He stayed quiet for a second before he nodded, running a hand through his hair. "I'm sorry, Baby."

I called him a cab and made sure he got in safe, before I went back in, hoping this week might give me time to come to a decision as to what to do about Charlie and my broken heart.

CHAPTER 35
Jordan

I didn't last a week though.

That Friday, I decided to listen to all the voicemails Charlie had left me over the last couple of weeks.

"Hey, Baby. I know you're probably not going to listen to this, but I just needed to talk to you, I guess. I'll say this every day for the rest of my life; I'm so incredibly sorry for the way I acted. I panicked, to put it simply. It's no excuse and I never should've said those things to you, but I wanted you to know. I love you."

I was in tears by the time I had listened to that last message, trembling hands lowering the phone.

"I love you, too," I whispered, staring at the floor for a minute before I sprinted to my bedroom. Throwing on some sneakers, I frantically searched my apartment for my keys, shrieking when I found them. *I am going to get my man.*

Stepping on the gas probably wasn't a good idea, especially since I got pulled over before I made it even halfway to Charlie's apartment.

"I'm sorry, officer," I said, handing him my license.

He raised a brow at me, walking back to his car. *I can pay for this ticket. It's ok. Charlie could wait a few minutes, right?*

Walking as slow as humanly possible, the police officer made his way back, returning my license and giving me a ticket. "Please keep the speed limit in mind, ma'am."

On my way to the love of my life, I'm on the clock, sir.

"I will." I smiled, throwing my license and the ticket on the passenger seat and driving off. I saw the officer shake his head, but I shifted my eyes back on the road. I was so nervous I had a hard time holding the wheel, shaking, clammy hands grabbing it for dear life. Butterflies were swarming my stomach, making me overthink my decision. *No, fuck that. I want him.*

Smiling at the doorman as I skipped into Charlie's building, I couldn't contain my excitement. Was I getting my happy ending after all?

Swiping the card I had never managed to throw away, I stepped into the elevator. I watched the numbers go by, impatiently tapping my foot on the bottom of the lift as it ascended. I took a deep breath when I reached his floor, almost jumping out when the doors rolled open.

He stood in the kitchen, leaning on the counter and swirling a spoon in a cup of coffee. Even though I was eager to touch him, feel him, I took a second to look at him. He looked better than he did last week, and I sighed inaudibly.

"Charlie," I croaked out, my face undoubtedly red.

His head shot up and his eyes widened when he saw me. "Baby?"

I didn't say anything. Instead, with tears running down my face, I ran up to him, jumping into his arms.

He let out a relieved moan as I pressed my lips on his, unable to be close enough. His hands grabbed the back of my legs and lifted me on the kitchen counter, parting my lips with his.

"I love you," I whispered in between kisses, pushing my tongue into his mouth and pulling him closer than humanly possible.

"I love you, too," he breathed, his hands roaming my body. "So Goddamn much."

I felt feverish with desire, but it went much deeper than that. I could breathe again. The weight had lifted off my shoulders, and Charlie had been the missing link.

Moaning softly, I threw my head back and gave him more access to my neck as he trailed kisses down. I curled my legs around his waist, pulling him against me and feeling his hard length against my core. "Shit."

"I've missed you, Baby." He grabbed the hem of my shirt, pulling it over my head and chucking it on the floor. I reached behind my back and undid my bra, throwing it over my shoulder.

Grabbing Charlie's shirt, buttons flew everywhere when I ripped it open. He didn't even say anything about it, or about the mess we were making in his apartment, and I couldn't help but smile against his lips as he captured them again.

"I need you." I felt his breath against my chest as he trailed kisses down, and I buried my hands in his hair.

"I need you, too. Please."

We quickly stripped each other until we were both naked, and I gasped when he pushed two fingers inside me. I was swiftly reminded of Charlie's expert knowledge of my body, and I had no idea how I ever made it so long without him.

"Oh, God." My eyes rolled back in my head and I grabbed his shoulder with force, digging my fingers into his skin. Pleasure surged through me as he worked my g-spot, my toes curling at the amazing sensation only *he* could make me feel.

"I want to—" I said, but Charlie interrupted me with a grin.

"I know." He carried me to the floor-to-ceiling windows, pushing me against one and digging his hands in my legs. With one arm up against the glass in an attempt to hold myself up, I moaned loudly when he entered me, filling me to the hilt.

"I missed your cock," I breathed out with a grunt, my brows furrowing as he started to move. God, he was so big, *I love it*.

"I missed everything about you," he said in a strained voice, thrusting me against the window. Our quick breaths became one, just like we did. I dug my heels in his ass, my free hand grabbing his neck.

"More." I arched my back and leaned my head against the cold glass behind me.

I couldn't contain my moans as he slammed into me harder, to the point where I would bruise for sure.

"Little more," I breathed out, feeling my orgasm building. He grabbed my ass and forced me harder onto him, pushing me over the edge.

"Fuck, fuck, fuck," I shrieked, my voice getting higher and higher as I came, my walls tightening around Charlie's dick.

He continued to thrust into me, riding out my orgasm while chasing his own. The groan he let out when he filled me was almost enough to make me come again, and he rested his forehead against mine when he came back down from his high.

We were both still panting, trying to catch our breath, and I cupped his face with my hands. I could drown in those beautiful light blue eyes of his as I looked at him, and I brought my lips back to his.

He kissed me tenderly, as if he was scared to ruin the moment, to lose me again, or to get woken up from a dream. *It's not a dream though. Thank God, it's not a dream.*

We stayed there for a minute, just kissing and getting lost in each other, oblivious to the fact that the people in the building across the street could see us, naked, in front of the window. We couldn't care less.

Letting out a sigh, I pulled back and brushed my fingers through his hair. "Want to take a shower with me?"

Charlie smirked and placed me back on the floor, grabbing my hand to pull me in the direction of his bathroom. I was eager to follow him, skipping to the shower.

We stood there under the hot water, kissing, touching each other. At one point, I was just leaning against his chest, enjoying the feel of his skin against mine and listening to his steady heartbeat.

"I love you," I said softly, feeling like I could utter the words every single day for the rest of my life.

Charlie kissed me on the top of my head, grabbing a bottle of shower gel and taking some in his hands. "I love you, too. I mean it, Baby."

I smiled up at him before he turned me around, rubbing his hands over my back to cover me in his scent. Standing there, I just decided to enjoy this moment, until he was done cleaning off all the soap suds, and it was my turn.

"Baby?" he said when I rubbed some shower gel over his shoulders.

"Hmm?"

I frowned when he stayed silent, and I turned him around in my hands, wrapping my arms around his waist. "What's up?"

He rolled his bottom lip between his teeth, studying my face as I rested my chin on his chest.

"Do you..." he paused, licking his lips before looking me straight in the eyes. "Do you want to move in with me?"

I swallowed hard, looking at him with wide eyes. I wasn't thinking about my answer though. I knew my answer. But I just wanted to be sure that I had heard him right before I would embarrass myself. "What?"

"Do you want to move in with me? Here, in this apartment. Or maybe we could get something of our own..."

"Yes!" I exclaimed, wrapping my arms around his neck and pressing my lips to his. My heart almost exploded from the amount of happiness I felt, and I swear I was going to pass out.

We finished our shower together, and I dressed in a pair of his sweats and a T-shirt, curling up against him on the bed while we watched a movie.

He drew circles over my arm, occasionally kissing my hair. I had closed my eyes, just smiling as I breathed in his scent.

"I think I've loved you since we first started our arrangement," Charlie suddenly said, and I rested my chin on his chest, looking up at him. He looked back with adoration, and I felt so much happiness I could cry all over again.

"You did?" I questioned, placing my hands on his chest and leaning on them.

"Hmm," he hummed, tucking a strand of hair behind my ear. "Oh, before I forget."

"Hey!" I scoffed when he pushed me off, jumping from the bed and walking out of the bedroom, only to return a few seconds later.

"I had it fixed." He showed me the pink stone of the necklace I had missed so much, and I smiled. He beckoned for me to turn around, and I held up my hair as he put the necklace back where it belonged.

His fingers lingered on my neck, and I closed my eyes. "I really *am* sorry, Baby," he said, brushing his hand over my shoulder. "What I said was wrong, hurtful, and most of all not true."

I turned, crawling onto his lap and placing my hands around his neck. "I forgive you." He opened his mouth to say something, but I interrupted him. "You get one chance though. Break my heart again and it's game over."

"Noted." He pecked me on the lips, grabbing my waist. "Want to go again?"

I pushed him back on the bed without another word, straddling his hips and leaning forward to kiss his chest. Sucking the skin, I created a trail of hickeys down. I was about to pull down his sweats and take him into my mouth when we heard the buzzer.

"For fuck's sake!" I exclaimed, rolling off of him.

Charlie chuckled, slapping me on the ass before he walked

out of the bedroom to see who was disturbing our peace. I flipped on my back, scrolling through my phone to kill the time, but I shot up when I heard a familiar voice.

"Jesus, Charlie." Ah, it's Ashley.

Giddy with excitement, I skipped off the bed and straightened out Charlie's shirt, tiptoeing to the living room.

"Nice to see you, too, baby sis," Charlie replied, and I was about to walk into the room when Ashley spoke up again.

"What the hell are you doing? Fucking around? You should be fighting for Jordan!"

I smiled, walking up to the pair. "Hey, Ash."

"Oh," she said, watching me curl my arm around Charlie's waist and rest my head against his chest. "Ew."

Charlie and I chuckled.

"So are you two..." She moved a finger between us.

I looked up at Charlie, realizing that we hadn't discussed that part. We were going to be a couple now, right? He looked down at me, a classic smirk paired with cute dimples plastered on his face. "Yes, we are. I'm never letting go of this woman."

Ashley shrieked, jumping toward us and wrapping her arms around the both of us. "This is so exciting! Gross, but exciting!"

"Yeah, yeah. Get off," Charlie huffed, pushing his sister off and snaking an arm around me to pull me tighter. "Why are you here anyway?"

"Right. I thought we could eat together."

"I already ate," Charlie retorted, giving me a quick look.

"Watch it, Pretty Boy," I scolded with a grin, slapping him playfully on the chest.

"I didn't need to know that." Ashley sighed, rolling her

eyes. "We'll have dinner another time." She turned on her heel, heading for the elevator, but just as Charlie grabbed my ass, she faced us again. "Oh, by the way."

I slapped Charlie's hand away, raising my brows. "Yes?"

Ashley ignored her brother's chuckle. "Mom invited us to dinner on Sunday. You too, Jordan."

Without saying anything else—*probably being ready to run out of this apartment*—Ashley made her way to the elevator. I loved her, but Charlie and I had time to make up for, so I was happy she didn't stick around.

"So..." I brushed a finger down his chest, following the grooves of his muscles.

"What do you want to do, Baby?" He smirked.

I licked his chest, standing on my toes to whisper in his ear. "What about number...sixty-nine?"

He startled me by throwing me over his shoulder and carrying me back to the bedroom where he threw me on the bed. "Come on, Jordan," he said, pushing off his joggers. "Get naked."

He honestly didn't have to tell me twice. *God, I had missed this.* Not just the sex, but our banter, his humor, and his charm. I thoroughly enjoyed the way we were together.

"Wait," I stated in confusion, thinking about the most comfortable way to do this. "How...?"

Charlie got on the bed, laying on his back. "Come sit on my face, lips around my cock."

I did as he said, admitting that this position sounded good in my head, but was harder to act out than I thought. *I swear I went to college.* Not that...whatever.

Digging my teeth in my lower lip, I straddled his head, feeling a little self-conscious about the proximity of his face to my pussy. "Relax, Baby. If you don't want to do this, just say the word."

I appreciated him comforting me, the action giving me the final push. *Let's fucking do this.*

It was hard not to gasp as I wrapped my lips around his hard length since Charlie was working his hot tongue around my clit in perfect swirls. It was even harder to focus on the task at hand as he ate me out like no tomorrow, the word *pleasure* not doing this feeling any justice.

"Hmm," I hummed, moaning against his dick, and I felt a bit more confident when I noticed that Charlie was getting a little distracted too.

After a couple of minutes of pleasuring each other, I had enough. It simply wasn't doing it for me. "Charlie," I breathed out, rolling off of him and spreading my legs. "Can you just fuck me?"

He didn't seem too bummed about the fact that I cut our little experiment short, especially when he pushed into me with force, showing me once again, what *real* pleasure felt like.

CHAPTER 36
Jordan

It was like we couldn't keep our hands off of each other. Somehow, we found a way to touch. Whether it was holding hands, leaning onto each other, or just randomly caressing a shoulder, it was all we did.

Looking at our intertwined fingers, I still felt a little nervous as we walked to the restaurant Charlie wanted to take to me for lunch.

People weren't staring, and I didn't hear any cameras, but I had to remind myself that it was ok. We didn't have to hide anymore.

I felt relieved everything turned out ok, even though I wasn't letting him forget about his little mistake any time soon. But at the same time, that's not what love is—keeping score of who hurt who and reminding someone every day about their wrongdoings.

I wouldn't go as far as saying I was suddenly a love expert. Far from it. But from what I've seen from my parents, and then Dad and Eliza, making mistakes was part of the ride. I loved Charlie, and he admitted his mistake in the end. That's a good start.

Charlie gave my hand a little squeeze, nudging his head in the direction of an Italian restaurant. *Of course.*

I smiled up at him, following him inside.

"Ah, Mr. Abbot," the hostess said, flipping her hair over her shoulder. "How are you?"

I probably looked like I just smelled something disgusting as she batted her fake eyelashes at *my* man, but I instantly relaxed when he spoke up. "Never been better. Let me introduce you to my *girlfriend.*"

Don't do a happy dance, Jordan.

"Hi, I'm Jordan," I said with a smile, holding out my free hand to the brunette.

She seemed surprised but quickly regained composure, shaking my hand. "I'm Vera, nice to meet you."

I ignored the lack of sincerity in her voice, getting back to sticking against Charlie's side, who didn't seem to mind all too much.

"Do you have a table for two?" He asked, and Vera nodded, grabbing some menus.

"Follow me." She weaved through the tables with ease until we reached a cute spot in the corner, tea lights already lit.

We got comfortable on the bench, the both of us flipping through the menu.

"Charlie?" I asked, biting my lip. "You called me your

girlfriend."

He looked up at me with a little worry in his eyes, and I placed my hand on his. "I'm sorry, I shouldn't have presumed—"

I interrupted him with a chuckle, shaking my head lightly. "No. I want to be."

He startled me by jumping up from the couch, his menu clattering on the table. "Listen up everybody!"

"Charlie." I tugged at his arm, trying to get him to sit down.

He ignored me, continuing his announcement. "This beautiful woman just agreed to be my girlfriend."

The restaurant stayed silent, apart from a few chuckles and awkward applause from one girl who probably didn't know how to react.

"Good for you, man," a guy replied before diving back into his risotto, and I rolled my eyes.

I smiled up to Charlie, though embarrassed, feeling happy and proud. I had my doubts about giving in to him, but it was safe to say that he wasn't afraid to show me off. Nobody ever did that before, and it felt great.

"I love you, Baby," he said when he sat back down, pecking me quickly on the lips.

"I love you, too." I smiled, watching a waitress walk over. *Shit, I have no clue what they even serve here.*

—

As I watched Charlie move the last set of boxes around his—*our*—apartment, I wouldn't have been surprised if people from miles away could see me glow.

No more money trouble, no more shady streets I had to cross to get home, and most of all, I was moving in with the man of my dreams.

"Are you just going to stand there or are you going to get your cute ass over here and help me unpack *your* stuff," Charlie said over his shoulder, catching me staring.

"I was enjoying the view," I muttered, watching him straighten up, his shirt stretching tightly over his shoulders.

"Hmm." He walked up to me and smiled, grabbing me by the hips and pulling me closer. "I'm so happy."

My eyes shot up to his, my heart bursting with joy and love. Of course, I felt the same, but I would never miss an opportunity to tease him. "Jesus, you're getting cheesy."

He chuckled, the low rumble making my insides tingle—*in a good way*. I pressed my lips on his, catching him off guard. Wrapping my arms around his neck, I pulled myself even closer, getting ready to devour him.

It's been all I wanted to do for the last couple of days.

"Baby," he mumbled against my mouth, pushing me back.

I looked up to him with a pout, waiting for him to tell me why the fuck he was cock blocking me. *And himself.*

"First we unpack, then we fuck in every room of the house."

My pout turned into a smirk, and I narrowed my eyes at him. "We've already fucked in every room of the house though."

He shook his head, biting his lower lip before he spoke. "You live here now, we've hit the reset button."

Rolling my eyes, yet amused, I walked past him, grabbing one of the boxes and ripping it open. We quickly emptied every last box, and a pizza and two glasses of wine later, we were done.

I couldn't contain my smile.

It was getting darker outside, and the lights of the city gave us a terrific view, something we often just stared at for an entire evening. This time it meant we were getting late for dinner at my dad's, though.

My eyes on the buildings, I took this moment. "Are you happy, Baby?" Charlie asked, walking up behind me and wrapping his arms around my waist.

"I am," I replied, resting my head back against his chest.

He brought his lips to my ear. "I love you."

I turned and gave him a quick kiss before I walked off. "Ew."

Charlie's laugh echoed through the apartment, making me very aware of the fact that the record in the player was done, and it was time for us to go.

I was nervous about introducing Charlie to my dad, but at the same time excited.

I couldn't contain my smile as I sat in the passenger seat of Charlie's Camaro fifteen minutes later, staring out the window as we made our way to my childhood home.

"Are you nervous?" he asked, placing a hand on my thigh.

I sighed, remembering that one night my dad had mentioned he was glad I didn't associate with people like Charlie. The very man I was now dating.

"I just hope my dad likes you," I replied, turning to him. He nodded, eyes still on the road and his other hand on the wheel, looking way too sexy as we arrived at our destination.

God, I wish we could just have a quick—

"Jordan?"

I broke from my daydream, noticing Charlie's smirk. "Let's get inside."

It was hard to mask my annoyance—*or rather, my frustration*—and he chuckled as he followed me out of the car.

"Are *you* nervous?" I asked when I noticed that he was rubbing his hands together, his breathing uneven and his jaw tensing.

"I guess I want your dad to like me, too." He pulled me against him for a final kiss, tenderly moving his mouth over mine. I huffed when the moment was over, leaning against his side as he pressed the doorbell.

Though I had told my father that I wanted to have dinner to introduce my boyfriend to him, I quickly stepped away from Charlie, anxiously waiting for the door to open.

"What?" Charlie asked, raising a brow at me.

"I don't—"

The door opened, and I held my breath as my father's dark eyes scanned over Charlie. "So," he said, crossing his arms. "You're dating my daughter?"

This was going to be great.

"Nice to meet you, sir," Charlie greeted, holding out his hand for my dad. "I'm Charlie Abbot."

I bit my lip at the mention of his last name and sighed when my dad realized what he just said. He narrowed his eyes at him before he spoke again. "Ashley's brother."

"Jordan!" Eliza pushed my father out of the way, wrapping her arms around me. "It's so good to see you."

I chuckled, hugging her back. "Likewise."

"And who is *this*?" She shot me a look.

"Charlie Abbot, ma'am. Jordan's boyfriend." He couldn't have said it with a wider smile, and I got giddy with excitement. My dad's face relaxed a little, and I could breathe again. *Maybe this wasn't going to be so bad.*

And I was right. Dad loosened up during dinner, and by the time we were ready to go, he and Charlie had flowed into conversation like it was second nature.

Of course, I knew Charlie was good with people, but I was still happily surprised.

CHAPTER 37
Charlie

Dinner with Jordan's father went better than expected. It took him about an hour to warm up to me, but eventually, he did. I didn't know I valued his opinion of me so much.

Eliza was a lot easier, and I thought that she was just very glad to see how happy Jordan was.

The next day, it was my parents' turn. Jordan had told me about her conversation with my mother, so I hoped that dinner was going to be bearable, though I was still furious about my dad's behavior.

"Are you ok, Baby?" I asked when we pulled up in front of the mansion.

Jordan was tapping her foot on the floor, her hands grabbing her thighs with so much force she was going to bruise herself. "What if your mother changed her mind? What if she hates me again? What if your dad throws me out? What if—" she rambled, and I interrupted her by placing my hand on one of hers.

"If they say even one thing to you that we don't like, we're leaving and getting McDonald's."

She smiled up at me, her leg relaxing. I kept my eyes on her, watching her smile change into a smirk, and her eyes sparkled with something else. Before I could register what was happening, she climbed over the console and straddled my legs, grabbing my face in her hands and pressing her lips on mine.

"I can't stop saying that I love you," she breathed through her kisses, and I grabbed her ass.

"Me neither," I replied, squeezing softly and deepening the kiss. "And I won't."

I pulled her closer onto me, moving my lips against hers and playing with her tongue. I would never get tired of kissing Jordan. *My* Jordan.

"How long do we have?" she breathed, one hand sliding down my chest and getting caught on one of the buttons.

"We can be fifteen minutes—oh, for fuck's sake."

We looked up when we heard a knock on the window, Ashley shielding her eyes as she mumbled something under her breath. Jordan climbed off of me and I flinched, having to adjust myself in my slacks after...well...anything to do with Jordan.

Cursing, I stepped out of the car.

"You guys are nasty," Ashley retorted, shaking her head and following Ryan into the house. I couldn't contain a smirk. *Yes, we were.*

"I know what we're doing straight after dinner," Jordan cooed, running a hand over my bicep before she took my hand.

"You're going to be the ruin of me, Jordan Sawyer."

"Hell yeah."

We walked into the house with probably the biggest smiles on our faces, and I took Jordan's coat.

"They're late," I heard my mother say from the dining room and I chuckled when Ashley replied.

"Oh, they're here. You don't want to know what they were up to in the car."

I rolled my eyes at her statement. I gestured for Jordan to walk ahead of me, and she frantically shook her head, pushing me forward. "Don't you dare do this to me."

"There they are," my mother exclaimed when we entered the room, the table already set. I gave my mom a hug, before stepping towards my sister.

"No, no, I don't know where those hands have been," she stated, avoiding my arms, and I chuckled.

I watched how Jordan walked up to Mom with a lot of hesitation in her step, the both of them not really knowing how to act around each other.

"Hi, Mrs. Abbot," Jordan croaked out, holding out her hand. My mom looked from her hand to her face, raising her brows. *Oh, no.*

Both Ashley and I gasped when she pulled Jordan against her chest, giving her a tight hug. "It's good to see you."

I smiled. Mom was really trying.

"Where's Dad?" I questioned, looking around the room. The table was set for five people and his chair was empty.

"He, erm…" Mom quickly looked up to Jordan before turning

back to me, clearly unsure how to approach this situation. "He couldn't—"

I sighed, angry at my father that he let my mother be the bad guy. "You don't have to lie for him."

Jordan and I took a seat next to each other, sliding our chairs a little closer together. It was safe to say we were addicted to each other. *And I love it.*

"Well, I'm proud of you, Mom," Ashley mentioned as she and Ryan sat opposite of us.

I cursed my dad for having the audacity to ask me to choose between the love of my life and my job, to not show up at dinner, and to continue to be an absolute ass to Jordan in general. *Fuck him.*

"So, how are you doing, Jordan?" Mom asked, diving into her dinner.

I looked to the gorgeous woman next to me, grabbing her hand that was laying on the table. She looked up at me with a smile, tucking a strand of hair behind her ear. "Never been better."

"Ugh," Ashley interrupted. "You guys are gross."

We chuckled, shifting our attention to our dinner as well.

—

The evening went better than expected, and surprisingly enough, Mom and Jordan seemed to really hit it off. Of course, there still was some tension, especially during certain subjects, but overall, everything seemed to fall into place.

We even stayed for a few drinks, not done with our conversations after we ate. It wasn't something we usually did, but maybe something really changed for the better.

I sipped my water, chatting with Ryan about work, but I couldn't help but look at Jordan every once in a while. She looked beautiful. She caught me staring and she smiled mischievously, gesturing to the hall. *What was she up to?*

"I'll ask about that position—" Ryan said but I cut him off, completely distracted. he was telling me about this job at his firm, but I only had eyes for one person.

"Yeah, great, give me a second."

I rose from my chair, ignoring the roll of Ryan's eyes and walking up to the three women. "Baby, what about a tour?"

Ashley looked up at me with her brows furrowed. "What do you mean? She's been here befo—ew."

Mom shook her head, walking over to Ryan, and Jordan jumped up. "Show me around, Pretty Boy," she squealed, grabbing my wrist and pulling me out of the living room.

"Where are we going, exactly?" I questioned with a chuckle, twirling her around when we arrived in the hall.

"Number seventy-seven?" She grinned, walking back towards the stairs.

I bit my lower lip, making my way to my childhood bedroom and tapping her on the ass before I sprinted past her. She giggled when I pulled her into my old room, her chest flush against mine and her lips inches from my neck.

"Now, what did you have in mind, Baby?" I cooed, grabbing her by the back of the legs and lifting her. She brushed her hands through my hair, capturing my lips in a toe-curling kiss and moving her hips against mine.

"You're so hot," I breathed, pushing her against the wall and sliding my hands to her ass. She smirked, unbuttoning the top few buttons of my shirt and bringing her lips to my chest, sucking and kissing as she went.

As much as I enjoyed her kisses, I enjoyed being the reason for her moans more.

Slapping her hand against her mouth when she let out a shriek, I threw her on the bed, crawling on top of her.

"Oh, God," she moaned when I pushed up her shirt and bra, desperate to touch her. I couldn't contain my smirk when she moaned again as I took a nipple into my mouth, humming against her skin.

"Charlie," she groaned, fumbling with my slacks, and I pulled her bra back down to get her comfortable.

"Alright, this is going to be quick," I breathed out, undoing her jeans and pulling them off. "And rough," she pushed down my slacks and underwear, taking my length in her hand. "But let's not scar my sister for life, ok?"

"Uh-huh," Jordan nodded with a moan, spreading her legs and grabbing the back of my neck.

I pushed into her slowly, trying not to hurt her before I received a frantic nod, telling me to continue. She gasped loudly as I started to move, and I covered her mouth with my hand, slamming into her harder.

—

About fifteen minutes later, we skipped down the stairs and made our way back to the living room.

"I hate you," Ashley hissed as she walked past us, moving to the kitchen to grab another drink. Jordan giggled, squeezing my ass before she followed her best friend, and I joined mine.

"I still can't believe it, man," Ryan said as I took a seat next to him on the couch.

I looked in the direction Jordan disappeared in. "Me neither."

I would never forget the way I spoke to her the first time she admitted her feelings, and my smile faded ever so slightly. I would spend the rest of my life making up for that massive mistake because she deserved the world. And I wanted to give it to her.

"You look happy," Mom mentioned as she sat across from me, placing her cup of tea on the table.

Jordan and Ashley walked back into the room, laughing about something. I flicked my eyes to the pair, letting out a breath before I answered. "I am."

Everyone looked up when we heard the front door close, and a few seconds later Dad walked in. He seemed surprised by the busy living room and clenched his jaw when his eyes landed on Jordan.

I knew it was jealousy with my Mom, but I was pretty sure it was all about reputation with my dad. Jordan didn't fit in his perfect image, and he couldn't handle it.

"Dad, good thing I saw you before we left," I said, walking up to Jordan and grabbing her hand. She shot me a questioning look, but I had made my decision. "I quit."

He gasped, furrowing his brows together and opening his mouth to say something, but I pulled Jordan with me out of the room. "We're leaving."

"Charles," my father warned, but I ignored him. I wasn't going to continue working for that sad excuse of a man. Jordan was going to do great things, and even if she wasn't, nobody deserved that kind of treatment.

"Babe?" Jordan said softly, brushing her hand over my arm as we walked outside.

"Hmm?"

"Are you sure?" She looked up to me with those big brown eyes, stopping me mid-step. I smiled at her. Staring at her full, perfect lips, smooth skin, and slightly messy hair. She looked beautiful no matter what happened or how much time she spent on herself, and I was more than ready to give up everything for her.

"I am."

She blushed, wrapping her arms around my waist and placing her head on my chest. "What are you going to do?"

I caressed a hand over her back, leaning my chin on her hair. "I've actually got an offer from a friend from college. It's been a few years, but you never know."

"Ok."

"And besides," I tilted her face up with two fingers, placing a soft kiss on her lips. "As long as you're in my life, nothing else matters."

Jordan scoffed with a slight blush on her cheeks, her eyes lowering to the gold watch around my wrist. "What about your money?"

She brought her lips to mine, smirking as she waited for me to answer. She had me there, but the job I was after actually paid more than my father ever did.

"Don't worry, we'll be fine."

CHAPTER 38
Jordan

I hadn't told anybody about my birthday. First of all, it was on Valentine's Day, and second, I didn't really celebrate it anymore. At work, there was no decoration for the holiday, but I heard everybody talking about having a romantic dinner and the amazing gifts they got for and from their significant other.

I stared at the clock on my screen, watching the final seconds of the day tick by, still not having received something from Charlie. It wasn't like I had anyone to celebrate with these last couple of years, but I guess I thought this year would be different.

"Jordan!" Nadine came running up to me with a magazine in her hands, her face red with excitement. I was sad that she was going back home in about two weeks, but I knew she needed to in order to make all her dreams come true.

"Are you ok?" I asked, logging off.

She tried to catch her breath when she reached my desk, holding out the tabloid. I took it from her, my eyes widening when my eyes fell on the page Nadine had it opened on.

There I was. My face plastered over the entire page, a small image of me and Charlie kissing in the corner. *Oh, God.*

I guess it didn't matter anymore, but I wasn't really used to being in the spotlight. Ashley had always managed to keep me somewhat out of the media, but of course, when Charlie Abbot kissed me in the middle of the street, I couldn't avoid it anymore.

"Are you guys dating?" Nadine questioned eagerly, almost bouncing on her feet.

I smiled at her, softly nodding my head. "Yes. I actually moved in with him."

She squealed, wrapping her arms around me. "Oh my God, finally!"

I shrugged. "Yeah, I guess everyone else knew we were in love with each other before we did, huh?"

Nadine released me, frowning at me. "Why are you still here? It's Valentine's Day!"

"Alright, I'm going." I grabbed my things, making sure my desk was tidy before I stood up. We made our way down together, chatting about her moving back to Sweden, and said goodbye at the front door.

I drove to Charlie's apartment—*I mean home*—mixed feelings swirling around in my stomach. Did he forget? Was he not going to do anything? *No, I shouldn't let it get to me.* I never told him when my birthday was, and maybe he just wasn't the type to be all romantic on this specific day.

Trying to stop overthinking, I took the elevator up, still wondering if I should say anything about it. Was it weird to want him to do something on Valentine's Day? To be fair, I hadn't prepared anything for him either. *Shit, I suck at being a girlfriend already.*

"No! Close your eyes!" Charlie yelled when the elevator doors rolled open, and I did as he said, a spark of happiness and relief going through me. *Ok, he didn't forget.*

He pulled me into the apartment, telling me to wait, and I heard the sound of a lighter and his footsteps. Just a few minutes later, I felt hands on my shoulders, and I grinned. "What are you up to, Pretty Boy?"

"Open your eyes, Baby."

I blinked a couple of times, not believing what I saw. The table was set up, complete with candles and wine, and Charlie had put on some music. Rose petals led to my seat, and I narrowed my eyes when I noticed actual food on the table.

"What..."

"Happy birthday."

My head shot up, looking into Charlie's beautiful blue eyes, and my breath hitched in my throat. "You...how?"

"Ashley." He shrugged and wrapped his arms around my waist, snuggling his face into my neck. "It's the first thing I asked when she found out."

I leaned back against him, my smile almost not fitting on my face.

"So, I tried to cook," he continued, leading me to the table and pulling out my chair. I dropped my bag on the couch and took a seat, looking at the plate of pasta with some hesitation. The last time he'd cooked, it didn't go very well. *Give him a chance Jordan, he tried.*

"Before we eat," he grabbed an envelope from the kitchen island, joining me at the table and holding it out to me. It didn't feel really heavy, and my curiosity was piqued. Charlie could be very unpredictable, so this could basically be anything.

I opened the envelope, taking out a folded piece of paper. Tears sprung into my eyes when I read the content, a two-week trip to Thailand staring back at me.

"Charlie..." I trailed off, reading on.

"It took me a while to figure everything out, but I thought it was important to you that we visited your family there."

I hadn't spoken to my Thai relatives in ages, especially since they weren't exactly thrilled that my mom got pregnant by an American, moved with him to the states, and decided to marry him. Therefore I never really knew my maternal grandparents, or any other relatives I had on that side of the family.

"But...what if they don't want to see me?" I choked out, wiping a few tears away and placing the envelope on the table.

"They do," Charlie reassured me, placing a hand on mine.

I looked up at him, happy tears streaming down my face. "I love you." I jumped up, hugging him in his seat and sobbing into his shoulder.

"I love you, too, Baby," he whispered in my ear, pulling me tighter against his chest.

We stayed like that for a few minutes until I had calmed down. Or, until he had calmed me down.

"So, what did you make?" I asked as I walked back to my seat, carefully wiping the remaining water from under my eyes.

Charlie looked from his plate to me, cocking his head to the side before he answered. "Remember that dish we ate on the square in Italy?"

I nodded, my lips curling into a smile when I realized that he tried to replicate it. My gaze moved to the pasta and red sauce that stared me in the face, my smile faltering when I remembered that Charlie couldn't cook anything other than pancakes.

"Uh..." I trailed off, looking up at him.

"Please try it first," he pleaded, and I picked up my fork. I slowly brought the pasta to my lips and took a bite, expecting an explosion of salt to hit me at any second. But, that didn't happen.

"Hmm," I hummed in satisfaction, enjoying the rich tomato and basil flavor.

Charlie's face lit up, and he started to devour his own plate.

"This tastes amazing," I admitted, nodding at him when he wanted to pour me a glass of wine. I watched the red liquid swirl around in my glass, and I quickly took a sip when Charlie was done pouring.

We talked about work and other little things as we finished dinner, and just before I had taken my last bite, he admitted that his mother had offered to teach him a few things. I found it absolutely adorable, and it made the evening even better.

"So, Pretty Boy, w-what's next?" I slurred, blaming the second bottle of red wine for my already drunken state.

Charlie chuckled, his cheeks almost as red as the sauce he had made for the pasta. "Whatever you want, Baby."

I kicked off my shoes, slowly standing from my chair while trying to stay upright. I walked up to him, climbing onto his lap. "I want you to rip my clothes off, bend me over the back of the couch and...and take me from behind."

He opened his mouth to say something, but I wasn't done yet. I wiped a hand over my face, feeling my hot skin under my fingers, and blurted out something I had wanted to do for the longest time, but now I was intoxicated enough to admit it. "And I want you to record it."

His eyes lit up like a Christmas tree, and before I knew what was happening, he had grabbed both sides of my blouse, ripping it open. Buttons flew everywhere, but Charlie was too busy trailing kisses down my neck to notice.

I moaned softly, enjoying the feel of his warm breath against my skin as I closed my eyes when the world started to spin around me.

"Fuck, you're so out of my league," he groaned, undoing my bra before placing me back on my feet.

I smiled, feeling powerful and incredibly desirable as I stood there, lightly swaying from side to side.

I giggled when Charlie jumped up and almost kicked over his chair, wrapping his arms around my waist and carrying me to the back of the sofa. He was probably the only man who could make me feel that way as he was throwing me around like a rag doll, bending me over the back of the couch and ripping off my thong.

"Stockings stay on. God, you're so hot." He slapped my ass, walking around the couch to set up his phone, and I grinned into the camera.

"Yes, s-sir," I purred, wiggling my ass against him when he returned behind me, managing to stay standing.

"Oh, hold on."

I huffed in annoyance, rolling my eyes when he disappeared into the bedroom, but that feeling quickly vanished when he held up a butt plug. He put it in with ease, rubbing his cock over my pussy to coat himself in my already flowing juices before he lined himself up with my entrance. It took him a few tries to get the tip of his dick into me, but I didn't care.

I felt his lips next to my ear and I swear he could hear my heartbeat as I waited for him to push further in. "Now, tell me," he slowly slid himself in, and I moaned loudly, the feeling of the plug and his big cock creating the perfect pleasurable tension. "What do you want?"

I squeezed my eyes shut, trying to cope with the pressure deep inside me. "I want you to fuck me hard. So hard, Pretty Boy," I groaned, grabbing the back of the couch with so much force my knuckles turned white.

"Hmm, like this?" He slammed into me, taking me by surprise, and I gasped loudly, my eyes shooting open.

"Oh, God. Harder," I managed to squeak out, my head falling back when he grabbed my hair in his fist and pulled. He pushed in harder, and I felt something uncomfortable.

"Bubble Gum, Bubble Gum," I said quickly, and Charlie froze inside me.

"Are you ok?" he asked, loosening his grip on my hair and brushing some out of my face. I tried to catch my breath, swallowing before I managed to speak again.

"Maybe not *that* hard." I chuckled, arching my back against him. "But continue."

Torturously slow, he started to move again, placing sloppy kisses over my back. At one point, we both lost our footing, and I giggled as we continued our little *workout* on the carpet. I felt my cheeks burn up, listening to our skin slapping together and

I spread my legs even further to take as much of him as I could.

"Oh, yes," I moaned, reaching over my head and grabbing the edge of the couch to try and steady myself.

"Come on, Baby," Charlie groaned, his voice strained and his thrusts getting a little sloppy.

He placed his hand on my throat and pushed me into the floor, and I felt my orgasm coming. Screaming out his name, I came hard, letting myself go entirely as I felt my legs shake with pleasure.

With a few final grunts, Charlie finished inside me, the fingers of his free hand digging into my thigh as he kept my leg wrapped around his waist. Our breathing heavy, we stayed in that position for a minute, our skin sticking together and our juices slowly dripping down my leg.

"I will never get tired of fucking you," he panted into my ear, and I chuckled.

When we had calmed down, we cleaned ourselves up and pulled on some comfy clothes, slouching on the couch in front of the TV.

"Oh," Charlie breathed out when he grabbed his phone. "I think I forgot to hit 'record.'"

We chuckled, deciding to cross that item off another day. Besides, we had plenty of time to finish the list anyway.

EPILOGUE

"We have ten minutes until Ashley's speech," I stated as Charlie pushed me into the men's room.

"She'll wait," he said, locking the door and crashing me against the opposite wall as he attacked my lips. I moaned into the kiss, fumbling with his belt as he grabbed my breasts in his hands.

It was hard to concentrate on what I was doing because Charlie had slid the straps of my dress off my shoulders, and was rubbing his thumbs gently over my nipples. "Hmm." I finally got his pants unbuttoned, and pushed them down, taking his briefs with them.

"Fuck, I love you," Charlie mumbled against my lips as I started to stroke his length.

"I love your massive dick," I breathed out, using my free hand to pull Charlie closer by the back of his neck.

"I know." He smirked.

Heavy breathing and gasps filled the air as he turned me towards the vanity, bending me over the counter. "Careful!" I scolded, grabbing a towel and placing it between me and the counter.

"Why do wedding dresses have so much fabric?" Charlie grumbled as he gathered the skirt and pulled it up, over my ass.

"Don't you *dare* rip my thong. It was expensive," I warned, looking over my shoulder. A grin crept onto Charlie's face.

"I can buy you a hundred thongs."

I rolled my eyes, turning back to the mirror and shooting him an air kiss. "This one's special."

"Alright," he sighed, pushing the underwear aside and positioning the tip of his cock at my entrance. I steadied myself by leaning one hand on the mirror in front of me and moaned loudly when Charlie grabbed my hips and pushed into me.

"Fuck, Charlie!" I gasped as he slammed into me, banging me against the counter, my breasts moving in sync with his shocks.

"Yes, moan my name, wife!" he groaned, his eyes staring at the reflection of my chest. I lifted my shoulders a little to give him a better view, smiling at the little *Pretty Boy* tattoo under my left boob. I chuckled softly at his comment, still not believing that we were actually married. Nor that he had *Baby* tattooed on his left pec, making us matching.

If someone would have told me two years ago that I would be getting fucked in the bathroom at my wedding by my husband, *Charlie Abbot*, I would've laughed in their face. But I couldn't be happier.

"Yes," I moaned, closing my eyes and moving my hips to meet his thrusts. "Oh, God."

"A little more, Baby," Charlie groaned, and my walls tightened, the euphoric feeling washing over me as I came, triggering his orgasm. We stayed there catching our breath, as we probably kept our guests waiting, but it was our wedding, so fuck it.

—

"I know it's your wedding and all, but gross," Ashley hissed when we walked back into the main room where the reception was being held.

"What can I say, I couldn't wait until our wedding night," Charlie retorted, and I playfully slapped him on the chest as he gave my ass a little squeeze.

"Oh, come on, Ash," Bailey said, clutching her husband's hand tighter. "You remember your wedding."

Ashley rolled her eyes, handing me a glass of bubbly. I knew she tried to hide it, but I could see the jealousy in her eyes when I took a sip.

"There you are," Mrs. Abbot said as she joined us, her cheeks flushed and a big smile on her face. Or was I supposed to say Ms. Johnson-Ray, since the divorce was just about final? *Doesn't matter.*

Over the last couple of years, she had really proven herself to me, showing us that she was serious when she said she wanted to make it up to me. I was grateful to have her here. We hadn't seen Mr. Abbot in months, and Charlie had made sure that he wasn't attending our wedding.

"Are you enjoying yourself, Mrs. Abbot?" I asked and she

chuckled softly.

"Oh, Jordan, please call me Nicole."

I nodded, playing with my mother's ring, the one Charlie had used to propose to me.

"Honey." Dad came walking up to us, stopping next to me and looking at Ashley's belly. "Am I going to get any grandkids?"

Charlie and I looked at each other, a smirk on our lips. "I'm sorry, Dad," I chuckled, patting him on the shoulder.

"I guess it's my own fault," he sighed, and I leaned against his chest. "Should've had more children."

"Excuse me," Mrs. Abbot said, her brows furrowed. "Am I *not* going to get any grandkids?"

"Uhm, Mom," Ashley replied, pointing to her protruding stomach.

"Oh, yes. I can always count on you."

They gave each other a hug before Ashley and Ryan walked off in search of a place to sit. I watched them walk away, feeling Charlie's arm pulling me against him. We had discussed the subject of children before and quickly came to the conclusion that we were fine with just being the rich and amazing aunt and uncle.

We were too busy completing the list anyway.

THE LIST

1. Threesome;
2. Edging;
3. Tying up;
4. Handcuffs;
5. Blindfolding;
6. Using a vibrator;
7. Nipple clamps;
8. Hair pulling;
9. Hot wax;
10. Ice;
11. Tickler;
12. Use a whip, paddle, riding crop, flogger or belt;
13. Butt plug;
14. Flavored lube/condoms;
15. Massages;
16. Spanking;
17. Roleplay;
18. Sex dice;
19. Choking;
20. Anal beads;
21. Finger in the ass;
22. Anal;
23. Phone sex;
24. Video chat-sex;

25. Sexting;
26. Sending nudes;
27. Go down on each other while on an important phone call;
28. A quickie in the office;
29. Car sex;
30. Sex in a pool;
31. Hot tub sex;
32. Sex outside;
33. Having sex when someone is watching;
34. Sex in a public place;
35. Sex in another country;
36. Hotel room sex;
37. Mile high club;
38. Sex on a boat;
39. Sex in the back of the movie theatre;
40. Sex on another continent;
41. Sex on the beach;
42. Sex in the wilderness;
43. Sex at a party without being heard;
44. Sex in a fitting room;
45. Sex in every room of the house;
46. Sex on a washing machine;
47. A quickie in the bathroom;
48. Sex in the bed of a pick-up;
49. Sex in someone else's bed;
50. Sex against the window;
51. Sex on the balcony;
52. Sex standing up;
53. Sex while fully clothed;

54. Vibrating panties;
55. Touch each other under the table;
56. Sex with food involved;
57. Edible underwear;
58. Only oral;
59. Only use your hands;
60. Without hands;
61. Nipple orgasm;
62. Super loud sex;
63. Silent sex;
64. Sex in the shower;
65. Sex without a condom;
66. Try hardcore, rough, sex;
67. Double penetration;
68. Roadhead;
69. I mean...
70. Rip each other's clothes off;
71. Naked workout;
72. Post-workout sex;
73. Stip tease;
74. Romantic candle lit sex;
75. Sex in front of a fireplace;
76. Sex while looking in each other's eyes;
77. Having sex in your childhood bedroom;
78. Masturbate in front of each other;
79. Coming over each other's faces;
80. Orgasm at the same time;
81. 12-hour sex;
82. Watch porn together;

83. Drunk sex;
84. Angry sex;
85. Period sex;
86. Midnight wake-up call;
87. Make a sex tape
88. Only about her/him;
89. Allow her to dominate for the night;
90. Sexy surprise;
91. Ceiling mirror;
92. Answer the door naked;
93. Try to make her squirt;
94. Leave at least three hickeys;
95. Sex on the lunch break;
96. Sex under the full moon;
97. Cum panties;
98. Doing everything the partner says for 24 hours;
99. Five orgasms in under 60 minutes;
100. Have sex a hundred times.

BONUS SCENE

"So our wedding anniversary is coming up," Charlie said with a shiver, walking around the kitchen island and turning on the coffee machine.

"Stop shivering when you say 'wedding'. *You* asked *me* to marry you, remember," I retorted, hopping onto one of the high chairs and watching him move around the kitchen without a shirt on.

"Yes, erm," he mumbled, grabbing two cups. "Well, I was thinking..." He played with one of the cups, keeping his eyes down. "We've never done the first item on the list."

I listened to the coffee machine as it poured, standing from my chair to grab it with a smirk. "Luna already said yes."

Charlie looked at me with his jaw to the floor. "I *knew* there was a reason I married you. But wait, Luna?"

"Hmm." I grabbed my cup, turned to leave, and sat down at the dinner table.

"But...but she's into women," he stuttered, watching me as I walked away.

"I know," I said with a smirk, shooting him a wink over my shoulder.

Naturally, when I thought of a threesome, I wanted to make sure I wasn't just going to watch while someone fucked *my* man. And Luna was all too eager to accept when I asked, so...

"I...ok," Charlie said, grabbing his own cup and joining me at the table. "When is this happening?"

I grinned, taking a sip from my coffee. "Next Saturday. I actually wanted to surprise you, but I guess now you have something to look forward to."

He smiled. "Hell yes."

―

While Charlie woke up excited and full of energy that following Saturday, I felt myself growing more anxious every hour.

"Baby?" he asked, moving to stand behind me as I poured a cup of tea and carefully wrapping his arms around my waist.

"Hmm?"

"Are you ok?"

I put the kettle down and turned, placing my head on his chest. "I'm just nervous."

He tightened his grip on me and I closed my eyes. It wasn't

that I didn't want to do this anymore. If I was being honest I had been thinking about a threesome with Luna since we first met, but it was something I had never done before.

"We don't have to do this, Baby," Charlie mumbled against my hair as he leaned forward to kiss me on top of my head.

I sighed. "I know." I looked up at him and smiled. "But I want to."

As if on cue, the buzzer sounded through the apartment, and I straightened up. "How are we even supposed to do this?" I questioned, my mind going a million miles per hour. "How do we start? Do I need to offer her a drink first? Will we—"

"Jordan," Charlie interrupted me, grabbing me by my jaw. "Just go with it. And the minute you want to stop, you tell us."

All my nerves disappeared into thin air when Luna came strutting in a few minutes later, her high heels clicking against the hardwood floor and her light ponytail swaying from side to side. "Hey," she purred, her gaze traveling over my red mini dress and down my legs, the look in her eyes alone sparking something inside me. Ok, this was definitely not going to be that bad.

"Yes, hi. I'm here too," Charlie said, dimming the lights before walking up to us.

"What's up, Abbot," Luna replied, grabbing my hand and pulling in the direction of the hall.

I smiled at him over my shoulder, following the blonde until she didn't know where to go. "In here." I led her to our bedroom, opening the door with slightly shaking hands.

Beyond that point, I was in uncharted territory. I never had a threesome in my life, nor taken a woman into my bedroom, so the next thing I did was just stand there awkwardly. "I actually don't—"

Luna didn't give me a chance to finish my sentence, interrupting me by pressing her lips on mine.

A soft squeaky sound left my throat, probably out of surprise, but after a few seconds, I managed to melt into her completely. I jumped slightly when I felt hands on my waist—different ones, bigger ones. *Thank God, Charlie is here.*

"Relax, Baby," he whispered into my ear, bringing his lips to my neck and sucking the skin between his teeth.

I let out a soft moan when Luna trailed kisses down my throat, her hand pushing the straps off my shoulder.

Shit, shit, this was really happening.

Unsure what to do with my hands, I decided to explore a little of Luna. As Charlie undressed me and Luna continued to kiss and lick every inch of skin she could find, I let my hands roam over her curves, playing with the hem of her dress.

She was quick to respond, pulling the flimsy piece of fabric over her head and throwing it on the floor. She hummed against my skin, hooking her fingers under the waistband of my thong before pulling it down.

Once I was completely naked, I turned to Charlie, feeling like I needed a little more of him to get thrown into the mix.

"Hey," he purred, smiling against my lips as he kissed me, and I gasped when I felt Luna's hand slide down my stomach.

I tried to undo Charlie's buttons, but I failed miserably when Luna's delicate fingers disappeared between my folds, quickly finding my clit.

So, I just wrapped my arms around my husband's neck and moaned against his mouth as he worked my nipples. "Oh, God." I leaned my forehead against Charlie's, the pleasure both him and Luna were causing to shoot through me almost getting the better of me.

Luna brushed my hair off my shoulder with her free hand, placing kisses in my neck as two of her fingers dipped into me, rubbing the perfect spot deep inside of me.

Charlie was just looking at me at that point, watching me as I came closer and closer to the edge, ready to get pushed over. I knew he enjoyed watching me come, but I never thought he'd enjoy it as much when it weren't *his* fingers that were providing me with an orgasm.

His pupils were enormous, the lust and love in his eyes shining through and adding to the tingle that started at the bottom of my spine. I took a deep breath, getting ready to explode over Luna's fingers way faster than I liked, and Charlie grabbed my jaw to keep me from looking away from him.

"Fuck, fuck, fuck," I breathed with my brows furrowed, my walls tightening and my fingers digging into Charlie's shoulders as I came.

Holy shit.

Luna hummed behind me, placing soft kisses on my shoulders as she rode out my orgasm with her fingers, and I swallowed hard when I came back from my high.

An idea popped up in my head and I turned to the gorgeous blonde behind me, slowly pushing her back onto the bed. She kept looking at me with those big blue eyes, the color darker and more vibrant than Charlie's.

I had always had an interest in exploring the bedroom with a woman, and even though this was literally Charlie's dream, I was doing this more for me.

Luna gasped, falling backward on the bed and I watched her abs flex as she steadied herself. "You're wearing too much," I said, my voice thick with desire.

"Alright, tell me what to do, tiger," she replied with a smirk, her light hair falling out of the ponytail she had been wearing.

I swallowed hard, taking a step in her direction. "Take off your underwear and get on your knees."

Charlie let out a soft groan, closing in at my side. Adrenaline coursed through me when Luna started to unhook her bra, and I totally understood why Charlie liked to bark orders at me in the bedroom so much. This was exhilarating.

I turned to my husband, cocking a brow. "You too."

His eyes sparkled as he unbuckled his belt and undid his slacks, pushing them down. He stripped off his shirt and boxers, getting on his knees beside Luna on the bed. They shared a look, and I sighed.

Come on. You got this. Pleasing two people at the same time. And a woman. Jesus, you are *a woman, Jordan.*

I crawled on the bed in front of them, lowering my face to Charlie's erection as my fingers trailed between Luna's thighs.

"Oh, Baby," Charlie moaned when I took his tip between my lips, and Luna gasped when I quickly found the bundle of nerves at the apex of her thighs.

"Jesus," she breathed out, rocking her hips against my hand as I swirled over her clit.

Charlie grabbed my hair as I sucked him off, wrapping it around his hand until his grip felt almost painful, and I moaned against him as I slid my fingers inside Luna. The sounds she let out turned me on even more and I suddenly felt the urge to bury my face between her legs, so why not?

She squealed when I pushed her on her back, and I spread her thighs with my hands before sharing a look with Charlie.

"Hmm, go on," he mumbled, grabbing his shaft and pulling himself off.

"Jordan," Luna started, but I silenced her by placing my mouth over her pussy and sucking. I had an idea of how to do this, thinking about the things I loved to feel myself.

My heart beat frantically in my chest as I continued to lick and suck, hesitating before burying two fingers inside her. She thrusted her hips against my face, and I couldn't help but let a small smirk dance on my lips as I felt her getting even wetter.

"Yes! Oh, God," she moaned, placing a hand on my head and running her fingers over my scalp as I brought her to her orgasm.

I felt almost euphoric when she came, her walls tightening around my fingers. I swirled my tongue around her core a little faster, waiting until her legs stopped shaking and she relaxed into the bed like a rag doll.

Sitting up, I licked my lips and watched the blush that spread over Luna's cheeks and chest. It was a truly erotic sight.

"My turn," Charlie said from behind me, sounding a little out of breath. He dropped himself on the bed beside Luna and pumped his cock once. "Hop on, Baby."

I obeyed with a grin, crawling on top of him and hovering my hips over his dick. I wiggled my brows, slowly lowering onto him and moaning at the feel of his thick length filling me to the hilt.

Luna propped up on her elbows, watching the spot where Charlie and I connected. She got on her knees and grabbed my hair in her hand, pulling my head back.

I tried to focus on Charlie as I rode him, but Luna made it exceptionally difficult when she lowered her mouth on my chest and started sucking on my rock-hard nipple. All the stimulation was overwhelming, and I felt myself getting ready for another orgasm way too fast. So, I pulled Luna's face to mine and pushed my tongue into her mouth.

Charlie placed his hands on my hips and dug his fingers in my flesh as he forced me harder onto him, and there was no keeping me from orgasming when I noticed Luna's hand going to her core. There was something so erotic about the way she pleased herself, and I moaned loudly when I came.

My walls tightened around Charlie and it triggered his release, yet he tried to keep pounding into me as he spilled himself inside me.

I dropped myself forward and rested a hand on his chest, feeling his rapid heartbeat under my fingers.

Luna moaned when she came again, and I chuckled when she let herself fall back into the sheets. I followed her lead and dropped beside her, turning my head. "This was one of the greatest gifts I've ever had in my life," I breathed, smiling at the blonde.

"I'll say," Charlie retorted as he sat up, leaning back on his palms as he watched us from the foot of the bed.

"You're *so* welcome," Luna replied, running a hand through her hair and shooting me a wink before grabbing her phone and scrolling through her messages as if nothing happened.

Charlie moved to my side and laid down on his chest, wrapping an arm around my waist and placing his cheek on my right boob.

"Happy anniversary, Baby," he mumbled against my skin, and I ran a hand through his hair.

"Happy anniversary, Pretty Boy."

ACKNOWLEDGMENTS

To the very first person to offer me her proofreading- and editing services, one of my best friends, and an amazing writer herself, Nikki. Thank you for helping me with the first draft, supporting me through ups and downs, and being an amazing friend with a lot of patience. Thanks to you, this book ended up getting finished in the first place, and I will be eternally grateful for your help with creating the list. That being said, I want to thank you, Brandon, for sharing some of your expertise with me too.

To my sister. Thank you for believing in me during one of the darkest times of my life, and keeping me grounded. Your support means the world to me, and since you are a book junkie, I hope this one is up to your standards. I love you.

To my best friend, Lotte. We've known each other for a long time, and I've never met a person as kind and passionate as you. You inspire me every day to do my best, and I can't thank you enough for always being there for me. Through thick and thin. I love you, and I apologize for all the chaotic rambling about my books you had to listen to over these last couple of months.

To Jessy, Leanne, Jessica, Michelle, Casey, and Nicki. Thank you for your friendship, being my lifelines, and encouraging me to get on this self-publishing journey. I will never forget how much you've helped me through the last year, in more ways than one. You guys kept me going and managed to sit through hours of my rambling, complaining, and me vocalizing my insecurities. I apologize. You all deserve the world and I can't wait to find out what the future will bring. I know I call myself an author, but words can never express how grateful I am for you.

To my beta-readers. All your comments, suggestions, and kind words have helped me tremendously with perfecting the story and making me grow as an author. I could never thank you enough for all your help.

To my parents. Mom, I know you will never read this, and it hurts me to my core that I never get to share this new part of my life with you, but I wanted to say thank you anyway. You have always encouraged me to chase my dreams, and, I did it, mama. Dad, please don't read this book, though if you made it this far, that's probably already happened. Thank you for supporting me and pushing me to be the best version of myself. I love you.

And lastly, to my readers. Thank you for supporting me, whether it's through reading, commenting, sending me positive messages, or sharing my work. I literally couldn't have done this without you.

Love,
Emma

FIND ME

Find out more about me, my merch and my other books on
www.emmamallory.com

www.instagram.com/authoremmamallory

Milton Keynes UK
Ingram Content Group UK Ltd.
UKHW041926131023
430523UK00004B/52